CANADA

MAINE
Montpelier
1
2
Augusta
Concord
Boston
3
4
Providence
5
Hartford
Paul
WISCONSIN
Madison
Milwaukee
MICHIGAN
NEW YORK
Rochester
Albany
Detroit
Lansing
New York
OWA
Chicago
es Moines
PENNSYLVANIA
Pittsburgh
Harrisburg
Trenton
OHIO
Baltimore
7
INDIANA
8
Dover
ILLINOIS
Columbus
WEST VIRGINIA
Washington,D.C.
Indianapolis
Annapolis
on City
Springfield
Charleston
VIRGINIA
St. Louis
SOURI
Lexington
Richmond
Frankfort
KENTUCKY
Greensboro
Raleigh
Nashville
NORTH CAROLINA
TENNESSEE
ANSAS
Memphis
SOUTH CAROLINA
Birmingham
Atlanta
ttle Rock
Columbia
ALABAMA
GEORGIA
MISSISSIPPI
eveport
Montgomery
Jackson
Jacksonville
OUISIANA
Tallahassee
on Rouge
New Orleans
FLORIDA
Miami
BAHAMAS
CUBA

1 VERMONT
2 NEW HAMPSHIRE
3 MASSACHUSETTS
4 RHODE ISLAND
5 CONNECTICUT
6 NEW JERSEY
7 DELAWARE
8 MARYLAND

Atlantic Ocean

★ National Capital
● State Capital
● City or Town

WORLD MAP

NORTH AMERICA

PACIFIC OCEAN

CARIBBEAN SEA

SOUTH AMERICA

PACIFIC OCEAN

ARCTIC OCEAN
EUROPE
ASIA
PACIFIC OCEAN
AFRICA
OCEANIA
INDIAN OCEAN
ANTARCTICA

THE UNITED STATES OF AMERICA

開口就會社交英語

Social English

實踐大學應用外語系專任講師
黃　靜　悅
Danny O. Neal ◎著

五南圖書出版公司 印行

前言

哈佛教授尼爾弗格森 (Niall Ferguson) 指出當今Chimerica (China加America) 已然形成：由中國與美國結合的中美經濟體未來將深遠地影響全世界，隨著中國經濟逐漸舉足輕重，國人與國際人士社交應對之機會與必要性亦將隨之倍增！與國際人士互相交流是了解世界的窗口，是個人視野與閱歷的開拓，更是做為世界村一員之必修課。

國人修習英語多年，多半擁有基礎或以上之對話能力，但常因缺乏練習而自信不足，待有機會與外籍人士交流時，經常緊張結巴或讓被動害羞阻礙了溝通及表達自我的機會。交流既是雙方面的，國人需能更進一步主動參與話題，有效率地表達回應或提問 (而非被動回答)，才能達到真正的溝通，共同創造愉悅的談話經驗。

本書帶領讀者到各式情境內實際對話演練，在國內外都能受用，展現自信主動開口與老外自然合宜地交談。書中以美國文化中的社交情境為主，並以華人文化的觀點為讀者指出社交互動中值得注意之處。了解兩種文化之間的歧異，能幫助讀者了解唐突、禁忌何以產生並加以避免，書中涵蓋美國社交禮儀常規及特定場合或派對裡合乎人們期待之應對進對之道。此外，「小祕訣」及「小叮嚀」裡包含世界其他文化之訊息。

另外必須一提的是人類文化有其普遍性，將任何文化貼上任何標籤無疑是不智的做法。世界各地不同文化的社交習慣或禮儀表現並不一定有道理可言，也無真正的對錯，遺憾的是人們常因本身成長背景而在潛意識裡對他人之行為舉止產生價值判斷。許多因素如地區、種族、語言、宗教信仰、風俗習慣，雖然使同一族群的人保有相同文化，但其他因素如世代變遷、教育程度、個人特質，當然也帶來不同的差異及獨特性。

因此，入境隨俗，遵守當地社交場合慣例以避免不必要的誤會，有其必要；另一方面開放心胸，將刻版印象 (stereotype) 放一邊，才能有所斬獲。世界歷史文化何其可貴，現代地球公民在開拓國際觀的同時，如果能觀察與比較世界上其他不同文化裡人們的社交行為，絕對是極為豐富又充滿趣味的學習！

推薦序

麥克魯漢 (Marshall McLuhan) 於上世紀六〇年代首度提出了「地球村」的概念，當時他原本用這個新名詞來說明電子媒介對於人類未來之衝擊，實不亞於古騰堡 (Johann Gutenberg) 印刷術對西方文明的影響；曾幾何時，「地球村」在今天有了新的涵義：天涯若比鄰！

現代科技進步昌明，往昔「五月花」號上的新教徒花了六十幾天，歷經千辛萬苦才橫渡大西洋，今日搭乘超音速飛機只要四個多小時就可完成；網際網路的普及，世界上任何角落所發生的事情對千里以外的地方都會有不可思議的影響，亦即所謂的「蝴蝶效應」；語言文字的互通理解；東方的「博愛」和西方的「charity」使得普天下心懷「人溺己溺」之心的信徒，都能為營造開創一個由愛出發、以和為貴的世界而一起努力！這一切都說明了一個事實：人與人之間不再因距離、時空、障礙和誤解而「老死不相往來」！

當然，在這一片光鮮亮麗的外表下，隱憂依然存在。「全球化」(Globalization) 對第三世界的人而言，竟成為新帝國主義和資本主義的同義字！造成這種誤解，甚至於扭曲的主要原因是對不同於自己的文化、風俗、傳統及習慣的一知半解；是不是用法文就顯得比較文明？使用義大利文就會比較熱情？德文，富哲理？英文，有深度？而美語，就「財大氣粗」？是不是有一套介紹書籍，雖不一定包含了所有相關的資訊，但至少對那些想要知道或了解異國風物的好奇者，能有所幫助的參考工具書？

放眼今日的自學書刊，林林總總，參差不齊。上者，艱澀聱牙或孤芳自賞；下者，錯誤百出或言不及意！想要找兼具深度和廣度的語言學習工具書，實屬不易。現有本校應用外語學系黃靜悅和唐凱仁兩位老師，前者留學旅居國外多年，以國人的角度看外國文化；後者則以外國人的立場，以其十數年寄居台灣的經驗，合作撰寫系列叢書，舉凡旅遊、日常生活、社交、校園及商務應用，提供真實情境對話，佐以「實用語句」、「字句補給站」讓學習者隨查隨用，並穿插「小叮嚀」和「小祕訣」，提供作者在美生活的點滴、體驗與心得等的第一手資訊。同時，「文化祕笈」及更為同類書刊中之創舉！

學無止境！但唯有輔以正確的學習書籍，才能收「事半功倍」之效。本人對兩位老師的投入與努力，除表示敬意，特此作序說明，並寄望黃唐兩位老師在教學研究之餘，再接再厲，為所有有志向學、自我提昇的學習者，提供更精練、更充實的自學叢書。

前實踐大學　校長

張光正

自序

學習外語的動機不外乎外在 (instrumental) 及內在 (intrinsic) 兩類：外在動機旨在以語言作為工具，完成工作任務；內在動機則是希望透過外語學習達成自我探索及自我實現的目標。若人們在語言學習上能有所成，則此成就也必然是雙方面的；一方面完成工作任務而得到實質上的利益報償，另一方面則因達成溝通、了解對方文化及想法而得到豐富的感受。

現今每個人都是地球公民中的一員，而語言則是自我與世界的連結工具。今日網路科技的發展在彈指間就可以連結到我們想要的網站，人類的學習心與天性因刺激而產生對未知的好奇心及行動力，使我們對於異國語言文化自然產生嚮往；增進對這個世界的了解已不是所謂的個人特色或美德，而是身處現代地球村的每個人都該具備的一種責任與義務！

用自己的腳走出去，用自己的眼睛去看、用自己的心靈去感受世界其他國家人們的生活方式，用自己學得的語言當工具，與不同國家的人們交談；或許我們的母語、種族、膚色、性別不同，或許我們的衣著、宗教信仰、喜好以及對事情的看法、做法不同，但人與人之間善意的眼神、微笑、肢體動作、互相尊重、善待他人的同理心，加上適切的語言，對世界和平、國際友邦間相互扶持的共同渴望，使我們深深體會到精彩動人的外語學習旅程其實是自我發現的旅程！只有自己親自走過的旅程、完成過的任務、通過的關卡、遇到的人們、累積的智慧經驗、開拓的視野、體驗過的人生，才是無可替代的真實感受。世界有多大、個人想為自己及世人貢獻的事有多少，學習外語完成自我實現內在動機的收穫就有多豐富！

今日有機會將自己所學與用腳走世界、用心親感受的經驗交付五南出版社出版叢書，誠摯感謝前實踐大學張光正校長慨為本叢書作序、前鄧景元主編催生本系列書，眾五南夥伴使本書順利完成，及親愛的家人朋友學生們的加油打氣。若讀者大眾能因本系列叢書增進英語文實力，並為自己開啟一道與世界溝通的大門，便是對作者最大的回饋與鼓勵！

願與所有立志於此的讀者共勉之。

作者　黃靜悅　謹誌

特點圖示

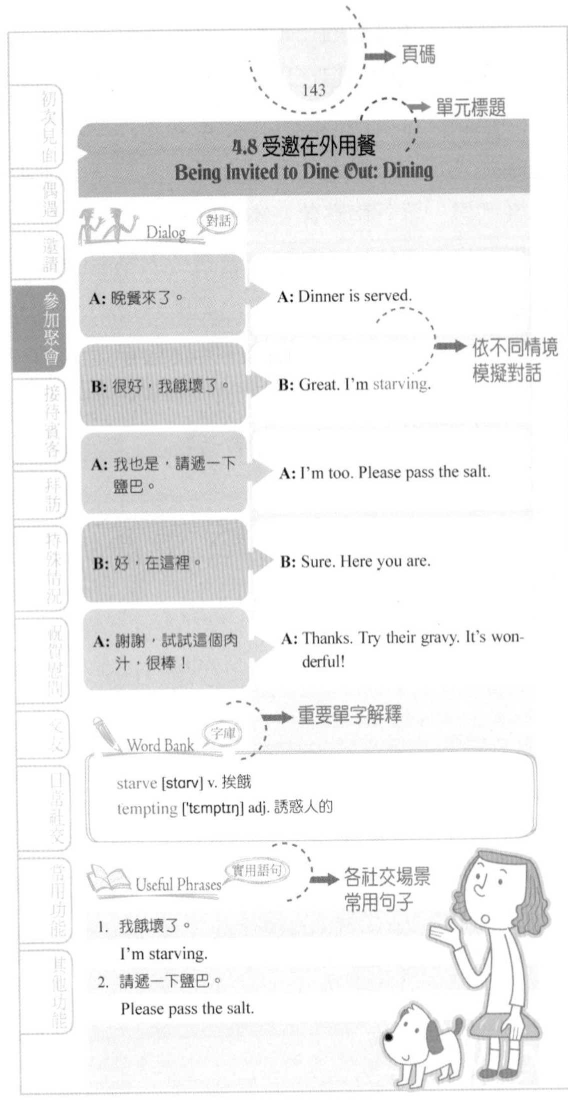

頁碼
143
單元標題
4.8 受邀在外用餐
Being Invited to Dine Out: Dining
初次見面
偶遇
邀請
參加聚會
接待賓客
拜訪
特殊情況
祝賀慰問
交友
日常社交
常用功能
其他功能
Dialog
對話
A: 晚餐來了。
A: Dinner is served.
依不同情境
模擬對話
B: 很好，我餓壞了。
B: Great. I'm starving.
A: 我也是，請遞一下鹽巴。
A: I'm too. Please pass the salt.
B: 好，在這裡。
B: Sure. Here you are.
A: 謝謝，試試這個肉汁，很棒！
A: Thanks. Try their gravy. It's wonderful!
重要單字解釋
Word Bank
字庫
starve [stɑrv] v. 挨餓
tempting ['tɛmptɪŋ] adj. 誘惑人的
Useful Phrases
實用語句
各社交場景
常用句子
1. 我餓壞了。
I'm starving.
2. 請遞一下鹽巴。
Please pass the salt.

Tips 小祕訣 ➡ 快速適應各國社交禮儀的妙方

真正的社交禮儀在於如何適切應對，使自己舉止合宜，而不在於背誦社交規則，如果心裡忐忑不知道該怎麼做才能不使自己困窘，不如坦承不了解社交禮儀 (social ettiquette)，請教主人該如何表現才恰當，例如：何種食物該用手吃（炸雞、蝦子、比薩、三明治）？或許其他賓客也不知道該怎麼辦，利用機會請問主人這些問題，可以讓大家自在地談論，有助於拉近距離，社交禮儀其實是實用又有趣的話題。

Language Power 字句補給站 ➡ 補充相關單字

◆ **音樂與歌曲 Music and Songs**

rock (and roll)	搖滾
pop	流行
reggae	雷鬼
salsa	騷莎
classical	古典

Notes 小叮嚀 ➡ 在美社交生活應注意事項

在美國致贈禮物沒有什麼禮數，將禮物交給對方，面帶微笑告訴他 [她] 是送給他 [她] 的禮物就行了，人們會欣喜的接受禮物。生日禮物何時打開，並無一定規則，小孩通常在玩一些遊戲或活動後打開禮物；大人則通常是壽星受到朋友慫恿時打開禮物。

➡ 介紹美國社交禮儀常規

聚會派對禮儀Party Etiquette

1　紳士行為

美國雖是平權社會，男士的紳士風度仍然存在，為女士開門，為最鄰近自己的女士拉椅子都是被期待的行為。紳士行為在世界各國同樣存在並且被期待 (含各種場合)，沒有紳士習慣的男士必須學習。

2　坐姿

坐直，勿彎腰駝背。坐下時就打開餐巾放在腿上。坐下時慣用右

目錄

Unit 1 初次見面 Meeting Someone the First Time

Unit 2 朋友(舊識)偶遇 Running into a Friend [Acquaintance]

Unit 3 邀請、受邀與回應 (非正式／正式) Invitations and Replies (Casual/Formal)

Unit 4 參加郊外聚會與生日 [晚餐] 派對 (非正式／正式) Attending Outings and Birthday [Dinner] Parties (Casual/Formal)

Unit 5 接待賓客（會議與晚宴派對）Receiving Guests (Conferences and Dinner Parties)

Unit 6 拜訪與受訪 Visiting People and Being Visited

Oh, No!

Unit 7 特殊情況 Special Situations

Unit 9 主動開口交友 Initiating Conversation to Make a New Friend

Unit 10 日常社交話題 Common Topics for Chatting and Socializing

Unit 12 其他功能性用語 Other Functional Expressions

附錄 Appendices

字句補給站 Language Power

Unit 1 Meeting Someone the First Time

初次見面

西方人經常因不確定語言能否溝通，或自認不了解亞洲文化而較少主動開口與陌生的亞洲人打招呼聊天。如果我們能主動說聲「hi」並報上姓名，打破沉默僵局 (break the ice)，多半會獲得正面回應，不必過於擔心自己的英文，微笑與禮貌友善的態度才是最重要的。在國外參加社交活動或商務拜訪時，主動認識他人並相互交談，除了交換資訊外，也被視為一種表達友善的方式，交談時注意聆聽對方並使用恰當的肢體語言。

1.1 與陌生人打招呼 Saying Hello to a Stranger

1.1a 與團體中的某人打招呼 With Someone in a Group

Dialog 1 對話1

A: 嗨，我是麥克斯陳。	**A:** Hi, I'm Max Chen.
B: 我是安迪柯林斯。	**B:** I'm Andy Collins.
A: 安迪，你從哪裡來？	**A:** Where are you from, Andy?
B: 德州，你呢？	**B:** Texas. And you?
A: 臺灣。	**A:** Taiwan.
B: 泰國？	**B:** Thailand?
A: 不是，是臺灣。	**A:** No. Taiwan.
B: 喔，是啊，我知道，抱歉。	**B:** Oh, yes. I know. Sorry.

A: 沒關係，也許我英文不夠好。

A: That's OK. Maybe my English is not good enough.

B: 不，不是那樣，我應該仔細聽才對。

B: No, no. It's not that. I should listen more closely.

1. 你從哪裡來？
   Where are you from?
2. 沒關係。
   That's OK.
3. 這是我第一次來。
   This is my first visit.
4. 也許我英文不夠好。
   Maybe my English is not good enough.
5. 我應該仔細聽才對。
   I should listen more closely.

臺灣在世界地圖上是很小的一點，儘管臺灣製造 (Made in Taiwan) 的各類產品在世界經濟上表現優異，許多外國人士未必知道臺灣在哪裡或將所有亞洲人都當作日本人；因為發音類似，將臺灣誤認為泰國 (Thailand) 或在曾經收容了許多難民的歐美國家被當作越南人 (Vietnamese)、柬埔寨人 (Cambodian) 也很常見。許多人一輩子的活動範圍仍僅限於自己的國家，對外國了解有限。萬一碰到外國人士問了好笑的問題，不要生氣反諷，要有耐性回答。外國人很難了解亞洲人有何差別，如同亞洲人看老外都差不多，或許你是他們第一個 (或極少數) 碰到的外國人。隨著地球村、網際網路、新興市場崛起及各國國民身為世界公民的自覺，情況應該會慢慢改變。

Dialog 2 對話2

A: 這位子有人坐嗎？	**A:** Is this seat taken?
B: 沒有，請便吧！我替你把東西拿開，我正在寫明信片。	**B:** No, go ahead. Let me put things away for you. I was writing some postcards.
A: 謝謝，現在甲板上好熱。	**A:** Thanks. The deck is scorching hot right now.
B: 我同意，在休息室裡好多了。	**B:** I agree. It's nicer to be in the lounge room.
A: 我是保羅，很高興認識你。	**A:** My name is Paul. Nice to meet you.
B: 我是南茜，也很高興認識你。	**B:** I'm Nancy. Nice to meet you, too.
A: 你晚點要去划獨木舟或游泳嗎，南茜？	**A:** Are you going to go kayaking or swimming later, Nancy?
B: 是，划獨木舟似乎很好玩，但一下子就很累，我大概就不游泳了，你呢？	**B:** Yes, kayaking seems a lot of fun, but can be pretty tiring after a while. I'll probably skip swimming. What about you?
A: 我想我會兩個都玩，如果我不需要划大部分的槳。	**A:** I guess I'll do both, if I don't have to do most of the paddling.

Word Bank 字庫

postcard ['post͵kɑrd] n. 明信片
deck [dɛk] n. 甲板
scorch [skɔrtʃ] v. 烤焦
lounge [laundʒ] n. 交誼廳，休息室
kayak ['kaɪæk] n. (一人或雙人前後座之) 獨木舟
skip [skɪp] v. 跳，略過
paddle ['pædl̩] v. 划槳

Useful Phrases 實用語句

1. 很高興認識你。
   Nice to meet you.
2. 我也是 (很高興認識你)。
   (Nice to meet) you too.
3. 這位子有人坐嗎？
   Is this seat taken?
4. 你晚點要去划獨木舟嗎？
   Are you going to go kayaking?
5. 划獨木舟可能會很累。
   Kayaking can be pretty tiring.

It is a friendly dog!

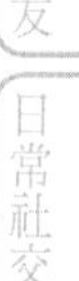

美國文化裡，陌生人之間點頭微笑，或說聲「嗨」打招呼已足夠，但美國人與萍水相逢的陌生人打招呼聊天甚至交換姓名也很常見，這與美國人(相對於其他歐美國家)直接、開放、熱情的文化背景有關。相對地，對於短暫同處一時空的陌生人保持沉默，可視為一種尊重對方，給對方距離，不打擾其寧靜的做法。

無論是否熟識，或透過何種方式認識他人，除了言談禮貌外，行進間勿忘基本禮儀，為下一位進出的人稍微拉住門並注意電梯禮儀，才不會讓門或電梯打到對方(男士為女士進出時拉門仍受歡迎)。除非在擁擠的空間，說話或排隊的距離以一手臂的距離丈量，注意不要入侵他人個人空間 (personal space)，談話內容也要避免問及個人隱私 (privacy)。

1.1b 與有寵物的人打招呼 Greeting Someone with a Pet

A: 嗨，你的狗是米格魯嗎？

A: Hi. Is your dog a Beagle?

B: 是的，你知道牠們嗎？

B: Yes, it is. Do you know about them?

A: 一點點，我姊姊也有一隻。

A: A little. My sister has one, too.

B: 她會帶牠來這個公園嗎？

B: Does she bring it to this park?

A: 不會，她住在香港。

A: No. She lives in Hong Kong.

B: 喔，我明白了，你是從那裡來的嗎？

B: Oh. I see. Is that where you are originally from?

A: 是的，我去年過來這裡讀書。

A: Yes, I came here to study last year.

1. 你的狗是米格魯嗎？

   Is your dog a Beagle?

2. 好漂亮的狗！

   What a beautiful dog!

3. 你的狗幾歲？

   How old is your dog?

4. 是什麼品種？

   What is the breed?

5. 你的狗是公的還是母的？

   Is your dog a he or she?

6. 牠 [他／她] 叫什麼名字？

   What is its [his, her] name?

7. 牠 [他／她] 喜歡跟小孩相處嗎？

   Does it [he, she] like to be with children?

8. 牠 [他／她] 是隻友善的狗！

   It [He, She] is a friendly dog!

都市人相較於小城鎮的人，多數比較冷漠，然而在較少人的郊外散步時、在電梯裡或排隊結帳時，陌生的人也有可能彼此打招呼，甚至短暫交談，帶著狗兒散步的人自然也容易與愛狗的人聊開來。

常見犬類 ①
Popular Dog Breeds

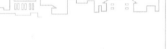

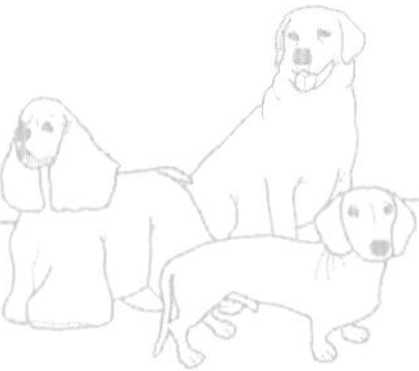

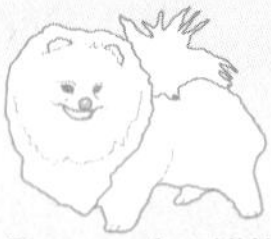

Pomeranian 博美 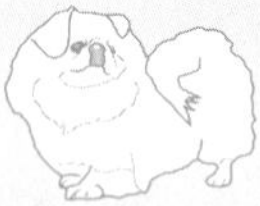 | Peikingese 北京狗 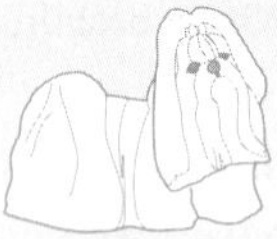 | Shih Tzu 西施犬

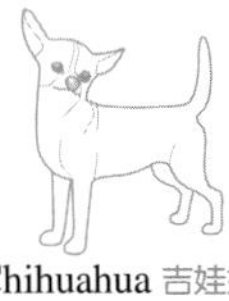

Chihuahua 吉娃娃 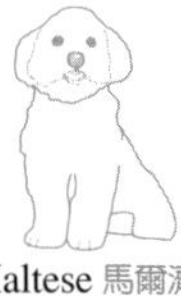 | Maltese 馬爾濟斯 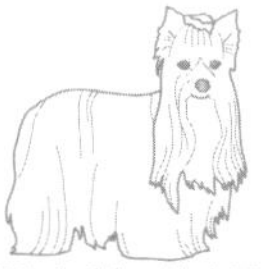 | Yorkshire 約克夏

- mixed-breed dog 混種犬
- working dog 工作犬
- guard dog 看守犬
- protection dog 護衛犬
- police dog 警犬
- pet dog 寵物犬

常見犬類 ② Popular Dog Breeds

Golden Retriever 黃金獵犬

Labrador 拉不拉多

Dalmatian 大麥町

Husky 哈士奇

Collie 牧羊犬

German Shepherd 德國狼犬

Chow Chow 鬆獅犬

Beagle 米格魯

Poodle 貴賓犬

Pug 巴哥

Bulldog 鬥牛犬

Cocker Spaniel 可卡

Shar Pei 沙皮狗

Dachshund 臘腸狗 (為德文，美國人暱稱Doxie 或 Sausage Dog)

Papillon 蝴蝶犬 (法文，美國人暱稱 Butterfly Dog)

1.1c 與行動不便人士碰面 (坐輪椅) Meeting Someone with a Disability (in a Wheel Chair)

Dialog 對話

A: 嗨，我是傑瑞黃。	**A:** Hi. I'm Jerry Huang.
B: 哈囉，我是尚恩史垂威克。	**B:** Hello, I'm Shane Stredwick.
A: 很高興認識你 (握手)。	**A:** It's nice to meet you (shaking hands).
B: 你需要幫忙弄那些東西嗎？	**B:** Do you need any help with those things?
A: 不用，沒關係，我可以的。	**A:** No, that's OK. I can handle them.
B: 好，我們該坐哪裡？	**B:** OK. Where should we sit?
A: 我們用那張桌子，我可以靠近一點。	**A:** Let's use that table. I can get close to it.
B: 好。	**B:** Sure.

Useful Phrases 實用語句

1. 你需要幫忙弄那些東西嗎？

   Do you need any help with those things?

2. 我們該坐哪裡？

   Where should we sit?

3. 這裡是個好位置嗎？

   Is here a good place to sit?

1.1d 與行動不便人士碰面 (視障) Meeting Someone with a Disability (Blind)

A: 嗨，我是泰瑞陳。	**A:** Hi. I'm Terry Chen.
B: 嗨，泰瑞，我是比爾柯林斯 (他是視障人士並且伸出右手)。	**B:** Hi, Terry. I'm Bill Collins (He is blind and puts out his right hand).
A: 我很高興認識你 (握手)，久仰了。	**A:** I'm pleased to meet you (shaking hands). I've heard a lot about you.
B: 希望是好事情？	**B:** Good things I hope?
A: 是的，都是好事。	**A:** Yes, yes, all good.

B: 我們找個地方坐下來。	**B:** Let's find a place to sit.
A: 好的。	**A:** Fine.
B: 你看到好地方了嗎？	**B:** Do you see a good place?
A: 是的，我看到了。	**A:** Yes, I do.
B: 好的，請繼續說，我會跟著你。	**B:** Great. Just keep talking and I'll follow you.
A: 沒問題。	**B:** No problem.

Useful Phrases 實用語句

1. 久仰了。
   I've heard a lot about you.
2. 希望是好事情？
   Good things I hope?
3. 我們找個地方坐下來。
   Let's find a place to sit.
4. 你看到好地方了嗎？
   Do you see a good place?
5. 請繼續說，我會跟著你。
   Just keep talking and I'll follow you.

與行動不便的人士會面，應該如對常人一般問候和對待他們，他們也希望被如此對待，以任何方式指出殘障人士之缺陷或是逗弄視障人士的導盲犬 (guide dog) 都是極度無禮的表現。如果你看到任何殘障人士有困難可能需要協助，不妨先問他們是否需要幫忙，不請自來就衝過去幫忙，可能使人感到不受尊重。

1.2 初遇同事
Meeting a Coworker for the First Time

A: 嗨，我是鮑伯胡。

A: Hi. I'm Bob Hu.

B: 嗨，鮑伯，我是陶德馬丁。

B: Hi, Bob. I'm Todd Martin.

A: 很高興認識你，這是我第一天上班，有人告訴你我今天開始在這個部門工作嗎？

A: Nice to meet you. This is my first day. Did anyone tell you I'd start working in this department today?

B: 有，人事部門告訴我今天有新人來。

B: Yes. The Personnel Department told me to expect a new person today.

A: 好。	**A:** That's good.
B: 我帶你繞一下，我會介紹你給其他同事。	**B:** Let me show you around a little. I'll introduce you to some of the other employees.
A: 謝謝。	**A:** Thanks.

Personnel Department n. 人事部門
expect [ɪk'spɛkt] v. 期待

初次見面招呼語 Greeting Someone the First Time

1. 哈囉，很高興認識你。
   Hello. It's nice to meet you.
2. 我是 (名字)。你的名字是？
   Hi. I'm (name). What's your name?
3. 嗨，你好嗎？
   Hi. How are you?
4. 你好嗎？我是 (名字)。(初次見面，正式)
   How do you do? I'm (name).
5. 我很高興認識你。(較正式)
   I'm very pleased to meet you.
6. 很高興見到你。
   Pleased to meet you.
7. 很榮幸認識你。
   It's a pleasure to meet you.

8. 很高興認識你。
   I'm so happy to meet you.
9. 很高興認識你。
   It's nice to make your acquaintance.
10. 我很高興認識你。
   I'm glad to make your acquaintance.
11. 讓我來介紹你。
   Let me introduce you.
12. 我想讓你見見某人。
   I'd like you to meet someone.
13. 我想讓你見見我朋友。
   I want you to meet a friend of mine.

介紹自己要簡短，讓別人也接的上話或回應問答，避免向初次見面的人提問嚴肅的問題。

1.3 初訪客戶辦公室
Meeting a New Client in His [Her] Office

A: 嗨，鮑伯，請進。	**A:** Hi, Bob. Please come in.
B: 哈囉，安德森先生，你今天好嗎？	**B:** Hello, Mr. Anderson. How are you today?
A: 還不錯，你呢？	**A:** Just fine. And you?

B: 很好，謝謝你見我。

B: Great. Thanks for seeing me.

A: 沒問題，現在你的想法是什麼呢？

A: No problem. Now, what's on your mind?

B: 那我直說了，我們相信我們今年開始可以降低你們10到15%的操作成本。

B: I'll get right to it then. We believe we can lower your cost of operations by 10 to 15% starting this year.

A: 那麼多，怎麼做呢？

A: That's a lot. How?

B: 我們傳輸服務公司至今已經為像你們這樣的公司著手及設計完善的流量系統好幾年了。

B: We at Streamserve have been working on and perfecting designed flow systems for companies like yours for several years now.

A: 進行的怎麼樣？

A: How has it been working?

B: 讓我為你展示這些圖表。

B: Let me show you these charts.

A: 聽起來這要花一些時間。

A: It sounds like this may take a while.

B: 我最多只需要一個小時。	**B:** I'll need an hour at most.
A: 那不是問題，我很有興趣聽你要說什麼。	**A:** Not a problem. I'm interested in hearing what you have to say.
B: 很好。	**B:** Great.
A: 但是先讓我點一些咖啡。	**A:** Let me order some coffee first though.
B: 謝謝。	**B:** Thank you.
A: 你的咖啡要加些什麼？	**A:** How do you take it?
B: 加奶精，如果有的話。	**B:** With cream if you have any.
A: 好，我打電話叫人送上來，我們再繼續。	**A:** Sure. I'll call out and have it sent up. Then, we'll continue.
B: 聽起來很好。	**B:** Sounds good.

Word Bank 字庫

lower ['loə] v. 降低
cost of operations n. 操作成本
perfect [pə'fɛkt] v. 使完美
chart [tʃɑrt] n. 圖表

Useful Phrases 實用語句

1. 謝謝你見我。
   Thanks for seeing me.
2. 那我直說了。
   I'll get right to it then.
3. 讓我為你展示這些圖表。
   Let me show you these charts.
4. 我來展示這個。
   Let me show this.
5. 我最多只需要一個小時。
   I'll need an hour at most.
6. 我大約需要一個小時。
   I'll need about an hour.
7. 這個不需要太久。
   This won't take long.
8. 我會把它寄來。
   I'll have it sent up.
9. 我會把它寄給你。
   I'll send it to you.
10. 你的咖啡要加些什麼？
   How do you take your coffee?
11. 我可以為你做什麼？
   What can I do for you?

12. 現在你的想法是什麼呢？

    What's on your mind?

13. 聽起來很好。

    Sounds good.

14. 我們繼續。

    Let's continue.

商務拜訪務必要準時，避免失禮。出發前要確認攜帶足夠數量的名片，衣著型式要適合商業場合及行業常規，乾淨整齊端莊不要太隨性或太時髦，香水的使用也要低調。

會面時，應使用先生 (Mr.) 或女士 (Ms.) 加上姓氏之正式稱呼 (Ms.為不涉及婚姻狀況之用法)，除非對方要你直呼其名或使用其他稱呼才改口，如果彼此年齡相仿，對方很快就會請你只稱呼名字；如果對方有博士或醫師資格，要使用 Dr. 加上姓氏稱呼以示尊重。如果不知對方的姓名如何發音，應該事先了解，避免見面時尷尬。

多數情況下，商業場合的禮物不包裝，並且在會面結束後贈與，送禮季節特別是在年底11月至年初1月。

1.4 初遇新鄰居 Meeting a New Neighbor

A: 哈囉，我是珍徐，我們剛搬到你隔壁。

A: Hello. I'm Jane Hsu. We just moved in next to you.

B: 嗨，我是雪莉泰勒，很高興認識你。

B: Hi. I'm Sherry Taylor. Nice to meet you.

A: 我也很高興認識你。

A: It's very nice to meet you, too.

B: 我和我先生、小孩才剛來兩三個禮拜。

B: My husband, children and I just arrived a few weeks ago.

A: 歡迎來到這社區。

A: Welcome to the neighborhood.

B: 謝謝，我可以問你關於本地服務的幾個問題嗎？

B: Thank you. Could I ask you a few questions about local services?

A: 當然囉，你想知道什麼呢？

A: Sure. What would you like to know?

Word Bank 字庫

neighborhood ['nebɚ,hud] n. 社區
local services n. 本地服務

Useful Phrases 實用語句

1. 嗨，我們剛搬來。
   Hi. We just moved in.
2. 我們打算在這裡住兩年。
   We plan to live here for two years.
3. 我先生在錢德勒公司工作。
   My husband works at Chandler Corporation.
4. 你可以告訴我怎麼申裝電話服務嗎？
   Can you tell me how to arrange phone service?

5. 你想知道什麼呢？

   What would you like to know?

6. 關於讓我們的小孩上學，我們要聯絡誰？

   Who should we contact about having our children enter school?

7. 這裡的商業區幾點打烊呢？

   What time do shopping districts close here?

8. 我們在等我們的東西從國外寄到這裡。

   We're expecting our things from overseas to arrive here soon.

9. 我可以偶爾向你請教嗎？

   May I ask for your advice sometimes?

10. 郵差什麼時候來呢？

    What time does the mail carrier come?

在國外認識新鄰居通常不難，但各地做法不同。一般而言，中小城鎮的人很容易碰到，這時你可以走過去自我介紹，或敲門自我介紹是這社區的一份子。在美國，有些鄰居會來你家自我介紹或送上歡迎禮，你也可以選擇要不要過去送個小禮，但你的鄰居不會認為你必須這麼做，送禮物也並不代表你就被新社區接受。在大城市，通常大家各管各的，所以鄰居多半不熟，但有些出租社區大家至少還知道鄰居是誰。

如果你受邀到別人家裡晚餐、烤肉或鄰居聚會，最好帶瓶酒或其他可以貢獻給這場合的東西，最好要準時，除非約定好要幫忙，不要早到，要讓主人有時間準備好會客。

1.5 初遇朋友 [同事，客戶] 之家人
Meeting a Friend's [Coworker's, Client's] Family

A: 爸，我想讓你見見我一個朋友。	**A:** Father. I'd like you to meet a friend of mine.
B: 好。	**B:** Great.
A: 爸，這是愛德李。	**A:** Father, this is Ed Lee.
B: 很高興認識你，愛德。	**B:** Pleased to meet you, Ed.
A: 愛德，這是我爸，藍道夫史登斯。	**A:** Ed, this is my Father. Randolf Stearns.
C: 很高興認識你，史登斯先生。	**C:** I'm pleased to meet you, Mr. Stearns.

在社交場合，除非是緊急狀況，馬上進入主題並不是社交慣例。人們通常在互相寒暄聊些愉快的事情之後，才會談公事，如果時間很趕，當然就會很快進入主題。

在商務場合，當然是為商務而會面，招呼完就談公事是慣例。

Dialog 2 對話2

A: 嗨，莎拉，請進。

A: Hi, Sarah. Come in.

B: 嗨，謝謝你邀請我來。

B: Hi. Thanks for inviting me over.

A: 這是我們的榮幸，讓我來介紹你給我的家人。

A: Our pleasure. Let me introduce you to my family.

B: 好，我很期待認識他們。

B: Sure. I've been looking forward to meeting them.

A: 好的，首先讓我介紹我的祖母。奶奶，這是我的一位同事，她的名字是莎拉宋。莎拉，這是我的奶奶，泰瑪塔特。

A: OK. First, let me introduce my grandmother. Grandma, this is one of my coworkers. Her name is Sarah Soong. Sarah, this is my grandmother on my father's side, Thelma Tot.

C: 我很高興認識你，莎拉。

C: I'm happy to meet you, Sarah.

B: 我也很高興認識你。

B: I'm happy to meet you, too.

A: 下一位是我的太太，克莉絲蒂。

A: Next is my wife, Christy.

B: 哈囉，克莉絲蒂，久仰大名。

B: Hello, Christy. I've heard so many nice things about you.

D: 我也是，歡迎你來我們家。

D: And I you. Welcome to our home.

B: 謝謝。

B: Thank you.

A: 輪到我的小孩，這是老大巴瑞，他旁邊的是我的小女兒莎莉，還有沙發上是我的大女兒卡羅。

A: Now for my children. This is my oldest, Barry, and next to him is my youngest daughter, Sally, and over there on the sofa is my oldest daughter, Carol.

B: 嗨，大家好。

B: Hi, everyone.

E: (大家同聲) 嗨！

E: (all three at the same time) Hi!

A: 我的爸媽還沒來，你晚點會看到他們。

A: My mom and dad aren't here yet, so you'll meet them later.

B: 好。

B: OK.

A: 坐下來並且讓自己舒服些。

A: Sit down and make yourself comfortable.

Word Bank 字庫

look forward to 期待

coworker ['koˌwɝkɚ] n. 同事

Useful Phrases 實用語句

1. 謝謝你邀請我來。

   Thanks for inviting me over.
2. 我們的榮幸。

   Our pleasure.
3. 歡迎你來我家。

   Welcome to our home.
4. 讓我來介紹你給我的家人。

   Let me introduce you to my family.
5. 我很期待認識他們。

   I've been looking forward to meeting them.
6. 久仰大名。

   I've heard so many nice things about you.
7. 我也是 (我也久仰你的大名)。

   And I you. (I've heard so many nice things about you, too.)
8. 讓自己舒服些。

   Make yourself comfortable.
9. (當作自己家) 不要客氣。

   Make yourself at home.

不同州的人對長輩有不同稱呼，習慣不一。如果自己有小孩，必須依照所在區域人們慣用的方式去教導小孩稱呼鄰居長輩或同學父母。傳統裡我們對同學、同事、家人或常見面的鄰居長輩使用泛稱，如王爸爸 (媽媽、爺爺、奶奶、婆婆、阿姨等)，有時素不相識的人 (如生意人) 為表示親切，也使用親屬之泛稱，但美國人認為父母及祖父母只有一個，並不如此稱呼外人 (偶有例外)。

除了區域性的習慣外，每個人對不同輩分間該如何稱呼的想法不盡相同，如果有疑問，可以問當事人希望如何被稱呼 (How would you prefer to be addressed?) 基本上，有禮貌的晚輩是受人歡迎的。Sir, Ma'am 或 Mr. Mrs. Ms. 加姓氏 (如 Mr. Jones)，是禮貌的用法。如果小孩還小，可以用表示親近的稱呼 (如 Uncle Bob, Auntie Jennifer) 來稱呼很熟悉的大人 (無論有無親戚關係)，待小孩長大到青少年時期，可能就會直接用名字稱呼大人了。此外，美國小孩稱呼繼父母或媳婦、女婿稱呼公婆、岳父母都是直呼其名，對於文化裡講求輩分倫理的人而言，可能會感到很吃驚。

稱呼不知名的陌生人 (尤其對長輩)，先生用 Sir，女士用 Ma'am，Miss 通常指相當年輕或十來歲的年輕女性，當然較年長者可能稱呼較自身年輕的女姓 Miss。

美國社交文化 Social Culture in America

不同文化及價值觀背後有其歷史、經濟及其他因素，個人與群體關係之不同，文化表現因此不同。與美籍人士互動，至少有下列幾項要注意：

1　自信、儀容、微笑與禮貌友善

參加國外旅遊、會議、表演活動、演講、商展或其他社交場合活動時，不需要太擔心自己的英文，在一些特定場合，如果要給陌生人良好的第一印象 (剛開始的 7 到 30 秒是關鍵)，必須有自信、儀容整潔、微笑並展現禮貌友善的舉止。自然地與他人交換跟當時情境、地

點有關的消息，將有助於增長自己的閱歷。

2 獨立的個人

在美國文化裡，每個人是自由、獨立且平等的個體，即使小孩也享有相同的權利，父母的責任在於訓練小孩獨立及其必須為自由所承擔的責任。因此以自信與積極的態度，為自己發聲並能說服別人，非但不是禁忌，反而是整個社會的期許。與美國人打交道務必要學習這一點，沒有人會知道你想要什麼，除非你為自己爭取。

與美國文化恰巧相反，傳統亞洲文化的群體意識及家庭親友的制約力量超越個人追求獨立自主的權利，身為家庭或其他團體的一份子，須以家庭 (團體) 或長輩 (權威) 意見為重，否則可能被認為是自私或不負責。團體意識下，眾人的關心幾乎包含任何話題，個人因此也難以保有隱私。

3 主動創造機會

美國人通常對他人有開放的態度，容易談話，但是對於新來的人，美國可能是個寂寞的地方。多數美國人因為不知道如何與文化不同的人開始交談，也不知道對方是否會說英語，除非有特定事由 (如教會人士請你去教堂聚會或某活動向你募款)，多半不會主動與不同種族的人說話，所以除非自己主動開口與別人交談，在美國可能不會有人主動來找你交朋友，社交機會也不會從天上掉下來。因此當你加入某個群體並且主動開口向美國人說英文，一開始通常會得到溫暖的回應，然而這種熱情經常不會持續，一個團體 (或個人的社交圈) 通常行之有年，已經有自己的文化，要融入任何團體，必須自立自強，讓他們知道你的熱誠與主動的態度，是最基本的生存法則。

4 英文不好不是藉口

英文不夠好，其實沒那麼嚴重，不需擔心要懂得每個字，而是了解其大致的含意。文法或發音不夠好也沒那麼要緊，犯錯是過程，主動的學習態度，加上練習及時間的累積，逐漸就會進步。如果有學校活動或其他邀請，就答應參加吧！不要因為擔心自己是否受歡迎或萬一去了不開心而拒絕。接受邀請會使你因此在新環境裡開始新的嘗試、認識新的人，將來也可主動邀請他人。

在討論商務的場合必須先直接說出重點，再補充事實、細節，不要打轉或拖延說出重點的時間。批評是可以被接受的，但必須是有建設性的批評 (constructive criticism)。

5 交流與學習

在大城市裡，有許多參與社交與文化交流的機會，體驗融入美國社交文化，每種嗜好幾乎都有社團與協會可以參加：旅遊、烹飪、寫作、餐飲、棋類、甚至駕船出海及其他水上活動等等。喜好大自然的人可參加健行或環境協會；參加運動社團可以維持健康也可認識新朋友，許多商界人士或同事們選擇打網球或高爾夫球健身和培養友誼；喜好靜態活動如閱讀或電影欣賞的人，也有各種活動可參與；有宗教信仰者可參加教會活動。

6 小孩的社交技能

有小孩的家長可參加學校的家長會 (Parent Teacher Association，簡稱PTA) 或志願參與學校其他的活動，小孩子可參加小聯盟 (Little League) 或女童軍 (Girl Scouts) 與其他小孩培養友誼。在新的文化、陌生的環境裡，小孩特別容易成為受害者，小孩如能參與學校或社區活動將受益良多，家長必須確認小孩在參與課後活動時能融入其他小朋友的活動，才不致於被孤立。

7 話題

運動和休閒在美國是很受歡迎的活動及很好的聊天題材，可以與對方聊自己這方面的活動或嗜好，但是如果我們將亞洲關心別人那一套的聊天話題 (如忠告他人減肥、戒煙，甚至結婚、早生貴子等) 拿來忠告追求個人獨立自主重視隱私的美國人，就是多管閒事 (nosy)，極不合宜。任何種族、膚色、政治、宗教、年齡、外貌、身材、收入、花費等敏感話題要避免，某些美國人可能開玩笑地反諷你勸他戒菸，而回答 Yes, Doc [doctor]. 或 Yes, Mom! (You sound like my Mom!) 意思是拜託，別管太多了。

8 幽默尺度

有些人喜歡搞笑，多數時候想要製造幽默效果，但是並非每個人都知道玩笑的尺度，難免有些人開種族或性別玩笑而不自知，如果這類玩笑持續，就離那樣的人遠點吧。

9 社交場合，記住他人名字要訣

(1) 在認識一群人之前，先讓自己冷靜。如果可以的話，先做功課，以便將名字及面貌連結。

(2) 當你被介紹時，直視對方並注意聽對方的名字，與對方握手時，馬上大聲說出對方名字。在與他 [她] 對話時，至少說出對方名字一次，在對方離去時，再重複一次。

(3) 重複在心裡說對方名字數次並與視覺連結，如對方名字是 James Jones，你可以想像對方與 James Bond 站在一起。或是想像對方的特徵與可能的連結，如對方名字為 Mary 且頭髮是紅色的，可以連結成 red hair Mary。

(4) 使用押韻，如 Stanley 很結實，可以 sturdy Stanley 記住，又 Tim 很瘦，可以用 thin Tim 記住。

(5) 最重要的是有機會再複習這些記憶，看對方的名牌、寫下名字或要對方的名片都是可用的辦法。

1.6 自我介紹 Self-Introduction

1.6a 不正式場合 Informal Settings

A: 哈囉 (握手)，我是朗尼蔡。	**A:** Hello (shaking hands). My name is Ronny Tsai.
B: 哈囉，朗尼，我是泰瑞莎卡登。很高興認識你。	**B:** Hello, Ronny. I'm Teresa Cardan. I'm pleased to meet you.
A: 我也很高興認識你。你喜歡這個聚會嗎？	**A:** I'm glad to meet you too. Are you enjoying this get together?
B: 喜歡，不錯，有佳肴、也有美酒。	**B:** Yes. It's not bad. Good food, and drinks are available too.
A: 是啊，我真的很喜歡他們提供的甜點。	**A:** True. I really like the desserts they provided.

B: 它們很棒，但是我擔心吃太多。

B: They are great, but I'm afraid of eating too many.

A: 我知道這種感覺，吃太多然後不運動就覺得很糟。

A: I know the feeling. Too many and then you feel bad about not exercising.

B: 對，即使有運動也是。

B: Right, even if you do.

A: 是的，正是如此。

A: Yes. That's exactly right.

B: 談到運動，你有運動嗎？

B: Speaking of exercise, do you?

A: 有，但是不夠規律。

A: Yes, but not regularly enough.

B: 你喜歡做哪一類運動？

B: What type of exercise do you like?

A: 我最喜歡健行，但是我經常沒時間健行，所以我上健身房。

A: I enjoy hiking the most, but I don't have time to do it usually, so I go to a gym.

B: 真的嗎？我也是。

B: Really? Me too.

available [ə'veləbḷ] adj. 可以得到的

dessert [dɪ'zɝt] n. 甜點

gym [dʒɪm] n. 健身房

Useful Phrases 實用語句

1. 你介意我稱呼你……嗎？

   Do you mind if I call you...?

2. 別人怎麼稱呼你？

   What do people call you?

3. 你喜歡這個聚會嗎？

   Are you enjoying this get together?

4. 我真的很喜歡他們提供的甜點。

   I really like the desserts they provided.

5. 你喜歡做哪一類運動？

   What type of exercise do you like?

6. 我最喜歡健行。

   I enjoy hiking the most.

7. 我經常沒時間健行。

   I don't have time to go hiking usually.

8. 我上健身房。

   I go to a gym.

在一個群體裡面，不認識的人並不是一道牆，而是一扇扇可以給你不同風景的窗戶。

參加不認識其他人的社交場合，向別人介紹自己時，可以這樣開始——「Hello. My name is Jack 」或「I'm Jack 」或「I'd like to introduce myself. I'm Jack. 」並加上握手。美國人握手外加上拍背或拍手臂來表示友善也很常見，德州人與熟人見面習慣加上擁抱。介紹自己時，不要加頭銜，即使別人以其他頭銜來稱呼你。別只報上姓名，加上一句讓人聽起來開心的「Good to see you. 」「Nice to meet you. 」或「Nice to see you again. 」很有必要。

美國人通常與對方談話時頗為輕鬆，所以在社交場合輕鬆自然就可以。在聚會的場合談論點心食物極為自然，談運動或興趣都是好話題，但要注意不要談論對方的身材、年齡、收入，也不要詢問對方某件物品的花費等敏感話題。

1.6b 正式場合 Formal Settings

Dialog 對話

A: 晚安，我是唐納唐。 → **A:** Good evening, I'm Donald Tang.

B: 唐先生，我是威廉杜勒斯。 → **B:** Mr. Tang, I'm William Dulles.

A: 我很高興認識您，杜勒斯先生。 → **A:** I'm very pleased to make your acquaintance, Mr. Dulles.

B: 我也是。 → **B:** And I yours.

A: 我以正式身分來此，我所代表的大學想要討論與貴機構合作國際研究計畫的可能性。

A: I'm here in an official capacity. The university I represent would like to discuss the possibility of collaborating with this institution on an international research project.

B: 很好，我們來決定談論此事的會面時間。

B: That would be fine. Let's decide on a time when we can meet to talk about it.

A: 您真是周到，這是我的名片。

A: That's very gracious of you. Here is my card.

B: 我的名片也在這裡。

B: Here is mine as well.

A: 我知道您很忙，何時是您會面最好的時間呢？

A: I know you are very busy. When would be the best time for you to meet?

Word Bank 字庫

collaborate [kə'læbə͵ret] v. 合作
institution [͵ɪnstə'tjuʃən] n. 機構
research project n. 研究計畫

Useful Phrases 實用語句

1. 我也是。(我也很高興認識您。)

   And I yours. (I'm very pleased to make your acquaintance, too.)

2. 我以正式身分來此。

   I'm here in an official capacity.

3. 我們來決定談論此事的會面時間。

   Let's decide on a time when we can meet to talk about it.

4. 您真是周到。

   That's very gracious of you.

5. 這是我的名片。

   Here is my card.

6. 何時是您會面最好的時間呢？

   When would be the best time for you to meet?

對於某些特定身分或職業，如醫師 (Doctor)，教授 (Professor)，軍官如將軍 (General)、上校 (Colonel)，政府官員如總統 (President)、首相 (Premier)、大使 (Ambassador)，宗教人士如教宗 (Pope)、神父 (Reverend (Father)) 及法官 (Justice (Judge)) 等職業，在姓氏前必須加上這些頭銜來稱呼他們，如 Doctor Jones, Colonel Brown。其他職業或身分以Mr. / Mrs. / Ms. 來稱呼。美國老師介紹自己時會加上希望學生稱呼的抬頭 (如 Mr. Smith or Dr. [Prof.] Smith)，但是會把全名 (John Smith) 寫在黑板上 (老師在英文裡是職業，不是稱謂)。中文裡職業頭銜直接當作稱謂的不勝枚舉 (如老師、經理、助理等)，但英文裡只有少數職業頭銜可以當作稱謂。

會面時如果沒見過某人，通常男士們會彼此握手。如果要與人握手，在說話前就先伸出手，握手時要注意力道及時間，千萬不可軟握一下就放開，顯得敷衍沒誠意。緊握對方的手並微笑，握手時介紹自己，不要握太久並讓他們口頭回應你的介紹。

如果會面時有身分上之差異，由位高者決定是否與對方伸手握手，男士與女士會面，傳統上由女士決定是否主動伸手握手，然而現今社會專業不分性別，女士與男士握手已經很普遍，女士們 (特別是某些專業人士) 也會彼此握手，在某些場合 (如會見久未碰面的朋友或親戚) 還會互相擁抱，男士們彼此間通常不擁抱，但這要看他們之間的交情或場合而定。如果有人已伸出手要與你握手，迎上去握手就對了，無論是否違反身分或社交慣例，讓對方的手懸在空中視若無睹可是社交大忌。

1.6c 向大人物自我介紹 Introducing Oneself to a VIP

Dialog 對話

A: 抱歉打擾您，安德魯先生，我的名字是席德王，我替HTS快捷工作。

A: Excuse me. Mr. Andrews. My name is Sid Wang. I work for HTS Express.

B: 嗨，席德，很高興認識你。

B: Hi, Sid. It's nice to make your acquaintance.

A: 我也很高興認識您，我想占用您幾分鐘時間與您談談我心中的一個新計畫。

A: It's nice to meet you too. I'd like to have a few minutes of your time to talk to you about a new project I have in mind.

B: 我明白了，是什麼計畫？

B: I see. What's the project for?

A: 設計客製化電腦程式來強化運輸效率及減低運輸成本。

A: To design customized computer programs to enhance shipping efficiency and lower costs of shipping.

B: 聽起來好極了。現在我必須離開，你打電話給我的祕書預定一個會面時間，我想多聽一些。

B: That sounds fascinating. Right now I have to go, but call my secretary and set up an appointment. I'd like to hear more.

A: 謝謝您，安德魯先生，我會照做。

A: Thank you, Mr. Andrews. I'll do that.

B: 好，再會。

B: Good. See you soon.

A: 是的，祝您有美好一天。

A: Yes. Good day to you, sir.

customized ['kʌstə,maɪzd] adj. 客製的
efficiency [ɪ'fɪʃənsɪ] n. 效率
enhance [ɪn'hæns] v. 強化
fascinating ['fæsn̩,etɪŋ] adj. 迷人的，極好的

1. 我想占用您幾分鐘時間談一個新計畫。

   I just want to use a few minutes of your time to talk about a new project.

2. 是什麼的計畫？

   What's the project for?

3. 聽起來好極了。

   That sounds fascinating.

4. 我想多聽一些。

   I'd like to hear more.

5. 我可以給您名片嗎？

   May I give you my card?

6. 祝您有美好一天。

   Good day to you, sir.

Tips 小祕訣

與大人物會面的難易度依自己的需求與環境而定，時機 (timing) 無疑是最難掌握的。在美國每個人都可以向任何人自我介紹，包含位高權重的人，只是大人物通常行程滿檔，而且隨從環繞很難接近，如果大人物出席的場合你也在場，才有可能利用機會向大人物自我介紹。

如果你身為大人物，應該禮貌回應，了解別人為何要與你打招呼並自我介紹，至少給每個人兩三分鐘的時間與注意力，將心比心。

如在電梯間與大人物 (如公司總裁) 偶遇，應該禮貌地打招呼 (Good morning, sir.)，視情形決定是否報上名字及工作部門 (My name is _______. I'm in the ______ Dept.)，讓大人物回應你的招呼，道別時可以這麼說「It was nice meeting you, sir. Have a nice day! 」(很高興遇到您，祝您有愉快的一天)。

1.7 介紹他人與被介紹 Introducing Someone and Being Introduced

1.7a 介紹某人給另一人 (不正式) Introducing Someone to Another Person (Informal)

Dialog 對話

A: 嗨，蘇珊，我想介紹一個我的朋友給你認識。

A: Hi, Susan. I'd like to introduce a friend of mine to you.

B: 好，很好。

B: Oh. Great.

A: 蘇珊，這是卡爾施。

A: Susan, this is Karl Shih.

B: 嗨，卡爾，很高興認識你。

B: Hi, Karl. I'm pleased to meet you.

C: 嗨，蘇珊，我也很高興認識你。

C: Hi, Susan, I'm happy to meet you too.

注意介紹的順序是禮貌對話的開始，先說女士、年長、位高、資深者的名字，將男士、年輕、資淺、位低者介紹給他們。如果不熟悉這個順序，找個朋友練習到流利無誤為止。如「Mom, this is my friend David. David, this is my mother, Barbara Jones.」。

1.7b 介紹某人給另一人 (較正式) Introducing Someone to Another Person (More Formal)

A: 歐爾森先生，我要介紹你給沙勒斯醫院的外科主任亞瑟范德爾斯醫師認識。

A: Mr. Olson. I would like to introduce you to the Head of Surgery at Salles Hospital, Dr. Arthur Vendars.

B: 我很高興能認識你，范德爾斯醫師，我是卡爾歐爾森。

B: I'm very happy to make your acquaintance, Dr. Vendars. I'm Karl Olson.

C: 我也很開心能認識你，歐爾森先生，久仰你及你公司的大名，但請叫我亞特就好。

C: I too am happy to meet you, Mr. Olson. I've heard much about you and your company. But please, call me Art.

B: 好，那你也叫我卡爾。

B: All right. I will. And you should call me Karl.

C: 好。

C: Fine.

surgery ['sɝdʒərɪ] n. 外科
head [hɛd] n. 主任，首長

1. 你希望我怎麼介紹你？
   How do you want me to introduce you?
2. 如果我稱呼他……會不禮貌嗎？
   Would it be rude if I called him...?
3. 我要介紹你給亞瑟范德爾斯醫師。
   I would like to introduce you to Dr. Arthur Vendars.
4. 我聽說許多你及你的公司的事。
   I've heard much about you and your company.
5. 但請叫我亞特就好。
   But please, call me Art.

Dialog 2 對話2

A: 約翰，你有空嗎？我想介紹你認識新來的編輯，艾美史密斯。

A: John, do you have a minute? I'd like you to meet our new editor, Amy Smith.

B: 好。

B: Sure.

A: 艾美從加州來，她是自由作家，剛完成加州大學洛杉磯分校的新聞碩士學位。

A: Amy is from California. She has been a freelance writer and has just completed her master's degree in journalism at UCLA.

B: 嗨，艾美。

B: Hi, Amy.

A: 艾美，這是約翰希爾頓，我們的藝術指導，約翰已經替我們出版社工作超過十年，我們沒他就活不下去。

A: Amy, this is John Hilton, our art director. John has been working for this publisher for over ten years. We can't live without him.

C: 很高興認識你。

C: Nice to meet you.

B: 我的榮幸。

B: My pleasure.

A: 約翰，艾美及其他編輯要一起午餐，如果你到時有空，加入我們吧。

A: John, Amy and the other editors are having lunch together. Join us if you have time then.

B: 好，應該沒問題！到時見。

B: Yeah. It should be no problem! See you guys then.

A: 好！待會見。

A: OK! See you later.

editor ['ɛdɪtɝ] n. 編輯
freelance writer n. 自由作家
master's degree n. 碩士學位
journalism ['dʒɝnḷ,ɪzṃ] n. 新聞
art director n. 藝術指導
publisher ['pʌblɪʃɚ] n. 出版社

1. 你有空嗎？
   Do you have a minute?
2. 我想介紹一個我的朋友給你認識。
   I'd like to introduce a friend of mine to you.

3. 我想介紹你認識新來的編輯，艾美史密斯。

   I'd like you to meet our new editor, Amy Smith.

4. 我們沒他就活不下去。

   We can't live without him.

5. 如果你到時有空，加入我們吧。

   Join us if you have time then.

1.7c 介紹某人給一組人認識 (較正式場合) Introducing Someone to a Group of People (at a More Formal Setting)

A: 各位，我要 (向大家) 介紹達爾德藥廠的執行長，理查華生先生。

A: Everyone. I would like to introduce the C.E.O. of Dard Pharmaceuticals, Mr. Richard Watson.

B: 哈囉，大家好。

B: Hello, everyone.

A: 華生先生，這是我們的行銷主任克爾文傑明森，財務主任雪洛費雪，國外股份規劃長大衛藍汀漢及人事部顧問凱思琳強生。(大家握手並且在被介紹時說哈囉)

A: Mr. Watson, this is our Marketing Director Calvin Jamison, our Director of Financial Services, Sheryl Fisher, our Chief Foreign Holdings Planner, David Landingham, and our Personnel Development Advisor, Kathleen Johnson. (Everyone would shake hands and say hello as they are introduced by name.)

A: 好，既然我們都介紹過了，最好開始談公事吧。

A: Well. Now that we have all been introduced, we'd better get on with business.

B: 聽起來很好。

B: Sounds good to me.

Word Bank 字庫

marketing ['mɑrkɪtɪŋ] n. 行銷
director [də'rɛktɝ] n. 主任
Financial Services n. 財務 (部門)
holdings ['holdɪŋz] n. 股份
advisor [əd'vaɪzɚ] n. 顧問

1.8 確認姓名 Clarifying Names

Dialog 對話

A: 哈囉，我的名字是潔西葉。

A: Hello. My name is Jessie Yeh.

B: 嗨，潔西，我是卡茲克雷韋曼。

B: Hi, Jessie. I'm Kaz Klevilm.

A: 是卡茲凱爾韋曼嗎？

A: Is that, Kaz Kelvilm?

B: 不太對，發音是克雷韋曼。

B: Not quite. It's pronounced Klevilm.

A: 我懂了，卡茲克雷韋曼。	**A:** I see. Kaz Klevilm.
B: 對，你說對了，你的名字念葉，對嗎？	**B:** Yes. You got it. And your name is Yeh, right?
A: 是的，潔西葉。	**A:** Yes. Jessie Yeh.
B: 好，很高興認識你。	**B:** Well, it's nice to make your acquaintance.
A: 我也很高興。	**A:** I'm pleased as well.

1. 不太對。
   Not quite.
2. 發音是……。
   It's pronounced ....
3. 你說對了。
   You got it.
4. 你的名字念葉對嗎？
   And your name is Yeh, right?
5. 可以請你再唸一次你的姓 [名] 嗎？
   Can you please pronounce your last [first] name again?
6. 「葉」是普遍的姓氏嗎？
   Is Yeh a popular last name?
7. 你的名字有含意嗎？
   Does your given name have a meaning?

8. 你是按照家裡的任何成員取名的嗎？

Are you named after anyone in your family?

9. 你的父母親如何為你取名呢？

How did your parents choose your name?

如果名字被唸錯，要清楚為對方重複，聽不懂或不知對方姓名如何發音，請對方教你或為你寫下來，不必不好意思，重複兩三遍直到你會為止，這麼做除了表示重視對方，還可增進彼此的了解，名字有文化上的意義，與姓名相關之討論有助於打開話題。

遇到舊識，卻忘記對方姓名時，先報上自己姓名「Hello. My name is ___ .」對方可能會回應姓名。如果不成，可以接著說「I'm sorry, I remember you, but I've forgotten your name.」表示「抱歉，記得人，但不記得名字」，讓對方回應。

肢體語言 Body Langauge

地球村的時代，人們有更多機會接觸不同文化，對於來自不同地區或宗教的人們有些基本認識是必要的。

美國是個大熔爐，在初次見面的介紹場合，最常見的是握手禮，將右手空出準備握手。被介紹時不要害羞，眼神要直視對方 (代表自信、誠實與熱誠) ，並且主動伸手與對方握手 (力道須展現熱誠，但避免誇張或草率)。朋友間以握手、拍肩表示鼓勵或熱誠，彼此不會稱兄 (姐) 道弟 (妹)，除非雙方都是非裔。男士間不會勾肩搭背，女士間不會勾手表示熱絡，除非是同性戀人。

除了握手禮之外，西方人表示關心與友好的禮節尚有擁抱禮、貼面禮與親吻禮，英國還有吻手禮。但在見面時是否適合要看人們的關係及場合而定，多數人不會在初次見面就與陌生人擁抱、貼面或親吻。擁抱禮可能出現在迎賓、祝賀、道謝、或道別的場合，平輩間的貼面禮與親吻禮是以貼面及親吻空氣 (air kiss) 表示友好。女士們與男女之間貼面與親吻次數各地不一城鄉有別，男士間是否貼面與親吻也有文化之別。

某些文化如泰國 (Thailand) 、印度 (India) 、尼泊爾 (Nepal) 、柬埔寨 (Cambodia) 等打招呼不用握手而是行雙手合十 (wai) 的合掌禮，從手放在胸前到眼前的程度表示尊敬的程度，慣於握手的人拜訪這些地區要入境隨俗。

許多亞洲與中東地區，對肢體碰觸相當保守，切記避免趨身向前與婦女握手，女士們可能感到受冒犯。回教文化中男女壁壘分明，異性之間即使是禮貌性的口頭稱讚 (如未婚男士稱讚已婚女士表示有興趣了解對方) 便可能惹惱對方配偶，與已婚女士照相更需取得對方先生同意，回教真主阿拉並無形象，所以保守的回教徒不拍照；阿拉伯文化熱情好客，但國人對其宗教、風俗與社會規範仍須多加了解。

此外，印度、尼泊爾、柬埔寨、阿拉伯地區或某些宗教 (如回教) 裡有禁用左手與他人互動的習俗，慣用左手的人一定要記住不用左手與來自這些文化的人握手、進食、付錢或傳遞物品。

某些文化肢體語言使用廣泛，美國人與義大利 (Italy) 南部人習慣說話時比手畫腳且表情豐富幫助語言傳達，中東男士間經常彼此碰觸，但英國人則少用肢體語言。國人經常使用的手勢在世界各地需要特別注意之處，列舉如下：

1. 豎起大拇指在許多地方是「棒極了」，但在澳洲、大部分中南美洲及義大利南部等於是比中指的髒話。
2. 拇指豎起朝後方比的搭便車 (hitchhiking) 的手勢，在希臘 (Greece) 與土耳其 (Turkey) 幾乎等同中指髒話。
3. 我們常比的「OK」手勢，在許多地方意為「沒問題」，在法國 (France) 代表「零」、「沒價值」，日本 (Japan) 代表「錢」或「零錢」 (年輕人代表OK) ，但在土耳其 (Turkey) 代表「同性戀」 (homosexual)，在德國某些地區與一些中南美洲國家如墨西哥 (Mexico) 、巴西 (Brazil) 、委內瑞拉 (Venezuela) 、巴拉圭 (Paraguay) 代表肛門，引申為「混蛋」。
4. 勝利的「V」手勢，手的背面要向著自己，如果在英國手背向著他人代表髒話，如果是在餐廳要點兩杯咖啡，比錯手勢，侍者不可能為你服務。
5. 在希臘 (Greece) 向別人比出數字「5」的手勢是侮辱之意，為歷史上侮辱戰敗敵人塗抹穢物的手勢，手掌朝對方臉越近，程度越嚴重。避免此手勢，要引起侍者注意、叫計程車或說再見，舉起手，手腕上下擺動。

6. 在馬來西亞 (Malaysia) 、印尼 (Indonesia) 、中東地區 (the Middle East)，以食指指他人是不禮貌的表現，要用拇指代替。
7. 在泰國及中東，人的腳是全身最低的地方，代表不乾淨，所以不要將腳底或鞋底示人，用腳推、指東西，也是不禮貌的表現。泰國人認為頭部最高也最神聖，所以不要摸任何人的頭部上方，當然包括小孩的頭。

肢體語言的重要性甚至比真正的語言還重要，尤其在言語不通的情形下，用錯了肢體語言將造成誤會，用對了使彼此心領神會盡在不言中，因此，學習並注意使用適切的肢體語言有助於溝通，超越語言的藩籬。

Unit 2 Running into a Friend
[Acquaintance]

偶遇朋友 [舊識]

打招呼不僅是友善的表示，也是禮貌的表現。在戶外、電梯間、走廊上等公共空間，相識的人們都會互相打招呼，簡短一聲嗨或微笑揮手致意皆可。沉默不發一語、面無表情或近距離卻視而不見，難免會被認為沒禮貌或不友善，適度寒暄 (making small talk) 可以拉近距離。

2.1 巧遇老同學
Bumping into an Old Classmate

A: 請問你是泰瑞莎林嗎？	**A:** Excuse me. Are you Teresa Lin?
B: 是的，我是。我是不是在哪裡認識你？	**B:** Yes. I am. Do I know you from somewhere?
A: 我是你的高中同學，吉米楊，綠湖高中。	**A:** I am your high school classmate, Jimmy Young, from Green Lake High School.
B: 喔！是啊！吉米，你現在看起來很不一樣。	**B:** Oh! Yes! Jimmy, you look so different now.

A: 是啊，我知道時間如何捉弄人，但另一方面，你一點都沒變，我完全可以在人群裡認出你來。

A: Yeah, I know how time can play tricks. On the other hand, you haven't changed a bit. I can recognize you in the crowd without a problem.

B: 嗯，我會把那當作是讚美。	**B:** Well, I'll take that as a compliment.
A: 當然，你有跟其他同學聯絡嗎？	**A:** Please do. Do you stay in contact with any other classmates?

B: 有，給我你的手機號碼及電子郵件地址，我會把你加入聯絡網。

B: Sure. Give me your cell-phone number and email address. I'll include you in our loop.

trick [trɪk] n. 詭計，把戲
recognize ['rɛkəg,naɪz] v. 認出
crowd [kraud] n. 人群
compliment ['kɑmpləmənt] n. 讚美
contact ['kɑntækt] n. 聯絡
loop [lup] n. 圈，環

1. 我是不是在哪裡認識你？
   Do I know you from somewhere?
2. 好久不見。
   Long time no see.
3. 我好久沒見到你了！
   I haven't seen you in ages!
4. 我沒認出你。
   I didn't recognize you.
5. 我一下子沒認出你來。
   I couldn't recognize you for a moment.
6. 我完全可以在人群裡認出你來。
   I can recognize you in the crowd without a problem.
7. 你現在看起來很不一樣！
   You look so different now!
8. 你一點都沒變。
   You haven't changed a bit.

9. 我知道時間真會捉弄人。
   I know how time can play tricks.
10. 我把那當作是讚美。
    I'll take that as a compliment.
11. 請這樣做。
    Please do.
12. 記得我們以前經常一起打球嗎？
    Remember we used to play sports together?
13. 你有跟其他同學聯絡嗎？
    Do you stay in contact with any other classmates?
14. 我會把你加入聯絡網。
    I'll include you in our loop.

問候他人時讚美對方是常見的美國文化，甚至可說是基本禮儀，人們不管交情如何，經常樂於讚美別人。例如：人們常讚美朋友看起來很好，使用「You look wonderful [marvelous, terrific, gorgeous, fabulous, fantastic, perfect]! 」等張力十足的字彙。異性之間的讚美很普遍也很直接，並不代表什麼暗示，與亞洲文化頗為不同；接受讚美不代表驕傲，自貶絕對不代表謙虛，一切以誠摯、不造作為原則，對於別人的讚美不要不好意思，大方的說「Thank you.」即可，或回覆對方「So do you.」(你也是)，不要說「No」否定別人對你的讚美，這樣會使對方很尷尬，學習真誠自然的讚美他人與接受讚美是重要的社交技巧。

2.2 巧遇朋友
Running into a Friend

2.2a 在書展 At a Book Show

Dialog 對話

A: 嘿，史丹！史丹蘇！	**A:** Hey, Stan! Stan Su!
B: 唐！好驚訝喔！你在這裡做什麼？	**B:** Dan! What a surprise! What are you doing here?
A: 我猜跟你一樣吧，我來看書展。	**A:** Same as you I suppose. I'm here for the book show.
B: 對，我想我早該猜到。	**B:** Right. I guess I should have figured that out.
A: 你會在這裡待多久？	**A:** How long will you be here?
B: 整整四天，你呢？	**B:** All four days. And you?
A: 一樣，我會在這裡多待幾天處理生意的事。	**A:** Same. I'm going to stay a few extra days to tend business.

B: 我們應該一起吃個晚餐。

B: We ought to get together for dinner.

A: 好主意，你何時有空？

A: Good idea. When are you free?

B: 我想今晚以後可以。你呢？

B: After tonight I think I'm OK. What about you?

A: 我應該可以，我們現在交換號碼吧，我必須立刻回到客戶那裡[回客戶電話]。

A: I can probably make it work. Let's exchange numbers now. I have to get back to some clients right now.

B: 好，我住在麗晶，房號是344，這是飯店的(電話)號碼。

B: Right. I'm staying at the Regent. My room number is 344. Here's the hotel number.

A: 我住在史坦斯佛，這是我的房間號碼以及櫃臺電話。

A: I'm at the Stansford. Here's my room number and their desk number.

B: 好，我們今晚聯絡一下，我想我11點左右會在。

B: Good. Let's get a hold of each other tonight. I'll be in around 11:00, I think.

A: 好，晚點再聊。

A: OK. Talk to you later.

B: 好。

B: Sure.

book show n. 書展
figure out 猜到
tend [tɛnd] v. 處理
get back to 回覆，回到
get a hold of 聯絡
exchange [ɪks'tʃendʒ] v. 交換

1. 你會在這裡待多久？
   How long will you be here?
2. 我們應該一起吃個晚餐。
   We ought to get together for dinner.
3. 我們現在交換號碼吧！
   Let's exchange numbers now.
4. 我必須立刻回到客戶那兒 [回客戶電話]。
   I have to get back to some clients right now.
5. 這是我的房間號碼以及櫃臺電話。
   Here's my room number and their desk number.
6. 我們今晚聯絡一下。
   Let's get a hold of each other tonight.
7. 我想我11點左右會在。
   I'll be in around 11:00, I think.
8. 晚點聊。
   Talk to you later.

微笑、握手、直視對方，這些是在美國主動開始與別人接觸時需要使用的肢體語言，記住不要給對方太多壓力，如果對方不想跟你說話，不必太在意 (Don't take it personally)。多數人用開放的態度回應別人的招呼，只是有時碰到的時機不對，不利交談，也可能他們的心思被太多事情占據，或是必須在短時間內匆促處理許多事情。

2.2b 在商店 At a Store

Dialog 1 對話1

A: 嘿，曼蒂！你在這裡做什麼？	**A:** Hey, Mandy! What are you doing here?
B: 哈囉，真是個驚喜！我正在購買生日禮物，你呢？	**B:** Hello. What a surprise! I'm just shopping for a birthday gift. What about you?
A: 我只是在看牙醫之前打發一點時間。	**A:** I'm just killing some time before I go to my dentist appointment.
B: 聽起來不太有趣。	**B:** That doesn't sound like much fun.
A: 喔，沒什麼，我今天只是要洗牙。	**A:** Oh, it's no big deal. I'm just having my teeth cleaned today.
B: 我明白了，你好嗎？	**B:** I see. How are things?

A: 不錯，我最近感覺很好，運動、工作以及晚上上課。	**A:** Not bad. I've been feeling good, exercising, working, and taking some classes at night.
B: 聽起來很好。	**B:** Sounds nice.
A: 你呢？最近怎麼樣？	**A:** And you? What have you been up to?
B: 沒什麼新鮮事，還是一樣在公立圖書館工作且在老人中心當義工。	**B:** Nothing new. I still work at the public library and volunteer at the Senior Center.
A: 真好，我們應該快點聚聚，一起吃個午餐。	**A:** That's good of you. We should get together soon and have lunch.
B: 好，這樣很好，我們可以聊聊近況。	**B:** Sure. That would be nice. We can catch up on things.
A: 對，你有我的手機號碼嗎？	**A:** Right. Do you have my cell phone number?
B: 好像沒有，我抄一下。	**B:** I don't think so. Let me write it down.
A: 我們也應該交換一下電子郵件地址。	**A:** We ought to exchange email addresses too.

B: 好主意。	**B:** Good idea.

Word Bank 字庫

dentist ['dɛntɪst] n. 牙醫
volunteer [ˌvɑlən'tɪr] v. 當義工
Senior Center n. 老人中心

Dialog 2 對話2

A: 嘿，麗莎！	**A:** Hey, Lisa!
B: 嗨，約翰，有一陣子沒見面囉。	**B:** Hi, John. It's been a while.
A: 是啊，你最近如何？	**A:** Yeah. How are you doing recently?
B: 還算不錯，我剛出版了第一本小說。	**B:** Really not bad. I just got my first novel published.
A: 哇，很棒喔！	**A:** Wow! That's wonderful.
B: 你呢？	**B:** How about you?

A: 我最近在找新工作，我有接到一些工作邀約，但沒一個讓我感興趣。

A: I've been looking for a new job. I've received some offers, but none of them interest me.

B: 我想以你的能力及經驗，你馬上就會找到工作。你有時間嗎？我們去吃個晚飯多聊聊。

B: I think with your ability and experience, you will find a job in no time. Do you have time now? Let's have dinner and catch up some more.

A: 好，走吧！

A: Sure. Let's do it!

Word Bank 字庫

publish ['pʌblɪʃ] v. 出版
offer ['ɔfɚ] n. 邀約

2.2c 在戶外 Outdoors

Dialog 1 對話1

A: 嗨，你好嗎？

A: Hi, how are you today?

B: 很好啊，你呢？

B: Just fine. And you?

A: 我也很好。	**A:** I feel fine, too
B: 你今天在忙些什麼呢？	**B:** What are you up to today?
A: 沒什麼，只是稍微觀光一下。	**A:** Not much, just a little sightseeing.
B: 聽起來不錯，要拍些照片喔。	**B:** Sounds good. Take some pictures.
A: 我一定會的。	**A:** I'll do that for sure.

Dialog 2 對話2

A: 嘿！你好嗎？	**A:** Hey! How are you doing?
B: 啊，真驚訝！我很好。	**B:** Well! What a surprise! I'm fine.
A: 你要去那裡呢？	**A:** Where are you going?
B: 這裡的一個歷史景點。	**B:** To a local historical site.

A: 好幾天沒見到你了。	**A:** I haven't seen you in a couple of days.
B: 我知道。我最近都自己四處亂跑。	**B:** I know. I've been running around by myself.
A: 很棒喔，你喜歡自由行。	**A:** Great! You like independent traveling.
B: 是啊。	**B:** Yes, I do.

Word Bank 字庫

sightseeing ['saɪtˌsiɪŋ] n. 觀光
historical [hɪs'tɔrɪkl̩] adj. 歷史的
independent [ˌɪndɪ'pɛndənt] adj. 獨立的
run around 到處走動

◆ **問候 Greetings**

1. 主動問候對方 Greeting: Initiating

①你近來好嗎？

How you been? (How have you been? 之簡語)

②最近怎麼樣啊？

What have you been up to (lately)?

③好久不見！

Long time no see!

④很高興見到你。

Great to see you.

⑤哈囉，很高興又見到你。

Hello. It’s so good to see you again.

⑥一切好嗎？

How’s everything?

⑦怎麼樣啊？

What’s up?

⑧有何新鮮事啊？

What’s new?

⑨順利嗎？

How’s it going?

⑩你好嗎？

How are you doing?

⑪你好嗎，夥伴？(牛仔間打招呼)

Howdy, partner? (heard in cowboy culture)

⑫你來這裡多久了？

How long have you been here?

⑬你來這裡很久了嗎？

Have you been here long?

⑭你有跟其他同學聯絡嗎？

Do you stay in contact with any other classmates?

⑮工作如何？

How’s work?

⑯學校如何？

How’s school?

⑰小孩好嗎？

How are the children?

⑱家人好嗎？

How’s the family?

⑲紐約天氣如何？

How’s the weather in New York?

⑳飛行順利嗎？

How was your flight?

㉑你現在住在哪裡？

Where do you live now?

㉒你住哪間旅館？

Where [which hotel] are you staying?

2. 回應問候 Greetings: Responding

①好一陣子沒見囉！

It's been a while.

②還可以 [好]。

OK. [All right].

③不錯。

Not bad.

④還可以。(英國人常用)

Not too bad.

⑤好。

(Just) fine.

⑥我很好。

I've been well.

⑦很忙，你呢？

Pretty busy, and you?

⑧我非常好 (不可能更好了)。

Couldn't be better.

⑨沒什麼。

Not much. [Nothing much].

⑩我 (一陣子) 不在。

I've been away.

⑪沒什麼新鮮事。

Nothing new.

⑫老樣子。

Same old (thing).

⑬(一樣) 忙。

Busy (as ever).

⑭聽起來沒什麼樂趣。

That doesn't sound like much fun.

⑮我只是在打發一點時間。

I'm just killing some time.

⑯我最近在運動。

I've been exercising.

⑰我最近感覺很好。

I've been feeling good.

⑱聽起來很好。

Sounds nice.

⑲我最近才搬家。

I've just moved.

⑳我剛出版了第一本小說。

I just got my first novel published.

㉑我最近在找新工作。

I've been looking for a new job.

㉒我一週兩次在老人中心當義工。

I volunteer at the Senior Center twice a week.

3. 後續聯繫 Keeping in Touch

①我們應該快點聚聚，一起吃個午餐。

We should get together soon and have lunch.

②我們可以聊聊近況。

We can catch up on things.

③你有我的手機號碼嗎？

Do you have my cell phone number?

④我們也該交換電子郵件 [即時通，Skype] 地址。

We ought to exchange email [Messenger, Skype] addresses too.

⑤我會把你加入聯絡網。

I'll include you in our loop.

⑥我會保持聯絡。

I'll be in touch.

中文的「你好嗎？」與英文的「How are you?」雖同樣是日常的問候語，但英文「How are you?」其實僅止於表面的形式，而非實質的問候；英美人士期待正面且制式的回答，如美國人多回答「Fine.」「Just fine.」「Pretty busy, and you?」；較年輕的英國人多回答「Not bad.」或「Not too bad.」；年長些的人多半回答「I am very well. Thank you.」；即使是交情不錯的朋友，也是報喜不報憂，老實報告生活瑣事，可是會讓朋友瞠目結舌、逃之夭夭呢！其他問題如：問工作如何「How's work?」、課程如何「How are your classes?」、感覺如何「How are you feeling?」才算是問句。

如果對方說我們該聚聚，別急著問什麼時候，有時這只是禮貌性道別的說法，此時只需附和說好即可。沒有下文的原因很多，但不必介意，如果想與對方聯絡感情，也可以視狀況，主動提出邀約。

2.3 偶遇鄰居
Running into a Neighbor

A: 嗨，彼得士先生。	**A:** Hi, Mr. Peters.
B: 哈囉，茱莉，你在做什麼呢？	**B:** Hello, Julie. What are you doing?
A: 我剛從商店回來。	**A:** I just got back from the store.

B: 買東西嗎？	**B:** Doing some shopping?
A: 是的，買了一些。	**A:** Yes. A little.
B: 呃，今天天氣很好，適合出去走走。	**B:** Well, it's a beautiful day to be out and about.
A: 確實如此！	**A:** It sure is.
A: 好，請代我向彼得士太太問好，再見了。	**A:** OK then, please say hello for me to Mrs. Peters. See you later.
B: 你也一樣，再見[保重]了。	**B:** Same to you. Take care.

Word Bank 字庫

be out and about 出去走走

Useful Phrases 實用語句

1. 今天天氣很好，適合出去走走。
   It's a beautiful day to be out and about.
2. 請代我向彼得士太太問好。
   Please say hello for me to Mrs. Peters.
3. 再見 [保重]。
   Take care.

禮貌及體貼的語言與行為是公民素養 (例如：行進間為他人拉住門或注意電梯禮貌，禮讓且不要催促老人，留意小孩等)，禮貌及體貼也會使人注意到你的需求，獲得人們的幫忙及所需資訊。

2.4 與同學打招呼 Saying Hello to a Classmate

A: 早安，南茜！

A: Good morning, Nancy!

B: 早安，羅德！你看起來非常開心！

B: Morning, Rod! You look psyched!

A: 對，我剛查了大學網頁裡我的成績，巴特利教授給我個體經濟學的成績是全班最高分。這對我來說是個好消息。

A: That's right! I just checked the university website for my grades. Professor Bartlet gave me the highest score in the microeconomics class. This is great news for me.

B: 哇…恭喜！我記得前兩天你很擔心這件事。

B: Wow... Congratulations! I remember you were concerned about it the other day.

A: 我知道，但是結果真的很好。

A: I know, but it turned out really fine.

Word Bank 字庫

psyched [saɪkt] adj. 開心的 (俚語)
grade [gred] n. 成績
concern [kən'sɝn] v. 使擔心
turn out 結果

1. 你看起來非常開心！
   You look psyched!
2. 恭喜！
   Congratulations!
3. 我記得前兩天你很擔心這件事。
   I remember you were concerned about it the other day.

2.5 與同事小聊
Making Small Talk with a Coworker

A: 吉米！吉米吳！	**A:** Jim! Jim Wu!
B: 嘿，巴瑞，怎麼啦？	**B:** Hey! Barry. What's going on?
A: 喔，沒什麼。我只是看到你想要和你聊聊。	**A:** Oh, nothing much. I just saw you and thought I'd catch up with you.
B: 好啊，你工作順利嗎？	**B:** Cool. Is your work going well?

A: 是啊，不錯，有時太多了，但整體而言還可以。

A: Yeah, not bad. Sometimes it's too much, but generally it's OK.

B: 很好。

B: That's good.

A: 你呢？生活裡有什麼新鮮事呢？

A: How about you? Anything new going on in your life?

B: 我在練空手道及瑜珈，對我很有幫助。

B: I've taken up karate and yoga. It's been good for me.

A: 哇，真了不起，你在哪裡學空手道？

A: Wow. That's really something. Where do you go to learn karate?

karate [kə'rɑtɪ] n. 空手道
yoga ['jogə] n. 瑜珈

1. 我想要和你聊聊。
   I thought I'd catch up with you.
2. 你工作順利嗎？
   Is your work going well?
3. 生活裡有什麼新鮮事呢？
   Anything new going on in your life?

主動與同事微笑打招呼或簡短聊上幾句是表達關心，也是禮貌。既然是「small talk」，話題當然就不宜太過深入。天氣、交通、休閒活動、工作動向、旅遊等都是適切的寒暄話題，切忌三姑六婆 (Don't be a busybody.)，探人隱私。

2.6 偶遇不同部門的同事
Running into a Coworker from a Different Department

A: 嘿，凱莉，怎麼樣啊？	**A:** Hey, Kelly. What's new?
B: 嗨，安迪，沒什麼，只是幫部門跑跑腿。	**B:** Hi, Andy. Nothing much. Just running errands for the department.
A: 我聽說那邊最近事情超忙的。	**A:** I hear things are crazy there these days.
B: 對啊，但這也不是新聞了，你怎麼樣呢？	**B:** Yes, but that's not new either. How's it going for you?
A: 很好，我還在做「南岸計畫」。	**A:** Well enough. I'm still working on the South End project.
B: 真不錯，我的樓層到了，再見。	**B:** Good. Here's my floor. See you.

A: 保重。

A: Take care.

errand ['ɛrənd] n. 跑腿
project ['prɑdʒɛkt] n. 計畫

1. 只是幫部門跑跑腿。
   Just running errands for the department.
2. 我聽說那邊最近事情超忙的。
   I hear things are crazy there these days.
3. 但這也不是新聞了。
   But that's not new.
4. 你怎麼樣呢？
   How's it going for you?
5. 我的樓層到了。
   Here's my floor.
6. 保重。
   Take care.

2.7 電梯內偶遇主管
Running into One of the Company Directors in the Elevator

A: 早安，摩根先生。

A: Good morning, Mr. Morgan.

B: 早安。	**B:** Good morning.
A: 您要到幾樓？	**A:** What floor are you going to, sir?
B: 10樓，謝謝。	**B:** To the 10th. Thank you.
A: 摩根先生，我是約翰布朗，在行銷部工作。	**A:** Mr. Morgan. My name is John Brown. I'm in the marketing department.
B: 我明白了，約翰，你跟行銷部的經理瑪格莉特雪納克一起(工作)。	**B:** I see, John. You're with Margret Sherak, the Manager in Marketing.
A: 是的，摩根先生，我們這個月在促銷「早鳥優惠」。	**A:** Yes, Mr. Morgan, we are promoting the Early Birds Special this month.
B: 希望事情進行順利，我的樓層到了。	**B:** I hope things are going well. Here's my floor.
A: 都進行得很順利，祝您有愉快的一天，摩根先生。	**A:** Things are going very well. Have a nice day, Mr. Morgan.

Word Bank 字庫

marketing department n. 行銷部
promote [prə'mot] v. 促銷
early birds n. 早起的鳥，早到的人 [顧客]

1. 您要到幾樓？

   What floor are you going to?

2. 我是約翰布朗，在行銷部工作。

   My name is John Brown. I'm in the marketing department.

3. 我們這個月在促銷「早鳥優惠」。

   We are promoting the Early Birds Special this month.

4. 希望事情進行順利。

   I hope things are going well.

A: 午安，葉慈女士！	**A:** Good afternoon, Ms. Yates!
B: 午安！	**B:** Good afternoon!
A: 恭喜你關於公司的報導！我是上星期在報紙上讀到的。	**A:** Congratulations on the story about the company. I read it in the newspaper last week.
B: 謝謝你，他們對我們很好。	**B:** Thank you. They were nice to us.
A: 我想你一定將訪問掌握得很好。	**A:** I think you must have handled the interview very well.
B: 或許吧。	**B:** Perhaps.

A: 我的樓層到了，祝你今天愉快。	**A:** My floor. Good day.
B: 你也是。	**B:** Same to you.

1. 恭喜你關於公司的報導！
   Congratulations on the story about the company.
2. 我想你一定將訪問掌握得很好。
   I think you must have handled the interview very well.
3. 報告 [演講] 很棒。
   It was a great presentation [speech].
4. 今天愉快！
   Good day!
5. 你也是。
   Same to you.

為了避免與主管一起搭電梯產生尷尬時刻，要避免不恰當的對話，在工作或商務場合就談論大家一起工作的事務。如果你的主管或老闆忽略了某些事情，你想反映，不要當面在電梯裡提起，以免使他 [她] 困窘，原因有幾項：一來電梯內可能有其他人，二來時間太短，三來電梯是密閉空間，原本就有些壓迫感。表達意見可以用其他的方式，例如：發電子郵件、留言或在其他適宜的場所談話。

與美國人的友誼 Making Friends with Americans

不論種族如何，人們都有社交的心靈需求。跨文化友誼因為牽涉不同文化，彼此間對友誼可能有完全不同的認知。因為對朋友的定義、成為朋友的時間與過程、對新環境的感受，以及人情味的不同，美國友誼可能令不熟悉美國文化的人感到困惑或灰心，跨文化的朋友交往在每個階段都可能因文化不同而產生誤會。因此，了解美國人如何定義、看待及維持友誼，是與美國人交流往來時相當切身的問題。

1　朋友的定義

(1) 美國 (主流) 觀點

美國人對朋友的定義很廣，儘管字典裡也有「acquaintance」(相識的人)，但美國人多半把初識不久的人 (在其他文化裡可能尚未到達朋友交情的人) 及各種熟識度的人統稱為「朋友」。美國對結交朋友的定義與其他文化比起來可以說相當務實：人們結交朋友可歸因於某一環境下滿足個人需求而產生的相互交流，務實並不表示美國人自私或只做表面功夫，而可以說是認清情勢。

(2) 華人觀點

華人通常較為安土重遷，傳統大家庭觀念使家庭親友的關係較為緊密，人與人間較有人情味，中國傳統裡還有「在家靠父母、出外靠朋友」的說法，朋友的產生是緣分，而非滿足彼此需求。

在華人的文化裡，從「陌生人」變成「相識的人」，進而變成「朋友」，經常需要經過一定程度的時間 (因此對陌生人與熟人的態度也截然不同)，「相識的人」彼此從互動中產生某種程度的熟悉與認可後才成為「朋友」，俗語說「百年修得同船渡」，所以能成為朋友是有緣，除非發生嚴重不愉快的事，朋友之間即使環境改變，彼此也會盡量維持情誼。

每個人當然也有不同程度不同場合結交的朋友，然而華人社會裡稱得上「朋友」的話，交往的本質是建立在情誼之上，而非為了其他需求。因為有朋友 (或如兄弟、姐妹) 之情，所以互相幫忙，珍惜友情是華人的共同價值。如果人們因為自己的需求以務實性 (practicality) 結交所謂的朋友 (通常會在朋友兩字之前冠以該務實理由做為區別，如「生意上的」朋友)，意味彼此互取所需，在華人文化裡並非真正的朋友。

2　三分鐘熱度？

一般而言，美國人並不像亞洲人或中東人好客、有人情味，但與其他文化相比，美國文化傾向對陌生人友善、健談、直接，甚至熱情(但較少主動與外國人打招呼，見1.8)，這些特性可能讓人誤以為在短時間內已與美國人成為好友，但是不久之後，熱情似乎就轉淡了，卻變成莫名的失落？

美國人之所以友善、健談、熱情是因為與陌生人開放隨興的交談方式允許他們打入新團體、結交新朋友，也因此友誼的移動很自由。一開始友善健談的美國人，後來卻顯得只有三分鐘熱度是很正常的，這可歸因於情勢使然。如果你要與美國人打交道，要採取自立自強的態度，了解美國友誼的存滅邏輯可以讓你不受挫折，並且知道如何因應。

3　隱私問題

華人文化裡友誼的進展經常代表著私人資訊的交換 (以定位儒家文化裡個人的位置與相處之道)，如：年齡、收入、婚姻家庭狀況、職業、宗教信仰等。然而在美國文化裡，不要誤把他人的友善當作可以詢問隱私，其友誼的進展模式並非如此。美國朋友間的相處之道是平權，而非以差序地位決定相處之道！

那就從談論自己開始吧！從一般話題開始，勿交淺言深，有技巧的問問題「I love to cook [eat out]. Do you?」如果時機合宜，問不失禮的問題「Do you have a family?」代替「Are you married?」及「It's a great dress. Where did you get it?」代替「How much is it？」如果對方願意談論自己私事，自然會吐露。善用觀察法，當然也有效。

4　友誼長存

美國是個高度變動的社會，到外地就學或高中畢業後就搬出父母家開始獨立、換工作、換室友、換住所、換車子等是每個人幾乎都會碰到的狀況；美國文化所隱含的價值由其建國原因 (追求自由、平等、獨立) 便可了解，改變與創造機會是使自己變得更好的必要手段。所以美國人交朋友常是各取所需，採取相當務實的態度，在不同階段 (環境)，有不同需求，交不同的朋友。因此與某些文化比起來，美國人的友誼可能有較明顯的階段性、目標性及務實性。一旦環境或需求改變，舊朋友就換成一批新朋友。例如：修同一門課程一起做報告的組員可能很快成為好友，但下學期修不同課程可能就冷淡了；同住一起感情融洽的室友，因為換地方了，也極可能就不再來往，這些結果因個人需求改變而自然而然形成。

總體而言，美國人的社交關係無非環繞著工作、興趣與宗教信仰。因此，偶遇舊識，如果美國友人說「We should get together soon.」通常是表示友善，可能就是說說而已，不見得會有下文，不必太在意。

5 跨文化友誼觀

跨文化種族的朋友交往 (交流) 必須彼此了解文化是平等的，雙方如發現任何文化差異的議題(包含交朋友之議題)，能透過了解或討論，彼此尊重進而產生對彼此都受用的方式是絕佳的文化學習及最好的交流結果。相信「百年修得同船渡」、珍惜情份的華人與較務實的美國朋友交友，不妨抱著隨緣的態度 (或許也可學學美國人的思維—朋友再交就有，人生要向前看)，了解美國人 (或其他國際人士) 的交友觀，便不會對跨文化友誼有不切實際的期待。幸運的是，現今科技的發達使遠距離朋友之間的聯繫變得容易許多。與美國人交朋友並不表示一定無法長久，但能交到好友並且變成老友，多少要看個人的運氣。

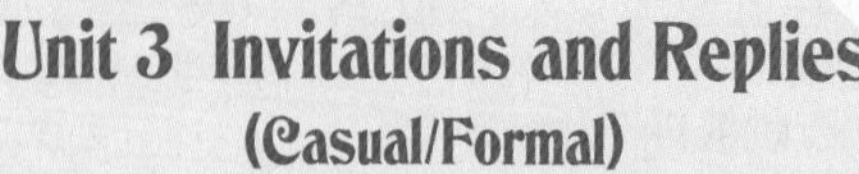

Unit 3 Invitations and Replies (Casual/Formal)

邀請、受邀與回應(非正式/正式)

日常生活裡，非正式的邀請占大多數，雖然提出非正式的邀請較輕鬆，但依然要注意禮貌。如果是請人來家裡開派對或到外面小聚，不需要準備卡片。正式邀請的場合較少，如果是你邀請別人參與正式活動，就要選擇適合的邀請卡，並且至少在一個月前寄出卡片，讓受邀者可以計畫時間。正式邀約通常需要加上 RSVP (請受邀者回覆 (來電或回函) 是否參加)。

3.1 當面邀請某人（不正式）：小孩生日派對
Inviting Someone in Person (Informal) : A Child's Birthday Party

Dialog 對話

A: 嘿，約翰！

A: Hey, John!

B: 嗨，比爾，你好嗎？

B: Hi, Bill. How are you doing?

A: 不錯，真的，潔咪和我下星期六要為席德辦六歲的生日派對，你跟你兒子可以來嗎？

A: Not bad, really. Listen, Jamie and I are holding a party for Sid's sixth birthday next Saturday. Will you and your son come along?

B: 當然，聽起來很好，小孩可以一起玩，派對是幾點？

B: Sure. That sounds great. The kids can have fun together. What time is the party?

A: 下午2點，在我家，到時候見了。

A: 2 p.m., at my place. See you then.

B: 沒問題。

B: No problem.

1. 我們要辦派對。

   We are holding a party.

2. 你跟你兒子可以來嗎？

   Will you and your son come along?

Notes 小叮嚀

如果小孩收到生日派對的邀請，家長通常只要接送小孩到派對地點即可，不需作陪，除非特別註明，否則給壽星的生日禮物通常是童書或玩具。小孩派對有許多不同的活動，天氣比較不好的時候可以在室內說故事、玩遊戲、唱歌、吃點心，在溫暖的天氣裡可以野餐，游泳或到動物園；大一點的小孩可能受同性友人邀請到家裡過夜 (overnights or sleepovers)，家長同樣將小孩送到朋友家，第二天接回即可。

3.2 籌畫郊外出遊 Setting Up an Outing

3.2a 計畫 Planning

A: 我想我們這個週末該找幾個朋友聚聚，玩一玩。	A: I think we should get some people together this weekend and have some fun.
B: 好啊，聽起來是個好主意，但我們該玩什麼呢？	B: Sure. It sounds like a good idea, but what should we do?
A: 我想我們該去銀瀑州立公園。	A: I think we should go to Silver Falls State Park.

初次見面
偶遇
邀請
參加聚會
接待賓客
拜訪
特殊情況
祝賀慰問
交友
日常社交
常用功能
其他功能

B: 我聽說那是個很好的地方。	**B:** I hear that's a nice place.
A: 是的，我們可以健行、野餐、玩樂，也可以看看美麗的瀑布。	**A:** Yes, it is. We can hike, picnic, play around, and see beautiful waterfalls, too.
B: 你要邀幾個人？	**B:** How many people do you want to invite?
A: 我不確定，我們打給我們認識的每個人並邀請他們。	**A:** I'm not sure. Let's just call everybody we know and invite them.
B: 好，就這麼做吧。	**B:** OK. Let's do it.

Word Bank 字庫

State Park n. 州立公園
waterfall ['wɔtɚ͵fɔl] n. 瀑布

Useful Phrases 實用語句

1. 我們這個週末該找幾個朋友聚聚。
   We should get some people together this weekend.
2. 你要邀幾個人？
   How many people do you want to invite?

3.2b 打電話邀請朋友
Calling Some Friends and Inviting Them

Dialog 對話

A: 哈囉。	**A:** Hello.
B: 哈囉，傑瑞嗎？	**B:** Hello. Is this Jerry?
A: 是的。	**A:** Yes, it is.
B: 嗨，傑瑞，我是馬丁施。	**B:** Hi, Jerry. This is Martin Shih.
A: 嗨，馬丁，什麼事？	**A:** Hi, Martin. What's up?
B: 我打電話來邀請大家這個週末到銀瀑去走走。	**B:** I'm calling people to invite them to an outing at Silver Falls this coming weekend.
A: 酷，什麼時候？	**A:** Cool. What time?
B: 週六早上大約10點。	**B:** Saturday, in the morning around ten.
A: 誰會去？	**A:** Who'll be there?

B: 目前聽來滿多人的，大約 15 人說他們會去。	**B:** So far it sounds like a lot of people. About fifteen have said they want to go.
A: 哇，聽來很棒，我們要在哪裡碰面呢？	**A:** Wow! Sounds great. Where should we meet exactly?
B: 公園南側入口，你有辦法到那裡嗎？	**B:** The south entrance of the park. Do you have a way to get there?
A: 喔，我正在想我能不能搭誰的便車。	**A:** Well, I was wondering if I could catch a ride with someone.
B: 我想沒問題，我會告訴你誰願意載人的。	**B:** I think it's no problem. Let me tell you who said they'd be willing to give rides.
A: 謝謝。	**A:** Thanks.

catch a ride 搭便車
give a ride 載人

1. 我們早點去，避開人群。
   Let's go early and beat the crowd.
2. 我們會在一個小時內到那裡。
   We'll be there in an hour.

3. 到那裡要四個小時。

   It will take about four hours to get there.

4. 我們得預訂飯店。

   We need to get hotel reservations.

5. 我們可以住我朋友家。

   We can stay at my friend's house.

6. 我們最好看天氣穿衣服。

   We'd better dress for the weather.

7. 明天會是又熱又陽光普照的天氣。

   It will be hot and sunny tomorrow.

8. 今晚將會又冷，風又大。

   The weather will be cold and windy tonight.

9. 帶把傘。

   Bring an umbrella.

不要太早或太晚打電話是基本禮貌，通常打電話給外國朋友的時間應在早上 9 點到晚上 9 點之間。如果提出的邀請被拒絕，不要放在心上。現在的人非常忙碌，不可能出席每個社交場合，而且朋友若有小孩要照顧，就不容易有空出席社交活動。

3.3 邀請朋友來家裡吃中國菜
Inviting Friends Over for Chinese Food

A: 哈囉，蘇珊，我想邀請你及你先生星期日過來吃中國菜。

A: Hello, Susan. I'd like to invite you and your husband over for Chinese food on Sunday.

B: 聽起來很棒，你要自己煮嗎？

B: That sounds good. Are you going to cook?

A: 是的，我想讓大家嚐嚐幾道我會做的菜。

A: Yes. I want everybody to taste some of the dishes I know how to make.

B: 我們該幾點到？

B: What time should we arrive?

A: 大約 5 點，我們會在 6 點左右用餐。

A: Around five will be fine. We'll eat at about six.

B: 我該怎麼穿呢？

B: How should we dress?

A: 輕鬆點就可以，到時會有六到八個人，來輕鬆一下就好。

A: Casual is fine. There will be six to eight people. Just come and have fun.

B: 聽起來很棒，星期天見。

B: Sounds great. See you on Sunday.

Word Bank 字庫

dish [dɪʃ] n. (一道) 菜
casual ['kæʒuəl] adj. 輕鬆的

1. 我想讓大家嚐嚐幾道我會做的菜。

   I want everybody to taste some of the dishes I know how to make.

2. 我們會在 6 點左右用餐。

   We'll eat at about six.

3. 有六到八個人。

   There will be six to eight people.

4. 來輕鬆一下就好。

   Just come and have fun.

雖然中式料理普遍受到外國人歡迎，但多數老外對中式食物認識有限，道地中式口味未必是他們喜歡或習慣的「中國菜」。美國人通常不喜歡食物裡有大蒜味 (garlic smell)，烹調時的味道彌漫極可能冒犯 (offend) 到老外鄰居，甚至讓廚房的油煙偵測器 (smoke detector) 大叫，引來騷動，按地區能源而定，美國住家烹調可能用電爐 (electric range) 而非瓦斯爐 (gas stove)，使烹調受限 (餐廳要營業，會用瓦斯爐)。不論是在家宴請或帶老外上中國餐館，食物切記不加味精 (MSG)，老外可能會因此過敏，一般美國人不太能吃辣，也要留意。

3.4 電話邀請：攝影展
Inviting Someone on the Phone: A Photo Show

A: 哈囉，傑羅姆，我是夏綠蒂布朗。	**A:** Hello, Jerome. This is Charlotte Brown.

B: 嘿，夏綠蒂，有什麼事嗎？

B: Hey, Charlotte. What's up?

A: 我下個月要在DK畫廊舉辦我第一場個人攝影展，開幕酒會是11月19日，週五晚上，希望你有空來參加，同時提供你的專業見解。

A: I'm having my first solo photo show next month at DK Gallery. The opening reception is on Nov 19th, a Friday evening. I hope you will have time to come by and provide your professional input.

B: 恭喜你舉辦個人展，我很高興你來電邀請我，我要跟我祕書查一下行程表，但是我真的希望可以參加，我會盡快讓你知道。

B: Congratulations on the solo show. I'm glad you called and invited me. I will need to check my schedule with my secretary. But I definitely hope I will make it. I'll get back to you as soon as possible.

A: 謝謝，我很感激。

A: Thank you. I really appreciate it.

B: 不客氣。

B: You are welcome.

solo show n. 個人展
gallery ['gælərɪ] n. 畫廊
opening reception n. 開幕酒會
professional input n. 專業見解

1. 我希望你有空來參加。
   I hope you will have time to come by.
2. 我很感激。
   I really appreciate it.

3.5 當面提出邀請：研討會主講
Inviting Someone in Person: A Seminar Keynote Speech

Dialog 對話

A: 強生教授。

A: Professor Johnson.

B: 林女士，你好嗎？

B: Ms. Lin. How are you?

A: 很好，我很高興你能出席這場會議。

A: Great. I'm glad you made time for this meeting.

B: 我可以為你做什麼？

B: What can I do for you?

A: 我最近為醫藥研究基金會作一項促進醫學倫理研究，我們明年四月將辦一個研討會。

A: I currently work for the Medical Research Foundation on a project to promote medical ethics, and we are holding a seminar next April.

B: 那幾乎是一年以後。

B: That's almost a year from now.

A: 是的，我們很誠摯地邀請您在開幕典禮時主講，您在這領域是最頂尖的，如果沒有您這場合就沒意義了。

A: Yes. We sincerely invite you to give a keynote speech at the opening ceremony. You are the best in this field. This event will mean nothing without you.

B: 真是過獎。

B: That is flattering.

A: 這是我們的提案，希望您能保留時間給我們。

A: Here's our proposal. We hope you can reserve the time for us.

B: 我會看看。

B: I'll read it through.

A: 如果您需要任何東西或有任何疑問，歡迎您聯絡我。

A: You are welcome to contact me if you need anything or have any questions.

B: 好，基本上我現在應該可以為這場研討會保留時間。	**B:** That's good. Basically, I can probably reserve the time for this event for now.
A: 好極了。	**A:** That's great.
B: 我們來看看，日期是幾號？	**B:** Let's see. What date will that be?
A: 4月25日，早上9點30分，是週六。	**A:** April 25th. 9:30 a.m. That's a Saturday.
B: 會場在哪裡？	**B:** Where is the event venue?
A: 臺北國際會議中心4樓。	**A:** 4th floor of the Taipei International Conference Hall.
B: 好，我會讓你知道我最後的決定。	**B:** All right. I will let you know my final decision.
A: 非常感謝您，強生教授。	**A:** Thank you very much. Professor Johnson.

Word Bank 字庫

seminar ['sɛmə͵nɑr] n. 研討會
flatter ['flætɚ] v. 誇獎，奉承
proposal [prə'pozl̩] n. 提案
venue ['vɛnju] n. 會場，地點

Useful Phrases 實用語句

1. 我們很誠摯地邀請您在開幕典禮時主講。
   We sincerely invite you to give a keynote speech at the opening ceremony.
2. 如果沒有您這場合就沒意義了。
   This event will mean nothing without you.
3. 這是我們的提案。
   Here's our proposal.
4. 希望您能保留時間給我們。
   We hope you can reserve the time for us.
5. 如果您需要任何東西或有任何疑問，歡迎您聯絡我。
   You are welcome to contact me if you need anything or have any questions.

3.6 電話邀請（正式）：保護動物活動
Inviting Someone on the Phone (Formal): A Wildlife Protection Campaign

Dialog 對話

A: 哈囉，我是山姆李。

A: Hello. This is Sam Lee.

B: 早，李總裁，我是艾咪包，野生動物協會執行長。

B: Good morning, President Lee. This is Amy Bo, Executive Director of the Wildlife Association.

A: 嗨，艾咪，我可以為你做什麼？

A: Hi, Amy. What can I do for you?

B: 我們協會發起進一步保護瀕臨絕種動物的活動，我們希望邀請您支持這活動，身為社會意見領袖，您的參與可以啟發大眾。

B: Our Association is initiating a campaign to demand further protection of endangered species. We would like to invite you to endorse this campaign. As an opinion leader in this society, your involvement will be inspiring to the public.

A: 我了解你的意思了，你先電郵寄給我活動聲明，我會仔細考慮並在週五前回覆你。

A: I see your point. Why don't you email me your campaign statement? I will give it a serious thought and get back to you by Friday.

B: 好，我會的。

B: Certainly, I will.

A: 除了支持背書外，我還要出席任何相關活動嗎？

A: In addition to the endorsement, will I need to attend any event in support of this initiative?

B: 是的，我正要提及，我們將在週六早上辦一場誓師大會，如果您可以來參加並對參加者演講就太好了。

B: Yes. I was about to mention that. We are holding a launch on Saturday morning. It will be great if you can attend it and address the participants.

A: 那你電郵活動聲明時，也請提供你要我演講的要點。

A: Then, when you email me the statement, please also provide the points you would like me to cover in the speech.

B: 沒問題，我期待您的最後決定，如果您有任何疑問，請與我聯絡。

B: No problem. I look forward to your final decision. Please feel free to contact me if you have any questions.

A: 好，再見。

A: Sure. Bye.

B: 再見。

B: Goodbye.

Word Bank 字庫

initiate [ɪ'nɪʃɪˌet] v. (主動的) 提議
endangered species n. 瀕臨絕種動物
endorse [ɪn'dɔrs] v. 支持
campaign [kæm'pen] n. 活動
inspire [ɪn'spaɪr] v. 啟發
launch (a launch party) [lɔntʃ] n. 發表會，誓師大會
initiative [ɪ'nɪʃɪˌetɪv] n. 發起
address [ə'drɛs] v. 演講

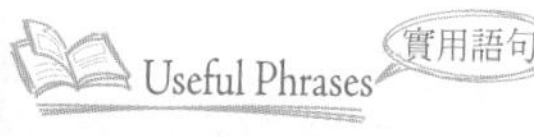

Useful Phrases 實用語句

1. 我們協會發起一項活動。

   Our Association is initiating a campaign.

2. 我們希望邀請您支持這活動。

   We would like to invite you to endorse this campaign.

3. 您的參與可以啟發大眾。

   Your involvement will be inspiring to the public.

4. 我們將在週六早上辦一場誓師大會。

   We are holding a launch on Saturday morning.

5. 如果您可以來參加並對參加者演講就太好了。

   It will be great if you can attend it and address the participants.

6. 我期待您的最後決定。

   I look forward to your final decision.

7. 如果您有任何疑問，請與我聯絡。

   Please feel free to contact me if you have any questions.

Language Power 字句補給站

◆ **不正式邀約 Less Formal**

①我們選個地方見面。

Let’s choose a place to meet.

②你今天想做什麼？

What do you want to do today?

③明天晚上來。

Come over tomorrow night.

④我要開派對，過來吧！

I’m having a party. Come over!

⑤請來參加我的生日派對。

Please come to my birthday party.

⑥我想邀請你的小孩來參加我兒子的生日派對。

I want to invite your kids to my son’s birthday party.

⑦派對大約晚上 8 點開始。

The party will start around eight in the evening.

⑧事實上，你什麼都不用帶。

Actually, you don’t need to bring anything.

⑨你不必帶任何東西，但是帶些點心或飲料也好。

You don’t have to bring anything, but some snack foods or something to drink would be nice.

⑩我需要為派對買些東西。

I need to buy some things for the party.

⑪我要弄些裝飾。

I want to get some decorations.

⑫最近的派對商店在哪裡？

Where is the nearest party store?

⑬你的生日派對在什麼時候？

When is your birthday party?

⑭我們要出去，跟我們去吧！

We’re going out. Come with us!

⑮我們待會在吉兒家碰面，要來喔！

We'll meet at Jill's place later. Be there!

⑯我們今晚出去吧。

Let's go out tonight.

⑰來派對吧！

Let's party!

◆ **正式邀約 Formal**

①我要邀請你。

I have an invitation for you.

②我要邀請你參加 (場合)。

I'd like to invite you to ______.

③希望你可以加入我們。

I hope you can join us.

④請來參加。

Please come.

⑤我 (們) 希望你可以來。

I [We] hope you can make it.

美國多數的社交活動包含飲食及聊天，有些則有禮物餽贈，如聖誕節、喬遷、畢業、準新娘禮物會及婚禮等，還有一些是需要特別打扮的活動，如萬聖節及扮裝派對 (costume party) 等。多數的邀約為不正式的場合 (casual event)，少數的場合要求較正式的穿著 (black tie event)，例如：退休歡送會、婚禮、公司開幕、畢業典禮等。到朋友家並不一定需要帶禮物，但是禮多人不怪，帶些飲料或酒都好。

3.7 邀請卡樣本 Invitation Card Samples

3.7a 正式邀請函樣本 Formal Invitation Sample

Alexander E. Gaston（邀請人）
President（頭銜）
requests the pleasure of your company（榮幸邀請您的參與）
at dinner（晚餐）
in honor of Margaret Tanmal（貴賓）
Friday, the tenth of March（日期）
at seven o'clock（時間）
in the Kyle Ballroom（地點）
The Ellsinore（地址）
Collins Hills Drive
Southmeadows
map enclosed（附地圖）
R.S.V.P. Office of University Relations（請回覆聯絡辦公室）
(345) 926-3407（聯絡電話）

3.7b 半正式邀請函樣本 Semi-Formal Invitation Sample

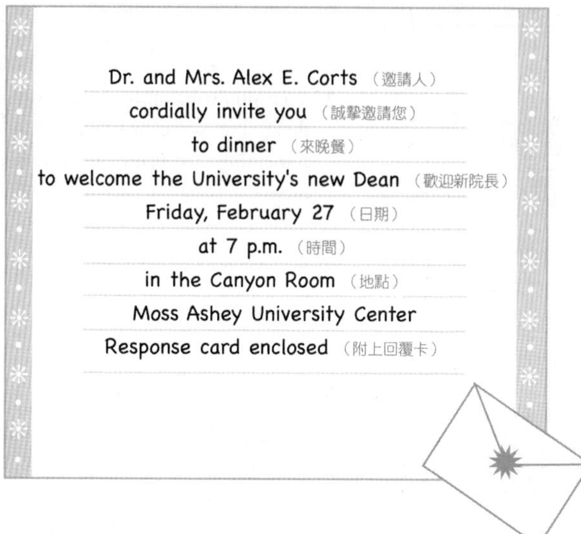

Dr. and Mrs. Alex E. Corts （邀請人）
cordially invite you （誠摯邀請您）
to dinner （來晚餐）
to welcome the University's new Dean （歡迎新院長）
Friday, February 27 （日期）
at 7 p.m. （時間）
in the Canyon Room （地點）
Moss Ashey University Center
Response card enclosed （附上回覆卡）

3.8 受邀 Being Invited to a Party

A: 嗨，約翰，我想邀請你參加星期六晚上的派對。

A: Hi, John. I want to invite you to a party on Saturday night.

B: 在哪裡？是什麼派對？

B: Where is it, and what's it for?

A: 大約晚上8點開始，好玩而已，在我家。

A: It will start around eight in the evening. It's just for fun. It's at my house.

B: 我該帶什麼嗎？	**B:** Should I bring something?
A: 你不必帶任何東西，但是帶些點心或飲料也好。	**A:** You don't have to bring anything, but some snack foods or something to drink would be nice.
B: 好的，沒問題，我會帶些東西來分享。	**B:** OK. No problem. I'll bring something to share.
A: 你記得怎麼來我家嗎？	**A:** Do you remember how to get to my place?
B: 我想我知道，或許你該再給我一次地址。	**B:** I think so. Maybe you should give me the address again.
A: 好的，確定一下你也有我的電話。	**A:** Sure. Let's make sure you have my phone number, too.

Useful Phrases 實用語句

1. 派對在哪裡？
   Where is the party?
2. 是什麼派對？
   What's it for?
3. 我該帶什麼嗎？
   Should I bring something?
4. 我會帶些東西來分享。
   I'll bring something to share.
5. 或許你該再給我一次地址。
   Maybe you should give me the address again.

6. 你記得怎麼來我家嗎？

   Do you remember how to get to my place?

7. 確定一下你有我的電話。

   Let's make sure you have my phone number.

你可能會接到口頭、電話或電子郵件的邀請，大多數的邀請是不正式的，但時間與地點會說清楚，不正式的邀約，如「有空來看我」(come see me sometime) 或「順道來走走」(drop in) 都意味著拜訪前要先打電話。當你接受電話上的邀請，要確認你記得時間與地點並且知道怎麼去，如果沒有交通工具，事先告訴邀請的人以便安排。

3.9 去電詢問所受邀請
Calling to Ask about an Invitation

Dialog 對話

A: 哈囉。 — **A:** Hello.

B: 嗨，瑪莉在嗎？ — **B:** Hi, is Mary there?

A: 我就是。 — **A:** This is she.

B: 嗨，我是巴瑞。 — **B:** Hi , Mary, this is Barry.

A: 嗨，巴瑞，什麼事？

A: Hi, Barry. What's up?

B: 我要問你關於你邀請我參加的晚餐派對。

B: I want to ask you about the dinner party you invited me to.

A: 當然，你的問題是什麼？

A: Sure. What's your question?

B: 我應該要帶什麼？

B: What should I bring?

A: 事實上，你什麼都不用帶。

A: Actually, you don't need to bring anything.

B: 真的？我以為大家都得帶些吃的或喝的。

B: Really? I thought people were supposed to bring something to eat or drink.

A: 這類晚餐派對不必，你可能以為是(大家各帶一道菜的) 便飯派對。

A: Not to this type of dinner party. You're probably thinking of a potluck.

B: 好，那我只需要到就好，對嗎？

B: OK. Then I only need to show up, right?

A: 這樣就可以了。

A: That's good enough.

B: 我可以帶女朋友去嗎？	**B:** Is it OK to bring my girlfriend?
A: 太好了，請帶她來。	**A:** That would be great. Please do.
B: 好，我們星期六晚上見。	**B:** OK. We'll see you on Saturday night.
A: 到時候見，再見。	**A:** See you then. Bye.
B: 再見。	**B:** Bye.

Word Bank 字庫

be supposed to 應該
potluck ['pɑt,lʌk] n. (大家各帶一道菜的) 便飯派對
show up 出現

◎ **請教派對問題 Asking about an Invitation**

1. 我要問你關於你邀請我參加的晚餐派對。

   I want to ask you about the dinner party you invited me to.

2. 我以為大家都得帶些吃的或喝的。

   I thought people were supposed to bring something to eat or drink.

3. 那我只需要到就好，對嗎？

   Then I only need to show up, right?

4. 我可以帶女朋友去嗎？
   Is it OK to bring my girlfriend?

◎ **電話用語 Telephone Expressions**

1. 我要找卡爾傑克森。
   I'm calling for Carl Jackson.
2. 卡爾傑克森在嗎？
   Is Carl Jackson in?
3. 他何時回來？
   When will he return?
4. 你可以打他手機。
   You can call his cell phone.
5. 你有他手機號碼嗎？
   Do you have his cell phone number?
6. 他何時會回來？
   What time will he be back?
7. 我可以留言嗎？
   Can I leave a message?
8. 請留言給他。
   Please give him a message.
9. 請告訴他我打電話過來。
   Please tell him I called.
10. 我的 (手機) 號碼是_________。
    My (cell phone) number is _________.
11. 我晚點再打。
    I'll call back later.
12. 請叫他打給我。
    Please ask him to call me.
13. 任何時間都可以打來。
    Call anytime.
14. 謝謝你的幫忙，再見。
    Thanks for you help. Good-bye.

在美國受邀參加派對，禮物通常不是必要的，除非是生日派對、準新生兒禮物派對或準新娘禮物派對。如果要到朋友家借住一晚，就有必要帶個禮物。參加聚會想送個禮物也可以，人們通常準備飲料或酒，主人會道謝並收下，如果主人在開門時收到禮物，會謝謝對方並表示待會再拆禮物。

如果要送主人禮物，必須知道對方的喜好且不要買太昂貴的物品，否則主人會很困擾。糖果、玻璃製品、盆栽 (相對地，比送花簡單) 及其他特別食品或酒類都是很好的選擇 (但注意喝酒不開車)。有民族或地方特色、代表自己國家的小東西也很適合；花可以當做禮物，但是要避免送整束玫瑰這種有特別意涵的花，選花時可以請教花店的人。

對美國人而言，除了整束玫瑰有特別含意外，不會在意其他花種，因此如果收到一些在亞洲或其他地區有不同含意的花 (如菊花 chrysanthemem、雛菊 daisy、康乃馨 carnation 等) 不必感到奇怪。如果是其他國籍的人士，除了花的寓意，顏色、數目、花種也是要注意的：白色的花經常用在葬禮 (白色百合用於追悼會，如英國、加拿大) 、黃色在智利代表輕視、法國表示不忠誠，紫色在墨西哥、巴西用於葬禮，菊花在許多國家用於葬禮，如中國、法國、西班牙、義大利。數目方面，單數在某些國家 (如前蘇聯國家以及一些歐洲國家) 被視為吉利，日本人、韓國人與華人一樣忌諱 4，基督教及天主教徒忌諱13，不要送德國及捷克人雙數的花，除非是一打，給德國人的花在主人開門後進入玄關處時，要先將包裝取下再交給主人。

3.10 拒絕邀約
Turning Down an Invitation

A: 嗨，山姆。	**A:** Hi , Sam.

B: 嗨，珊蒂。	**B:** Hi ,Sandy.
A: 山姆，我們晚點要去「爵士狂歡時光」。	**A:** Sam, we're all going to the Razz-MoJazz later.
B: 聽起來很好玩。	**B:** Sounds like fun.
A: 一定會，你能來嗎？	**A:** No doubt. Can you come?
B: 我想去，但我得加班。	**B:** I'd like to, but I've got to work late.
A: 你確定嗎？大家都會到。	**A:** Are you sure? Everyone will be there.
B: 對，我確定，我真的得把那件工作完成。	**B:** Yeah, I'm sure. I really have to get that work done.
A: 好，那或許就下次吧。	**A:** A:OK, then maybe next time.
B: 一定。	**B:** For sure.

Useful Phrases 實用語句

1. 聽起來很好玩。

   Sounds like fun.

2. 毫無疑問。

   No doubt.

3. 你能來嗎？

   Can you come?

4. 我想去，但我得加班。

   I'd like to, but I've got to work late.

5. 我真的得把那件工作完成。

   I really have to get that work done.

6. 或許下次吧。

   Maybe next time.

Notes 小叮嚀

拒絕邀約是很正常的，工作忙碌的人們不可能參加每項受邀的活動，但要注意拒絕時的禮貌，才不會使邀請人覺得不舒服或尷尬。

3.11 回覆：接受及拒絕邀請
Reply: Accepting and Declining the Invitation

Useful Phrases 實用語句

口頭接受 Accepting (Verbal)

1. 感謝你邀請我，我一定會到。

   Thanks for inviting me. I'll be there for sure.

2. 聽起來很棒，我們到時見。

   Sounds wonderful. We'll see you then.

口頭拒絕 Declining (Verbal)

1. 感謝邀請我，但我有另外的約會要參加。(正式)

   Thanks for inviting me, but I have another engagement to attend. (Formal)

2. 聽起來很棒，但我那天晚上不行。

   That sounds great, but I can't make it that night.

書面接受 Accepting (Written)

1. 謝謝，我們在那裡見。(簽名)

   Thanks. We'll see you there. (sign your name)

2. 期待見到大家。(簽名)

   Looking forward to seeing you all. (sign your name)

書面拒絕 Declining (Written)

1. 謝謝你的邀請，我們那晚不能參加，希望很快能在另一個聚會再見。(正式)

   Thank you for the invitation. We cannot attend that night. Hope to see you again soon on another date. (Formal)

2. 謝謝，但是恐怕我們沒辦法到。抱歉，以後見了。

   Thanks, but I'm afraid we can't make it. Sorry. See you later though.

Please come to my birthday party.

Notes 小叮嚀

收到口頭的邀請，要清楚表示是否參加。如果有困難應該提出，主人可以因應，如果不能參加，要向邀請人解釋 (I am very sorry, but I will be out of town that day.) 並致謝，並且建議另外的安排 (Thanks for inviting me. Maybe we can get together the next weekend.)。

如果接到註明RSVP的邀請，表示你必須回覆是否參加，回覆應當盡早，不要拖延，有些邀請只要求不參加者回覆 (for regrets only)；大型的公眾活動通常不需回覆是否參加。

辦一場派對或聚會並不容易，如果沒有心理準備好好參加受邀的活動，不要勉強接受邀請；接受了別人的邀請，就要守信，否則主人會感到懊惱。萬一接受了邀請，後來發現沒辦法赴約或不能出席派對的話，要及早聯繫主人 (至少24小時前，主人或許還未開始準備食物或購買其他物品)，以便及早因應。

Unit 4 Attending Outings and Birthday [Dinner] Parties (Casual/Formal)

參加郊外聚會與生日 [晚宴] 派對 (非正式/正式)

社交活動可以活絡朋友情誼並認識新朋友，因此不要只與熟識的人談話，而冷落他人。朋友間通常會互相介紹其他朋友一起聊天，如果朋友不在，也可以主動對同去參加聚會派對的人問好寒暄，這是被期待的社交行為；而工作機構所舉辦的 (家人) 聚會，預期員工參加，以增加彼此的了解及向心力，有利將來共事。在歡樂的派對氣氛下，增進人際關係比平日要容易得多。

初次見面
偶遇
邀請
參加聚會
接待賓客
拜訪
特殊情況
祝賀慰問
交友
日常社交
常用功能
其他功能

4.1 參加郊外聚會 At the Outing

A: 今天超過 30 個人來到這裡。

A: More than thirty people are here today.

B: 希望我們帶來野餐的東西夠吃。

B: I hope we brought enough food for the picnic.

A: 沒問題，每個人都帶了一或兩樣東西來跟大家分享。

A: No problem. Everybody brought one or two things for everyone to share.

B: 是的，就算我們需要更多，公園內有間商店，雖然那裡的東西很貴。

B: Yes, and even if we need more there is a store here at the park, although things there are pretty expensive.

A: 對，可以的話，我們最好不要在那裡買東西。

A: Right. We'd better avoid buying things there if possible.

B: 我們在瀑布旁走走之後，或許可以打棒球。

B: After we do some hiking around the waterfalls, maybe we can play baseball.

A: 山姆帶了球網及排球。

A: Sam brought a volleyball net and ball.

B: 好，那可能更好，不需要太多空間。

B: Good. That's probably better. It won't use up so much room.

A: 對，而且每個人都會打排球。

A: Right, and anyone can play volleyball.

B: 當然，我們只是為了好玩而已。

B: Sure. We just want to play for fun anyway.

A: 我們也可以在旁邊煮東西。

A: We can cook close to the game, too.

Word Bank 字庫

volleyball ['vɑlɪˌbɔl] n. 排球
net [nɛt] n. 網子

Useful Phrases 實用語句

1. 那可能更好。
   That's probably better.
2. 我們只是為了好玩而已。
   We just want to play for fun anyway.

Notes 小叮嚀

如果朋友邀請到郊外或外面聚會，可以問該帶多少費用 (How much money should I bring?) 及該穿些什麼 (What should I wear?)。

4.2 照相 Photo Taking

A: 我們來拍團體照。	**A:** Let's have agroup photo.
B: 大家過來這裡。	**B:** Everybody, come over here.
A: (這是) 拍照的好地點，大樹成了好背景。	**A:** Goodspot for a photo. The big trees make a nice background.
B: 每個人都靠近點了嗎？	**B:** Everybody, get closer together?
A: 嘿，你呢？傑瑞，你不在照片裡。	**A:** Hey!What about you Jerry? You won't be in the photo.
B: 我要找個人幫我們照相。	**B:** I'm going to ask someone to help us take the picture.

Word Bank 字庫

group photo n. 團體照
spot [spɑt] n. 地點
background ['bæk,graund] n. 背景

1. 我們來拍團體照。

   Let's have a group photo.

2. 大家過來這裡。

   Everybody, come over here.

3. (這是) 拍照的好地點。

   Good spot for a photo.

4. 大樹成了好背景。

   The big trees make a nice background.

5. 每個人都靠近點了嗎？

   Everybody, get closer together?

6. 我要找個人幫我們照相。

   I'm going to ask someone to help us take the picture.

美國人的派對聚會邀請可能包含被邀請人的配偶，但一般而言並不包含小孩，除非是不正式的聚會 (如烤肉Barbecue parties或街坊派對Block parties)。如果邀請人希望小孩參加，會明白表示小孩受到邀請，如果不確定，就問邀請人。小孩們有屬於他們自己的派對 (通常是生日派對)，小朋友間會自行互相邀請，受邀小孩的家長們除了接送外，通常不參加。

4.3 參加正式晚宴 Attending a Formal Dinner Party

A: 大家晚安！

A: Good evening, everyone!

B: 晚安，連先生。	**B:** Good evening, Mr. Lien.
A: 我可以坐這裡嗎？	**A:** May I sit here?
B: 當然可以，請坐。	**B:** Yes, of course. Please do.
A: 我看大家都已經到了，我想我有點晚了。	**A:** I see everyone is here already. I'm afraid I'm a little late.
B: 沒有沒有，我們只是在為大家倒酒，你要一些嗎？	**B:** No, not really. We were just pouring wine for everyone. Would you like some?
A: 好的，謝謝。	**A:** Yes, please.
B: 我們現在喝紅酒，你可以喝嗎？	**B:** We're having a red right now. Is it alright for you?
A: 可以，謝謝。	**A:** That will be fine, thank you.
B: 你公司最近如何？	**B:** How are things going at the company these days?
A: 事實上不錯。我該告訴你我們明年的計畫。	**A:** Not bad actually. I should tell you about our plans for next year.

B: 我想知道，請說。	**B:** I'd like to know. Please go on.

Notes 小叮嚀

美國人很重視時間，上課遲到可能得低分，上班遲到表示工作態度有問題。依照晚宴的時間準時到達最好，不要早到，主人可能還沒準備好。遲到幾分鐘沒關係，若超過10分鐘就有必要向主人解釋一下，不要遲到超過15分鐘，否則要先打電話 (菜肴涼掉，主人的辛苦就白費了)；如果約在外面，超過15分鐘朋友可能就走了，除非很要好，很少有人會等超過半個小時。

餐桌禮儀在美國並不難理解，特別是在輕鬆的場合。在餐桌上與他交談是多數人的期待，但不會在滿口食物時交談，也要避免在別人剛將食物送入口時問問題。餐巾通常是拿來擺在腿上而不是只放在桌上用。想拿遠一些的食物時要讓別人幫你傳過來，而不是自己伸長手去拿，否則就顯得失禮。

出席正式場合必須穿著得體、坐姿端正及說些禮貌性的對話，有敬酒祝賀及外燴服務時，別給小費，說聲「謝謝」即可；有演講時避免用餐，但可以繼續喝東西，以禮貌及保守的言談舉止共同創造出令人愉悅的交誼環境。

◆ **晚餐派對 Dinner Parties**

formal	正式
casual	不正式的
potluck	一人帶一道菜的便飯派對
dish	一道菜肴
deli	熟食
soda	汽水飲料
juice (orange, grape, grapefruit, apple, cranberry)	果汁 (柳橙，葡萄，葡萄柚，蘋果，小紅莓)
wine	葡萄酒

brandy	白蘭地
champagne	香檳
cocktail	雞尾酒
whiskey	威士忌
beer	啤酒
cup	杯子 (裝熱飲)
glass	玻璃杯 (裝冷飲及酒)
goblet	高腳杯
knife	刀子
steak knife	牛排刀
fork	叉子
salad fork	沙拉叉
spoon	湯匙
soup spoon	湯匙
utensils	餐具
plate	盤子
napkin	餐巾
placemat	桌墊
salt	鹽
pepper	胡椒
sugar	糖
coffee	咖啡
cream	奶精
creamer	奶精罐
gravy	肉汁 (調味用的滷汁)
gravy boat	盛肉汁 (調味用滷汁) 的船型盅
salad	沙拉
salad dressing	沙拉醬
ice	冰
ice cube	冰塊
refill	續 (杯)
pass the...	遞…

4.4 聊天話題 Topics for Chatting

天氣 Weather

1. 今天天氣很好。

   The weather is good today.

2. 天氣真好！

   Lovely weather!

3. 你覺得今天天氣如何？

   What do you think of the weather today?

4. 天氣如何？

   How's the weather?

5. 今天多雲。

   It's cloudy today.

6. 我希望雨停。

   I hope the rain stops.

7. 我希望別下雨了。

   I hope it stops raining.

8. 我希望不要下雨。

   I hope it doesn't rain.

9. 這裡的天氣通常如何？

   What's the weather like around here usually?

10. 今天真熱。

    It's really hot today.

11. 今天有點涼。

    It's a little cool today.

12. 你想今天會下雪嗎？

    Do you think it will snow today?

13. 今天天氣真棒。

    The weather is great today.

美國人談論天氣其實多為談話的開場，真正談論天氣的狀況其實並不多。在天氣多變的英國，談論天氣更為頻繁。天氣之所以是個好話題，不僅在於其普遍性，更是測試雙方是否投緣的風向球。如果別人開頭說「It's a bit cold day, isn't it? 」另一方最好同意「Yes, it is. 」一旦同意規則 (agreement rule) 確立，雙方可以一搭一唱繼續聊下去；如果另一方說「Really, I don't think so. It's kind of hot today. 」那第一句話就夠對方判斷非我族類，話不投機半句多了。

● **工作 Jobs**

1. 你 [您] 從事什麼職業？
   What do you do? [What is your job?]
2. 你在哪裡工作？
   Where do you work?
3. 你在那裡工作多久了？
   How long have you worked there?
4. 你喜歡那裡嗎？
   Do you like it there?
5. 你打算住那裡嗎？
   Do you plan to stay there?
6. 那是個有趣的工作嗎？
   Is it an interesting job?
7. 你 [您] 公司 [辦公室] 有多少人？
   How many people are in the company [your office]?
8. 我喜歡我的工作。
   I like my job.
9. 我的工作普通。
   My job is so so.

10. 我想換工作。

I'd like to change my job.

11. 我必須加班。

I have to work overtime.

12. 你經常加班嗎？

Do you work much overtime?

13. 你的老闆如何？

How's your boss?

14. 有升遷的機會。

There are chances for promotion.

15. 你可以升遷嗎？

Can you get promotions?

16. 它是一個很好的工作場所。

It's a pretty good place to work.

關於房子 About a House

1. 你有一個可愛的家。

You have a lovely home.

2. 這桌子很漂亮。

This is a beautiful table.

3. 你一定喜歡住這裡。

You must like living here.

4. 誰漆的油漆？

Who did these paintings?

5. 你自己布置的嗎？

Did you decorate yourself?

6. 你家很舒適。

Your home is so comfortable.

7. 你的庭院看來很棒。

Your yard looks great.

8. 你的後院很棒。

Your backyard is very nice.

9. 你房子裡面很寬敞。

   You have a lot of room inside.

10. 我喜歡你布置的方式。

    I like the way you have decorated.

家庭照片 **Family Pictures**

1. 看一下我的家庭相簿。

   Have a look at my family photo album.

2. 這些相片很好。

   These photos are nice.

3. 這些人是誰？

   Who are these people?

4. 你有很多好照片。

   You have a lot of nice pictures.

5. 還有嗎？

   Do you have any more?

有禮貌是對話的關鍵，衡量與對方的交情，不要太咄咄逼人 (pushy) 或與剛認識的人交淺言深 (too personal)，注意對方的個性，試著了解對方對什麼樣的話題感到自在或不自在。

聊天話題Topics for Chatting

不管是正式或輕鬆的社交活動，談話內容最好不要牽涉個人隱私，在與對方不熟的情況下，更要避免有關婚姻或政治話題，運動、工作、娛樂(電影、戲劇、音樂活動、歌手、演員等)、值得一去的好地方、個人嗜好、慶典活動等都是可以交談的好話題。

一個人是否已婚，通常看手就知道 (美國人在婚後就戴著婚戒)。若仍想肯定，可以問的安全問題是「Do you have a family?」如果單刀直入的問「Do you have a boy [girlfriend] ?」「Are you married?」對方會誤以為你對他 [她] 有興趣，或者要替他 [她] 介紹對象。

詢問美國人某件衣物或配件的價錢，等同打聽對方的經濟能力，是很失禮的。所以寒暄時可以先讚美該物品，再詢問在何處購買「What a beautiful watch! Where did you get it?」，對方可能回答你購買處，或是禮物太久、忘記了等等。轉個彎的問法，可以避掉尷尬的價格問題。

敏感話題 (touchy topics) 因文化而異，除了政治、宗教、婚姻、金錢、體重、年齡之外，某些文化還包含家庭、工作在內 (如法國、西班牙)，職業確實意味著社會階級，有些文化對此較為敏感，並非每個人都樂意 (尤其與不算熟的人) 談論自己或家人的工作及出身背景。另外，不要對西班牙人批評鬥牛 (bull fighting)，不要在反美的地方談論美國等都是國際公民常識。總而言之，「禮貌」最基本的定義在於不使人感到困窘。

4.5 參加生日派對 Going to a Birthday Party

4.5a 在外開派對——生日問候 Party Out — Birthday Greetings

Dialog 對話

A: 生日快樂，莎拉。	**A:** Happy birthday, Sarah.
B: 謝謝，你怎麼知道的？	**B:** Thank you. How did you know?
A: 卡蘿告訴我的。	**A:** Carol told me.

B: 我了解了，我要開一個派對，我在「開瓶」訂了位，你應該順道來參加。

B: Isee. I'm having a party. I reserved tables at the Open Bottle. You should stop by.

A: 好，派對什麼時候開始？

A: OK. What time will it get started?

B: 大家大概9點來，我們會待到他們打烊。

B: People will probably show up around nine, but we'll be there until they close.

A: 那是幾點？

A: What time is that?

B: 早上 3 點。

B: 3 a.m.

A: 聽起來是個通宵派對。

A: Sounds like an all night party.

B: 是的！

B: Sure!

Word Bank 字庫

reserve [rɪ'zɝv] v. 保留
stop by 順道過來

1. 你怎麼知道的？

   How did you know?

2. 你應該順道來參加。

   You should stop by.

3. 派對什麼時候開始？

   What time will it get started?

4. 我們會待到他們打烊。

   We'll be there until they close.

4.5b 派對中 At the Party

A: 嘿，珍妮佛，你好嗎？	**A:** Hey, Jennifer. How are you?
B: 嗨，班，我很好，你好嗎？	**B:** Hi, Ben. I'm fine. How are you?
A: 很好。	**A:** Good.
B: 這是個開派對的好地方。	**B:** This is a good place to have a party.
A: 是的，你最近在做什麼？	**A:** Yes, it is. What have you been doing lately?

B: 新工作讓我很忙碌。	**B:** Keeping busy with my new job.
A: 你現在在哪裡工作？	**A:** Where are you working now?
B: 我現在在「有米樂」餐廳當經理。	**B:** I'mthe Manager at the Ol' Mill Restaurant.
A: 真的？真好，恭喜你。	**A:** Really?That's good. Congratulations.
B: 謝謝。你呢？	**B:** Thanks. How about you?
A: 我還是在「阿嬤果汁公司」工作。	**A:** I'm still working at Grannies Juice Company.
B: 我聽說那是一個很好的工作場所。	**B:** Ihear that's a nice place to work.
A: 是的，還不錯。	**A:** Yeah. It's not bad at all.

Useful Phrases 實用語句

1. 新工作讓我很忙碌。

   I've been keeping busy.

2. 恭喜。

   Congratulations.

3. 還不錯。

It’s not bad at all.

4.5c 結束 Closing Time

Dialog 對話

A: 那是最後廣播。

A: That was last call.

B: 他們快打烊了。

B: They’ll be closing soon.

A: 對，派對要移到提姆家裡。

A: Right. The party is moving to Tim’s apartment.

B: 好，在哪裡？

B: OK.Where is that?

A: 從這裡過去大約兩三條街左右。

A: It’sjust a couple of blocks from here.

B: 好，你要走了嗎？

B: Great.Are you going soon?

A: 是的，要跟我一起去嗎？

A: Yes.Want to come with me?

B: 好。

B: Sure.

初次見面
偶遇
邀請
參加聚會
接待賓客
拜訪
特殊情況
祝賀慰問
交友
日常社交
常用功能
其他功能

A: 很好，等其他的人幾分鐘，好嗎？

A: Cool.Wait a few minutes for the others, OK?

B: 沒問題。

B: No problem.

1. 那是最後廣播。
   That was last call.
2. 他們快打烊了。
   They'll be closing soon.
3. 你要走了嗎？
   Are you going soon?
4. 等其他的人幾分鐘，好嗎？
   Wait a few minutes for the others, OK?
5. 派對要換到提姆家裡。
   The party is moving to Tim's apartment.
6. 從這裡過去大約兩三條街左右。
   It's a couple of blocks from here.

Let's have a group photo.
Everybody, come over here.

Tips 小祕訣

美國的生日壽星不分年紀大小，通稱 birthday boy [girl]。年齡算實歲，16 歲可在有人陪同下開始學開車，一年後可以考駕照；18 歲可以投票、買菸及當兵，但要滿 21 歲才能買酒、進酒吧，擁有完整成年人的權利，因此，21 歲生日是美國人的大生日，壽星喝酒慶祝邁入「成年」極為普遍；過了 30 歲後，體力及心境會漸走下坡 (over the hill)，多數人不再喜歡過生日，所以也有朋友、家人會給壽星來個驚喜派對 (surprise party)。Milestone birthdays 指的是像 30、40、50 這樣整數年紀的生日，Over the hill 表示過了忙碌奮鬥的幾年，到了可以舒緩一下的年紀了。中文裡「人生 70 才開始」的說法，在英語裡則是「人生 40 才開始」(Life begins at 40。)

4.5d 家裡的生日派對——在門口
Birthday Party at a House — At the Door

A: 嗨，吉兒。	**A:** Hi, Jill.
B: 哈囉，亨利。謝謝你來。	**B:** Hello, Henry. Thanks for coming.
A: 來這裡很開心，生日快樂，這是送你的禮物。	**A:** Happy to be here. Happy birthday. Here's your gift.
B: 哇，多謝，進來吧。	**B:** Wow. Thanks so much. Come on in.

A: 好。

A: OK.

B: 我想你認識這裡大部分的人。

B: Ithink you know most of the people here.

A: 大概，我會向所有不認識的人自我介紹。

A: Probably. I'll introduce myself to anyone new.

B: 這裡有派對帽及派對小禮物，拿一些吧。

B: There are hats and party favors here. Take some.

A: 酷，這些很好玩，我也帶了些烈酒。

A: Cool. These are fun. I brought some booze too.

B: 好，我會把它放在廚房裡，我們晚點會切蛋糕，現在那邊有小點心和飲料。

B: Great.I'll put it in the kitchen for now. We'll have cake later. Right now there are snacks and drinks over there.

A: 好，我餓了。

A: Good. I'm hungry.

Word Bank 字庫

party favor n. 派對小禮物 [紀念品]
booze [buz] n. (俚語) 烈酒

1. 謝謝你邀請我來。

   Thanks for inviting me.

2. 謝謝你來。

   Thanks for coming.

3. 這是送你的禮物。

   Here's your gift.

4. 我帶了這個 (禮物) 給你。

   I brought this (gift) for you.

5. 我希望你會喜歡。

   I hope you like it.

6. 享受它吧。

   Enjoy it.

7. 我會向所有不認識的人自我介紹。

   I'll introduce myself to anyone new.

8. 拿一些吧。

   Take some.

9. 我帶了些烈酒。

   I brought some booze.

10. 我該坐哪裡？

    Where should I sit?

11. 讓我來自我介紹。

    Let me introduce myself.

12. 嗨，我是班，你呢？

    Hi, my name's Ben. What's yours?

13. 洗手間在哪裡？

    Where is the bathroom?

14. 我可以把大衣掛在哪裡？

    Where can I hang my coat?

15. 這個我該放哪裡？

    Where should I put this?

16. 放在廚房水槽 [垃圾筒] 裡。
Put it in the sink [garbage can].
17. 拿給我，我會替你處理。
Give it to me. I'll take care of it for you.

4.5e 切蛋糕 Cutting the Birthday Cake

Dialog 1 對話1

A: 等一下，他們正把蛋糕拿出來。	**A:** Wait, they're bringing out the cake.
B: 看看那些蠟燭！你幾歲了？	**B:** Look at all those candles! How old are you?
A: 很 (不) 好笑，來吧，我來吹熄它們。	**A:** Very funny. Come on. I'll blow them out.
B: 你得先許個願。	**B:** You have to make a wish first.
A: 我知道。	**A:** I know that.
B: 還有你得一次就吹熄所有蠟燭。	**B:** And you have to blow out all the candles on the first try.
A: 為什麼？	**A:** Why?

B: 不然願望不會實現。

B: Otherwise the wish won't come true.

A: 我不知道還有這回事。

A: I didn't know that.

Dialog 2 對話2

A: 好，各位，現在要切蛋糕了。

A: OK, everyone. It's time to have cake.

(點蠟燭 Light the candles.)

A: 首先我們要唱生日快樂歌。

A: Firstwe have to sing "Happy Birthday."

(每個人唱 everyone sings)

B: 許個願然後吹熄蠟燭，吉兒。要確定全部吹熄，否則願望不會實現。(她吹熄後大家歡呼)

B: Makea wish and blow out the candles, Jill. Make sure you blow all the candles out or your wish won't come true. (She does and everyone cheers.)

A: 我們來切蛋糕。

A: Let's cut the cake.

Useful Phrases 實用語句

生日蛋糕儀式 Birthday Cake Rituals

1. 點蠟燭。

   Light the candles.

2. 許個願！

   Make a wish!

3. 吹熄蠟燭。

   Blow out the candles.

4. 我們來切蛋糕。

   Let's cut the cake.

賀詞 Congratulatory Expressions

1. (30歲) 生日快樂！

   Happy (30th) Birthday!

2. 祝你 (60歲) 生日快樂！

   Congratulations on your (60th) birthday!

◆ **生日賀卡樣本 Birthday Cards Sample**

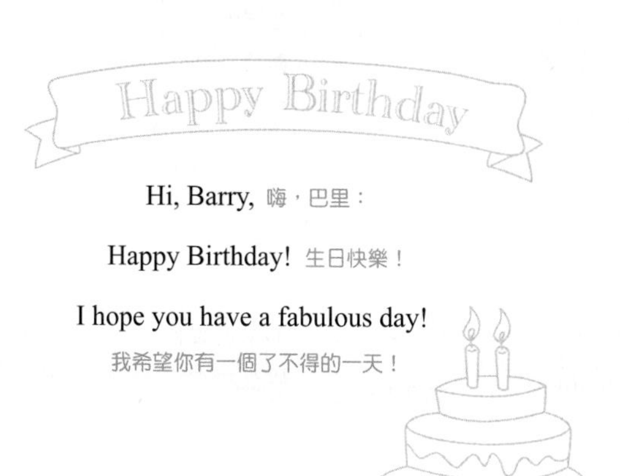

Hi, Barry, 嗨，巴里：

Happy Birthday! 生日快樂！

I hope you have a fabulous day!

我希望你有一個了不得的一天！

Dear Jill, 親愛的吉兒：

Have a great birthday! 祝你有很棒的生日！

We love you and wish you all the best.

我們愛你並且祝福你一切都很好。

◆ **歡樂派對 Fun Parties**

birthday boy [girl]	壽星 (男 [女])
birthday, b-day	生日
birthday cake	生日蛋糕
birthday card	生日卡
invitation	邀請
candles	蠟燭
present, gift	禮物
noisemaker	發出聲響的物品
party [funny] hat	派對帽
balloon	氣球
ribbon	彩帶，緞帶
confetti	碎紙片
glow stick	螢光棒
surprise party	驚喜派對
gift wrapping paper	包裝紙

4.6 送禮與打開禮物 Gift Giving and Opening a Gift

Dialog 1 對話1

A: 嗨，傑夫，請進。	**A:** Hi, Jeff. Come on in.
B: 謝謝，我帶了這個給你。	**A:** Thanks. I brought this for you.
A: 嘿，謝謝，我會把它與其他禮物放在一起。	**A:** Hey, thanks. I'll put it with the others.

Dialog 2 對話2

A: 嗨，壽星，你該拆你的禮物了。

A: Hi, Birthday Boy. You should open your gifts.

B: 好，我想現在是個好時機。

B: OK. I guess this is as good of a time as any.

A: 對，先開我的。

A: Right. Open mine first.

B: 好。

B: Sure.

Dialog 3 對話3

B: 嘿，這是那件皮夾克，我上星期帶你去看的。

B: Hey! It's that the leather jacket I showed you last week.

A: 對！試試看。

A: Right on! Try it on.

B: 很完美，我看起來如何？

B: It's perfect. How do I look?

A: 帥，老兄，真的很帥。

A: Sharp, man. Really sharp.

B: 太棒了，太感謝了。

B: This is great. Thanks a million.

A: 很高興你喜歡它。

A: Glad you like it.

leather jacket n. 皮夾克
sharp [ʃɑrp] adj. 帥氣的，時髦的

1. 我帶了這個給你。
   I brought this for you.
2. 我帶了一份禮物給這房子。
   I brought a gift for the house.
3. 我會把它與其他禮物放在一起。
   I'll put it with the others.
4. 你該拆你的禮物了。
   You should open your gifts.
5. 現在是個好時機。
   This is as good of a time as any.
6. 試試看。
   Try it on.

在美國致贈禮物沒有什麼禮數，將禮物交給對方，面帶微笑告訴他 [她] 是送給他 [她] 的禮物就行了，人們會欣喜的接受禮物。生日禮物何時打開，並無一定規則，小孩通常在玩一些遊戲或活動後打開禮物；大人則通常是壽星受到朋友慫恿時打開禮物。

4.7 受邀到朋友家用餐 Being Invited to a Friend's Home for Dinner

A: 傑瑞，自己來喔，你喜歡西式食物嗎？

A: Help yourself, Jerry. Do you like Western food?

B: 我漸漸習慣了，有時候我不是很確定怎麼吃西式食物。

B: I'm getting used to it. Sometimes I'm not sure how to eat it.

A: 真的嗎？什麼意思呢？

A: Really? What do you mean?

B: 呃，有時候我不太確定到底該怎麼吃。

B: Well, sometimes I'm not sure how to actually get the food.

A: 我不懂。

A: I don't understand.

B: 我想是文化 (問題)，舉鹽巴與胡椒的例子來說，在這裡我看你放在桌上，但是在餐廳裡有時有，有時你必須主動要求，為什麼呢？

B: It's cultural I think. Take salt and pepper for example. Here I see it on your table, but at restaurants sometimes it is there, but sometimes you have to ask for it. Why?

A: 好問題，我真的不知道，我想有些餐廳認為他們給顧客是比較特別的服務，其他餐廳不想這麼正式。

A: Good question. I don't know really. I think some restaurants consider it to be a special service they can give to their customers. Other restaurants don't want to be so formal.

B: 那三明治呢？那也很讓人困惑。

B: What about sandwiches? That's confusing too.

A: 是嗎？

A: It is?

B: 是啊，漢堡是一種三明治，你可以拿起來吃，沒問題，但是兩星期前我點了叫做雞汁三明治的東西，我就無法把那東西拿起來吃。

B: Yes. A hamburger is a sandwich and you can pick it up and eat it no problem. But a couple of weeks ago, I ordered something called a chicken gravy sandwich. There was no way I could pick that thing up and eat it.

A: 是的，我想我開始了解你的問題了，這是文化 (問題)。我的意思是有些陪我們長大的東西是很沒有一致性的。光用聽的會發現你期待的東西與結果並不同，但因為它陪著我們長大，所以我們並不覺得奇怪。

A: Yes. I'm beginning to see the problem. It is cultural. I mean some things we grow up with are really inconsistent. What you expect it to be when you hear about it turns out to be different, but since we grew up with it we don't think of it as being strange.

B: 對，那當然有道理，只是對一個局外人而言，有時很令人困惑。

B: Right. Of course that makes sense. It's just confusing to an outsider at times.

A: 嗯，你讓我注意到這個挑戰，而且那就是答案。既然現在我了解你面臨的情形，如果你有任何不確定的或有任何問題，隨時問我吧！

A: Well, you made me aware of the challenge, and that's where the answer is. Now that I know what you are up against, just ask anytime you aren't sure or have a question.

B: 好的，謝謝。

B: OK. Thanks.

Word Bank 字庫

gravy ['grevɪ] n. 肉汁

inconsistent [ˌɪnkən'sɪstənt] adj. 不一致的

outsider [aut'saɪdɚ] n. 局外人

challenge ['ʧælɪndʒ] n. 挑戰

up against 面臨的

Useful Phrases 實用語句

1. 你喜歡西式食物嗎？

   Do you like Western food?

2. 自己來喔。

   Help yourself.

3. 我漸漸習慣了。

   I'm getting used to it.

4. 我不太確定到底該怎麼吃。

   I'm not sure how to actually get the food.

5. 結果卻不同。

   It turns out to be different.

6. 那有道理。

   That makes sense.

7. 我了解你面臨的情形。

   I know what you are up against.

真正的社交禮儀在於如何適切應對，使自己舉止合宜，而不在於背誦社交規則，如果心裡忐忑不知道該怎麼做才能不使自己困窘，不如坦承不了解社交禮儀 (social ettiquette)，請教主人該如何表現才恰當，例如：何種食物該用手吃（炸雞、蝦子、比薩、三明治）？或許其他賓客也不知道該怎麼辦，利用機會請問主人這些問題，可以讓大家自在地談論，有助於拉近距離，社交禮儀其實是實用又有趣的話題。

許多公共場所全面禁菸，私人聚會要抽菸要先問主人在屋內抽菸是否妥當，如果主人家沒有菸灰缸 (ash tray)，他們可能不希望你抽菸，或你必須在外面抽。

4.8 受邀在外用餐
Being Invited to Dine Out: Dining

Dialog 對話

A: 晚餐來了。	**A:** Dinner is served.
B: 很好，我餓壞了。	**B:** Great. I'm starving.
A: 我也是，請遞一下鹽巴。	**A:** I'm too. Please pass the salt.
B: 好，在這裡。	**B:** Sure. Here you are.
A: 謝謝，試試這個肉汁，很棒！	**A:** Thanks. Try their gravy. It's wonderful!

B: 好，每樣東西看起來都很好吃。	**B:** OK. Everything looks delicious.
A: 我常來。	**A:** I come here often.
B: 難怪，食物看起來很吸引人。	**B:** I see why. The food is so tempting.
A: 如果你還覺得餓的話，我們晚點可以再看看菜單。	**A:** We can look at the menu again later if you are still hungry.
B: 我們應該留點肚子吃點心。	**B:** We should both leave room for dessert.
A: 對。	**A:** Yes.

Word Bank 字庫

starve [stɑrv] v. 挨餓
tempting ['tɛmptɪŋ] adj. 誘惑人的

Useful Phrases 實用語句

1. 我餓壞了。
I'm starving.
2. 請遞一下鹽巴。
Please pass the salt.

3. 試試這個肉汁，很棒！

   Try their gravy. It's wonderful!

4. 食物看起來很吸引人。

   The food is so tempting.

5. 我們應該留點肚子吃點心。

   We should both leave room for dessert.

如果異性邀你一起參加幾次活動或外出用餐等，不一定有什麼暗示。美國人的約會對象可能是一對一或一對多，與相同對象約會數次沒有所謂忠誠問題，也不要錯誤解釋異性之間因場合而起的隨性擁抱或握手。跨文化的異性朋友關係與個人成長文化有關，某些美國文化習以為常的舉動可能使不同文化的人感到困惑，如果有必要，可以與當事人討論這些感受，以避免產生任何誤會。

聚會派對禮儀Party Etiquette

1 **紳士行為**

美國雖是平權社會，男士的紳士風度仍然存在，為女士開門，為最鄰近自己的女士拉椅子都是被期待的行為。紳士行為在世界各國同樣存在並且被期待 (含各種場合)，沒有紳士習慣的男士必須學習。

2 **坐姿**

坐直，勿彎腰駝背。坐下時就打開餐巾放在腿上。坐下時慣用右手的人要將左手放在腿上，而不是桌上，否則會被認為是不體貼或是水準欠佳 (法國人則是雙手置於桌上)。

3 **用餐時間**

美國人用餐時間與臺灣差不多，但不重視午餐也不午休，晚餐是一天中最豐盛的一餐。

許多歐洲、中東、拉丁美洲、東南亞國家晚1-3小時才用餐，有些國家重視午餐，用餐時間長很多 (還包含午休)，晚餐則是8、9點以後才開始，所以黃昏時會先吃點心。晚餐後如有派對可能在晚上10點後 (甚至更晚) 才開始。

4　用餐禮儀

(1) 有些家庭用餐前要先祈禱 (say grace)，別急著開動。

(2) 注意 (女) 主人是否開動了才開動，因為 (女) 主人要花時間為大家上菜，如果上菜時賓客已經都開動了，(女) 主人準備許久要與大家共餐，(她) 才開始用餐時，大家卻已經吃飽了，(女) 主人可能會感到很失落。

(3) 餐巾打開表示開始用餐，中途離開時餐巾放椅子上，用餐結束放桌上。

(4) 用餐及喝湯時，身體不要向前傾，而是坐正將食物送入口中。

(5) 體貼地將食物或餐盤傳給較遠的一方，或請對方傳過來，而不是伸長手去取食物。

(6) 用餐時不要先聞食物，否則美國人會感到受冒犯。如果不確定使用哪個刀叉，看主人怎麼做。

(7) 要有「公筷母匙」的概念：如果奶油是共用的，使用奶油刀將奶油放在自己的麵包盤上，再用晚餐刀在麵包上塗上奶油。直接將共用的奶油塗上你的麵包感覺不太衛生。麵包要先撕成小片再入口。

(8) 不要滿口食物時說話，咀嚼時要閉口，也不要在他人正放入食物要咀嚼時問問題。要使用刀叉，不要用手拿起食物兜在刀叉上食用，湯匙是為喝湯及甜品專用，食用主菜時不使用。

(9) 美國人不喜歡帶骨或刺的菜肴 (除非是牛排或肋骨)，所以碰到骨頭與刺的機會不多，如果有的話，要用叉子接著放在自己的盤子邊(水果有籽也一樣)，不可直接吐在盤子上或放在桌上。

(10) 刀叉擺放要注意，如將刀叉各擺在 5 及 7 點鐘位置，表示仍在進食。兩者擺在 5 點鐘位置為用餐完畢，兩者都在 7 點鐘位置表示食物不合胃口或不好吃，可能會讓主人很難過 (在法國若將麵包沾醬料完全吃完，主人會很高興，但在埃及留一小口表示不貪心)。

5　其他

擤鼻涕、剔牙或女士補妝要到洗手間，萬一打噴嚏 (sneeze)、打嗝 (hiccup)、打哈欠 (yawn) 都要說抱歉 (Excuse me)，最好再加個解釋。他人道歉時可說沒關係 (It's OK.)，別人打噴嚏時，可以說 (上帝) 保佑你 ((God) Bless you.) 或保重 (Take care.)。

4.9 在派對道別
Leave-Taking at a Party

Dialog 1 對話1

A: 幾點了？	**A:** Do you have the time?
B: 現在10點30分。	**B:** Yes. It's 10:30 now.
A: 哇，真的很晚了，我現在得走了，我明天早上有會議。	**A:** Wow! It's really late. I have to go now. I have an early meeting tomorrow.
B: 真可惜，我們一向喜歡你的陪伴。	**B:** That's too bad. We enjoy your company, as always.
A: 我今晚真的很愉快，多謝。	**A:** I certainly had a great time tonight. Thanks for everything.
B: 沒什麼，別忘了你的外套，小心開車。	**B:** No problem. Don't forget your coat and drive safely.
A: 好，晚安。	**A:** OK. Good night.
B: 晚安。	**B:** Good night.

1. 幾點了？

   Do you have the time?
2. 真的很晚了。

   It’s really late.
3. 我現在得走了。

   I have to go now.
4. 我明天早上有會議。

   I have an early meeting tomorrow.
5. 我今晚真的很愉快。

   I certainly had a great time tonight.
6. 我們一向喜歡你的陪伴。

   We enjoy your company, as always.
7. 請問我的大衣在哪裡？

   Where is my coat, please?
8. 別忘了你的外套，小心開車。

   Don’t forget your coat and drive safely.

A: 人家什麼時候會來接你呢？	**A:** So what time will your ride get here?
B: 應該隨時會到。	**B:** Should be here any moment.
A: 別擔心禮貌問題了，有必要就離開吧。	**A:** Well, don’t worry about being polite. Take off when you have to.

B: 好的，謝謝。我不想沒禮貌。	**B:** OK, thanks. I don't want to be rude.
A: 沒什麼。	**A:** No problem.
B: 嘿，我的便車來了，我得走了。	**B:** Hey, my ride is here. I've got to run.
A: 再見。	**A:** See you later.

1. 人家什麼時候會來接你呢？
   What time will your ride get here?
2. 別擔心禮貌問題了。
   Don't worry about being polite.
3. 有必要就離開吧。
   Take off when you have to.
4. 我的便車應該隨時會到。
   My ride should be here any moment.
5. 我的便車來了。
   My ride is here.
6. 我不想沒禮貌。
   I don't want to be rude.
7. 我得走了。
   I've got to run.

Tips

派對的道別通常是很不正式的，除非是很正式的場合，否則無須特別注意說什麼道別語。倒是要注意表現禮貌，道別再離開。

必須離開時，可以說明理由。例如：

「It's getting late.」(有點晚了)或「I need to pick up my laundry.」(我得去取衣服)，「I've got to go.」「I have to go.」「I've got to get going.」(我得走了)。

4.10 道別：提早離開
Farewell: Leaving Early

A: 羅伯特，很抱歉，我剛接到一通辦公室打來的電話，明天我得比先前想的更早起去底特律。很抱歉，我今晚就到此為止了。

A: Robert. I'm terribly sorry, but I just got a call from my office. I'll have to get up much earlier than I thought in order to go to Detroit. I'm very sorry, but I will have to call it a night.

B: 沒問題，我了解，我們盡快再聚聚。

B: No problem. I understand. Let's do this again soon.

A: 好，好。我明天打電話給你，我真的很抱歉。

A: Sure, sure. I'll call you tomorrow. I'm really sorry about this.

B: 別擔心，誰都可能發生這種情形。

B: Don't worry. It can happen to anybody.

B: 我告訴你怎麼出去，你每樣東西都帶著了嗎？	**B:** Let me show you out. Do you have everything?
A: 我想是的，改天見。	**A:** I think so. I'll see you soon.
B: 改天見，小心開車。	**B:** Yes. Drive carefully.
A: 我會的，晚安。	**A:** I will. Good night.
B: 晚安。	**B:** Goodnight.

◎ 結束語 **Phrases for Closure**

1. 我得比先前想的更早起。
   I'll have to get up much earlier than I thought.
2. 很抱歉，但我今晚就到此為止了。
   I'm very sorry, but I will have to call it a night.
3. 我們應該盡快再聚聚。
   We should get together soon.
4. 我們盡快再聚聚。
   Let's do this again soon.
5. 跟你聊聊很棒。
   It's been great talking to you.
6. 我很享受今天的派對。
   I really enjoyed today's party.

7. 派對很棒。

   It was a great party.

8. 我玩得很開心。

   I had a lot of fun.

9. 俱樂部會員提供非常好的協助。

   The club members offered wonderful assistance.

10. 我明天打電話給你。

    I'll call you tomorrow.

11. 我會很快寫信給你。

    I'll write to you soon.

12. 改天見。

    I'll see you soon.

13. 我真的對此很抱歉。

    I'm really sorry about this.

14. 多謝。

    Thanks for everything.

15. 我了解，別擔心。

    I understand. Don't worry.

16. 誰都可能發生這種情形。

    It can happen to anybody.

17. 我告訴你怎麼出去。

    Let me show you out.

18. 請再來。

    Please come again.

19. 你每樣東西都帶著了嗎？

    Do you have everything?

20. 這裡是派對小禮物 (道別時送給客人)。

    Here are some party favors.

道別語 Phrases for Farewells

1. 再見。

   Good bye.

初次見面
偶遇
邀請
參加聚會
接待賓客
拜訪
特殊情況
祝賀慰問
交友
日常社交
常用功能
其他功能

2. 再見。

See you / See ya.

3. 再見 [待會見]。

Catch you later. / See you later. / Later.

4. 再見。

Bye for now./So long.

5. 回頭見。

See you around.

6. 保重。

Take Care.

7. 很快再見到你。

See you again soon.

8. 放輕鬆。

Take it easy.

9. 請代我向你家人問好 [道別]。

Please say hello [goodbye] for me to your family.

10. 很高興與你聊聊。

It's been good talking with you.

11. 保重，下次再來。

Take care, and come again.

12. 再見了 [直到下次碰面再見了]。

Until we meet again.

13. 小心開車。

Drive carefully.

14. 保持聯絡。

Keep in touch.

15. 別變成陌生人了。

Don't be a stranger.

16. 你進城時，打電話給我。

Call me when you're in town.

Language Power 字句補給站

◆ **道別 Farewells**

外語道別語很常見 (如國人常講日語 Sayonara)，尤其拉丁裔在美國人數不少，使用外語可能令人感覺俏皮、好玩或親切，但對不熟的人或長輩可能感覺不同，應避免使用。

在美國常用的外語道別語如下：

西班牙語Spanish	Adiós ['adɪ'os] 再見 (goodbye)
	Adiós, amigo. [ˌadɪ'os, a'migo] 朋友，再見了 (goodbye, friend)
	Hasta la Vista ['hastə lə 'vistə] 待會見 (see you later)
法語 French	Au revoir [ˌourə'vwar] 再見 (goodbye)
德語German	Auf wiedersehen [auf'vidər,zeɪən] 待會見 (see you later)
夏威夷語Hawaiian	Aloha [a'loha] 哈囉及再見 (hello and good bye)
義大利語Italian	Ciao [ʧau] 哈囉及再見 (hello and good bye)

4.11 失禮的道別 Impolite Farewell

Dialog 對話

A: 謝謝你邀請我來，傑瑞。 → **A:** Thanks for inviting me over, Jerry.

B: 是啊，沒問題，別客氣。 → **B:** Yeah, sure. Any time!

A: 我們應盡快再聚聚。 → **A:** Let's get together again soon.

B: 好，隨便，我明天要早起，所以你現在得快點離開。

B: Sure. Whatever. I have to get up early tomorrow, so you need to leave now.

A: 喔！當然，抱歉。

A: Oh! Of course. Sorry.

B: 好，再見。

B: Right. Later.

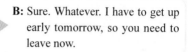

在社交場合，禮貌表現出來的重點在於體貼對方的需要、犧牲及有耐性，有時我們失禮而不自知，迎接及道別的時候尤其要用禮貌、體貼的語言。避免說 whatever 來結束談話，給人冷漠敷衍的感覺，這是全美公認 (2009調查) 最令人討厭的口頭禪。為了避免派對的時間成為問題，及早計畫並告知主 [客] 人，如果時間突然變成問題，立即與主 [客] 人開誠布公討論。

4.12 感謝主人 Thanking the Host [Hostess]

A: 謝謝你邀請我來，吉兒。

A: Thanks for inviting me to your party, Jill.

B: 謝謝你來，並謝謝你的好禮物。

B: Thanks for coming. And thanks for the great gift.

A: 我希望你喜歡。

A: I hope you like it.

B: 真的很好，我很喜歡。	**B:** It's really nice. I love it.
A: 好，享受它吧，再見了。	**A:** OK. Well, enjoy it. I'll see you later.
B: 好，再見了。	**B:** Sure. Bye for now.
A: 晚安。	**A:** Good night.

Useful Phrases 實用語句

1. 謝謝你邀請我來。
   Thanks for inviting me to your party.
2. 我得走了。
   I have to go now.
3. 我很享受這個派對。
   I've enjoyed the party.
4. 食物很棒！
   The food was great!
5. 每樣東西都很棒。
   Everything was wonderful.
6. 謝謝你來。
   Thanks for coming.
7. 謝謝你的好禮物。
   Thanks for the great gift.
8. 我希望你喜歡。
   I hope you like it.

9. 享受它吧！

Enjoy it!

10. 謝謝你，並且希望很快能再看到你。

Thank you and hope to see you soon.

道別與問候的肢體語言相同，依照人們的關係與文化，包含握手、擁抱、親吻、拍肩(或鞠躬、合掌)等。

4.13 賓客感謝卡
Thank-You Card from the Guest

接受別人盛情款待後，親自寄張感謝卡給主人表達誠摯感謝是必要的。

◆ 感謝卡樣本 Thank-You Card Sample

感謝邀請

Dear John and Mary,
Thank you for inviting me to your dinner party. I had a wonderful evening with everyone there. You two are definitely great cooks! Thanks again.

Best,
Steven

親愛的約翰與瑪麗：
謝謝你們邀請我參加晚餐派對，我與大家度過一個很美好的夜晚，你們真的很會做飯！再次感謝你們。

獻上最好的祝福，
史蒂文

Unit 5 Receiving Guests (Conferences and Dinner Parties)

接待賓客(會議與晚宴派對)

接待工作需要相當的事前準備，從場地動線、議程活動規劃、場地布置、到準備來賓名牌、所需文件、電腦設備、點心、飲水、休息區等。活動當天接待來賓協助他們順利參與活動，並使所有賓客感到舒適愉悅，以達到活動互相交流的目的。

5.1 接待賓客：開幕典禮
Receiving Guests: At an Opening Ceremony

Dialog 對話

A: 艾爾登博士，謝謝您今晚過來。	**A:** Dr. Alton. Thanks for coming this evening.
B: 很高興來到這裡，我不想錯過。	**B:** Great to be here. I wouldn't want to miss it.
A: 謝謝你，我們對今晚的活動都感到很興奮。	**A:** Thank you. We're all very excited about tonight's event.
B: 是的，我想每個人都如此。	**B:** Yes. I think everyone is.
A: 請跟著我到您的座位。	**A:** Please follow me to your seat.
B: 謝謝。	**B:** Thank you.

Useful Phrases 實用語句

1. 我們對今晚的活動都感到很興奮。
   We're all very excited about tonight's event.
2. 請跟著我到您的座位。
   Please follow me to your seat.
3. 謝謝您今晚過來。
   Thanks for coming this evening.

4. 我帶您看看這裡的環境。

Let me show you around.

5.2 接待研討會來賓
Receiving Guests: At a Conference

A: 嗨，我是瑪莉奇頓，我已經報名。	**A:** Hi, my name is Mary Keaton. I've registered.
B: 好的，我來找一下你的名牌。	**B:** OK, let me find your name badge for you.

(幾秒鐘後 a few seconds later)

B: 抱歉，這裡沒有，我馬上替你做一個新的。	**B:** Sorry, it is not here. I'll make a new one right away.
A: 好。	**A:** OK.
B: 我應該寫奇頓女士[小姐] 或太太？	**B:** Should I put Ms. or Mrs. Keaton?
A: 是奇頓博士。	**A:** It's Dr. Keaton.

B: 好的，奇頓博士，你的名牌在這裡，請拿一份議程，研討會的入口就在那邊。

B: OK, Dr. Keaton. Here you are. Please take a copy of the agenda with you. The conference entrance is right there.

A: 謝謝。

A: Thank you.

Word Bank 字庫

conference ['kənfərəns] n. 研討會
register ['rɛdʒɪstɚ] v. 報名
name badge [tag] n. 名牌
agenda [ə'dʒɛndə] n. 議程

Useful Phrases 實用語句

1. 我已經報名。
I've registered.
2. 我來找一下你的名牌。
Let me find your name badge for you.
3. 我應該寫奇頓女士 [小姐] 或太太？
Should I put Ms. or Mrs. Keaton?
4. 請拿一份議程。
Please take a copy of the agenda with you.

5.3 在會場接待主講人 Receiving the Keynote Speaker at the Venue

A: 強生教授，歡迎您。	**A:** Prof. Johnson. Welcome.
B: 謝謝。	**B:** Thank you.
A: 這裡會不會很難找？	**A:** Did you have any trouble finding this place?
B: 喔，不會，每件事都很順利。	**B:** Oh, no. Everything has been very smooth.
A: 您的住宿呢？	**A:** How is your accommodation?
B: 我住在老朋友那裡，很完美。	**B:** I'm staying with an old friend from days gone by. It's perfect.
A: 太好了，跟我來，我會帶您到大廳。	**A:** Great to hear it. Come with me. I'll show you to the lounge.
B: 謝謝。	**B:** Thank you.

Word Bank

smooth [smuð] adj. 平順的
accommodation [əˌkɑmə'deʃən] n. 住宿
lounge [laundʒ] n. 大廳

1. 這裡會不會很難找？
   Did you have any trouble finding this place?
2. 您的住宿呢？
   How is your accommodation?
3. 跟我來，我會帶您到大廳。
   Come with me. I'll show you to the lounge.

5.4 在畫廊接待舉辦展覽的藝術家
Receiving the Artist at the Gallery

Dialog 對話

A: 亨利，看到你真好。	**A:** Henry. Hello. Nice to see you.
B: 很開心來到這裡，很興奮，對吧？	**B:** Good to be here. Very exciting, right?
A: 是的，每個人都迫不及待想看到你的作品。	**A:** Yes, it is. Everyone is anxious to see your collection.
B: 畫展的門何時打開？	**B:** When will the gallery doors open?

A: 晚上7點30分。

A: 7:30 p.m.

B: 看來很多人聚在前面。

B: It looks like a lot of people are gathering out front.

A: 是啊，我想你的展出相當受到期待。

A: Yes. I think your show is very anticipated.

B: 聽你這麼說我很高興。

B: I'm happy to hear that.

A: 我們也都很替你開心，你值得得到肯定。

A: Well, we're all happy for you. You deserve recognition.

B: 多謝你，我很感動。

B: Thank you so much. I'm touched.

A: 這是真的。來，我帶你去一個你可以放鬆並準備今晚展出的地方。

A: It's all true. Come. I'll show you to a place you can relax and prepare for tonight's showing.

B: 聽起來很棒，我要準備好自己。

B: Sounds good. I need to collect myself.

A: 當然，跟我來。

A: Sure. Follow me.

Word Bank 

collection [kə'lɛkʃən] n. 收藏
anticipate [æn'tɪsə,pet] v. 期待
deserve [dɪ'zɝv] v. 值得
recognition [,rɛkəg'nɪʃən] n. 認可
touch [tʌtʃ] v. 感動

Useful Phrases 實用語句

1. 每個人都迫不及待想看到你的作品。
   Everyone is anxious to see your collection.
2. 我想你的展出相當受到期待。
   I think your show is very anticipated.
3. 我們都很替你開心。
   We're all happy for you.
4. 你值得得到肯定。
   You deserve recognition.

5.5 喬遷派對 Housewarming Parties

Dialog 1 對話1

A: 嗨，傑瑞，請進。	**A:** Hi , Jerry. Come on in.
B: 謝謝，我來的太早了嗎？	**B:** Thanks. I'm not too early, am I?

A: 不會，已經有幾個人來了。	**A:** No. Several people are here already.
B: 我帶了一份禮物給新房。	**B:** I brought a gift for the house.
A: 太好了，謝謝，我把它跟其他的放在一起。	**A:** Great. Thanks. I'll put it over here with the others.
B: 好。	**B:** OK.
A: 我幫你把外套掛起來。	**A:** Let me take your coat. I'll hang it up for you.
B: 謝謝。	**B:** Good. Thank you.
A: 那邊有些食物及飲料，請自行取用。	**A:** There is some food and drinks over there. Please help yourself.
B: 好，我會的。	**B:** OK. I will.
A: 我來介紹你給一些人。	**A:** Let me introduce you to some people, too.
B: 好，謝謝。	**B:** Great. Thanks.

Dialog 2 對話2

A: 傑瑞，我來向你介紹傑克王。

A: Jerry, I'd like to introduce Jack Wong to you.

B: 嗨，很高興見到你，我是傑瑞克拉克。

B: Hi. Pleased to meet you. I'm Jerry Clark.

C: 哈囉，我是傑克王，我也很高興認識你。

C: Hello. I'm Jack Wong. I'm glad to meet you, too.

A: 我要去看看其他客人，我讓你們倆聊聊。

A: I'm going to check on some other guests. I'll leave you two to chat.

C: 沒問題，我想待會再與你多聊一些。

C: No problem. I hope to talk to you more later.

A: 喔，當然，我很快就過來，我想把你介紹給大家。

A: Oh, for sure. I'll be back soon. I want to introduce you to everyone.

B: 別擔心，我會讓他覺得自在。

B: Don't worry. I'll make him feel at home.

Useful Phrases 實用語句

1. 進來吧。
   Come on in.
2. 很高興你能來。
   Glad you could make it.
3. 請坐這裡。
   Please sit here.

4. 我來帶你看看 (我家)。

   Let me show you around (the house).

5. 讓我來介紹你給大家認識。

   Let me introduce you to everyone.

6. 喝點東西。

   Have something to drink.

7. 你要喝點東西嗎？

   Would you like something to drink?

8. 我來幫你拿夾克。

   Let me take your jacket.

9. 我想待會再與你多聊一些。

   I hope to talk to you more later.

不同文化裡對收受禮物有不同規定，諸如用哪一隻手或雙手送禮或收禮，是否要先拒絕再接受，禮物的單雙數等等。一般而言，美國人的收禮與送禮都很直接，沒有這些繁瑣禮數，對顏色及數字 (除了 13 之外) 也沒有什麼忌諱。

5.6 輕鬆晚餐派對 Casual Dinner Parties

A: 請自行取用。

A: Please help yourself to everything.

B: 每道菜看起來都很美味。那是什麼？

B: Everything looks delicious. What is that?

A: 是肉條，我用我媽媽的食譜。

A: That's meatloaf. I used my mom's recipe.

B: 我從沒有吃過。

B: I've never tried it before.

A: 請拿一些，我會遞給你。

A: Please take some. I'll pass it to you.

B: 謝謝。

B: Thanks.

A: 你要喝什麼？

A: What would you like to drink?

B: 你們有果汁嗎？

B: Do you have any fruit juice?

A: 有，我們有柳橙汁及葡萄汁。

A: Yes. We have orange and grape.

B: 我要葡萄汁。

B: I'd like grape.

A: 好，也請拿些馬鈴薯泥。

A: Sure. Be sure to take some mashed potatoes, too.

recipe ['rɛsəpɪ] n. 食譜

mashed potatoes n. 馬鈴薯泥

1. 請自行取用。

   Please help yourself to everything.

2. 我用我媽媽的食譜。

   I used my mom's recipe.

3. 請拿一些，我會遞給你。

   Please take some. I'll pass it to you.

4. 你要喝什麼？

   What would you like to drink?

5. 吃些蛋糕吧。

   Have some cake.

6. 你看來很好。

   You look well.

7. 你看起來很棒！

   You look great!

8. 你的家人好嗎？

   How is your family?

9. 很開心又看到你。

   Great to see you again.

10. 你穿得很好看。

    You're dressed well.

11. 你的洋裝很可愛。

    Your dress is lovely.

12. 你的衣服很棒。

    Your clothing is very nice.

13. 我覺得不錯。

I feel OK.

14. 你的身體還好嗎？

How’s your health?

15. 還不錯。

Not bad.

16. 最近不怎麼好。

Not so good lately.

17. 我想很好。

Pretty good I think.

18. 我的健康還可以，謝謝。

I’m well enough, thanks.

賓客到家裡拜訪前，確認家裡有冰塊及冰鎮的 (chilled) 碳酸飲料、果汁或啤酒 (許多美國人喝飲料非冰不可，用餐時也必先準備一杯冰飲料再進食)，賓客到這就為他們倒飲料並請他們坐下來，如果賓客彼此不熟識，介紹每個人給彼此認識也很重要。安排好地方讓賓客可以自己倒飲料及有合適的空間坐下來聊天。

5.7 正式晚宴派對 Formal Dinner Parties

5.7a 寒暄與安排座位 Greeting and Seating the Guests

A: 哈囉，詹姆士，看到你真好。	**A:** Hello, James. It’s so good to see you.

B: 謝謝你，艾蜜莉，你看起來容光煥發。	**B:** Thank you, Emily. You look radiant.
A: 謝謝你的稱讚，請跟我來。	**A:** Thank you for the compliment. Please come with me.
B: 好。	**B:** All right.
A: 你將坐在湯瑪士桑柏格旁邊。	**A:** You're going to be seated next to Mr. Thomas Sandburg.
B: 太好了，我聽過許多他的趣事。	**B:** Wonderful. I've heard interesting things about him.
A: 是的，他是個很有趣的人。	**A:** Yes. He's a very interesting person.

radiant ['redjənt] adj. 容光煥發的
compliment ['kɑmpləmənt] n. 稱讚

1. 你看起來容光煥發。
   You look radiant.
2. 請跟我來。
   Please come with me.
3. 你將坐在湯瑪士桑柏格旁邊。
   You're going to be seated next to Mr. Thomas Sandburg.

正式宴會必須事先安排座位以顯示對賓客的尊重，座位的安排要看桌子形狀而定，圓桌在互動上比長型桌容易。如果是圓桌，夫婦毗鄰而坐；長條桌則是夫婦面對面坐，且習慣上將男士與女士坐位交錯。如果是有小孩參加的派對，安排小孩與父母坐在一起，大一點的小孩可以自成一桌。另外，將年齡或興趣相仿的賓客排在一起，可以增進賓客的互動。

5.7b 正式晚宴 Dining: Formal Dinner Parties

A: 各位，請注意，晚餐即將開始，在那之前我想感謝大家今晚的光臨，我們為大家準備了美味佳肴，如果你有任何需要，請立刻告訴我們，謝謝你們並請好好享用。

A: Everyone, your attention please. Dinner is about to be served. Before that I want to thank all of you for being here tonight. We have prepared a delicious arrangement of dishes for you. If there is anything you need, please do not hesitate to ask. Thank you and please enjoy.

1. 各位，請注意。
   Everyone, your attention please.
2. 我想感謝大家今晚的光臨。
   I want to thank all of you for being here tonight.
3. 如果你有任何需要，請立刻告訴我們。
   If there is anything you need, please do not hesitate to ask.

4. 謝謝你們並請好好享用。

Thank you and please enjoy.

多數的人都了解料理宴會菜肴是很辛苦的事情，所以不要把老中的客套說法用在宴會上，不要說家裡是寒舍，亂七八糟，也不要說自己隨便煮煮，沒什麼好菜之類的話，自然大方地告訴受邀的賓客如何準備佳肴，能使他們更享受食物的滋味與被宴請的光榮。

5.7c 主人招呼使賓客交流 Introducing Guests and Having Them Mingle

A: 桑柏格先生，這是詹姆士邱。	**A:** Mr. Sandburg. This is James Chiu.
B: 很高興見到你，邱先生，這是我太太，卡拉。	**B:** Pleased to meet you, Mr. Chiu. This is my wife, Carla.
C: 桑柏格夫人，(認識你是)我的榮幸。	**C:** Mrs. Sandburg. A pleasure.
D: 謝謝。	**D:** Thank you.
A: 我去招呼其他人，讓你們三位彼此熟悉一下。	**A:** I'm going to let you three get to know each other while I tend to a few other people.

B: 沒問題，艾蜜莉。您是哪裡人，邱先生？

B: No problem, Emily. Where are you from originally, Mr. Chiu?

C: 我在上海出生，但我家後來搬到香港。

C: I was born in Shanghai, but my family later moved to Hong Kong.

B: 真的！香港是個很棒的城市，我去出差過幾次。

B: Really? Hong Kong is a great city. I've been there on business a few times.

C: 是真的嗎？您上次去是什麼時候？

C: Is that right? When was the last time you were there?

B: 我想是2001年7月。

B: I think it was in 2001, July I believe.

C: 那裡已經改變了很多。

C: The city has changed much since then.

B: 我想也是，但我聽說不如上海改變那麼大。

B: I suppose, but from what I hear it hasn't changed as much as Shanghai.

D: 我聽說上海現在是個大都市，非常現代而且開放。

D: I hear Shanghai is a great city now, very modern and open.

C: 桑柏格夫人，這是真的，你們兩位應該去那裡 (看看)，我想你們會喜歡那裡的。

C: That's true, Mrs. Sandburg. You both should go there. I think you would like it.

B: 邱先生，您從事哪一行？

B: What line are you in, Mr. Chiu?

C: 我在電腦硬體業，我為格蘭科技工作，這是我的名片。

C: I'm in the computer hardware field. I work for Grand Tech. Allow me to give you my card.

B: 謝謝，我沒有帶名片，我是史班電信通的行銷長。

B: Thank you. I'm afraid I don't have any of mine, but I should tell you I'm head of marketing for Spanntel Tonne.

C: 是的，我有聽過你，即使是在香港跟上海，這家公司都很有名。

C: Yes. I've heard about you. That company is very well known, even in Hong Kong and Shanghai.

B: 聽到這樣真好。

B: That's nice to hear.

A: 我看你們全都相處融洽。

A: I see you are all getting along well.

D: 邱先生最初是從上海來，艾蜜莉，很浪漫吧？

D: Mr. Chiu is from Shanghai originally, Emily. Isn't that romantic?

A: 是，卡拉，我也覺得是的，我可以替你們拿點什麼嗎？

A: Yes, I'd say it is, Carla. Can I get any of you anything?

B: 我不用。	**B:** I'm fine.
C: 我也不用，桑柏格夫人呢？	**C:** I'm fine too. Mrs. Sandburg?
D: 我不用，我聊得很開心。	**D:** I'm all right. I'm enjoying the conversation.
A: 很好，那我晚點再找你們聊。	**A:** Wonderful. I'll talk to all of you later then.

Word Bank 字庫

hardware ['hɑrdˌwɛr] n. 硬體
marketing ['mɑrkɪtɪŋ] n. 行銷
romantic [rə'mæntɪk] adj. 浪漫的

Useful Phrases 實用語句

1. 我的榮幸。

   A pleasure.

2. 我去招呼其他人，讓你們三位彼此熟悉一下。

   I'm going to let you three get to know each other while I tend to a few other people.

3. 您是哪裡人？

   Where are you from originally?

4. 您上次去是什麼時候？

   When was the last time you were there?

5. 您從事哪一行？

   What line are you in?

6. 這城市已經改變了很多。

   The city has changed much since then.

7. 是真的嗎？

   Is that right?

8. 很浪漫吧？

   Isn't that romantic?

9. 我想你們會喜歡。

   I think you would like it.

10. 我看你們全都相處融洽。

    I see you are all getting along well.

11. 我可以替你拿點什麼嗎？

    Can I get any of you anything?

12. 我不用。

    I'm all right.

13. 我聊得很開心。

    I'm enjoying the conversation.

如果你邀請不同團體的人到家裡，確定要邀請能和別人打成一片 (mingle) 的人，並且讓每個人隨時都感到自在。正式餐點前，要供應小點心和飲料，如果是派對形式的晚餐，整晚都要有餐點及飲料。有些人可能會帶食物及飲料來分享，但是主人不該這麼打算，主人也不該期待客人帶禮物來，那並非美國文化。

5.8 招待朋友在外享用中國菜
Taking Friends to a Chinese Restaurant

A: 你有吃過這裡的食物嗎？	**A:** Have you tried the food here?

B: 我從未在美國吃過中國菜。	**B:** I've never had Chinese food in America.
A: 嗯，跟亞洲的中國菜不一樣。	**A:** Well, it's different from Chinese food in Asia.
B: 真的嗎？	**B:** Really?
A: 對，這裡的中國菜是為了滿足美國人的口味偏好。	**A:** Yes. It's designed to satisfy the tastes Americans prefer.
B: 嗯，我想我現在吃一些就會發現。	**B:** Well, I guess I'll find out by eating some right now.
A: 對，你要筷子嗎？	**A:** True. Do you want chopsticks?
B: 這裡有嗎？	**B:** Do they have them here?
A: 有，多數在美國的中國餐館都有，但你可能必須開口要求。	**A:** Yes. Most Chinese restaurants in the U.S. have them, but you'll probably need to ask for them.
B: 我會記住，現在我只要用刀、叉跟湯匙就好。	**B:** I'll remember that. For now I'll just use a knife, fork, and spoon.
A: 好。	**A:** OK.

Word Bank 字庫

satisfy ['sætɪsˌfaɪ] v. 滿足
taste [test] n. 口味
prefer [prɪ'fɝ] v. 偏好
chopsticks ['tʃɑpˌstɪks] n. 筷子

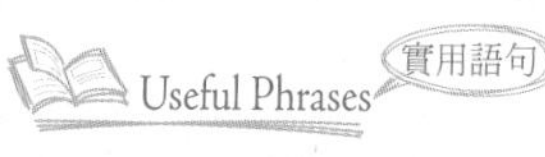

Useful Phrases 實用語句

1. 跟亞洲的中國菜不一樣。
   It's different from Chinese food in Asia.
2. 我吃了就會發現。
   I'll find out by eating.
3. 你要筷子嗎？
   Do you want chopsticks?
4. 你可能必須開口要求。
   You'll probably need to ask for them.

Notes 小叮嚀

除了華人聚集的大城市有機會找到道地的 (authentic) 中國菜之外，海外的「中國」餐館雖普遍但多已加入當地人的口味，菜肴通常是酸甜 (sweet and sour) (有時還混雜東南亞) 口味，米飯幾乎都是泰國米，感覺不中不西；如果帶老外到中國餐館用餐，要告訴餐廳不要放味精 (MSG)，許多老外對味精過敏 (allergic to MSG)。在美國的中國餐館用餐後要結帳時，服務生會送來幸運餅 (fortune cookies)，內有處事格言或運勢預測，後又加入樂透明牌。許多老外到中國或臺灣才知道原來這是海外的中國餐館吸引顧客的手法 (gimmick)，海外的中國餐館的另一個特點是戶外皆懸掛紅燈籠。

5.9 中國菜晚宴
Chinese Dinner Parties

A: 哈囉，蘇珊，很高興看到你，這一定是你的先生。

A: Hello, Susan. Nice to see you. This must be your husband.

B: 是的。鮑伯，這是我們今晚的主人傑生胡。

B: Yes, it is. Bob, this is our host this evening, Jason Hu.

C: 很高興認識你，傑生。

C: I'm pleased to meet you, Jason.

A: 我也很高興認識你，請進。

A: I'm very pleased to meet you as well. Please come in.

C: 謝謝。

C: Thank you.

Dialog 2 對話2

B: 食物看起來很美味，但其中有些東西我不知道是什麼。

B: The food looks delicious, but I don't know what some of it is.

A: 我來解釋，這是炸豆腐，在我的國家很普遍。你可能沒見過這種料理的方式。

A: Let me explain. This is fried tofu. It's very popular in my country. You've probably never seen it prepared this way.

C: 對。

C: You're right.

A: 這些是粽子，在美國這裡很少見，但是在我的文化裡很普遍，特別是在我們的一個特定慶典。

A: These are sticky rice dumplings, also uncommon here in the States, but very popular in my culture, especially during a certain celebration we have.

B: 什麼慶典？

B: What celebration?

A: 這個慶典叫做端午節。

A: It's called Dragon Boat Festival.

C: 喔，是的，我聽過那個節日。

C: Oh, yes, I've heard of that festival.

B: 我們可以用筷子嗎？

B: Can we use chopsticks?

A: 喔，當然，我來拿給你。	**A:** Oh sure. Let me get some for you.
C: 我在練習用筷子。	**C:** I've been practicing using them.
B: 我也是，但是有時我會掉下去。	**B:** Me too, but sometimes I drop them.
A: 用筷子並不容易，別擔心。	**A:** Everybody has some trouble with chopsticks. Don't worry.
C: 對，我們來享受食物吧！	**C:** Yeah. Let's just enjoy the food!

Word Bank 字庫

sticky rice dumplings n. 粽子
Dragon Boat Festival n. 龍舟節，端午節

Useful Phrases 實用語句

1. 其中有些食物我不知道是什麼。
I don't know what some of food is.
2. 炸豆腐在我的國家很普遍。
Fried tofu is very popular in my country.
3. 粽子在美國這裡很少見。
Sticky rice dumplings are uncommon here in the States.
4. 我聽過那個節日。
I've heard of that festival.

5. 我們可以用筷子嗎？

   Can we use chopsticks?

6. 我在練習用筷子。

   I've been practicing using chopsticks.

7. 你需要叉子嗎？

   Do you need a fork?

8. 用筷子並不容易。

   Everybody has some trouble with chopsticks.

9. 別擔心。

   Don't worry.

食物準備須知 for Preparing Foods

美國人不喜歡帶骨或刺的菜肴 (除非是牛排或肋骨)，多數人不能吃辣，且頂多只能接受一點點辣，宴請美國客人當然要投其所好，使賓主盡歡，設計菜單要盡量使賓客方便食用。在國外宴請中國菜就先上湯吧，雖然這是美國人的西餐順序，多數美國人能用筷子，但不要讓他們用餐時為難或必須要動手吃，所以選擇雞胸肉會比選擇帶骨頭的翅膀或雞腿好。

如果要煮魚或蝦，要去掉魚頭、蝦頭，魚蝦最好做成魚片、魚排或蝦鬆，沒有魚刺或蝦殼最受歡迎。如果沒有特別的原因，要避免請他們吃不敢吃的食物。美國人不希望看到或吃到家畜、家禽或海鮮的頭部或其他如內臟 (intestines, guts)、血 (blood)、蹄 (hooves)、腦 (brains) 等部分，以減少對食物的罪惡感 (肝臟算是例外，如牛肝、鵝肝醬)，西方許多國家如希臘、德國、法國等食材或多或少都包含以上一些部分，並非完全排斥。主流的美國文化認為除了衛生問題外，食用這些部位與人類獸性有關。附帶一提，除了西方國家外，東南亞 (如泰國、越南、柬埔寨) 及一些拉丁美洲 (如墨西哥、巴西)、非洲 (如辛巴威) 國家有吃蟲的文化。

在國外烹飪中國菜時，要特別注意廚房的油煙，盡量使用少油煙的方式做菜，不要讓油煙變成公害或造成警報器亂叫，才能與鄰居和睦相處。如果朋友稱讚自己費心打點的家及菜肴，就大方接受，不要客套抹煞自己，適度說一些自己準備菜肴的過程可以顯示自己對賓客與派對的重視。

如果友人是素食者 (vegetarian)、佛教徒 (Buddhist)，當然必須為其準備素菜；如果賓客來自其他文化及宗教 (如猶太教徒Jews、回教徒Muslims、印度教徒Hindus，對於可食肉類種類、來源、宰殺方式、食用部位、飲食器具都有特別規定，此外，回教徒不可飲酒及吸菸，每日必須按時朝拜並有齋戒月 (Ramadan) 等風俗，要當主人之前必須先做功課或詢問客人以避免觸犯禁忌 (taboo) 造成尷尬。

5.10 送客
Seeing Guests Off

（另見 4.9-4.12）

A: 太棒了，謝謝你邀請我們。	**A:** It's been great. Thanks for inviting us.
B: 謝謝你們兩位過來。	**B:** Thank you both so much for coming.
A: 一點也不麻煩。	**A:** No problem at all.
B: 你確定每樣東西都帶了嗎？	**B:** Are sure you have everything?
A: 是的，我們檢查過了。	**A:** Yes. We checked.
B: 很好，那我希望可以很快再見到你們。	**B:** Very well then. Hope to see you again soon.

A: 我們也是，晚安。

A: We hope so too. Good night.

B: 晚安，小心開車。

B: Good night. Drive safely.

記住自己不要喝酒開車，也不要讓喝酒的人開車載你，酒駕 (drunk driving) 是危險及違法的行為，如果被警察抓到酒駕，可能導致逮捕 (arrest)、罰款 (fine) 或吊照 (loss of driver's license) 的結果。

5.11 活動主人之感謝卡
Thank -You Card from the Host [Sponsor]

在邀請之貴賓出席活動後，要寄出感謝卡向對方致意，親手寫張卡片比寄電子郵件更有誠意。

(a) 感謝卡樣本 (正式) Thank-You Card Sample (Formal)

Dear Prof. Johnson,
Thank you for attending on Saturday, October 20th.
We greatly appreciate your participation in our conference and hope to have you again in the future.

Sincerely,
(signature)
Rodger Liu

親愛的強生教授：
謝謝您10月20日星期六的出席。
我們非常感謝您出席我們的研討會，並希望將來有您的再次參與。

誠摯地，
(簽名)
羅傑劉

(b) 感謝卡樣本 (不正式) Thank-You Card Sample (Informal)
感謝朋友參與聚會

Thanks for coming last weekend, Jerry. 謝謝你上週末來，傑瑞。

Stay in touch. 保持聯絡，

Give me a call anytime. 隨時打電話給我。

Thanks again. 再次感謝。

Sue 蘇

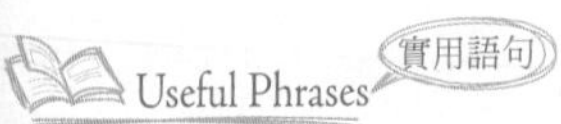

1. 謝謝你上星期幫我。

   Thanks for helping me out last week.

2. 謝謝你做的一切。

   Thanks for everything.

3. 活動很棒，謝謝你到場。

   The event was great. Thanks for being there.

4. 謝謝你的光臨，如有任何需要請來電。

   Thank you for attending. Please call if you have any needs.

5. 我們希望將來再次邀請您。

   We hope to have you again in the future.

6. 謝謝你，並希望很快能再看到你。

   Thank you and hope to see you again soon.

Unit 6 Visiting People and Being Visited

拜訪與受訪

拜訪朋友通常在晚上或週末，通常是受邀或自己打電話知會對方，時間大約 2 到 4 小時，尊重朋友的家 (及家人)，不要亂碰物品 (包括任何遙控器或冰箱)。吃吃東西、聊聊天、聯絡感情且放鬆一下，週末也可以一起外出運動，多數美國人家裡不須脫鞋，帶一些點心或一些飲料大家一起喝是個好主意，但不一定非帶不可。

6.1 依約拜訪老友
Visiting an Old Friend by Appointment

Dialog 1 對話1

A: 嗨，安迪。	**A:** Hi, Andy.
B: 嗨，艾力克。	**B:** Hi, Eric.
A: 進來坐吧，你要喝點什麼嗎？可樂、啤酒還是咖啡？	**A:** Come on in and have a seat. Do you want anything to drink? Coke, beer, or coffee?
B: 可樂好了。	**B:** Coke is fine.
A: 我很高興你打電話並來拜訪我，我好久沒見到你了，你近來好嗎？	**A:** I'm glad you called and came to visit me. I haven't seen you in ages. How have you been?
B: 很好，你呢？	**B:** Pretty good. How about yourself?
A: 不錯，但最近忙著工作。	**A:** Not bad. I've been busy with work though.
B: 我也是。	**B:** Me, too.

Useful Phrases 實用語句

客人 Guest

1. 我好久沒見到你了。

   I haven't seen you in ages.

2. 我最近忙著工作。

   I've been busy with work.

主人 Host

1. 你要喝點什麼嗎？

   Do you want anything to drink?

2. 我很高興你打電話並來拜訪我。

   I'm glad you called and came to visit me.

3. 你近來好嗎？

   How have you been?

Dialog 2 對話2

A: 你的工作進行得如何？

A: How are things going with your job?

B: 我想還好，我與一組同事在做一個大案子，有點趕。

B: OK, I think. I've been working with a group of colleagues on a big project. It's been kind of hectic.

A: 真的？為什麼？

A: Really? Why?

B: 嗯，例如，公司中途改變預定日期，他們將截止期限提前了兩個月。

B: Well, for example, the company changed the target date half way through the project. They cut two months off the deadline.

初次見面
偶遇
邀請
參加聚會
接待賓客
拜訪
特殊情況
祝賀慰問
交友
日常社交
常用功能
其他功能

A: 噢，這樣差很多。	**A:** Ouch. That is a lot.
B: 對，我很討厭這樣，但是有時就是這樣。	**B:** Yeah. I hate it, but that's the way it goes sometimes.
A: 真的，事實上我也因為截止期限在工作上有很多麻煩。	**A:** True. Actually I have been having a lot of trouble at work because of deadlines as well.

Word Bank 字庫

colleague ['kɑlig] n. 同事
hectic ['hɛktɪk] adj. 忙亂的
target date n. 預定 (開始或完成之) 日期
deadline ['dɛd,laɪn] n. 截止期限

Useful Phrases 實用語句

1. 你的工作進行得如何？
   How are things going with your job?
2. 我在做一個大案子。
   I've been working on a big project.
3. 有點趕。
   It's been kind of hectic.
4. 有時就是這樣。
   That's the way it goes sometimes.

6.2 個人拜訪道別
Farewell at a Personal Meeting

A: 真可惜你明天要搭機離開了，你下次何時再回到城裡來？

A: Too bad you are flying out tomorrow. When will you be back in town next time?

B: 那要等到明年夏天了。

B: That will be next summer.

A: 我該讓其他同學知道嗎？或是開個同學會？

A: Should I let other classmates know about it, and maybe have a class reunion?

B: 好主意，我很想和一些人聊聊。

B: Good idea. I'd love to catch up with some of them.

A: 好，我會留意 (站起來擁抱)，那我們明年夏天再見面了，請幫我向你愛妻致意。

A: Good. I will see to that. (Stand up and hug) So, I will see you next summer. Please give my regards to your lovely wife.

B: 好的，保持聯絡，再見。

B: Sure. Keep in touch. See you.

Word Bank 字庫

fly out 搭機離開
class reunion n. 同學會
regards [rɪ'gardz] n. 問候，致意

Useful Phrases 實用語句

1. 你下次何時再回到城裡來？
   When will you be back in town next time?
2. 或許我們該開個同學會？
   Maybe we should have a class reunion?
3. 我很想和一些人聊聊。
   I'd love to catch up with some of them.
4. 請幫我向你愛妻致意。
   Please give my regards to your lovely wife.
5. 替我向您家人致意。
   Give my best to your family.
6. 希望你一切順利。
   I hope everything goes well with you.
7. 保持聯絡。
   Keep in touch.

6.3 臨時拜訪 Visiting Someone by Chance

Dialog 對話

A: 你在嗎，安迪？

A: Are you in, Andy?

B: 在，(開門) 嗨，吉姆。怎麼樣啊？	**B:** Yes, (open the door) Hi, Jim. What's up?
A: 啊，安迪，你最近做了些什麼好玩的事嗎？	**A:** So, Andy, what have you been doing for fun lately?
B: 我上週去了一間很好的夜店。	**B:** I went to a good nightclub last week.
A: 真的？哪裡？	**A:** Really? Where?
B: 市區的北邊，一間叫「亮點」的店。	**B:** The north side of the city. A place called High Lights.
A: 很好的地方，真的嗎？	**A:** Nice place, really?
B: 真的，好飲料、好音樂、好D.J.，裝潢也很好。	**B:** Yes. Good drinks, good music, good D.J. Really cool decor too.
A: 有娛樂費嗎？	**A:** Is there a cover charge?
B: 沒有，週三晚上女士可得到三杯飲料的兌換券。	**B:** No, and on Wednesday nights women get vouchers good for three drinks.
A: 喔，聽起來很棒。	**A:** Oh! That sounds good to me.

B: 對，對女士很好，但男士也喜歡，因為這做法吸引很多女士。

B: Yeah, it's great for the girls, but guys like it too because it attracts a lot of ladies.

A: 我相信。

A: I'll bet.

Word Bank 字庫

decor [de'kɔr] n. 裝潢
cover charge n. 娛樂費
voucher ['vautʃɚ] n. 兌換券

Useful Phrases 實用語句

1. 有娛樂費嗎？
   Is there a cover charge?
2. 兌換券可以換三杯飲料。
   Vouchers are good for three drinks.

除了學生宿舍外，沒有事先約定的拜訪 (無論何種情形) 很可能給自己跟別人惹來尷尬或麻煩。嚴重的情況下甚至可能導致喪命！美國是可以合法擁有槍枝的國家，如果被誤認為擅闖私人土地可能遭致槍擊，多年前日本學生在美國萬聖節敲門問路被槍殺即因此而來。如果是不請自來的人又是屋主不歡迎的人 (如追討欠款)，屋主拿槍完全合法！對於習慣住在沒有槍械威脅，從來沒有槍械戒心的國人而言，實在難以想像這種極端情形，但事實確實如此，攸關生命大事，國人不能不知！

同樣的，在國外開車被警察攔下，一定要盡速停車，務必坐在車內不要亂動，等待警察過來指示你開窗、拿證件 (要在車內尋找證件、開手套箱要先告知警察你下一步的動作)，千萬不可在警察未走到時就在車內亂找東西或打開車門出來，否則警察以為你在找槍、藏毒品或要挑釁、攻擊，極可能馬上就開槍。

6.4 借住國外朋友家
Staying at a Friend's House in Another Country

6.4a 約定拜訪 Visiting Someone by Appointment

Dialog 對話

A: 哈囉。	**A:** Hello.
B: 嗨，珊蒂，我是凱莉王。	**B:** Hi, Sandy. It's Kelly Wang.

A: 嗨，凱莉，你好嗎？	**A:** Hi, Kelly. How are you?
B: 好，你呢？	**B:** Good. And you?
A: 我也好，怎麼了？	**A:** I'm OK. What's going on?
B: 呃，我六月要去你那邊，希望能去探望你。	**B:** Well, I need to fly to your city in June and was hoping to visit you.
A: 真的嗎？那就太棒了！你可以住在我這裡。	**A:** Really? That would be so cool! You can stay at my place.
B: 不是開玩笑吧？	**B:** No kidding?
A: 當然不是，我們會很盡興！	**A:** Of course no kidding. We'll have a blast.
B: 你確定這樣沒問題？我會在那裡待兩個星期。	**B:** Are you sure it would be OK? I'm going to be there for a couple of weeks.
A: 太棒了！非常歡迎你。	**A:** Terrific! You're more than welcome.
B: 太好了！	**B:** Great!

blast [blæst] n. 爆破，(俚語) 盡興
terrific [tə'rɪfɪk] adj. 很好的

Useful Phrases 實用語句

1. 怎麼了？
   What's going on?
2. 不是開玩笑吧？
   No kidding?
3. 我會在那裡待兩個星期。
   I'm going to be there for a couple of weeks.
4. 你確定這樣沒問題？
   Are you sure it would be OK?
5. 太棒了！
   Terrific!
6. 我們會很盡興的！
   We'll have a blast.
7. 非常歡迎你。
   You're more than welcome.

6.4b 抵達 Arriving

A: 嗨，凱莉，請進。	**A:** Hi, Kelly. Come on in.
B: 謝謝，珊蒂。	**B:** Thanks, Sandy.

A: 你的 (航班) 飛行如何？

A: How was your flight?

B: 不錯，但是很久。

B: Not bad, but long.

A: 你餓嗎？

A: Are you hungry?

B: 有一點。

B: Yes, a little.

A: 我為你準備了一些食物。

A: I have some food ready for you.

B: 謝謝。

B: Thanks.

A: 我們把行李放到你房間再用餐。

A: Let's put your luggage in your room before we eat.

B: 好。

B: OK.

A: 我有一間不錯的客房給你用，跟我來。

A: I have a nice guest room for you to use. Follow me.

B: 好，我希望我在這住幾天不會給你造成麻煩。

B: Sure. I hope I'm not creating any problems for you by staying a few days.

A: 你在開玩笑嗎？我盼望你來已經好幾個月了。	**A:** Are you kidding? I've been looking forward to your coming here for months.
B: 真好，我很興奮終於來到這裡。	**B:** Great. I'm excited to finally be here.
A: 好，就把這當作是自己的家，任何事情都可以問我。	**A:** Well, be sure to make yourself at home, and don't hesitate to ask me anything.
B: 謝謝你準備的一切。	**B:** Thanks for everything.
A: 沒什麼。	**A:** No problem.

◎ 客人 **Guest**

1. 希望我不會給你造成麻煩。
   I hope I'm not creating any problems for you.
2. 我很興奮終於來到這裡。
   I'm excited to be here finally.
3. 謝謝你準備的一切。
   Thanks for everything.

◎ 主人 **Host [Hostess]**

1. 你的 (航班) 飛行如何？
   How was your flight?
2. 你餓嗎？
   Are you hungry?

3. 我有一間不錯的客房給你用。

   I have a nice guest room for you to use.

4. 我盼望你來已經好幾個月了。

   I've been looking forward to your coming here for months.

5. 當作是自己的家。

   Make yourself at home.

6. 任何事情都可以問我。

   Don't hesitate to ask me anything.

到朋友家作客要帶伴手禮，拜訪以前要先問該注意到的問題，因為多數的主人不會用客人的角度去想事情，所以不會在第一時間發現有什麼不對，要問的包含朋友及家人幾點就寢、晚餐時間、寵物、小孩、聽不聽音樂等等。主人通常會諒解客人的需要和對環境的不熟悉，但是客人當然也要為主人著想；除非非常要好的朋友，否則借住短短幾天就好，別讓自己變成不受歡迎 (Don't wear out your welcome.) 才是上策。

6.5 拜訪親戚 Visiting Relatives

A: 哈囉，潔西阿姨。(擁抱)	**A:** Hello, Aunt Jessie. (hugging)
B: 嗨，葛洛莉亞，很高興看到你。	**B:** Hi, Gloria. It's so nice to see you.
A: 我也很高興看到你。	**A:** Nice to see you too.

B: 你的姨丈大約一個小時後會回來，坐下吧。	**B:** Your uncle will be here in an hour or so. Have a seat.
A: 好，但是首先我要給你這個。	**A:** OK, but first I want to give you this.
B: 花瓶，好可愛。	**B:** A flower vase. It's lovely.
A: 我希望你喜歡。	**A:** I hope you like it.
B: 我喜歡，很好看，你知道我們喜歡新鮮的花。	**B:** I do. It's very nice. And you know how much we love fresh cut flowers.
A: 我知道。	**A:** Yes, I do.
B: 現在我們去花園剪一些，好嗎？	**B:** Let's go out to the garden and cut some flowers right now, OK?
A: 好主意。	**A:** Great idea.

Word Bank 字庫

vase [ves] n. 花瓶
fresh cut flowers n. 新鮮的花

初次見面
偶遇
邀請
參加聚會
接待賓客
拜訪
特殊情況
祝賀慰問
交友
日常社交
常用功能
其他功能

Useful Phrases 實用語句

客人 Guest

1. 首先我要給你這個。

   First I want to give you this.

2. 我希望你會喜歡它。

   I hope you like it.

主人 Host [Hostess]

1. 坐下吧。

   Have a seat.

2. 我喜歡，很好看。

   I like it. It's very nice.

3. 你不用帶任何東西來。

   You didn't have to (bring anything).

不要買昂貴的禮物送人，多數人會覺得好像欠你什麼而感到很不舒服，而且會因為覺得要回送你等值的東西而擔憂。

6.6 拜訪顧客 Visiting a Client

A: 哈囉。	**A:** Hello.
B: 嗨，我可以為你效勞嗎？	**B:** Hi. May I help you?

A: 可以，我是傑瑞王，我約了時間跟安德森先生見面。

A: Yes, I'm Jerry Wang. I have an appointment to see Mr. Anderson.

B: 好，我去告訴他你到這裡了。

B: OK. Let me tell him you are here.

B: (接待員打電話) 他說他會在幾分鐘後見你。你可以在那裡等一下嗎？

B: (receptionist calls Mr. Anderson) He said he will see you in a few minutes. Would you please wait over there?

A: 當然可以，沒問題。

A: Yes, of course. No problem.

B: 那邊的桌子上有咖啡。

B: There is coffee available over there on that table.

A: 好，謝謝。

A: Great. Thank you.

Dialog 2 對話2

A: 早安，安德森先生。

A: Good morning, Mr. Anderson.

B: 哈囉，傑瑞，請進。

B: Hello, Jerry. Come in.

A: 謝謝，我希望這是個見面的好時間。

A: Thank you. I hope this is a good time to meet.

B: 是的，沒問題，我正在等你。

B: Yes. No problem. I was expecting you.

A: 你的秘書說你很忙，但還是排了時間給我。

A: Your secretary said you're very busy, but gave me an appointment.

B: 是真的，我們需要談一談，所以開始吧。

B: It's true, but we need to talk, so let's get started.

A: 好，我準備了在電話中告訴過你的那一項新設備，同時我也想要知道你是否滿意我們目前為止賣給你的 (設備)。

A: Fine. I have that new piece of equipment I told you about on the phone, and I also want to know if you're satisfied with what we have sold you so far.

B: 好，我們晚點再談第二部分，現在我要知道你之前說的那項新設備。

B: Good. Let's talk about the second part later. Right now I want to know about that new piece of equipment you told me about the other day.

A: 好。

A: Sure.

Useful Phrases 實用語句

拜訪者 Visitor

1. 我跟安德森先生約了時間見面。

   I have an appointment to see Mr. Anderson.
2. 我希望這是個見面的好時間。

   I hope this is a good time to meet.
3. 目前為止…。

   ...so far.

接待員 Receptionist

1. 你可以在那裡等一下嗎？

   Would you please wait over there?
2. 那邊的桌子上有咖啡。

   There is coffee available over there on that table.
3. 請等幾分鐘。

   Please wait a few minutes.

客戶 Client

1. 我正在等你。

   I was expecting you.
2. 我們開始吧。

   Let's get started.

拜訪客戶時，如果由男士來倒咖啡，女士作簡報或擔任主管事務，應習以為常，避免在性別及工作領域上作任何評論。

美國人做生意直來直往，利潤是最高指導原則，與面子無關，所以不需先建立「關係」再談生意。強力推銷、爭辯、挑錯的策略是常態，提案被直接拒絕也是家常便飯，直接了當是美國人做生意的不二法門，也可避免浪費彼此時間；如果提案被接受了，就要守信用，雙方也會互訂合約 (contract) 或備忘錄 (memorandum) 規範。

如果美國人拿到你的名片後把它塞在褲子的後面口袋，不必生氣，對美國人而言這樣的舉動完全是方便考量，雖然在許多文化裡，這樣做對遞名片的人是很無禮的。如果美國人沒有給你名片，也不要覺得不受重視，如果有必要，請他給你一張，美國人不像其他文化一樣注意名片文化，有時他們並不交換名片，結束會面要離開時覺得有必要，才以名片留下自己的聯絡方式；總之一切都是方便考量，而不是面子問題。

6.7 訪問市府官員
Visiting a City Official

A: 這是市長辦公室，我可以為你服務嗎？

A: This is the Mayor's office. May I help you?

B: 可以，我是羅傑蘇，我想要安排與市長會面。

B: Yes. My name is Rodger Su. I would like to schedule a meeting with the Mayor.

A: 我明白了，你與市長見面是想談論關於什麼呢？

A: I see. What is it you want to see the Mayor about?

B: 我們最近談過關於新機場的計畫，他要我來拜訪並跟他談談這件事。

B: We recently spoke to each other about plans for the new airport. He asked me to stop by and talk to him about it.

A: 很好，你可以等一下嗎？

A: Very well. Can you hold a minute?

B: 可以，沒問題。

B: Yes, no problem.

Dialog 2 對話2

A: 蘇先生？

A: Mr. Su?

B: 是的。

B: Yes.

A: 市長很樂意與你見面。

A: The Mayor would be happy to meet with you.

B: 太好了，他何時有空呢？

B: Wonderful. When is he available?

A: 16日星期二下午2點好嗎？

A: Is Tuesday the 16th at 2 p.m. good?

B: 那時我恐怕會在公司開會，3點半可以嗎？

B: I'm afraid I'll be in a meeting at my company then. How about 3:30?

A: 可以。

A: That will be fine.

B: 好，我會準時到。

B: Great. I'll be there.

A: 喔，等等，你的聯絡電話是？

A: Oh, wait. What is your contact number?

B: 我公司電話是343- 6677，手機是6743453399。

B: My office number is 343-6677. My cell is 6743453399.

A: 好，蘇先生，我把你放入16日市長星期二下午3點半的行程。

A: All right, Mr. Su. I have you written in to the Mayor's schedule for Tuesday the 16th at 3:30 in the afternoon.

B: 好，多謝。

B: OK. Thank you very much.

A: 祝你有愉快的一天！

A: Have a nice day!

B: 謝謝，你也是，再見。	**B:** Thank you. You too. Bye.

A: 哈囉，市長先生。我是羅傑蘇。	**A:** Hello, Mr. Mayor. I'm Rodger Su.
B: 我很高興與你會面，蘇先生。	**B:** I'm very pleased to meet you, Mr. Su.
A: 我也很高興與你會面。	**A:** I'm pleased to meet you also.
B: 你來本市多久了？	**B:** How long have you been in our city?
A: 我和家人兩年前搬過來的。	**A:** My family and I moved here two years ago.
B: 我希望到目前為止都很好。	**B:** I hope it's been good so far.
A: 是的，很好，這是很適合居住的城市。	**A:** Yes, it has. It's a great city to live in.
B: 聽到這樣真好，你從事哪一行呢？	**B:** That's nice to hear. What do you do?

A: 我是泰勒兄弟建築公司的會計師。

A: I'm an accountant for Taylor Brothers Construction Company.

B: 那是本市重要的公司之一，他們僱用很多人。

B: That's an important company in our city. They employ a lot of people.

A: 是的，我們是本地的大公司。

A: Yes, we're a big company, locally.

B: 嗯，我希望待會我們可以多聊一些。我知道你來這裡是想參與興建新機場的協商部分。

B: Well, I hope we can talk more later. I know you are here to participate in negotiations with the city about the new airport we want to build.

A: 對，我是泰勒兄弟的代表之一。

A: That's right. I'm one of the representatives for Taylor Brothers.

B: 好，我們一定很快會再次碰面。

B: Good. We'll cross paths again soon no doubt.

A: 我很期待。很榮幸與您會面，市長先生。

A: I'm looking forward to it. It's been a pleasure to meet you, Mr. Mayor.

B: 謝謝，跟你會面也很好，蘇先生。

B: Thank you. It's been very fine to meet you too, Mr. Su.

accountant [ə'kauntənt] n. 會計師
construction company n. 建築公司
participate [pɑr'tɪsəˌpet] v. 參與
negotiation [nɪˌgoʃɪ'eʃən] n. 協調
representative [ˌrɛprɪ'zɛntətɪv] n. 代表

1. 目前為止都很好。
   It's been good so far.
2. 我很期待。
   I'm looking forward to it.
3. 我希望待會兒我們可以多聊一些。
   I hope we can talk more later.
4. 我們一定很快會再次碰面。
   We'll cross paths again.

Notes 小叮嚀

與市府官員會面要穿著正式服裝並表現成熟舉止，不需過度拘謹或客套，保持禮貌，如果能在接待或與市府官員 (或其他大人物) 會面的場合參與有趣的談話則會更好。

6.8 升遷祝賀及拜訪
Congratulating and Visiting at a Promotional Event

A: 我要謝謝你今天來這裡。

A: I want to thank you for being here today.

B: 我的榮幸，我很高興你今天邀我來拜訪。

B: My pleasure. I'm very glad you invited me to visit today.

A: 你來參加我公司的升遷活動對我意義重大。

A: It means a lot to me that you have come to my company's promotional event.

B: 真的，我很高興來參加，恭喜你升遷。

B: Really, I'm happy to attend. By the way, congratulations on your promotion.

A: 謝謝，我對這件事感到很興奮。

A: Thank you. I'm very excited about it.

B: 你會繼續在這辦公室工作嗎？

B: Will you continue to work in this office?

A: 會，再六個月，然後就搬到城市的另一邊。

A: Yes, for the next six months, then I'll move across town.

Useful Phrases 實用語句

拜訪及祝賀 Visiting and Congratulating

1. 我很高興你今天邀我來拜訪。
   I'm very glad you invited me to visit today.
2. 我的榮幸。
   My pleasure.
3. 我很高興來參加。
   I'm happy to attend.
4. 恭喜你升遷！
   Congratulations on your promotion!
5. 你會繼續在這辦公室工作嗎？
   Will you continue to work in this office?

接受祝賀 Accepting Congratulations

1. 我要謝謝你今天來這裡。
   I want to thank you for being here today.
2. 它對我意義重大。
   It means a lot to me.
3. 我對這件事感到很興奮。
   I'm very excited about it.

Tips 小祕訣

美國文化裡祝賀升遷可以用卡片祝賀，如果是女性友人升遷可以送花，但這些做法是個人情誼，與傳統或期待無關。如果是大公司的高階職位，卡片、祝賀信或花都可能是賀禮。

It's been great. Thanks for inviting us.
Good night. Drive safely.

Unit 7 Special Situations

特殊情況

生活裡總是有意料之外的特殊情形發生，如果因自己的緣故而耽誤到他人的時間，必須盡早告知。萬一借來的物品有損傷，要據實以告並提供補救措施或賠償，誠實有禮對待他人是不二法門。

7.1 取消約定
Canceling an Appointment

A: 哈囉，尼爾森醫師辦公室，我可以幫你嗎？	**A:** Hello, Doctor Nelson's office. May I help you?
B: 可以，我是安妮潘，我要取消明天下午的預約。	**B:** Yes. My name is Annie Pan. I have an appointment for tomorrow afternoon I need to cancel.
A: 我明白了，潘女士，你要改約別的時間嗎？	**A:** I see, Ms. Pan. Would you like me to give you another appointment time?
B: 不，我要離開城裡幾星期，我回來後會再打來。	**B:** No. I have to leave the city for a few weeks. I'll call again after I return.
A: 好，潘女士，祝你旅途平安！	**A:** Very well, Ms. Pan. Have a safe journey!
B: 謝謝你。	**B:** Thank you.

1. 我要取消明天下午的預約。
   I need to cancel an appointment for tomorrow afternoon.
2. 你要改約別的時間嗎？
   Would you like me to give you another appointment time?
3. 祝你旅途平安！
   Have a safe journey!

7.2 打電話請病假
Calling in Sick

A: 哈囉，史密斯傑利公司。	**A:** Hello. Smith Jally Company.
B: 嗨，我是傑瑞蘇，我今天沒辦法上班，我生病了。	**B:** Hi. This is Jerry Su. I can't come to work today. I'm sick.
A: 你的主管是誰，傑瑞？我會告訴他。	**A:** Who is your supervisor, Jerry? I'll inform him.
B: 我的主管是席德蘭德斯。	**B:** My supervisor is Sid Landers.
A: 好，祝你早日康復。	**A:** OK. Get well.
B: 謝謝，再見。	**B:** Thanks. Bye.

Word Bank 字庫

supervisor ['supɚˌvaɪzɚ] n. 主管
inform [ɪn'fɔrm] v. 通知

Useful Phrases 實用語句

1. 我打電話來請病假。

   I'm calling in sick.

2. 我今天生病了。

   I'm sick today.

3. 你的主管是誰？

   Who is your supervisor?

4. 祝你早日康復。

   Get well (soon).

7.3 會議遲到 Late for a Meeting

Dialog 1 對話1

A: 哈囉，我是傑克魏，我跟安德斯女士有約但遲到了。

A: Hello. I'm Jack Wei. I'm late for an appointment with Ms. Anders.

B: 是的，魏先生，她在等你。

B: Yes, Mr. Wei. She's been expecting you.

A: 很抱歉，我遲到了，我不知道搭計程車過來要這麼久。

A: I'm sorry. I'm late. I didn't think it would take so long to get here by taxi.

B: 我會告訴她，請等一下。

B: I'll tell her. Just a moment please.

A: 謝謝。

A: Thank you.

1. 我跟安德斯女士有約但遲到了。

   I'm late for an appointment with Ms. Anders.

2. 我不知道搭計程車過來要這麼久。

   I didn't think it would take so long to get here by taxi.

3. 她在等你。

   She's been expecting you.

4. 很抱歉，我遲到了。

   I'm sorry. I'm late.

A: 哈囉，波登士公司。

A: Hello, Boltons Incorporated.

B: 哈囉，我是羅伯特李，我與托伯特先生約了9點見面，但是我會遲到。

B: Hello. This is Robert Lee. I have an appointment to see Mr. Talbot at 9:00, but I'm going to be late.

A: 好，李先生，你要另約新時間嗎？

A: All right, Mr. Lee. Would you like to make a new appointment?

B: 不了，事實上我只會遲到大約 30 分鐘。

B: No. Actually I'll only be about thirty minutes late.

A: 請等一下，我打電話給托伯特先生通知他你的情況。

A: Please hold a moment. I'll call Mr. Talbot and inform him of your situation.

B: 謝謝。

B: Thank you.

Dialog 3 對話3

A: 李先生？

A: Mr. Lee?

B: 是的。

B: Yes.

A: 托伯特先生說他還是可以見你，但是他必須參加 10 點 15 分的會議。

A: Mr. Talbot says he can still see you, but he must go to a meeting at 10:15.

B: 好，我只要花他 20 分鐘的時間。

B: That's fine. I'll only need twenty minutes of his time.

A: 好，我會告訴他你 9 點半會到。

A: Very well. I'll tell him you'll be here at 9:30.

B: 好，多謝了。

B: Great. Thank you very much.

A: 沒什麼，待會見。

A: No problem. See you soon.

B: 是的，再見。

B: Yes. Good bye.

Useful Phrases 實用語句

1. 我會遲到一下。

   I'm going to be a little late.

2. 你要另約新時間嗎？

   Would you like to make a new appointment?

3. 我只要花他20分鐘的時間。

   I'll only need twenty minutes of his time.

4. 請等一下。

   Just a moment please.

5. 請等一下 (不要掛斷)。

   Please hold a moment.

6. 待會見。

   See you soon.

7.4 因遲到另約時間
Rescheduling an Appointment Due to Lateness

Dialog 對話

A: 嗨，我是彼得謝，我跟肯斯先生有約但遲到了，塞車塞得很嚴重。

A: Hi. I'm Peter Hsieh. I'm late for an appointment with Mr. Kanns. I got stuck in heavy traffic.

B: 我來打電話給他。

B: Let me call him.

(一分鐘後 a minute late)

B: 他正在等你而且了解你的情況，但是他行程太忙今天沒辦法見你。

B: He was expecting you and understands your situation, but won't be able to see you today due to his busy schedule.

A: 我了解，我非常抱歉造成不方便，有可能改約別的時間嗎？

A: I understand. I'm terribly sorry for causing this inconvenience. Would it be possible to reschedule the appointment?

B: 當然可以，你何時可以再來？

B: Of course. When would you like to return?

A: 最快可以見他的日期是哪一天？

A: What is the earliest date I could see him?

B: 他這星期的行事曆都滿了，下週二早上會有時間。

B: His calendar is full for the rest of this week. He'll have time in the morning on Tuesday of next week.

A: 好，幾點？

A: That's fine. What time?

B: 早上 10 點。

B: 10 a.m.

A: 好，我一定會到。

A: OK. I'll be here for sure.

B: 好，我把你寫進去(行事曆)。

B: All right, I'll write you in.

A: 謝謝。

A: Thank you.

Word Bank 字庫

due to 因為
inconvenience [ˌɪnkən'vinjəns] n. 不方便
reschedule [ri'skɛdʒul] v. 重新訂時間

Useful Phrases 實用語句

1. 我塞車塞得很嚴重。
   I got stuck in heavy traffic.
2. 我非常抱歉造成不方便。
   I'm terribly sorry for causing this inconvenience.
3. 有可能改約別的時間嗎？
   Would it be possible to reschedule the appointment?
4. 最快可以見他的日期是哪一天？
   What is the earliest date I could see him?
5. 他的行事曆滿了。
   His calendar is full.
6. 你何時可以再來？
   When would you like to return?
7. 我一定會到。
   I'll be here for sure.
8. 我把你寫進去 (行事曆)。
   I'll write you in.

初次見面 偶遇 邀請 參加聚會 接待賓客 拜訪 特殊情況 祝賀慰問 交友 日常社交 常用功能 其他功能

7.5 報告壞消息
Telling Someone Bad News

Dialog 對話

A: 莎莉，我有事要跟你說。	**A:** Sally, I need to talk to you a minute.
B: 好，你需要什麼？	**B:** Sure. What do you need?
A: 我恐怕有些壞消息。	**A:** I'm afraid I have some bad news.
B: 怎麼了？	**B:** What's wrong?
A: 羅伯特剛打電話來，發生了車禍，海倫受傷了。	**A:** Robert just called. There has been an accident. Helen has been injured.
B: 什麼？真的嗎？多嚴重？	**B:** What? Really? How badly?
A: 他說救護車現在正送她去醫院。	**A:** He said an ambulance is taking her to the hospital now.
B: 我最好打電話到醫院。	**B:** I'd better call the hospital.

A: 好，用我的電話。

A: Sure. Use my phone.

injure ['ɪndʒɚ] v. 受傷
ambulance ['æmbjələns] n. 救護車

1. 我有事要跟你說。
   I need to talk to you.
2. 我恐怕有些壞消息。
   I'm afraid I have some bad news.
3. 怎麼了？
   What's wrong?
4. 發生了車禍。
   There has been an accident.
5. 海倫受傷了。
   Helen has been injured.
6. 多嚴重？
   How badly?
7. 我最好打電話到醫院。
   I'd better call the hospital.

報告壞消息時加上「I'm afraid」(恐怕)，給對方心理準備。

7.6 遺失借來物品
Losing a Borrowed Item

A: 嗨，喬登。	**A:** Hi , Jordan.
B: 嗨，辛蒂。	**B:** Hi , Cindy.
A: 喬登，記得我跟你借的腳踏車嗎？	**A:** Jordan, remember the bike I borrowed from you?
B: 記得。	**B:** Yes.
A: 我要跟你說關於它的一些事。	**A:** I have to tell something about it.
B: 什麼？	**B:** What?
A: 我弄丟了。	**A:** I lost it.
B: 什麼？怎麼會？在哪裡丟的？	**B:** What? How? Where?

A: 別擔心，我會買一臺新的還你。	**A:** Don't worry. I'll buy you a new one.
B: 什麼時候？	**B:** When?
A: 現在，如果你要的話。	**A:** Now if you like.
B: 我現在沒時間，但是我很快就會需要一臺 (腳踏車)。	**B:** I don't have time now, but I'm going to need one very soon.
A: 告訴我你要什麼，我明天會去買給你。	**A:** Tell me what you want, and I'll buy it and give it to you tomorrow.
B: 你人真好。	**B:** That's very nice of you.
A: 沒什麼，我欠你的。	**A:** No problem. I owe it to you.

Useful Phrases 實用語句

1. 我要跟你說關於它 (腳踏車) 的一些事。

   I have to tell something about it.

2. 我弄丟了。

   I lost it.

3. 我會買一臺新的還你。

   I'll buy you a new one.

4. 你人真好。

   That's very nice of you.

5. 我欠你的。

   I owe it to you.

鄰居通常會向彼此借東西，如果弄壞了借來的東西，一定要據實以報並且公平地賠償對方。

7.7 損壞借來物品 Damaging a Borrowed Item

A: 嗨，吉姆，我要還你梯子，但是我想我弄壞它了。	**A:** Hi, Jim. I brought your ladder back, but I think I damaged it.
B: 真的嗎？發生什麼事？	**B:** Really? What happened?
A: 我弄斷了它底部的一隻腳。	**A:** I broke one of the feet off the bottom of it.
B: 我明白了，呃，我們看一下。	**B:** I see. Well, let's look at it.
A: 好，在這邊。它啪的一聲突然斷掉了，我不確定為什麼。	**A:** Sure. It's over here. It snapped off. I'm not sure why.

B: 呃，別擔心了，是個小問題。

B: Well, don't worry about it. It's a small problem.

A: 我會付任何必要的修理費用。

A: I'll pay for any repair needed.

B: 沒關係，算了。

B: That's OK. Forget about it.

Word Bank 字庫

ladder ['lædɚ] n. 梯子
snap [snæp] v. 突然斷掉

Useful Phrases 實用語句

1. 我弄壞這東西了。
   I damaged this thing.
2. 它啪的一聲突然斷掉了。
   It snapped off.
3. 對不起，我弄壞了。
   I'm sorry. I broke it.
4. 我會付修理費。
   I'll pay for the repairs.
5. 關於這件事，真抱歉。
   Sorry about this.
6. 我真的很抱歉，我意外地弄壞了你的梯子。
   I'm really sorry, but I accidentally broke your ladder.
7. 我明天會換一個新的給你。
   I'll replace it tomorrow.

8. 我買了一個新的給你。

   I bought you a new one.

9. 沒關係。

   That's OK.

10. 算了。

    Forget about it.

7.8 在派對裡身體不舒服 Not Feeling Well at a Party

A: 傑瑞，你的派對很好玩，但是我得走了。	**A:** Jerry. Your party is fun, but I have to leave.
B: 為什麼？	**B:** Why?
A: 我真的覺得不太舒服。	**A:** I really don't feel well.
B: 怎麼了？	**B:** What's wrong?
A: 我覺得很累，也許我快生病了。	**A:** I feel very tired. Maybe I'm coming down with something.
B: 你需要人送你嗎？	**B:** Do you need a ride?

A: 不用，沒關係，我走路回家。	**A:** No. That's OK. I'll walk home.
B: 這樣不好，我送你回家，你不舒服的話走回家太遠。	**B:** That's no good. Let me take you home. It's too far for you to walk feeling ill.
A: 好，謝謝。	**A:** All right. Thanks.
B: 走吧，我的車就在旁邊。	**B:** Come on. My car is close by.

come down with 感染，得到

1. 我真的覺得不太舒服。
   I really don't feel well.
2. 也許我快生病了。
   Maybe I'm coming down with something.
3. 你需要人送你嗎？
   Do you need a ride?
4. 我送你回家。
   Let me take you home.

7.9 朋友失去寵物
Friend Losing a Pet

A: 嗨，瑪莉，你好嗎？	**A:** Hi, Mary. How's it going?
B: 我想還可以。	**B:** OK, I guess.
A: 你看起來心情不太好，怎麼了？	**A:** You look a little down. Anything wrong?
B: 我的貓死了。	**B:** My cat died.
A: 喔，真的嗎？聽到這件事我很難過，發生了什麼事？	**A:** Oh, really? I'm sorry to hear that. What happened?
B: 牠生病了，我帶牠去看獸醫，但牠還是死了。	**B:** It got sick. I took it to the vet, but it died anyway.
A: 我真的很遺憾。	**A:** I'm really sorry.
B: 謝謝。	**B:** Thanks.

Word Bank 字庫

down [daʊn] adj. 沮喪的
vet [vɛt] n. 獸醫 (= veterinarian)

Useful Phrases 實用語句

1. 一切都還好嗎？
   Is everything OK?
2. 你沒事吧？
   Are you all right?
3. 怎麼了？
   What's wrong?
4. 你看起來很困擾。
   You look troubled.
5. 聽到這件事我很難過。
   I'm sorry to hear that.
6. 我真的很遺憾。
   I'm terribly sorry.

7.10 拜訪鄰居商借某物
Visiting a Neighbor to Borrow Something

Dialog 1 對話1

A: 嘿，早安，史蒂芬。

A: Hey. Good morning, Steven.

B: 嗨，羅賓，你好嗎？

B: Hi, Robin. How are you?

A: 好，怎麼了？

A: OK. What's up?

B: 呃，我就有話直說了，我可以借你的割草機嗎？

B: Well, I'll get to the point. I'm wondering if I can borrow your weed eater.

A: 嗯，我不確定，它有點難用，因為引擎可能很難啟動。

A: Hmmm. I'm not sure. It's a little hard to use because the engine can be hard to start.

B: 引擎？你有汽油啟動的割草機？我以為我看到你用臺電力發動的。

B: Engine? You have a gas powered weed eater? I thought I saw you using an electric one.

A: 喔，那臺小的，對，你當然可以用那臺。

A: Oh! That one. The little one. Yeah, sure you can use it.

B: 我不知道你有汽油動力的割草機，我不需要像那樣的，我只有一些小地方需要割草。

B: I didn't know you had a gas powered one. I don't need anything like that. I only have a few small areas that I need to weed whack.

A: 沒問題，在車庫，我拿給你。

A: No problem. It's in the garage. I'll get it for you.

weed eater n. 割草機
gas [gæs] n. 汽油 (= gasoline)
electric [ɪ'lɛktrɪk] adj. 電力的
whack [hwæk] v. 重擊 (用割草機割草)

Useful Phrases 實用語句

借入者 Borrower

1. 我就有話直說了。
   I'll get to the point.
2. 我可以借你的割草機嗎？
   I'm wondering if I can borrow your weed eater.
3. 我想請你幫一個忙。
   I have a favor to ask.
4. 你就是我要的人 [就是你可以幫我]！
   You are just the man I need!

借出者 Lender

1. 我不確定。
   I'm not sure.
2. 它有點難用。
   It's a little hard to use.
3. 你當然可以用那個。
   Sure you can use it.
4. 沒問題。
   No problem.
5. 我拿給你。
   I'll get it for you.

Dialog 2 對話2

A: 在這邊。	**A:** Here you go.
B: 多謝。	**B:** Thanks.
A: 你有延長線嗎？	**A:** Do you have an extension cord?
B: 有，我有兩條，所以我接到要用的地方應該沒問題。	**B:** Yes, I do. I have a couple of them, so I should have no problem reaching the area I need to get to.
A: 好。	**A:** OK, good.
B: 我明天晚上還你，可以嗎？	**B:** I'll bring it back tomorrow. Is that OK?
A: 不急，你可以借整個星期。	**A:** No need to hurry. You can keep it all week.
B: 謝謝，我下週末前一定會還。	**B:** Thanks. I'll certainly return it before next weekend.
A: 很好。	**A:** Great.

B: 再次感謝。

B: Thanks again.

extension cord n. 延長線
hurry ['hɝɪ] v. 匆忙

Useful Phrases 實用語句

借入者 Borrower

1. 我明天晚上還你。
   I'll bring it back tomorrow.
2. 我下週末前一定會還。
   I'll certainly return it before next weekend.
3. 可以嗎？
   Is that OK?
4. 再次感謝。
   Thanks again.

借出者 Lender

1. 不急。
   No need to hurry.
2. 你可以借整個星期。
   You can keep it all week.

borrow 為借入，lend 是借出，不要搞混了。向別人借東西盡量早點歸還，因為那是別人的財物。如果借用使用汽油的割草機，歸還時應先加滿油再歸還，借用其他東西除小心使用外，也要整理乾淨再歸還。

因為保險 (insurance) 的緣故，美國人多半不會借車給別人，也不會開口向別人借車，以免出了狀況後續理賠很複雜，還可能進一步造成車輛出借人之保險公司將來拒保或大幅調高保費的代價！

◆ 提出請求 Making a Request

借東西跟請人幫忙一樣，別人較不願出借的物品、不容易幫的忙、請不算熟的人幫忙都需要用比較正式的問法，在語言上顯現體貼及禮貌，才有可能讓人答應幫忙。

下列句子中文看來雖然差不多，但英文句子由上到下越來越正式。

1 借入物品 Borrowing Something

①我可以借你的割草機嗎？

Can I borrow your weed eater? (使用現在式，直接，句子短，不正式的用法)

②你的割草機可以借我嗎？

Could you lend me your weed eater?

③我可否借你的割草機？

Is it OK if I use your weed eater?

④你介意我借你的割草機嗎？

Do you mind if I borrow your weed eater?

⑤我想知道你是否可以借我你的割草機？

I'm wondering if you can lend me your weed eater?

⑥是否可以借我你的割草機？

Would it be OK if I borrowed your weed eater? (使用假設語氣，有點正式)

⑦如果我借你的割草機，你會介意嗎？

Would you mind if I borrowed your weed eater?

⑧你會介意借我你的割草機嗎？

Would you mind lending me your weed eater?

⑨我想知道我是否可以借你的割草機？

I wonder if I could borrow your weed eater?

⑩我想知道你是否介意借我割草機。

I was wondering if you'd mind lending me your weed eater. (使用假設語氣且拉長句子，極正式)

2 英文的正式與否必須透過助動詞的使用：

(1) 使用現在式句子最短也最直接，沒有給對方考慮的時間，適用於與自己很熟的人或物品價值不高的情況。

(2) 使用過去式是假設法，因為把想借物品的想法說成一種假設，即使主人不答應，因為是個假設的提議，雙方也不會尷尬。用假設法且句子拉長是給對方心理準備應答，用在不太熟的人、物品價值高或東西很新的情況。

3 回答 Responding to a Request

按照問句之助動詞回答。

(1)肯定

①可以。

Yes, you can.

②可以。

Yes, it's OK.

③我不介意。

No, I don't mind.

④可以。

Yes, it would be OK.

⑤我不介意。

No, I wouldn't mind.

(2)否定，須加上不能出借的原因聽來較友善。

①恐怕不行，它不是我的。

No, I'm afraid not. It's not mine.

②很不巧，它壞了。

Too bad. It's broken.

③我還沒時間去修理它。

I haven't got time to fix it yet.

④事實上你可以租一部。

You can rent one actually.

⑤我這兩天在用，你可以等嗎？

I'm using it these days. Can you wait?

⑥很抱歉，我要用。

Sorry, I can't. I have to use it.

⑦很抱歉，我真的很喜歡我的 _______ 。

Sorry, I can't. I really like my_______.

7.11 請朋友看家
Asking a Friend to Housesit

A: 嗨，卡蘿。我可以和你談一下嗎？	A: Hi, Carol. Can I talk to you for a few minutes?
B: 當然可以，珊蒂，怎麼了？	B: Sure, Sandy. What's up?
A: 我要請你幫個大忙，你是第一人選。	A: I have a big favor to ask. You are my first choice.
B: 真的嗎？你需要什麼？	B: Really? What do you need?
A: 我需要有人幫我看家兩個星期。	A: I need someone to housesit for me for two weeks.

B: 我懂了，什麼時候？

B: I see. When?

A: 下個月，我為了我姊姊的婚禮要回家。

A: Next month. I have to go back home for my sister's wedding.

B: 真的嗎？要一個月嗎？

B: Really? Will that take a month?

A: 不用，但是我要跟我家人聚一聚，因為我飛回亞洲。

A: No, but I should spend some time with my family as I'm flying all the way back to Asia.

B: 當然，有道理，好，我需要做什麼？

B: Sure. That makes sense. Well, what do I have to do?

A: 不會很難，我只需要有人澆花及房子看來有人住，你知道，收郵件、開燈，諸如此類。

A: It won't be too difficult. I just need some plants watered and the place looking lived in. You know, pick up the mail, lights on, that kind of thing.

B: 聽起來沒問題。

B: Sounds OK to me.

A: 完全當做自己的家，使用每件或任何你要用的東西。我會付所有費用，不必擔心電費或其他費用。

A: Feel free to make yourself totally at home. Use everything and anything you want to use. I'll pay for everything, so don't worry about electricity or other utilities.

B: 好，聽起來我可以為你處理。

B: Great. It sounds like I can handle it for you.

A: 太好了，真多謝。

A: Wonderful. Thanks so much.

Word Bank 字庫

housesit ['haus,sɪt] v. 看家
electricity [ɪ,lɛk'trɪsətɪ] n. 電力
utilities [ju'tɪlətɪz] n. 水電等公用設備

Useful Phrases 實用語句

屋主 Home Owner

1. 我要請你幫個大忙。
   I have a big favor to ask.
2. 你是第一人選。
   You are my first choice.
3. 我可以和你談一下嗎？
   Can I talk to you for a few minutes?
4. 我需要有人幫我看家。
   I need someone to housesit for me.

5. 收郵件。

   Pick up the mail.

6. 開燈。

   Lights on.

7. 給盆栽澆水。

   Water the plants.

看家者 Housesitter

1. 我需要做什麼？

   What do I have to do?

2. 聽起來沒問題。

   Sounds OK to me.

為別人看家，要尊重屋主的家當，並確實做到被請求的事情，如收報紙、郵件、澆花、餵寵物等。通常屋主會請看家的人將房子當成自己的家，可以請朋友過來聊聊天，但絕對不行開派對狂歡。

7.12 拒絕請求
Turn Downs at Work

A: 傑瑞，我得去城鎮的另一頭跟客戶談談。	**A:** Jerry, I have to go across town to talk to a client.
B: 好，再見。	**B:** OK. See you later.
A: 事實上我想知道你是否可以幫我一個忙。	**A:** Actually I'm wondering if you can do me a favor.

B: 什麼忙？

B: What is it?

A: 我在一小時後要去機場接另一個客戶。

A: I have to pick up another client at the airport in an hour.

B: 我明白了，我願意去接，但是我沒辦法離開辦公室，我得在今天下午開會前完成這份報告。

B: I see. I'd do it, but there's no way I can leave the office. I have to get this report done before this afternoon's meeting.

A: 只要半個小時就好。

A: It would only take a half hour.

B: 抱歉，我真的不行。

B: I'm sorry. I really can't.

A: 好，還是謝謝你。

A: OK. Thanks anyway.

1. 我想知道你是否可以幫我一個忙。
   I'm wondering if you can do me a favor.
2. 我願意去接，但是我沒辦法離開辦公室，
   I'd do it, but there's no way I can leave the office.
3. 抱歉，我真的不行。
   I'm sorry. I really can't.

4. 還是謝謝你。

Thanks anyway.

7.13 朋友借錢 Friend Borrowing Money

7.13a 答應幫忙 Agreeing to Help

Dialog 對話

A: 嗨，安琪拉。	**A:** Hi, Angela.
B: 嗨，傑瑞。	**B:** Hi, Jerry.
A: 安琪拉，我有一個忙要請你幫，這個忙有點大。	**A:** Angela, I have a favor to ask. It's sort of big.
B: 是什麼？	**B:** What is it?
A: 我要借錢付一筆醫藥費。	**A:** I need to borrow money to pay a doctor bill.
B: 我明白了，你要借多少？	**B:** I see. How much do you need to borrow?
A: 300 元。	**A:** $300.

B: 你何時可以還？	**B:** When can you pay it back?
A: 下個月中。	**A:** The middle of next month.
B: 你確定嗎？	**B:** Are you sure?
A: 確定，我那時會收到家裡的錢。	**A:** Yes. I'll have money from my family by then.
B: 好。	**B:** OK.

Word Bank 字庫

doctor bill n. 醫藥費

Useful Phrases 實用語句

1. 我需要幫忙。
   I need a favor.
2. 我有一個忙要請你幫。
   I have a favor to ask.
3. 我需要借點錢。
   I need to borrow some money.
4. 我要付一筆醫藥費。
   I need to pay a doctor bill.
5. 我會在 10 號還你。
   I'll pay you back on the 10th.

6. 你要借多少？
   How much do you need to borrow?
7. 你何時可以還？
   When can you pay it back?
8. 你確定嗎？
   Are you sure?

7.13b 無法幫忙 Unable to Help

A: 抱歉，傑瑞，我無法幫忙，我得付房租，你為何不打電話回家呢？

A: Sorry, Jerry. I can't help. I have to pay the rent. Why don't you ever call home?

B: 我不喜歡打電話回家。

B: I hate to call home.

A: 為什麼？

A: Why?

B: 我媽媽跟爸爸太會替我操心了。

B: My mom and dad worry too much about me.

A: 所以呢？

A: So?

B: 他們問我太多問題，並且誤解我說的每件事。

B: They ask me too many questions and misinterpret everything I say.

A: 真的嗎？

A: Really?

B: 真的，他們把我告訴他們的每句話聽成不好的或是潛在性的壞事，真讓我抓狂。

B: Yes. They hear every word I tell them as some bad or potentially bad thing. It drives me nuts.

A: 呃，你知道父母親都這樣。

A: Well, you know how parents are.

B: 對，我知道他們關心我並且只是對我表現他們的愛，但是我仍然不喜歡。

B: Sure, I know they care about me and are just showing their love, but I still, don't like it.

A: 你應該打電話給他們。

A: You should call them.

B: 算了，我知道你是對的，但我現在沒有心情做那件事。

B: Forget it. I know you are right, but I'm in no mood for that right now.

Word Bank 字庫

misinterpret [ˌmɪsɪn'tɝprɪt] v. 誤解，誤譯
potentially [pə'tɛnʃəlɪ] adv. 潛在性地
mood [mud] n. 心情

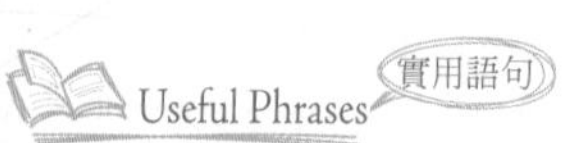

1. 你應該打電話回家。

   You should call home.

2. 你知道父母親都這樣。

   You know how parents are.

3. 我現在沒有心情做那件事。

   I'm in no mood for that right now.

4. 我只能借你 100 元。

   I can lend you $100 only.

5. 我也沒有現金。

   I'm short on cash too.

6. 我下星期要繳房租。

   My rent is due next week.

7. 你要開一張支票給我。

   You will need to write me a check.

8. 支票會在下個月中被提示付款。

   The check will be presented for payment in the middle of next month.

9. 你還錢的時候，我會把支票還你。

   I'll give the check back to you when you pay the money back.

俗語說「Lend your money and lose a friend.」(錢借出去就失去朋友) 也說「A friend in need is a friend indeed.」(患難見真情)。借錢給朋友當然可以，但最好確定你了解並能信任借錢的人，無論國籍、種族，有些人就是會占別人便宜。借錢給好友是一回事，另外有些詐騙高手 (con artist) 宣稱他們認識一些你也認識的人，說他們替需要借錢的朋友帶口信，不要理會這些人，只與自己的朋友接觸，也不要覺得有人情壓力而被迫答應；如果你不能或無法負擔借錢給他人，不必為此覺得對不起朋友，或覺得不自在而感到羞愧，美國文化就是如此乾脆。

7.14 朋友被解僱 Friend Being Laid Off

Dialog 對話

A: 怎麼了，莎拉？	**A:** What's up, Sarah?
B: 我被解僱了。	**B:** I got laid off.
A: 真不好。	**A:** That's not good.
B: 對，我很懊惱。	**B:** Yeah. I'm bummed out.
A: 別難過了，我請你吃午飯。	**A:** Come on. I'll buy you lunch.

B: 謝謝，你真好。 → **B:** Thanks. That's very nice of you.

A: 我的榮幸。 → **A:** My pleasure.

Word Bank 字庫

lay off 解僱
bum out 使懊惱

◎ **尋求幫忙 Looking for Help**

1. 我很懊惱。
   I'm bummed out.
2. 我需要幫忙。
   I need a favor.
3. 我需要幫忙。
   I need some help.

◎ **鼓勵 Phrases for Encouragement**

1. 以你的能力及經驗，你馬上會找到工作。
   With your ability and experience, you will find a job in no time.
2. 不會有事的。
   Things will be alright.
3. 事情會好轉的。
   Things will get better.

因為經濟情況使然，企業裁員時有所聞，金融風暴下大批在美國遭解僱的人苦中作樂，紛紛到夜店加入粉紅單派對 (pink slip party)，意指拿到粉紅色解僱單的失業一族去酒吧喝酒解悶，參加被解僱派對 (laid off party)，吐苦水之餘，順道交換消息並開發人脈。

7.15 替朋友照顧寵物
Taking Care of a Pet for a Friend

Dialog 對話

A: 嗨，泰瑞。	**A:** Hi, Terry.
B: 哈囉，吉兒。	**B:** Hello, Jill.
A: 謝謝你答應照顧我的烏龜。	**A:** Thanks for offering to take care of my turtle.
B: 當然，我以前養過一隻烏龜，所以沒問題。	**B:** Sure. I used to have a turtle so no problem.
A: 牠在這裡，在烏龜箱裡。	**A:** Here he is. He's in his terrarium.
B: 很好，我們把牠放在這裡。	**B:** Very nice. Let's put him here.

A: 好，這裡也有烏龜的食物。	**A:** OK. Here is the turtle food too.
B: 喔，好，我會放在牠箱子的旁邊。	**B:** Oh, good. I'll keep it next to his home.
A: 一天餵牠兩次，但是不要太多。	**A:** Feed him twice a day, but not too much.
B: 好，別擔心，我會照顧牠。	**B:** OK. Don't worry. I'll take good care of him.
A: 我知道你會，謝謝。	**A:** I know you will. Thanks.

turtle ['tɝtl̩] n. 烏龜

terrarium [tɛ'rɛrɪəm] n. 飼養所，栽培或飼養的容器

feed [fid] v. 餵

1. 一天餵牠兩次。

   Feed it twice a day.

2. 牠很容易照顧。

   It's easy to take care of.

3. 我很感謝你的幫忙。

   I really appreciate your help.

4. 如果你有問題或疑問，打這個電話。

   Call this number if you have a problem or question.

5. 這是我獸醫的電話。

This is the number of my vet.

6. 如果有問題，打電話給我。

Call me if there's a problem.

7.16 替朋友顧小孩 Babysitting for Friends

Dialog 對話

A: 哈囉。	**A:** Hello.
B: 哈囉，凱麗，我是雪莉。	**B:** Hello, Kylie. This is Shelly.
A: 嗨，雪莉，怎麼了？	**A:** Hi, Shelly. What's going on?
B: 我有個問題，我今晚要加班，我的小孩需要人幫忙。	**B:** I have a problem. I have to work late tonight. I need help with my kids.
A: 你需要什麼？	**A:** What do you need?
B: 你今晚可以看顧我的小孩嗎？	**B:** Can you watch my kids tonight?
A: 好，在哪裡？	**A:** Sure. Where?

B: 你可以到我家嗎？	**B:** Can you go to my house?
A: 好，我幾點要到？	**A:** Yes. What time do I need to be there?
B: 他們6點左右會到家。	**B:** They'll be home around 6.
A: 沒問題，我會騎我的腳踏車過去。	**A:** No problem. I'll ride my bike over there.
B: 很好，我真的很感謝。	**B:** Great. I really appreciate this.
A: 很高興我可以幫忙，我要餵他們吃東西嗎？	**A:** Glad I can help. Do I need to feed them?
B: 不用，我會叫外送並且留下錢。	**B:** No. I'll have food delivered, and I'll leave money for it.
A: 我會看到你嗎？	**A:** Will I see you?
B: 會，如果你在6點前到的話。	**B:** Yes, if you are there before 6.
A: 好，我知道了，在你家見了。	**A:** OK. Got it. See you at your house.

B: 十二萬分感謝！	**B:** Thanks a million!
A: 好，我現在就過去。	**A:** Sure. I'll leave now.
B: 好，再見。	**B:** OK. Bye.

Word Bank 字庫

babysit ['bebɪˌsɪt] v. 看顧小孩
deliver [dɪ'lɪvɚ] v. 遞送

Useful Phrases 實用語句

1. 我今晚要加班。
   I have to work late tonight.
2. 我的小孩需要人幫忙。
   I need help with my kids.
3. 你今晚可以看顧我的小孩嗎？
   Can you watch my kids tonight?
4. 你可以到我家嗎？
   Can you go to my house?
5. 你可以 6 點前到嗎？
   Can you be here by 6?
6. 我會叫外送晚餐。
   I'll have dinner delivered.
7. 我會留錢給你。
   I'll leave money for you.

8. 我真的很感謝。

I really appreciate this.

9. 謝謝你的幫忙。

Thanks for your help.

10. 感激不盡。

I can't thank you enough.

11. 我會帶他們到你家。

I'll bring them to your house.

12. 我會在 10 點左右回來。

I'll be back around 10.

13. 你需要什麼？

What do you need?

14. 我幾點要到？

What time do I need to be there?

15. 我要餵他們吃東西嗎？

Do I need to feed them?

7.17 幫朋友搬家 Helping a Friend Move

A: 嘿，鮑伯，我可以和你說一下話嗎？	**A:** Hey, Bob, can I talk to you a minute?
B: 可以，什麼事呢？	**B:** Yes. What's up?
A: 我要搬家，我需要人幫忙搬兩件東西。	**A:** I'm moving and I need some help moving two things.
B: 你何時要搬？	**B:** When are you moving?

初次見面
偶遇
邀請
參加聚會
接待賓客
拜訪
特殊情況
祝賀慰問
交友
日常社交
常用功能
其他功能

A: 下週末，但我只需要你幫忙兩個鐘頭。	**A:** Next weekend, but I'll only need your help for a couple of hours.
B: 我星期六下午可以幫你。	**B:** I can help you on Saturday afternoon.
A: 那很好，幾點？	**A:** That would be great. What time?
B: 嗯，大約 2 點吧？	**B:** Say around two?
A: 星期五我會打電話跟你確認。	**A:** I'll call you on Friday to confirm.
B: 聽起來不錯。	**B:** Sounds good.
A: 再見了。	**A:** See you later.
B: 好。	**B:** Right.

Word Bank 字庫

say [se] int. 嗯 (語助詞)
confirm [kən'fɝm] v. 確認

1. 我需要人幫忙搬家。

   I need help moving.

2. 這個星期六你可以幫我嗎？

   Can you help me this coming Saturday?

3. 我會買午餐。

   I'll buy lunch.

4. 你幾點可以來這裡？

   What time can you be here?

7.18 幫朋友代班
Substituting Work for a Friend

Dialog 對話

A: 嗨，崔兒喜。	**A:** Hi, Chelsey.
B: 嗨，唐。	**B:** Hi, Dan.
A: 我有事要問你。	**A:** I have something I need to ask you.
B: 好，是什麼呢？	**B:** OK. What is it?
A: 我下週要去紐約，所以需要代理人。	**A:** I have to go to New York next week, so I need a sub.

B: 你整個星期都不在嗎？ | B: You'll be gone all week?

A: 對，但是我只需要人代理週三的會議。 | A: Yes, but I only need a sub to cover the Wednesday meeting for me.

B: 嗯，我想我可以幫你。 | B: Well, I suppose I can cover for you.

A: 我會替你準備好所有東西，而且，我欠你一次(人情)。 | A: I'll have everything prepped for you, and, I owe you one.

B: 是的，沒錯。 | B: Yes, you do.

A: 你需要紐約的什麼東西嗎？ | A: Anything you want from New York?

B: 讓我驚喜吧。 | B: Surprise me.

A: 好，沒問題，謝謝你幫我忙。 | A: Sure. No problem. Thanks for helping me out.

B: 我相信改天你也會幫我。 | B: I trust you'll do the same for me someday.

A: 一定會！ | A: You bet!

sub [sʌb] n. 代理人 (= subtitute)
cover ['kʌvɚ] v. 代理
prep [prɛp] v. 準備 (= prepare)

1. 這是緊急事件。
   It's an emergency.
2. 我需要代理人。
   I need a sub.
3. 你可以代理我 (的工作) 嗎？
   Can you cover for me?
4. 我會離開一週。
   I'll be gone a week.
5. 我欠你一次 (人情)。
   I owe you one.
6. 我下次會代理你 (的工作)。
   I'll cover you next time.
7. 我會替你準備好每樣東西。
   I'll have everything ready for you.

Unit 8 Congratulations and Congolences

祝賀與慰問（含賀詞、賀卡格式）

祝賀與慰問是日常生活的一部分，有時伴隨著禮物及卡片，言語很重要，關係著接受者的感受，本單元包含美國生活裡各類祝賀派對與慰問場合之應對。

8.1 單身派對 Bachelor's Parties

8.1a 派對開始 Starting the Party

A: 嘿，大衛，進來吧，派對正好開始。	**A:** Hey, David. Come on in. The party is just starting.
B: 好，今晚的計畫是什麼？	**B:** Great. What's the plan for tonight?
A: 我們有好多食物和飲料，當然還有電影。	**A:** We've got plenty of food and drinks, and of course movies.
B: 電影，老天！哪種電影？	**B:** Movies. Gee! What kind of movies?
A: 我想你知道。	**A:** I think you know.
B: 是啊，開個玩笑。	**B:** Yeah. Just kidding.

1. 今晚的計畫是什麼？

   What's the plan for tonight?

2. 老天！

Gee!

8.1b 確認派對物品 Checking on Party Supplies

A: 你買了多少啤酒？	**A:** How much beer did you buy?
B: 別擔心，我們有一小桶。	**B:** Don't worry. We have a keg.
A: 好，我猜那代表我們不會沒啤酒。	**A:** Great. I guess that means we won't run out of beer.
B: 對，我們也有雪茄。	**B:** Right. We have cigars too.
A: 真的？我從沒抽過雪茄。	**A:** Really? I've never smoked a cigar before.
B: 我們有一些牙買加雪茄。	**B:** We got some from Jamaica.
A: 我們也有萊姆酒嗎？	**A:** Do we have rum too?
B: 有。	**B:** Yes.

keg [kɛg] n. 小桶 (5-10加崙)
cigar [sɪ'gɑr] n. 雪茄
rum [rʌm] n. 萊姆酒

8.1c 派對中 At the Party

A: 傑瑞撲克玩得不錯。	**A:** Jerry did well playing poker.
B: 是的，他贏了全部的錢。	**B:** Yes. He won all the money.
A: 我們沒萊姆酒了。	**A:** We're running out of rum.
B: 我們可以走去酒店買一些。	**B:** We can walk down to the liquor store to buy more.
A: 我們一起出錢。	**A:** Let's take up a collection.
B: 不，沒關係，我會付酒錢。	**B:** No, that's ok. I'll pay for it.
A: 你確定嗎？	**A:** Are you sure?

B: 是的，沒什麼。	**B:** Yeah. No big deal.
A: 我也會出一點。	**A:** I'll pitch in too.

poker ['pokɚ] n. 撲克牌
liquor ['lɪkɚ] n. 酒
pitch in 分攤 (金錢)；貢獻

Useful Phrases 實用語句

1. 我們一起出錢。
   Let's take up a collection.
2. 沒什麼。
   No big deal.
3. 我也會出一點。
   I'll pitch in too.

8.1d 派對結束 Ending a Party

Dialog 對話

A: 湯姆跟史丹利剛離開，他們搭計程車。	**A:** Tom and Stanley just left. They took a taxi.
B: 他們還有一點醉。	**B:** They're still a little drunk.

A: 我明白了，這是好主意，安全總比後悔好。	**A:** I see. It's a good idea. Better safe than sorry.
B: 你呢？你覺得怎麼樣？	**B:** How about you? How do you feel?
A: 我覺得一點飄飄然，但我覺得我可以騎我的腳踏車。	**A:** I'm kind of tipsy, but I can ride my bike I think.
B: 什麼？不行！你今晚可以待在這裡。	**B:** What? No way! You can stay here tonight.
A: 我不想麻煩你。	**A:** I don't want to bother you.
B: 胡說八道，不麻煩，我有很多空間。	**B:** Nonsense. It's no bother. I have plenty of room.
A: 謝謝，也許我可以就倒在這裡睡。	**A:** Thanks. Maybe I should just crash here.
B: 當然，讓我帶你去看你可以睡在哪裡。	**B:** No doubt about it. Let me show you where you can sleep.
A: 謝謝。	**A:** Thanks.

tipsy ['tɪpsɪ] adj. 微醉
crash [kræʃ] v. 碰撞、倒下；(俚語) 睡

1. 安全總比後悔好。
   Better safe than sorry.
2. 我覺得一點飄飄然。
   I'm kind of tipsy.
3. 你可以倒在這裡睡。
   You can crash here.
4. 我不要麻煩你。
   I don't want to bother you.
5. 胡說八道
   Nonsense.

派對與習俗說明：結婚 / 生子
Parties and Traditions: Getting Married / Having a Baby

準新娘派對及準新生兒派對 Bridal Shower & Baby Shower

準新娘派對及準新生兒派對都是女士的派對，送禮物給準新娘和準新生兒、吃簡單的點心並聊很多女士們的話題，是很輕鬆隨性的派對。

單身派對 Bachelor's Party

單身派對是準新郎作為單身的最後一個派對，喝酒、進食、限制級的笑話及男士間的話題，隨意穿著即可，會有一些很活躍或較瘋狂的活動。

結婚派對 Wedding Party

收到結婚派對的邀請卡要盡早回覆，並且準備禮物；如果不能參加婚禮，也要寄出禮物祝福新人。婚禮儀式時，不要談天說笑，要尊重新人的婚禮與賓客的感受。招待派對時與其他賓客共同享受新人結婚的喜悅，但切記不要貪杯。

結婚週年派對 Wedding Anniversary Party

通常是結婚多年夫妻邀請至親好友在一些好餐廳舉辦的平靜晚餐，因此需要合宜的穿著打扮，飲酒及舉杯祝福是很平常的。

8.2 準新娘派對 Bridal Showers

A: 嗨，凱倫，你興奮嗎？	**A:** Hi, Karen. Are you excited?
B: 我暈頭轉向，這麼多事要做。	**B:** My head is spinning. There is so much to plan.
A: 你是說婚禮，對嗎？	**A:** You mean the wedding, right?
B: 對。	**B:** Yes, I do.
A: 我知道你的意思，我姊姊結婚時真的忙翻了。	**A:** I know what you mean. When my sister got married, it was crazy.
B: 我不知道我要做這麼多選擇及決定。	**B:** I had no idea I'd have to make so many choices and decisions.
A: 對，顏色、式樣、地點、邀請誰，一大串清單。	**A:** Right, colors, styles, places, who to invite. The list is long.

B: 我看到其他女生來了。	**B:** I see some of the other girls are here.
A: 對，我們都在聊婚禮。	**A:** Yes. We're all chatting about the wedding.
B: 那不令人驚訝。	**B:** I guess that's no surprise.

8.3 婚禮 Weddings

8.3a 迎接賓客 Receiving Guests

Dialog 對話

A: 哈囉，琴。	**A:** Hello, Jean.
B: 你來了！	**B:** You made it!
A: 是的，我不確定我可以到這裡。	**A:** Yes. I was not sure I'd get here.
B: 搭機到這裡還順利嗎？	**B:** How was your flight?

A: 很好，很平順，也準時。	**A:** Good. Very smooth, and on time.
B: 我帶你到你的座位。	**B:** Let me show you to your seat.
A: 儀式會準時開始嗎？	**A:** Will the ceremony start on time?
B: 我想會準時。	**B:** Yes. I think so.
A: 招待派對在哪裡？	**A:** Where is the reception?
B: 在教堂這裡。	**B:** Here at the church.
A: 很方便。	**A:** That's convenient.

1. 你來了！
   You made it!
2. 我帶你到你的座位。
   Let me show you to your seat.
3. 儀式會準時開始嗎？
   Will the ceremony start on time?

4. 招待派對在哪裡？

Where is the reception?

婚禮邀請卡會註明 RSVP 回覆期限，因為新人要統計參加賓客人數以做準備，所以收到邀請卡要盡早回覆。如果在新人已經確定人數後才回覆參加，會造成新人的不便，是失禮的表現。如果邀請卡信封上註明你的名字及「and guest」表示可以攜伴，如果沒有註明，就不要攜伴，也不要打電話問新人是否可以攜伴，因為派對費用是以人數計算，新人如果沒有預計攜伴的費用，將導致費用的增加。另外與亞洲傳統可能不同之處為婚禮邀請卡之邀請人為即將新婚之夫婦，而婚禮費用傳統上由女方父母負擔開銷，但現今雙方父母會討論，而新婚夫婦也會盡量避免豪華婚禮，控制開銷，使結婚不致於造成負擔。

8.3b 婚禮禮物 Wedding Gifts

A: 我有個婚禮禮物，要放在哪裡？	**A:** I have a wedding gift. Where should I put it?
B: 我拿去跟其他的放在一起。	**B:** I'll take it and put it with the others.
A: 謝謝。	**A:** Thanks.

美國傳統思維 (traditional sense) 是否給新人贈禮以及贈送何種禮物 (習慣上避免將俗氣的現金及支票當賀禮) 為賓客的自由意志，新人不能置喙。但時代改變，為避免禮物重複並免去賓客挑選禮物之麻煩，新人可列出結婚禮物清單 (wedding gift registry) 供賓客參考。因賓客仍可自行決定送禮事宜，所以將禮物項目與邀請卡放在一起在今日仍是禁忌。現今受到亞洲移民影響，美國人對原本被認為俗氣的貨幣型禮物 (monetary gifts) 態度已漸漸改變，尤其年輕一代的接受度頗高。

婚禮前就寄出禮物是比較好的，也有些賓客會於婚禮結束後將準備的禮物寄給新人，避免在婚禮當天給新人增添載運禮物的麻煩。許多賓客婚禮當天會準備百貨公司禮券 (gift certificates) 或是寫上新郎新娘名字之支票或現金當賀禮。現金因有遺失風險，支票其實是較好的形式。如果不能參加婚禮，還是要寄出禮物祝福新人才合乎禮儀。

參加婚禮時會有放禮物的桌子及負責收禮物的人員，新婚夫婦會在蜜月後打開禮物並寄出感謝卡。

8.3c 祝賀新人 Congratulating the Bride and Groom

A: 恭喜兩位，我真替你們高興。

A: Congratulations, you two, I'm so happy for you.

B: 謝謝你，蓋瑞。謝謝你來。

B: Thanks, Gary. And thanks for coming.

A: 沒什麼，我不想錯過。

A: No problem. I wouldn't miss it for anything.

B: 我們知道你路途遙遠，我們很榮幸。

B: We know you had to come a long way. We're honored.

A: 不用客氣，我很樂意來這裡。

A: Don't mention it. I'm really happy to be here.

B: 我們看來如何？

B: How do we look?

A: 就像熱戀中的伴侶。

A: Like a couple in love.

1. 恭喜！
   Congratulations!
2. 我不想錯過。
   I wouldn't miss it for anything.
3. 我們知道你路途遙遠。
   We know you had to come a long way.
4. 我們很榮幸。
   We're honored.

8.3d 婚禮招待派對 At the Wedding Reception

A: 你有通過招待動線嗎？

A: Did you go through the reception line?

B: 當然，你呢？	**B:** Sure. Did you?
A: 有，我親到新娘。	**A:** Yes. I got to kiss the bride.
B: 那是傳統，對嗎？	**B:** That's the tradition, right?
A: 是的。	**A:** Yes, it is.
B: 我們去拿些蛋糕。	**B:** Let's get some cake.
A: 嗯，看來新娘要開始切蛋糕了。	**A:** Yeah. It looks like the bride is about to start cutting it.

Useful Phrases 實用語句

1. 親新娘。
   Kiss the bride.
2. 那是傳統。
   That's the tradition.

8.3e 敬酒祝賀新婚夫婦 Toasting the Couple

A: 各位請注意，我想為神仙眷侶敬酒。

A: Your attention please. I'd like to toast the couple.

A: 莎莉，傑瑞，我祝福你們幸福快樂長長久久，你們是完美的一對，敬你們 (舉杯敬酒)！

A: Sally. Jerry. I want to wish you many years of happiness and health, and say that you two are a perfect match. To you! (lifting his/her glass to toast)

B: 各位先生女士，我要恭喜新婚夫妻並為他們的將來敬酒。傑瑞，恭喜你有一位美麗的妻子；莎莉，你嫁了一個好男人。

B: Ladies and gentleman. I want to congratulate the Newlyweds and toast their future. Congratulations, Jerry. You have a beautiful wife. And Sally, you have married a fine man.

B: 祝你們幸福 (舉杯敬酒)！

B: To your happiness! (lifting his/her glass to toast)

◆ **祝福語 Words of Blessing**

①恭喜！

Congratulations!

②恭喜新婚！

Congratulation on your marriage.

③祝美好人生！

Have a great life!

◆ **新婚賀卡樣本 Sample Cards to the Newlyweds**

May your lives be filled with
joy and happiness.
願你的人生充滿喜樂與幸福。
Congratulations! 恭喜！
(sign your name)（簽名）

Love and joy to you both! 祝福你倆愛與喜悅！

Good luck! 祝好運！

(sign your name)（簽名）

教堂婚禮 White Weddings

傳統的美國婚禮在教堂舉行，儀式簡短，婚禮儀式在新娘的家人、祖母、母親坐定位後開始，新郎在神父前方等待新娘及陪伴人員出場，伴娘伴郎人數沒有規定，出場的順序是招待人員 (伴郎)、伴娘、主伴娘、戒指男童、花童入場，接下來是新娘父親挽著新娘入場，走到神父面前。神父主持婚禮帶領新郎新娘完成結婚誓言並交換戒指儀式，由神父宣示新郎新娘從此成為夫妻，典禮至此完成，新婚夫婦在兩位證人陪同下到側室內簽下結婚證書，成為合法佳偶，新婚夫婦回到教堂後接受眾賓客灑下花瓣、彩紙之祝福，並與賓客拍照留念。

隨後賓客齊聚招待派對地點，開始婚禮派對，新娘與新郎開舞、新娘與父親共舞、來賓參與舞蹈、新婚夫婦合切結婚蛋糕、簡短致詞 (新娘父親、新郎、主伴郎)、向新婚夫婦舉杯祝賀等都是派對內容，傳統上美國的婚禮開銷由新娘父親支付。派對進行數小時後，新婚夫婦即將離開前，新娘背對未婚女賓客將捧花丟出，據說接到捧花之幸運女賓客將成為下一位新娘。有些新人保留扔吊襪帶之習俗，新娘扔完捧花後坐下，由新郎取下新娘之右側吊襪帶 (上綴有心型圖案) 扔向未婚男賓客，接到吊襪帶的男士據說將與接到捧花的女士成為佳偶，或將成為下一位新郎。隨後新婚夫婦坐上綁上瓶罐彩帶及寫有新婚 (just married) 字樣的禮車，叮咚作響宣告新婚喜悅及新婚夫婦即將展開蜜月。

結婚典禮和宴客準備可能累壞新人，所以有些人選擇到隨處都有小禮堂和牧師，並且 24 小時提供婚禮服務的著名賭城拉斯維加斯 (Las Vegas) 快速結婚。

◆ 教堂婚禮 White Weddings

bride	新娘
groom	新郎
chapel/church	(小) 教堂/教堂
white wedding	傳統白紗婚禮
father of the bride	新娘的父親

walk up the aisle	步上教堂走道；結婚
priest	神父，牧師
bestman	主伴郎
groomsmen	伴郎群
maid of honor	主伴娘
bridesmaids	伴娘群
flower girl [boy/child]	花童 (多由女童擔任)
page boy	聽差少年
ring bearer	攜帶戒指者 (多由5到10歲左右男童擔任，攜帶上縫有 (假) 婚戒之絲綢抱枕走紅毯)
wedding vow	結婚誓言
bouquet	新娘花束
wedding ring	婚戒
wedding dress [gown]	新娘禮服
head piece	頭紗
veil	面紗
garter	吊襪帶
tuxedo	新郎禮服
a toast	舉杯敬酒
speech	演說、致詞
bridal waltz	新婚夫婦開舞華爾滋
wedding favors	婚禮賓客紀念品
honeymoon	蜜月
limo	禮車
newlyweds	新婚夫婦
marriage license	結婚證書
confetti	彩紙
petals	花瓣

8.4 準新生兒派對 Baby Showers

Dialog 1 對話1

A: 嗨，唐娜，恭喜！	**A:** Hi, Donna. Congratulations!
B: 謝謝，西莉亞。	**B:** Thanks, Celia.
A: 你可以將這禮物加入這 (禮物) 堆裡。	**A:** You can add this gift to the pile.
B: 好，謝謝，請進來。	**B:** OK. Thanks. Come on in.
A: 我也帶了些點心。	**A:** I brought some snacks too.
B: 你不必費心張羅。	**B:** You didn't need to do that.
A: 沒關係	**A:** It's OK.

Dialog 2 對話2

A: 是男生還是女生？	**A:** Is it going to be a boy or a girl?

B: 我們不知道。	**B:** We don't know.
A: 真的嗎？為什麼？	**A:** Really? Why?
B: 吉姆和我決定我們想要驚喜。	**B:** Jim and I decided we want to be surprised.
A: 好甜蜜！我想那是正確的決定。	**A:** How sweet! I think that's the right decision.
B: 我媽認為我們應該現在就知道，這樣幫小寶貝買東西會容易些。	**B:** My mom thinks we should find out now so it will make shopping for baby things easier.
A: 那也有道理。	**A:** That makes sense, too.
B: 對，但是我們想要喜愛這個經驗的每個時刻，而且驚喜很有趣。	**B:** Yes, but we want to love every moment of this experience, and surprises are fun.
A: 不錯喔 [你真行，真有你的]！	**A:** Good for you.

Useful Phrases 實用語句

1. 你可以將這禮物加入這 (禮物) 堆裡。
   You can add this gift to the pile.

2. 你不必費心張羅。

You didn't need to do that.

3. 是男生還是女生？

Is it going to be a boy or a girl?

4. 我們想要驚喜。

We want to be surprised.

5. 好甜蜜！

How sweet!

6. 我想那是正確的決定。

I think that's the right decision.

7. 不錯喔 [你真行，真有你的]！

Good for you.

◆ 卡片祝福新生兒語句 **Expressions on a Sample Card**

①恭喜你獲得新生寶貝！

Congratulations on your new born baby!

②我聽到你寶貝的好消息了，祝大家健康快樂！

I heard the great news about your baby. Health and happiness to all!

③祝你家裡的新成員快樂久久。

Years of happiness to the new member of your family.

8.5 結婚週年 Wedding Anniversary Parties

8.5a 參加結婚週年派對 Attending a Wedding Anniversary Party

A: 哈囉，瑪莉，這是舉辦派對的地方嗎？	**A:** Hello, Mary. Is this where the party is being held?
B: 哈囉，肯恩，是的，過來加入我們。	**B:** Hello, Ken. Yes, it is. Come join us at our table.
A: 謝謝，那對神仙眷侶在哪裡？	**A:** Thanks. Where is the happy couple?
B: 他們馬上到這裡，他們在外面拍照。	**B:** They'll be here soon. They're outside having their picture taken.
A: 我明白了，我應該把禮物放哪裡？	**A:** I see. Where should I put this gift?
B: 那邊桌上。	**B:** Over on that table.
A: 好。	**A:** OK.

B: 我們喝些調酒。	**B:** Let's have some punch.
A: 裡頭有酒精成分嗎？	**A:** Is there any alcohol in it?
B: 有酒精跟沒有酒精的調酒都有。	**B:** They have punch with and without alcohol.
A: 好，走吧。	**A:** Good. Let's go.

anniversary [ænə'vɝsərɪ] n. 週年
punch [pʌntʃ] n. 調酒
alcohol ['ælkə,hɔl] n. 酒精

1. 這是舉辦派對的地方嗎？
   Is this where the party is being held?
2. 那對神仙眷侶在哪裡？
   Where is the happy couple?
3. 我應該把禮物放哪裡？
   Where should I put this gift?
4. 我們喝些調酒。
   Let's have some punch.
5. 裡頭有酒精成分嗎？
   Is there any alcohol in it?

8.5b 恭喜神仙眷侶 Congratulating the Happy Couple

Dialog 對話

A: 史丹，瑪莎，恭喜你們結婚30週年。	**A:** Stan. Martha. Congratulations on your thirtieth wedding anniversary.
B: 謝謝，傑瑞，謝謝你來和我們一起慶祝。	**B:** Thank you, Jerry. And thanks for coming to celebrate with us.
A: 我的榮幸，我真為你們兩位開心。	**A:** It's my pleasure. I'm so happy for both of you.
A: 你們的小孩在這裡嗎？	**A:** Are your kids here?
B: 女兒在，但兩個兒子沒辦法來。	**B:** Our daughters are, but our two sons couldn't make it.
A: 喔，真不巧，在忙什麼？	**A:** Oh, too bad. What's keeping them away?
B: 大兒子是海軍官員，在海上。另一個兒子為公司到亞洲出差。	**B:** Our oldest son is an officer in the Navy. He's at sea. Our other son is on a business trip for the company he works for in Asia.
A: 那我想他們有不能來的理由。	**A:** I guess they have good excuses then.

B: 對，如果他們在就好了，但是他們沒辦法。	**B:** Yes. We'd love it if they were here, but they really couldn't do anything about it.
A: 好，我想你們一定以他們為榮。	**A:** Well, I bet you are really proud of them.
B: 是啊。	**B:** Yes, we are.

officer ['ɔfəsɚ] n. 官員
Navy ['nevɪ] n. 海軍

1. 恭喜你們結婚30週年。
   Congratulations on your thirtieth wedding anniversary.
2. 我真為你們兩位開心。
   I'm so happy for both of you.
3. 你們的小孩在這裡嗎？
   Are your kids here?
4. 謝謝你來和我們一起慶祝。
   Thanks for coming to celebrate with us.
5. 加入我們。
   Come join us.
6. 喔，真不巧。
   Oh, that's too bad.
7. 我有好理由。
   I have a good excuse.

8. 你被什麼絆住了？

 What kept you away?

9. 我沒辦法。

 I couldn't do anything about it.

10. 我想你們一定以他們為榮。

 I'll bet you're proud of them.

◆ 舉杯祝賀 Toasting

舉杯祝賀在社交活動時是很平常的，敬酒文化 (toast culture) 各地有所不同，記住喝酒小酌即可，切記不可對老外勸酒。舉杯時用一隻手拿著杯子就好，葡萄酒或香檳之高腳杯以三根手指握著杯腳，白蘭地之矮腳大肚杯則以手握杯體暖酒，看著對方 (而不是酒杯) 敬酒祝賀，常說的祝賀內容及場合如下：

1. 祝你健康！(退休時)	To your health!
2. 好好享用美食！(法文，晚餐活動時)	Bon Appetit! [ˌbɔnɑpe'ti]
3. 旅途平安！	Safe voyage!
4. 旅途愉快！	Bon voyage!
5. 恭喜！ (畢業、升遷、婚禮時)	Congratulations!
6. 敬好友！(朋友聚會時)	Here's to good friends!
7. 乾杯！(任何活動)	Cheers!

派對與習俗說明：節日與其他主題
Parties and Traditions: Holidays and Other Themes

除了每年都會輪到一次的生日與各式節日派對外，朋友或鄰居間的派對聚餐也很常見，聯絡感情之餘，對於不同主題的派對，人們也有不同的期待。

生日派對 Birthday Party

如果是小孩的生日，帶份禮物並準備唱歌及玩遊戲；如果是 21 歲生日，通常會喝很多酒，因為在美國 21 歲是一個人可以合法喝酒的開始。雖說個人慶祝生日有差異，一般而言，快到 30 歲時，生日派對就會平靜許多。

餞行派對 Farewell Party

類似週年派對，但多與公司有關，飲酒及舉杯祝福升遷而必須搬到另一城市或州的人 (們)，需要正式的穿著打扮。

開放參觀及親師會 Open House & Parent-Teacher Events

這類的聚會都是較安靜的活動，人們藉此機會在友善的氣氛裡碰面並詢問學校、教會或其他場所的情況，可以穿著舒適衣著前往，會場備有飲料及點心。

喬遷之喜 Housewarming

這是參觀某人新房子或新鄰居家裡的聚會，習慣上要帶份禮物，且是新房子或新家用得到的東西。

畢業派對 Graduation Party

這是家裡有人畢業或畢業生們舉辦的派對，不管是哪一種都少不了香檳及狂歡，為畢業生準備小禮物，穿舒適的衣著並準備照相吧！此派對和 21 歲生日頗為類似。

萬聖節及裝扮派對 Halloween and Costume Parties

這些是有趣的派對，可以打扮成任何你想要的樣子，萬聖節時的巫婆、骷髏、鬼及其他怪物相當受歡迎，但也可以打扮成其他你喜歡的樣子；除了奇怪的飲料、食物及糖果外，如果是成年人的派對，有時也會有酒精飲料。

感恩節 Thanksgiving

這是家庭成員聚在一起用餐團圓的日子，如果受邀參加感恩節晚餐，穿著乾淨舒適輕便的衣著，享受家庭氣氛的用餐及談話，不需帶禮物。

耶誕節 Christmas

像感恩節一樣，耶誕節也是家庭團聚的日子，但是要交換禮物，因此受邀參加耶誕節晚餐時，要準備一份給邀請者全家的禮物並帶著開心和善的態度，享用耶誕晚餐。

新年派對 New Year Party

這是狂歡慶祝新年到來的時刻，暢飲、跳舞、祝賀、聊天及從事任何可以讓你開心的活動對一年最後一晚而言都是合適的，有些派對是正式的，但大多數不是，享受美好時光就對了。

街坊聚會 Block Party

這是大型的鄰居聚會，大夥兒到一戶或幾戶人家拜訪，大部分是在戶外舉辦，每個人帶些食物來與大家分享，通常會有啤酒及其他冷飲，鄰居們聊天、用餐及照相，穿著完全以舒服輕便為原則。

聚餐派對 Potluck Party

通常美國人會辦聚餐派對及烤肉活動，參加這類活動，每個人要準備一道菜或買些飲料或從熟食店帶來的食物、點心，聚餐派對類似街坊派對，但是規模比較小一點。

8.6 萬聖節派對 Halloween Parties

Dialog 1 對話1

A: 噗！嗨，卡蘿。	A: Boo! Hi, Carol.
B: 嘿，你嚇到我了，嗨，伊森。	B: Hey! You scared me. Hi, Ethan.
A: 你覺得我的裝扮如何？	A: What do you think of my costume?
B: 很好，我想。你是什麼？	B: Nice. I guess. What are you?
A: 我是一罐啤酒。	A: I'm a can of beer.
B: 什麼？真的嗎？那很怪。	B: What? Really? That's weird.

A: 嗯，你看看自己，你是女忍者。	**A:** Well. Look at you. You're a girl Ninja.
B: 我不是，我是隻貓。	**B:** I am not! I'm a cat.
A: 貓？	**A:** A cat!?
B: 是的，忘記裝扮這事，我們加入派對吧！	**B:** Yes. Forget about this stuff. Let's join the party!

Word Bank 字庫

boo [bu] int. 噗、噓聲
costume ['kɑstjum] n. 服裝
weird [wɪrd] adj. 怪異的
Ninja ['nɪndʒə] n. 忍者

1. 你嚇到我了。
   You scared me.
2. 你覺得我的裝扮如何？
   What do you think of my costume?
3. 那很怪。
   That's weird.

Dialog 2 對話2

A: 我們喝點調酒。	**A:** Let's have some punch.
B: 好。	**B:** OK.
A: 這裡，我拿一杯給你。	**A:** Here, I'll get you a glass of it.
B: 謝謝。	**B:** Thanks.
A: 這是你的。	**A:** Here you are.
B: 是紫色跟綠色。	**B:** It's purple, and green.
A: 是的，這是鬼怪果汁。	**A:** Yeah. It's Spook Juice.
B: 看起來很恐怖。	**B:** It looks creepy.
A: 喝喝看。	**A:** Taste it.

B: 嘿！很好喝。	**B:** Hey! It's good.
A: 看，吉姆在那裡。	**A:** Look. There's Jim.
B: 哪裡？	**B:** Where?
A: 那裡，看起來像條大蟲的傢伙。	**A:** There, the guy that looks like a big worm.
A: 真奇怪。	**A:** That's strange.

Word Bank 字庫

Spook Juice n. 鬼怪果汁
creepy ['kripɪ] adj. 恐怖的

Useful Phrases 實用語句

1. 看起來很恐怖。
   It looks creepy.
2. 很好的裝扮。
   Nice costume.
3. 你裝扮成什麼？
   What are you?
4. 喝喝看。
   Taste it.

8.7 公司耶誕派對
Company Christmas Parties

8.7a 派對中 Party Time

A: 耶誕快樂，辛蒂！	**A:** Merry Christmas, Cindy!
B: 耶誕快樂，麗莎。	**B:** Merry Christmas, Lisa.
A: 每個人都在這裡嗎？	**A:** Is everyone here?
B: 是的，每個人都參加了公司的耶誕派對。	**B:** Yes. Everybody attends the company Christmas party.
A: 我們何時交換禮物？	**A:** When will we exchange gifts?
B: 晚一點，現在是吃吃喝喝及唱一些耶誕歌曲的時間。	**B:** A little later. Right now it's time for food and drink, and singing a few Christmas carols.
A: 今年的耶誕老人是誰？	**A:** Who's Santa Claus this year?

B: 我想是約翰，去年也是他。	**B:** I think it's John. He did it last year, too.
A: 我聞到蛋酒。	**A:** I smell eggnog.
B: 是的，我們有蛋酒以及萊姆酒。	**B:** Yes. We've got eggnog and rum.
A: 那樣很傳統。	**A:** That's traditional.
B: 當然囉，我們來一些吧。	**B:** Sure is. Let's have some.

Christmas carols n. 耶誕歌曲
Santa Claus n. 耶誕老人
eggnog ['ɛg,nɑg] n. 蛋酒

Useful Phrases 實用語句

1. 我們何時交換禮物？
   When will we exchange gifts?
2. 今年的耶誕老人是誰？
   Who's Santa Claus this year?
3. 晚一點。
   A little later.

4. 現在是吃吃喝喝及唱一些耶誕歌曲的時間。

   It's time for food and drink, and singing a few Christmas carols.

5. 我們有蛋酒以及萊姆酒。

   We've got eggnog and rum.

6. 那樣很傳統。

   That's traditional.

蛋酒 (eggnog) 是冬季裡聖誕節及新年期間很受歡迎的傳統飲品，由蛋、牛奶、糖製成，因為蛋經過打的程序 (beaten eggs) 所以飲料成泡沫狀。冬季尤其到過節時市面上有不含酒精 (non-alcoholic) 的蛋酒可購買，也有許多人自製或依照配方 (eggnog recipes) 調入不同種類酒精 (萊姆 rum、白蘭地 brandy 或威士忌 whisky) 的蛋酒。

8.7b 交換禮物 Exchanging Gifts

Dialog 對話

A: 交換禮物時間到了。

A: It's time to exchange gifts.

B: 好，我想知道拿到我禮物的人是否喜歡。

B: Great. I want to see if the person who gets mine likes it.

A: 首先每個人要從盒子裡抽一個號碼。

A: First everyone has to pull a number out of the box.

B: 號碼與我們的禮物相符，對嗎？

B: The number goes with the gift we'll get, right?

A: 對。	**A:** Right.
B: 耶誕樹下有許多禮物。	**B:** The Christmas tree has a lot of gifts under it.
A: 對，要花很長時間才能全部發出去。	**A:** Yeah. It will take a long time to hand them all out.
B: 好，可以玩久一點。	**B:** Good. The fun will last a long time.
A: 對，我們再去拿杯飲料。	**A:** Right. Let's get another drink.
B: 好。	**B:** OK.

1. 交換禮物時間到了。
   It's time to exchange gifts.
2. 從盒子裡抽一個號碼。
   Pull a number out of the box.
3. 號碼與禮物相符。
   The number goes with the gift.
4. 要花很長時間。
   It will take a long time.
5. 可以玩久一點。
   The fun will last a long time.

Language Power 字句補給站

◆ 耶誕卡樣本 Sample Greetings

美國人喜歡送耶誕卡給親朋好友，到商店選張好朋友會喜歡的卡片親手寫上祝福：

①佳節問候大家，願你們有個好年！

Seasons Greetings to all of you. Wish you well for the new year!

②佳節快樂！祝你有一個美好的假期。

Happy Holidays! Have a wonderful holiday season.

③耶誕快樂，新年快樂！

Merry Christmas and Happy New Year.

④在此祝福你耶誕快樂！

Here's wishing you a Merry Christmas.

⑤嗨，_________！祝你有一個很棒的假期。

Hi, __________! Have a great holiday season.

⑥願新年帶給你歡樂及長久的幸福。

May the New Year bring you joy and continued happiness.

⑦願你的新年歡樂光明！

May your new year be happy and bright.

⑧(獻上) 新年最好的祝福。

Best of wishes for the New Year.

⑨我在此祝福你這個新年只有成功。

Here's hoping you only success for this New Year.

⑩有個很棒的一年！

Have a great year!

8.8 畢業典禮與派對
Graduation Ceremonies and Receptions

A: 我們的區在哪裡？	**A:** Where is our section?
B: 在那邊，所有化學系學生都坐在那區。	**B:** Over there. All the Chem. Students sit in that section.
A: 今天的演講來賓是誰？	**A:** Who will be the guest speaker today?
B: 巴瑞特路卡，「旅行袋」的創辦人及執行長。	**B:** Barry Tellooka. He is the founder and C.E.O. of Travel Bag.
A: 你是說旅行供貨連鎖。	**A:** You mean the travel supplies franchise?
B: 是的。	**B:** Yes.
A: 我想聽他演講應該很有趣。	**A:** I think he will be interesting to listen to.
B: 我想也是。	**B:** I think so too.

A: 嘿，在宣布我們畢業之後，別忘了將你的帽穗移到左邊。

A: Hey. Don't forget to move your tassel to the left side of your cap after it's been announced that we've graduated.

guest speaker n. 演講來賓
founder ['faundə˞] n. 創辦人
C.E.O. n. 執行長
franchise ['fræn͵tʃaɪz] n. 連鎖
tassel ['tæsl̩] n. 帽穗

1. 我們的區在哪裡？
   Where is our section?
2. 今天的演講來賓是誰？
   Who will be the guest speaker today?
3. 聽他演講應該很有趣。
   He will be interesting to listen to.
4. 別忘了將你的帽穗移到左邊。
   Don't forget to move your tassel to the left side.

A: 恭喜你，凱倫！

A: Congratulations, Karen!

B: 謝謝，吉姆。你也是。

B: Thanks, Jim. Same to you.

A: 你要去參加今晚的派對嗎？

A: Are you going to the party tonight?

B: 要，我希望大家都去。

B: Yes. Everyone is, I hope.

A: 是的，我想每個人都會在那裡。

A: Yes. I think everyone will be there.

Dialog 3 對話3

A: 乾杯！

A: Cheers!

B: 乾杯！

B: Cheers.

A: 這是個很棒的派對。

A: This is a great party.

B: 是的，我真高興我終於畢業了。

B: Yes, it is. I'm so glad I've finally graduated.

A: 我也是。

A: Me too.

B: 接下來你要做什麼？

B: What are you going to do next?

A: 我想先旅行一下吧，你呢？	**A:** Travel a little I think. What about you?
B: 我不知道，但現在我要去參加派對！	**B:** I don't know, but right now I'm going to party!
A: 對！	**A:** Yeah!

1. 何時畢業典禮？
   When is Graduation?
2. 戴上你的帽子並穿上長袍。
   Put on your cap and gown.
3. 我們去畢業後派對吧。
   Let's go to the after ceremony party.
4. 乾杯！
   Cheers!
5. 做得好！
   Good job!
6. 恭喜！做得好！
   Congrats! Great job!
7. 做得好！
   Way to go!
8. 恭喜 (你畢業)！
   Congratulations (on your graduation)!
9. 好！讚！出色！
   Great! Super! Outstanding!

8.9 頒獎場合
Awards Events

8.9a 較不正式：學生社團頒獎
Less Formal Occasion: Student Club Awards

A: 大家注意，我要宣布今年的「最有影響力會員」，得獎的是金王！金，請過來。

A: Your attention, everyone. I want to make an announcement. This year's award for "Most Influential Member" goes to Kim Wang! Kim, come here, please.

B: 謝謝大家，這完全是個驚喜，我真的很榮幸，再次感謝你們。

B: Thank you, everybody. This a total surprise. I'm really honored. Thanks again.

A: 金，你還有什麼話要說嗎？

A: Kim, is there anything else you'd like to say?

B: 我真的要謝謝每個幫過我的人，沒有他們我不可能辦到。

B: I really need to thank everyone that helped me. I couldn't have succeeded without them.

A: 好。恭喜你，金！

A: OK. Congratulations, Kim!

announcement [ə'naunsmənt] n. 宣布
award [ə'wɔrd] n. 獎
Most Influential Member n. 最有影響力會員

Useful Phrases 實用語句

1. 我要宣布一件事。
   I want to make an announcement.
2. 這完全是個驚喜。
   This is a total surprise.
3. 我真的很榮幸。
   I'm really honored.
4. 我真的要謝謝每個幫過我的人。
   I really need to thank everyone that helped me.
5. 沒有他們我不可能辦到。
   I couldn't have succeeded without them.
6. 你還有什麼話要說嗎？
   Is there anything else you'd like to say?

8.9b 較正式頒獎 More Formal Award Giving

A: 各位女士先生，我很榮幸頒發今年的翰林亞頓優秀傑出學生研究獎學金，瑞秋王小姐！

A: Ladies and Gentlemen. I'm honored to present this year's recipient of the Hamlin-Alton Scholarship Award for excellence in student research. Miss Rachael Wong!

B: 謝謝大家，我非常高興被選為今年的受獎人，我必須要感謝大家在我研究期間在學校裡給我的支持及肯定，我也要謝謝我的家人，特別是我的雙親這幾年來給我的愛及支持。

B: Thank you, everyone. I'm very pleased to be chosen as this year's recipient. I must thank everyone for the support and recognition I have received while doing my research here at the university. I also want to thank my family, especially my parents for all their love and support over these years.

present [prɪ'zɛnt] v. 頒發
recipient [rɪ'sɪpɪənt] n. 受獎人
recognition [ˌrɛkəg'nɪʃən] n. 肯定

1. 我很榮幸頒發這個獎。
   I'm honored to present this award.
2. 我非常高興被選中。
   I'm very pleased to be chosen.
3. 我必須感謝大家的支持與肯定。
   I must thank everyone for the support and recognition.

正式場合意味著正式的氣氛，參加者要穿著端莊，合宜之舉止與有禮自制是當天的準則。

8.9c 祝賀 Giving Congratulations

Dialog 1 對話1

A: 嗨，蓋瑞。	**A:** Hi, Gary.
B: 嗨，麥克斯。你認識金嗎？	**B:** Hi, Max. Do you know Kim?
A: 是的，我幾個月前與她一起工作。	**A:** Yes, I worked with her a couple of months ago.
B: 她得獎真是太好了。	**B:** It's great that she won the award.
A: 是的。	**A:** Yes, it is.
B: 我們過去恭喜她吧。	**B:** Let's go over and congratulate her.
A: 好主意。	**A:** Good idea.

Useful Phrases 實用語句

1. 她得獎真是太好了。
   It's great that she won the award.
2. 我們過去恭喜她吧。
   Let's go over and congratulate her.

Dialog 2 對話2

A: 嗨，金，恭喜你得獎！	**A:** Hi, Kim. Congratulations for winning the award!
B: 謝謝，我不認為我該得。	**B:** Thanks. I don't think I deserve it.
A: 當然是你應得的，你很努力。	**A:** Sure you do. You work hard.
B: 謝謝，活動結束後我要去慶祝，一起來吧。	**B:** Thanks. I'm going to celebrate after the event. Join me.
A: 沒問題。	**A:** No problem.

恭喜 Congratulatory Phrases

1. 恭喜你的成功！
   Congratulations to your success!
2. 恭喜你獲獎！
   Congratulations for winning the award!
3. 做得好！我真替你高興。
   Great job. I'm very happy for you.
4. 恭喜，我想他們確實作對了決定。
   Congratulations! I think they certainly made the right choice.
5. 你應得的，恭喜！
   You really deserve it. Congratulations!

6. 當然是你應得的，你很努力。
   Sure you do. You work hard.
7. 你確實是最好的人選，恭喜！
   You're the best choice for sure. Congratulations!
8. 正確的選擇，做得好！
   The right choice. Good work!
9. 他們選對人了，恭喜！
   They picked the right one! Congrats!

舉杯祝賀 Toasting

1. 做得好 [敬工作成就]！
   To a job well done!
2. 恭喜你的成功！
   Congratulations to your success!
3. 乾杯！
   Cheers!
4. 敬你及你的成就！
   To you and your success!
5. 敬今年的傑出得主！
   To this year's outstanding winner!

同伴祝賀 Peer Students to the Award Recipient

1. 恭喜！
   Congratulations!
2. 做得好！
   Good work!
3. 做得好！
   Way to go!
4. 太棒了，恭喜！
   This is so great! Congratulations.
5. 可以碰你嗎？(開玩笑口氣，因得獎者像神一般榮耀)
   Can I touch you?

6. 我可以看這個獎嗎？

   Can I see the award?

回應 Responses

1. 謝謝。/ 謝謝大家。/ 非常感謝。

   Thank you. / Thank you, everyone. / Thank you so much.

2. 我很榮幸。

   I'm honored.

3. 我配不上這個 (獎)。

   I don't deserve this.

4. 我不認為我該得。

   I don't think I deserve it.

5. 我不知道要說什麼，我很幸運。

   I don't know what to say. I'm very fortunate.

6. 這是很大的榮耀。

   This is a great honor.

得獎人對教授 Award Winner to a Professor

1. 謝謝你，教授。

   Thank you, Professor.

2. 為這個榮耀，謝謝你

   Thank you for this honor.

3. 我很榮幸。

   I'm honored.

4. 我配不上這個 (謙虛地說)。

   I don't deserve this.

頒獎儀式 (Awards Ceremony) 可能是正式也可能是非正式場合，要依照獎項的層級而定。

8.9d 正式頒獎 Formal Award Giving

A: 各位先生女士，我非常榮幸頒發今年的克拉森畢爾斯研究獎給得主安東基特教授，讓我們熱烈歡迎他。

A: Ladies and Gentlemen. It's my honor to present this year's winner of the Clarkson-Beals Research Award to Professor Anton Kitt. Let's all give him a warm welcome.

B: 謝謝各位，謝謝。讓我先感謝校內生物研究系的教職員們，他們在我研究期間給我全力支持，當然我必須感謝我的太太，奈莉，她忍受我的缺席以及沒有人受得了的脾氣。

B: Thank you, everyone. Thank you. Let me start by thanking the staff of the Department of Bio Research here at the University. They have been extremely supportive throughout the period of time of my research. I of course must thank my wife, Nelly. She has put up with my absence and temper far more than anyone should ever have to.

supportive [sə'pɔrtɪv] adj. 支持的

temper ['tɛmpɚ] n. 脾氣

1. 非常榮幸頒發 (獎名) 給 (受獎人)。

   It's my honor to present (name of award) to (person).

2. 讓我們熱烈歡迎他。

Let’s all give him a warm welcome.

8.9e 祝賀 Giving Congratulations

A: 恭喜，基特教授！我真為你高興。	**A:** Congratulations, Professor Kitt! I’m very happy for you.
B: 謝謝你，班。	**B:** Thank you, Ben.
A: 我真的很開心學校選了你。	**A:** I’m really happy the school chose you.
B: 非常感謝你，希望你留下來開慶祝會。	**B:** Thank you very much. I hope you’ll stay for the reception.
A: 當然。	**A:** Yes, of course.
B: 太好了，在那裡見了。	**B:** Great. See you there.

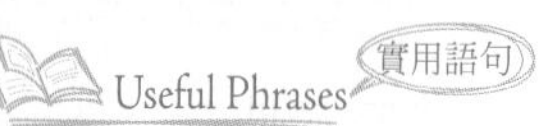

1. 恭喜！

   Congratulations！

2. 我真為你高興！

   I’m really happy for you!

3. 恭喜你贏得這個獎！

   Congratulations on winning this award!

4. 我真的很開心學校選了你。

   I'm really happy the school chose you.

5. 希望你留下來開慶祝會。

   I hope you'll stay for the reception.

6. 贏得這個獎是很大的光榮，而你值得獲獎！

   Winning this award is a great honor, and you deserve to win it.

7. 我認為你值得 (這個獎)，恭喜！

   I think you really deserve it. Congratulations!

8.10 順風派對 Bon Voyage Parties

8.10a 與參與派對者聊天 Chatting with Others in the Party

A: 每個人似乎都處得很好。	**A:** Everyone seems to be getting along well.
B: 當然，這裡每個人都透過提姆跟貝琪認識其他人。	**B:** Sure. Everyone here knows each other through Tim and Becky.
A: 我想你是對的。	**A:** I guess you are right.
B: 他們何時前往歐洲？	**B:** When are they leaving for Europe?

A: 這個星期五。	**A:** This coming Friday.
B: 我幫他們打包很多東西放到倉庫。	**B:** I helped them pack up a lot of their stuff and place it in storage.
A: 真的，他們東西放哪裡？	**A:** Really. Where did they put everything?
B: 他們向本地的倉儲公司租了倉庫。	**B:** They rented a storage space at one of the local storage rental businesses.
A: 那樣很好，那裡每樣東西會很安全。	**A:** That's good. Everything will be safe there.
B: 對，不必擔心，而且每件東西都有保險。	**B:** Right. No worries, and everything's insured.

Word Bank 字庫

pack [pæk] v. 打包
storage ['storɪdʒ] n. 倉庫
insure [ɪn'ʃur] v. 保險

1. 他們相處得很好。
   They are getting along well.
2. 他們何時前往歐洲？
   When are they leaving for Europe?

3. 不必擔心。

No worries. / Don't worry.

順風派對的旅行時間至少在兩週以上，但是旅行時間長短不是派對最主要的考量，父母親或許會為第一次出門旅行的子女舉行順風派對，慶祝他們可以獨立出遠門了。有些高中生畢業後會空出一年時間 (gap year) 旅行、打工或做國際志工 (international volunteering)，確定自己的志向。年輕人時間較充裕，多數自己旅行 (independent travel) 或到國外當背包客 (backpacker)，其後隨著年齡、時間限制、體力、經濟等條件，而考慮套裝行程 (package tour) 或跟團 (group tour) 等選項。

順風派對的大布條會為主角寫出「Bon Voyage, (人名) ！」主角可能會收到賓客們共同購買的機票作為禮物，並且在順風派對上一起盡歡。

派對的氣氛很重要，所以派對上的杯、盤、餐巾等紙製品圖案多配合旅程主題，使大家共享歡樂時光；派對布置方面，如果是西部牧場 (dude ranch) 之旅，牧草捲裝飾可以顯現西部風味的主題；如果是郵輪 (cruise) 之旅，沙罐可用來顯示熱帶氣息。此外氣球、彩帶、餐具、甚至化妝室的裝飾布置都可以增加順風派對的歡樂氣氛。

8.10b 與準旅行者聊天 Chatting with the "Will Be" Travelers

A: 嗨，提姆。嗨，貝琪。	**A:** Hi, Tim. Hi, Becky.
B: 嗨，泰瑞。你喜歡這個派對嗎？	**B:** Hi, Terry. Are you enjoying the party?

A: 喜歡，很好玩。	**A:** Yes. It's fun.
B: 很高興聽到你這麼說。	**B:** Good to hear it.
A: 我聽說你們兩個很快就要出發了，我只想說一路順風。	**A:** I hear you two are leaving soon. I just wanted to say Bon Voyage.
B: 謝謝，對於這趟旅行，我們很興奮，我們已經計畫很久了。	**B:** Thanks. We really are excited about this trip. We've been planning it for a very long time.
A: 我相信旅行會很棒。	**A:** I'm sure it will be great.
B: 我們希望是趟好的冒險。	**B:** We hope it's a good adventure.
A: 呃，像人們說的，冒險就是看你如何處理那些預料之外的事情。	**A:** Well, like they say, an adventure is made from how you deal with those things you didn't expect to happen.
B: 對，可能這趟旅程會有很多那樣的事。	**B:** Right. And there will probably be plenty of that on this trip.
A: 好，呃，好好玩，多拍些照片。	**A:** OK. Well. Enjoy, and take pictures.

B: 別擔心，我們旅行時會貼到部落格上。

B: Don't worry. We'll be posting them on our blog as we travel.

Word Bank 字庫

adventure [əd'vɛntʃɚ] n. 冒險
blog [blɑg] n. 部落格

Useful Phrases 實用語句

1. 你喜歡這個派對嗎？
   Are you enjoying the party?
2. 很高興聽到 (某事)。
   Good to hear it.
3. 我們希望是趟好的冒險。
   We hope it's a good adventure.
4. 我們已經計畫很久了。
   We've been planning it for a very long time.
5. 我相信會很好。
   I'm sure it will be great.
6. 好好玩，多拍些照片。
   Enjoy, and take pictures.
7. 一路順風。
   Bon voyage. / Have a nice trip.
8. 順風。
   Good speed.

8.10c 談論旅行 Chatting about Travel

Dialog 對話

A: 我好嫉妒他們。	A: I'm really envious of them.
B: 我也是，但願我有時間去旅行。	B: Me too. I wish I had time to travel.
A: 時間跟金錢，兩者總是最大的問題。	A: Time and money, they are always a problem.
B: 是啊，如果可以，你要去哪裡？	B: True. Where would you go if you could?
A: 柬埔寨。	A: Cambodia.
B: 不是開玩笑吧？為什麼？	B: No kidding? Why?
A: 我想看吳哥窟。	A: I'd love to see Angkor Wat.
B: 是的，一定很棒。	B: Yes. It must be great.
A: 我三年前要去，但訂不到機位。	A: I was going to go three years ago, but couldn't get a flight.

B: 真糟糕。	**B:** Too bad.
A: 是啊，我應該早點訂。	**A:** Yeah. I should have booked earlier.
B: 嗯，也許我們很快會為你開一個順風派對。	**B:** Well, maybe soon we'll be having Bon Voyage party for you.
A: 真好！	**A:** Sweet!

Word Bank 字庫

envious ['ɛnvɪəs] adj. 嫉妒的
Cambodia [kæm'bodɪə] n. 柬埔寨
Angkor Wat n. 吳哥窟
book [buk] v. 訂位

Useful Phrases 實用語句

1. 我好嫉妒他們。
   I'm really envious of them.
2. 但願我有時間去旅行。
   I wish I had time to travel.
3. 如果可以，你要去哪裡？
   Where would you go if you could?
4. 我真的很想看看。
   I'd love to see it.
5. 提早訂位。
   Book early.

6. 真好！

Sweet!

美國人喜歡旅遊，但是多數人必須工作，對於工作與休閒的態度是「努力工作，有機會時盡量玩樂」(work hard, play when you can)。相對於許多歐洲國家，美國人的休假時間算是少的，一年中較長的假期是從耶誕節到新年期間的年假，家人們聚在一起享受佳肴、交換禮物或出遊。週休二日加上少數放假或補假的星期一才有 long weekend，許多節日並不休假，想有長一點的假期並不容易，旅遊因此受到限制，許多美國人也只能在國內旅遊 (請參見附錄 4 美國假日)。

8.11 歡送派對
Farewell Parties

8.11a 與參與派對者聊天
Chatting with Others in the Party

A: 我不敢相信莎拉要搬到阿根廷。	**A:** I can't believe Sarah is moving to Argentina.
B: 我知道，我很難想像我不能隨時看到她。	**B:** I know. I have a hard time imagining not seeing her anytime I want to.
A: 是啊，感覺怪怪的，不知我們何時可以再見到她？	**A:** Yeah. It's weird. I wonder when we'll see her again.

初次見面 偶遇 邀請 參加聚會 接待賓客 拜訪 特殊情況 祝賀慰問 交友 日常社交 常用功能 其他功能

B: 我猜我們可以去阿根廷。	**B:** I guess we can go to Argentina.
A: 是的，我打賭她會讓我們住在她那裡。	**A:** Yes. I'll bet she would let us stay at her place.
B: 對，你知道她很友善，而且她也喜歡支持旅行的人。	**B:** I'm sure. You know how friendly she is. And she likes to support travelers.
A: 無論如何，我確定這派對會很好玩。	**A:** Anyway. I'm sure this party will be fun.
B: 是的，我們來喝一杯。	**B:** Yes. Let's get a drink.
A: 對，我們也要複習西班牙語了，拜託。	**A:** Right. Let's also brush up our Spanish, por favor.

Word Bank 字庫

Argentina [ˌɑrdʒən'tinə] n. 阿根廷
brush up 複習
por favor (西語) 請，拜託

1. 我不敢相信。
   I can't believe it.
2. 很難想像。
   It's hard to imagine.

3. 感覺怪怪的。

It's weird.

4. 不知我們何時可以再看見她？

I wonder when we'll see her again.

5. 我打賭她願意。

I'll bet she would.

6. 我確定這派對會很好玩。

I'm sure this party will be fun.

8.11b 與派對主角聊天 Chatting with the Person Moving Abroad

A: 莎拉，我會很想念你。	**A:** Sarah, I'm really going to miss you.
B: 我也會很想念你。	**B:** I'm going to miss you too.
A: 我希望你可以有時回來。	**A:** I hope you come back some time.
B: 我會，我會想探望我爸媽以及老朋友。	**B:** I will. I'll want to visit my mom and dad and old friends too.
A: 好。	**A:** Good.
B: 我希望這裡的人也會來探望我。	**B:** I hope people here will come visit me.

A: 那會很棒，我很希望去你去的地方。

A: That would be so cool. I'd love to go where you're going.

B: 如果這樣，你知道你有地方住。

B: If you do, you know you have a place to stay.

A: 太好了，你是說真的嗎？

A: Wonderful. Are you serious?

B: 是的，當然，非常歡迎你。

B: Yes, of course. You'll be more than welcome.

A: 嗯，我一定會記住。

A: Well, I'll certainly keep that in mind.

B: 好的。

B: Please do.

1. 來探望我。
   Come visit me.
2. 那會很棒。
   That would be so cool.
3. 非常歡迎你。
   You'll be more than welcome.
4. 你是說真的嗎？
   Are you serious?
5. 我會記住。
   I'll keep that in mind.

6. 後會有期。

Farewell.

7. 如果你到……，一定要聯絡我 [打電話給我]。

If you're ever in..., you must get in touch [give me a call].

8.11c 以鼓勵道別 Farewell with Encouragement

A: 鮑伯，我認為你搬到非洲去嘗試完全不同的東西很棒。

A: Bob, I think it's great that you are moving to Africa to try something totally new.

B: 事實上，我有時候覺得這樣做很瘋狂。

B: Actually, sometimes I think it's crazy of me to do this.

A: 你不應該這麼覺得，這是件好事，很有挑戰性。

A: You shouldn't feel that way. It's a great thing to do. Challenging.

B: 我希望如此，我有一些朋友覺得這樣很怪。

B: I hope so. Some of my friends think it's weird.

A: 是因為這樣很令人害怕，他們無法想像做出這樣的事，他們沒有準備好做那樣的事。

A: It's just scary to them. They can't imagine doing something like that. They aren't ready for anything like that.

B: 我想也是。我想從這樣做中學習並成長。

B: I guess so. I want to learn and grow from doing this.

A: 毫無疑問，你會的，你有正確的態度而且你很聰明，一切都會很好的。

A: You will. No doubt about it. You've got the right attitude, and you're smart. It will all be fine.

B: 謝謝你的鼓勵，我很感激。

B: Thanks for your encouragement. I really appreciate it.

challenging ['tʃælɪndʒɪŋ] adj. 有挑戰性的

1. 你有正確的態度。

   You've got the right attitude.

2. 你很聰明。

   You're smart.

3. 你的計畫很好。

   You have a good plan.

4. 一切都會很好的。

   It will all be fine.

5. 這是個新機會。

   It is a new opportunity.

8.12 探病
Visiting Someone at a Hospital

8.12a 在櫃臺 At the Reception

A: 哈囉，你可以告訴我艾力克強生在哪一間房嗎？	A: Hello. Can you tell me which room Eric Johnson is in?
B: 好，他在133號房，從這條走廊直走下去左轉，然後跟著箭頭走。	B: Yes. He is in room 133. Go down this hall, turn left, and then follow the arrows.
A: 謝謝，探視時間幾點開始幾點結束？	A: Thank you. When do visiting hours start and end?
B: 早上10點開始晚上9點結束。	B: Visiting hours start at 10 a.m. and end at 9 p.m.
A: 我明白了，謝謝。	A: I see. Thanks.

Word Bank 字庫

hall [hɔl] n. 走廊
arrow ['æro] n. 箭頭
visiting hours n. 探視時間

1. 艾力克強生在哪一間房？
   Which room is Eric Johnson in?
2. 探視時間幾點開始幾點結束？
   When do visiting hours start and end?

看到親朋好友在醫院因病痛受苦並不好受，有些人因此不去探視病人，但病人沒有別人的關心，非常不利心理及身體的復原，即使到醫院探病可能令人感到手足無措，不知該說什麼或做什麼，只要想像病人的需要，將心比心，病人會感受到你的關心。

8.12b 病房探視 Visiting Someone in a Hospital Room

Dialog 對話

A: 嗨，艾力克。	**A:** Hi, Eric.
B: 嘿，真是驚喜！	**B:** Hey. What a surprise!
A: 呃，我聽說那場意外了，所以我想最好來看看你怎麼樣了。	**A:** Well, I heard about the accident, so I thought I'd better see how you are.
B: 謝謝，我很感激。	**B:** Thanks. I appreciate it.

A: 你覺得怎樣？	**A:** How do you feel?
B: 還好，我斷了兩根肋骨跟左手臂。	**B:** Not too bad. I broke two ribs and my left arm.
A: 唉唷，聽起來好像很糟糕。	**A:** Ouch. That sounds bad to me.
B: 意外時我昏過去了，所以沒有任何感覺。	**B:** I was knocked out in the accident, so I didn't feel anything.
A: 我想那算好事，對吧？	**A:** I guess that's good, right?
B: 應該算吧，問題是在救護車上醒來時我能感受到全部，我以為我要死了。	**B:** Sort of. The problem is that when I woke up in the ambulance I could feel everything. I thought I was dying.
A: 後來呢？	**A:** So what happened then?
B: 急救小組馬上給我打止痛針。	**B:** The EMT immediately gave some type of shot that killed the pain pretty fast.
A: 很好。	**A:** Good.

B: 對，後來我就進了醫院，之後我不太記得了，因為他們幫我麻醉。	**B:** Yeah. After that I was taken into the hospital. I don't remember much past that as they put me out.
A: (雖然很不幸) 那你現在覺得還好嗎？	**A:** You feel OK now though, right?
B: 好多了。	**B:** Much better.
A: 聽起來很可怕。總之，我帶了幾樣東西給你，一些雜誌跟甜食。	**A:** It all sounds scary to me. Anyway, I brought you a few things. Some magazines and sweets.
B: 很棒，謝謝你，我需要一些可以讀的。	**B:** Great. Thank you. I need something to read.
A: 我帶了兩本汽車雜誌跟一本新聞週刊。	**A:** I got a couple of car magazines, and a weekly news mag.
B: 好酷，謝謝。	**B:** Really cool. Thanks.

Word Bank 字庫

rib [rɪb] n. 肋骨
be knocked out 昏倒
shot [ʃɑt] n. 注射
put out 麻醉
mag [mæg] n. 雜誌 (= magazine)

Useful Phrases 實用語句

1. 我想最好來看看你怎麼樣了。

   I'd better see how you are.

2. 你覺得怎樣？

   How do you feel?

3. 聽起來很糟糕。

   That sounds bad to me.

4. 看到你真好。

   It's good to see you.

5. 我已經想念你了呢。

   I've missed you.

6. 後來呢？

   So what happened then?

7. 那你現在覺得還好嗎？

   You feel OK now, right?

8. 意外時我昏過去了。

   I was knocked out in the accident.

9. 他們馬上給我打針。

   They immediately gave me a shot.

10. 他們幫我麻醉。

    They put me out.

11. 好多了。

    Much better.

8.12c 離開 Leaving

A: 我想我該走了，我得回去工作。

A: I suppose I'd better get going. I have to get to work.

B: 嘿，沒問題，我真高興你來。

B: Hey, no problem. I'm really glad you stopped by.

A: 我的榮幸，我希望人們也會這樣對我。

A: My pleasure. I hope people would do the same for me.

B: 下次你出意外我會出現。

B: Next time you're in an accident I'll show up.

A: 哈，謝謝，我想我不需要那樣獲得朋友的注意。

A: Ha! Thanks. I hope I don't have to do that to get attention from friends.

B: 只是開玩笑，如果可以的話再過來吧，我還要待在這裡一個禮拜。

B: Just kidding. Stop by again if you can. I'm going to be stuck in here for another week.

A: 當然好，我也會帶一些人來。

A: For sure. I'll bring along some others too.

B: 好，再次謝謝你。

B: Great. Thanks again.

A: 小事一樁，我很快會再見到你。

A: Piece of cake. I'll see you again soon.

B: 對，再見。

B: Right. Bye.

A: 再見。

A: See you.

1. 我該走了。

   I'd better get going.

2. 小事一樁。

   Piece of cake.

3. 沒有你很無趣。

   It's no fun without you.

4. 快好起來。

   Get well.

5. 我可以幫你做什麼嗎？

   Is there anything I can do for you?

6. 如果你要我帶什麼來，打電話給我。

   Call me if you need me to bring anything.

7. 我很高興你來。

   I'm really glad you stopped by.

8. 你如果可以的話再過來。

   Stop by again if you can.

探視病人前可先電話詢問護理站可否帶些病人可以吃的食物過去，因為醫院的伙食多半不美味，病人看到外帶的食物會很開心。另外帶些讓病人忘記病痛打發無聊的東西，如雜誌、電玩都是不錯的選擇。探病時間不要太久，讓病人多休息，也不要坐在病床上使病人空間侷促不舒服，避免令人傷心的話題，給病人正面愉悅的情緒才有利病人恢復健康。

美國人不忌諱拿意外或死亡說笑，也不認為這樣會招厄運或增加意外發生的機會，但對其他文化的人不見得如此。病人住院生活一定受到影響，主動詢問病人是否需要幫忙，可以讓病人減輕焦慮，病人也會感受到友情的珍貴，加速復原。

◆ 慰問病人卡片樣本 **Sample Get-Well Cards**

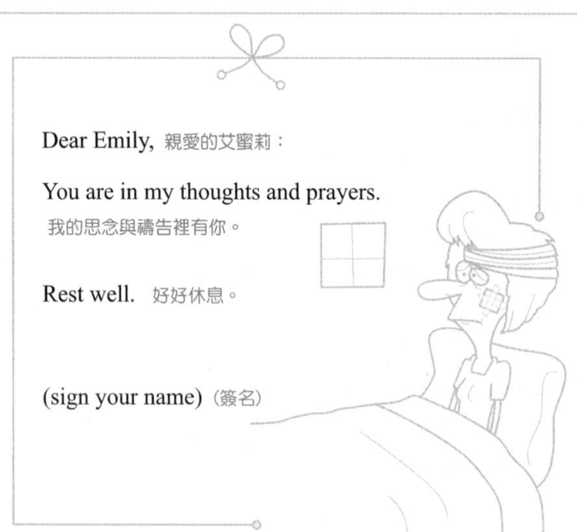

Dear Emily, 親愛的艾蜜莉：

You are in my thoughts and prayers.
我的思念與禱告裡有你。

Rest well. 好好休息。

(sign your name)（簽名）

Dear Jackie, 親愛的傑克：

I'm sending a special wish to you.
我寄來特別的願望給你。

Have a speedy recovery! 快快康復！

(sign your name)（簽名）

8.13 喪禮
Funerals

A: 珍妮，我為你失去重要的人感到很遺憾。	**A:** I'm very sorry for your loss, Jenny.
B: 謝謝你的安慰。	**B:** Thank you for your kind words.
A: 你知道我很了解約翰，而且大家都為他的去世感到很悲傷。	**A:** I knew John well as you know, and everyone is sad about his passing.
B: 謝謝。	**B:** Thank you.

1. 我為你失去重要的人感到很遺憾。
   I'm very sorry for your loss.
2. 大家都為他的去世感到很悲傷。
   Everyone is sad about his passing.
3. 如果我可以幫上任何的忙，請讓我知道。
   Let me know if I can do anything to help.
4. 我們聽到消息很傷心。
   We are saddened to hear the news.
5. 我們的想念與祈禱與你同在。
   Our thoughts and prayers are with you.

喪禮是沉重的場合，參加喪禮必須著黑色衣服，一句「I am sorry」及一個擁抱就足夠表達對家屬的情感支持，傾聽家屬對往生者的回憶，做個好的傾聽者，不必多說什麼。殯儀館 (funeral home) 的喪禮儀式包含了神職人員、家屬、朋友對往生者的追憶禱告以及親友們列隊對往生者 (the deceased) 最後瞻仰致意，隨後車輛啟程到墓地 (cemetery) 土葬 (burial)。越來越多人選擇火葬 (cremation)，並且將骨灰 (ashes) 灑在生前選擇之處，選擇以此方式告別人間的許多人也選擇不舉行喪禮。

◆ **慰問喪家卡片樣本 Sample Condolence Cards**

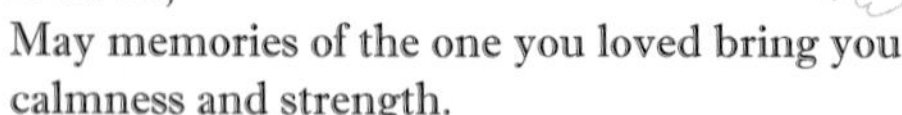

Dear …,
May memories of the one you loved bring you calmness and strength.
I'm thinking of you with sympathy.

(sign your name)

親愛的…：
願回憶你所愛的人帶給你平靜和力量，
我感同身受地想念你。

(簽名)

Dear…,
You are in many thoughts and prayers.
May peace be with you and around you at this difficult time.

(sign your name)

親愛的…:
許多的思念與禱告裡有你，
但願在這艱難的時候，平靜與你同在。

(簽名)

對需回家鄉奔喪的朋友或同事主動伸出援手，詢問並提供幫忙對他 (她) 是最受用的，例如：分擔請假時的工作或無人在家時需要的幫忙，可大為減輕朋友面對喪慟的衝擊。

There hase been an accident.
Helen has been injured.

Unit 9 Initiating Conversation to Make a New Friend

主動開口交友

與他人交友必須有開放的心胸，在國外更是如此，挑選那些你認為看來誠懇可靠的人，勇於主動開口(但不要讓人感受到壓力)，才能增加認識新朋友的機會。

9.1 跨出第一步
Taking the First Step

9.1a 在學校社團辦公室 At a School Club Office

Dialog 1 對話1

A: 嗨，我想獲得你們社團活動的資訊。	**A:** Hi. I'd like to get some information about your club's activities.
B: 我們有小冊子你可以看，我也可以回答你的問題。	**B:** We have this brochure you can read, and I can answer your questions too.
A: 我想了解費用。	**A:** I'm wondering about cost.
B: 我們有一年10元的會費來付房租。	**B:** We have a $10 annual membership fee to help pay for rent.
A: 有其他費用嗎？	**A:** Are there any other fees?
B: 如果你要參加我們的特別活動才要。	**B:** Only if you want to join one of our special events.
A: 那要多少費用？	**A:** What do those cost?

B: 不一定，但通常10到15元。	**B:** It varies, but usually it's around \$10 to \$15.
A: 社團聚會是何時？	**A:** When are the club meetings?
B: 我們一個月2次在第一、三週的週二晚上 7 點左右聚會。	**B:** We meet twice a month on the first and third Tuesdays around 7 p.m.
A: 好，謝謝你的資訊。	**A:** OK. Thanks for the information.
B: 沒什麼。	**B:** No problem.

A: 嗨，我先前來過，我還有幾個問題。	**A:** Hi. I was here earlier. I have a few more questions.
B: 好的，你想知道什麼呢？	**B:** Sure. What would you like to know?
A: 我可以在這辦公室做什麼？	**A:** Is there anything I can do here in the office?
B: 是的，我們有許多社團內你可以幫忙的事。	**B:** Yes. We have many things you can help out with in the club.

A: 我想這是比較好認識人的方式。	**A:** I think it would be a better way to meet people.
B: 你是對的，讓我介紹你認識我們的義務協導。	**B:** You're right. Let me introduce you to our volunteer coordinator.
A: 謝謝。	**A:** Thanks.

Word Bank 字庫

annual membership fee n. 會員年費
brochure [bro'ʃur] n. 小冊子
volunteer coordinator n. 義務協導

Useful Phrases 實用語句

1. 我想了解費用。
   I'm wondering about cost.
2. 有其他費用嗎？
   Are there any other fees?
3. 社團聚會是何時？
   When are the club meetings?
4. 我可以在這辦公室做什麼？
   Is there anything I can do here in the office?

Tips 小祕訣

參加社交活動與其他人共度時間、擁有共同經驗是放諸四海皆準的交友準則，在新場合要交上朋友需要時間，如果是在校園裡就比較容易。

9.1b 在 DVD 出租店 At a DVD Rental

A: 嗨，我看到你要租一些那部新電視影集的光碟。	**A:** Hi. I see you are going to rent some DVDs from that new TV series.
B: 對。	**B:** Yes.
A: 我沒有看過這個節目，但我有讀過(報章雜誌) 它很不錯。	**A:** I've never seen the show, but I've read it's not bad.
B: 對，我覺得這個影集很好笑。	**B:** Yeah, I think it's pretty funny.
A: 我喜歡那影集裡的女生，我在一部電影裡看過她。	**A:** I like the girl in that series. I saw her in a movie.
B: 是莎莉達爾斯嗎？	**B:** Sally Dolls?
A: 對，是她。	**A:** Yes. Her.
B: 是的，她很可愛又有趣，你在哪部電影看過她？	**B:** Yeah, she's cute and funny. What movie did you see her in?

A: 「12天的星期一」。	**A:** *Twelve Days of Mondays*.
B: 我看過那部片子，她在那部電影裡很棒。	**B:** I saw that. She was good in that movie.
A: 我認為她讓那部戲有看頭。	**A:** She sort of made the show worth seeing, I think.
B: 對，電影的情節簡單，但是她的演出讓電影有娛樂性。	**B:** Right. It had a simple plot, but her acting made it entertaining.
A: 對，古溫巴斯在那部電影裡也不錯。	**A:** Yes. Goodwin Bass was good in that movie, too.
B: 我認為他因為那電影變有名了。	**B:** I think he became pretty famous because of that film.
A: 對，你應該沒錯，順便一提，我名字是布萊德郭。	**A:** Yeah, you're probably right. By the way, my name's Brad Guo.
B: 我是席德哈伍。	**B:** I'm Sid Harwood.
A: 很高興認識你。	**A:** Nice to meet you.
B: 我也是。	**B:** Nice to meet you, too.

TV series n. 電視影集
acting ['æktɪŋ] n. 演技
entertaining [ˌɛntɚ'tenɪŋ] adj. 有娛樂性的

Useful Phrases 實用語句

1. 我看到你要租一些那部新電視影集的光碟。
   I see you are going to rent some DVDs from that new TV series.
2. 我喜歡那影集裡的女生。
   I like the girl in that series.
3. 我在一部電影裡看過她。
   I saw her in a movie.
4. 她讓那部戲有看頭。
   She made the show worth seeing.
5. 你在哪部電影看過她？
   What movie did you see her in?
6. 我覺得它很好笑。
   I think it's pretty funny.
7. 電影的情節簡單。
   It had a simple plot.
8. 她的演出讓電影有娛樂性。
   Her acting made it entertaining.
9. 順便一提，我名字是布萊德郭。
   By the way, my name's Brad Guo.

Tips 小祕訣

讓對話持續的關鍵在於注意聆聽，並且在腦海裡記住說話者提到的人、地、事，如此你可以對這些你注意到的要點提出問題(或關於這些要點的問題)，讓對話保持新鮮。

9.1c 在二手書店 At a Used Book Store

Dialog 對話

A: 對不起打擾你，我注意到你在讀卡爾蒙地的書，你讀過很多他的書嗎？	**A:** Sorry to bother you, but I noticed you are reading that Carl Monty book. Have you read many of his books?
B: 讀過一些，我喜歡他的作品。	**B:** A few. I like his writing.
A: 我只是好奇，朋友說我可能會喜歡他的風格。	**A:** Just wondering. A friend said I might like his style.
B: 他的寫作節奏很快並且寫實。	**B:** His writing is fast paced and real life too.
A: 真的，我想我應該挑一本來讀。	**A:** Really. I guess I should pick one to read.
B: 從這本開始吧，我讀過，我想這是他最好的書之一。	**B:** Start with this one. I read it. I think it is one of his best.
A: 謝謝，我會讀讀看。順道一提，我的名字是羅傑蔡。	**A:** Thanks. I will. My name is Rodger Tsai, by the way.
B: 我是提姆桑德森。	**B:** I'm Tim Sunderson.

A: 很高興跟你聊天。

A: Nice to chat with you.

B: 我也有同感。

B: Same here.

fast paced 節奏很快的
real life n. 寫實

Useful Phrases 實用語句

1. 對不起打擾你，(原因……)。

   Sorry to bother you, but...

2. 我只是好奇 (某事)。

   Just wondering.

3. 朋友說我可能會喜歡他的風格。

   A friend said I might like his style.

9.1d 在旅途上 On a Trip

A: 請問，你知道我們還要等船等多久嗎？

A: Excuse me. Do you know how much longer we will have to wait for the boat?

B: 我不確定，船應該現在要到了。

B: I'm not sure. It ought to be here now.

A: 我也這麼想，呃，我想是誤點了。	**A:** That's what I thought. Well, I guess it's late.
B: 等等，我看到了，在那邊！	**B:** Wait. I see it. There it is over there!
A: 好，我想再幾分鐘就到這裡了。	**A:** Oh. OK. It will be here in a few minutes I guess.
B: 是的，看起來船員正在準備。	**B:** Yes. It looks like the crew is still preparing it.
A: 你搭過這輪船嗎？	**A:** Have you been on this cruise?
B: 沒有，沒搭過，你呢？	**B:** No, not this one. How about you?
A: 一次，但是好久以前了，我想對我而言會像個新的經驗。	**A:** Once, but that was a while back. I think it will be like a new experience for me.
B: 那很好。	**B:** That's nice.
A: 對。	**A:** Yes, it is.
B: 我是達倫蘇。	**B:** I'm Darin Su.

A: (我是) 蘭迪黃。	A: Randy Huang.
B: 看起來你住這附近。	B: It seems you live around here.
A: 是的，我住在這城市七年了。	A: Yes, I've lived in this city for seven years.
B: 你從事哪一行？	B: What do you do?
A: 我是記者。	A: I'm a journalist.
B: 我也是。	B: Me, too.
A: 真的嗎？我們在船上有很多可以聊的。	A: Really? We'll have plenty to talk about on the cruise.
B: 沒錯。	B: No doubt.

Word Bank 字庫

cruise [kruz] n. 乘船巡遊
crew [kru] n. 船員

1. 你知道我們還要等船等多久？

   Do you know how much longer we will have to wait for the boat?

2. 應該現在要到了。

   It ought to be here now.

3. 我想是誤點了。

   I guess it's late.

4. 我想再幾分鐘就到這裡了。

   It will be here in a few minutes I guess.

5. 你搭過這輪船嗎？

   Have you been on this cruise?

6. 我想對我而言會像個新的經驗。

   I think it will be like a new experience for me.

7. 我們在船上有很多可以聊的。

   We'll have plenty to talk about on the cruise.

每個文化對陌生人有不同的對待方式，有些文化對外地或外國人好客有人情味 (hospitality)，但其他文化則不然，除文化背景外，大都市的人們通常也較小鄉鎮的人冷漠，而個人因素及場合也會決定人們是否與陌生人交談。

9.1e 在展覽場 At an Exhibition

A: 對不起，你可以告訴我在哪裡買展覽的票嗎？

A: Sorry. Can you tell me where to buy tickets for the exhibition?

B: 可以，跟我來，我也要買票。

B: Yes. Come with me. I have to buy some too.

A: 謝謝。

A: Thanks.

B: 沒什麼。

B: No problem.

A: 這邊人很多。

A: There's a lot of people here.

B: 對，這是個大活動，很多宣傳。

B: Yes. This is a big event. It was heavily promoted.

A: 我是莎倫，莎倫丁。

A: My name is Sharon. Sharon Ting.

B: 我是威廉史東，大家叫我比爾。

B: I'm William Stone. Everybody calls me Bill.

A: 你從哪裡來，比爾？

A: Where are you from, Bill?

B: 英國，你呢？

B: England. And you?

A: 臺灣。

A: Taiwan.

B: 我了解，我外甥幾年前在臺灣教英文。	**B:** I see. I have a nephew who taught English in Taiwan a few years ago.
A: 他在哪個城市工作？	**A:** Which city did he work in?
B: 我相信是個叫做啊，嗯，我似乎忘了。	**B:** I believe it was a place named, uh, hmmm. It seems I've forgotten.
A: 沒關係，我只是好奇。	**A:** No matter. Just curious.
B: 喔，等等，我想起什麼，他經常叫它「新的竹子」。	**B:** Oh, wait. I remember something. He often called it New Bamboo.
A: 什麼？喔，我知道了，他是說新竹。	**A:** What? Oh. I know. He means Hsin Chu.
B: 是的，對，它的意思是新的竹子，對嗎？	**B:** Yes. That's it. It means new bamboo, right?
A: 不盡然，但是如果你直譯成英文，那就是這樣。	**A:** Not exactly, but if you literally translated it into English, that's what you'd get.
B: 有點好玩。	**B:** Kind of funny.
A: 是的。	**A:** Yes, it is.

exhibition [ˌɛksə'bɪʃən] n. 展覽
literally ['lɪtərəlɪ] adv. 字面上地
translate [træns'let] v. 翻譯

Useful Phrases 實用語句

1. 這是個大活動。
   This is a big event
2. 很多宣傳。
   It was heavily promoted.
3. 沒關係
   No matter. /It doesn't matter.
4. 我只是好奇。
   Just curious.
5. 不盡然。
   Not exactly.
6. 有點好玩。
   Kind of funny.

9.1f 在咖啡廳 At a Coffee House

A: 對不起，我注意到你在讀約翰塔克曼最新的小說。	**A:** Excuse me. I noticed that you are reading John Tekman's latest novel.
B: 是的，我是他的頭號粉絲。	**B:** Yes. I am a big fan of his.

A: 我也是，他的作品不只有趣也很聰明。

A: I am, too. His writing is not only intriguing, but also intelligent.

B: 我也這麼想，它也提供簡單的方法來學到重要的法律概念。

B: I think so too. It also provides an easy way to pick up important legal concepts.

A: 我完全同意，身為法律系學生，我覺得他的書對我的課業有幫助。

A: I couldn't agree more. As a law school student, I find his books helpful for my studies.

B: 知道這個很有意思。

B: That's interesting to know.

A: 順帶一提，我是葛瑞格吳，很榮幸遇到你。

A: By the way, my name is Greg Wu. Pleasure to meet you.

B: 我是艾莉西亞連，也很高興遇到你。

B: I am Alicia Lian. Nice to meet you, too.

A: 我和一些朋友一個月在這裡碰面一次討論這類的小說，你有興趣加入我們嗎？

A: A few friends and I meet here once a month to discuss these kinds of novels. Are you interested in joining us?

B: 呃，他們也是法律系學生嗎？

B: Well, are they also law students?

A: 喔，他們不是，聚會不是關於專業法律分析，你就過來看看吧！	A: Oh! They are not. The meetings aren't about professional legal analysis. Just come and check it out.
B: 好，我不認為有何不可？	B: Ok. I don't see why not.
A: 好，下一次會面是 12 月 5 日下午 3 點，到時候見。	A: Great! The next meeting is on Dec. 5th at 3 p.m. I'll see you then.
B: 好。	B: You bet.

Word Bank 字庫

latest novel n. 最新小說
intriguing [ɪn'trigɪv] adj. 引人入勝的
intelligent [ɪn'tɛlədʒənt] adj. 聰明的
legal concept n. 法律概念
analysis [ə'næləsɪs] n. 分析

Useful Phrases 實用語句

1. 我注意到你在 (做某事)。
   I noticed that you are (doing something).
2. 我是他的頭號粉絲。
   I am a big fan of his.
3. 我完全同意。
   I couldn't agree more.
4. 你有興趣加入我們嗎？
   Are you interested in joining us?

5. 你就過來看看吧！
   Just come and check it out.
6. 我不認為有何不可？
   I don't see why not.
7. 好。
   You bet.

9.1g 在健身房 At the Gym

A: 嗨，我是珍林，我是健身房的新會員，我對有氧課有興趣。	**A:** Hi. My name is Jane Lin, I'm a new member of this gym. I'm curious about this aerobic class.
B: 進來吧，珍，老師還沒來。	**B:** Come on in, Jane. The instructor is not here yet.
A: 呃……會很難嗎？	**A:** Well... Is it difficult?
B: 這個課我只來上過兩次，前 30 分鐘算是基礎，容易進入狀況。	**B:** I've been in this class twice only. I find the first 30 minutes basic and easy to get into.
A: 所以後半部比較有挑戰性。	**A:** So the latter half of the class is more challenging.
B: 對，但老師很有耐心也很仔細。	**B:** That's right, but the instructor is quite patient and detailed.

A: 聽起來對像我一樣學得慢的人很好。	**A:** Sounds good for a slow learner like me.
B: 如果你跟不上，不要氣餒，不只是你，我也學得慢。	**B:** If you can't catch the steps, don't feel bad. You won't be alone. I'm a slow learner, too.
A: 非常感謝你，我可以知道你的名字嗎？	**A:** Thank you so much. May I have your name?
B: 喔，我是凱西，凱西莫克。	**B:** Oh, I am Kathy, Kathy Mok.
A: 很高興遇到你，凱西。	**A:** Nice meeting you, Kathy.
B: 我的榮幸，或許我們可以一起去挑一些其他的課。	**B:** My pleasure. Maybe we can go over other classes and choose some together.
A: 好主意，上完這堂課之後如何？	**A:** Great idea. How about doing it after this class?
B: 好！	**B:** Sure.

Word Bank 字庫

aerobic [ˌeə'robɪk] adj. 有氧的
instructor [ɪn'strʌkɚ] n. 老師，教練
patient ['peʃənt] adj. 有耐心的
detailed [dɪ'teld] adj. 仔細的

初次見面
偶遇
邀請
參加聚會
接待賓客
拜訪
特殊情況
祝賀慰問
交友
日常社交
常用功能
其他功能

1. 我對這有氧課有興趣。
   I'm curious about this aerobic class.
2. 聽起來對像我一樣學得慢的人很好。
   Sounds good for a slow learner like me.
3. 我可以知道你的名字嗎？
   May I have your name?

要主動與不相識的人開始交談，談論所處的環境是最恰當的話題，因此談論天氣最常見「Do you like this warm weather? 」(你喜歡這樣暖和的天氣嗎)。稱讚別人也是打開話題常見的方式，接下去再問相關的問題「I like your glasses. Where did you get glasses like those? 」(我喜歡你的眼鏡，你在哪裡找到這樣的眼鏡)，問開放性的問題可以使對方持續與你交談，當然要避免問價錢。請人幫個小忙「Could you tell [help, show] me how to ..., if you have a minute? 」(如果你有一點時間，可以告訴 [幫 / 示範] 給我看……) 也是一種方式。

9.1h 在夜店 At a Night Club

Dialog 對話

A: 嗨，我想我們在優太普科技的同一個部門工作，對嗎？	**A:** Hi. I think we work in the same department at Utep Tech., right?
B: 喔，對，我看過你。	**B:** Oh, yes. I've seen you.

A: 我是湯姆孫。	**A:** My name's Tom Sun.
B: 嗨，湯姆，我是瑪莎泰勒。	**B:** Hi, Tom. I'm Martha Taylor.
A: 你跟其他朋友一起嗎？	**A:** Are you with some friends?
B: 沒有，我只是下班後順道喝東西。	**B:** No. I just stopped by for a drink after work.
A: 有點晚，你剛才才下班嗎？	**A:** It's kind of late. Did you just leave work?
B: 對，黑爾斯波恩案讓我很忙。	**B:** Yes. The Hells Point Project is keeping me busy.
A: 我知道，也快換我了，我想我很快就要加班。	**A:** I know. It's about to hit me too. I imagine I'll be working late soon too.
B: 你呢？你跟誰一起來這裡嗎？	**B:** How about you? Are you here with anyone?
A: 我跟傑瑞古曼來，你認識他嗎？	**A:** I came with Jerry Goodman. You know him?
B: 當然，他在人事室工作。	**B:** Sure. He works in personnel.

A: 對，就是他，雖然他剛才已經走了。	**A:** Yeah, that's him. He left a while ago though.
B: 所以，你一個人囉？	**B:** So you're alone?
A: 我想是吧，我可以加入嗎？	**A:** I suppose. Can I join you?
B: 當然，我很樂意。	**B:** Sure. I'd like that.

Useful Phrases 實用語句

1. 你跟其他朋友一起嗎？
   Are you with some friends?
2. 我只是下班後順道來喝東西。
   I just stopped by for a drink after work.
3. 你剛才才下班嗎？
   Did you just leave work?
4. 你跟誰一起來這裡嗎？
   Are you here with anyone?
5. 那麼你一個人嗎？
   So you're alone?
6. 我可以加入嗎？
   Can I join you?
7. 我很樂意。
   I'd like that.

9.1i 在節慶場合 At a Festival

Dialog 對話

A: 喔，抱歉，我踩到你的腳。	**A:** Oh, sorry. I stepped on your foot.
B: 別擔心。	**B:** No worries.
A: 這裡有很多人，我不太能動。	**A:** There are so many people here. I can't move much.
B: 我知道你的意思，真的很擠。	**B:** I know what you mean. It's really crowded.
A: 音樂何時開始呢？	**A:** What time does the music start?
B: 快了，舞臺燈已經亮了。	**B:** Any minute now. The stage lights are on.
A: 他們在那裡，樂團！	**A:** There they are. The band!
B: 哇，撐住！	**B:** Whoa! Hang on.
A: 每個人都蜂擁向前。	**A:** Everyone is surging forward.

B: 別跌倒了。	**B:** Don’t fall.
A: 小心！	**A:** Be careful!
B: 好，我們現在安全了。	**B:** OK. We’re safe now.
A: 剛才好恐怖。	**A:** That was scary.
B: 對，音樂開始了。	**B:** Yes. The music’s starting.
A: 你的名字是？	**A:** What’s your name?
B: 艾蜜莉，你呢？	**B:** Emily. And yours?
A: 我是唐。	**A:** I’m Don.
B: 大家準備跳舞了，我們加入吧。	**B:** Everybody’s going to dance. Let’s join in.
A: 好。	**A:** Let’s.

crowded ['kraudɪd] adj. 擁擠的

band [bænd] n. 樂團

surge [sɝdʒ] v. 蜂擁而至，(波浪) 猛衝

1. 抱歉，我踩到你的腳。

   Sorry. I stepped on your foot.

2. 我不太能動。

   I can't move much.

3. 真的很擠。

   It's really crowded.

4. 音樂何時開始呢？

   What time does the music start?

5. 舞臺燈已經亮了。

   The stage lights are on.

6. 撐住 [堅持下去]！

   Hang on.

7. 別跌倒了。

   Don't fall.

8. 剛才好恐怖。

   That was scary.

9. 音樂開始了。

   The music's starting.

10. 我們加入吧。

    Let's join in.

11. 好。

    Let's.

主動認識他人，自信絕對是關鍵，無需感覺彆扭，讓自己保持隨意自然的態度。如果一個人出席陌生的聚會，可以直說不認識他人，並在不給他人壓力下展開談話，注意禮貌，並避免對不熟的人說不開心的事，保持話題輕鬆。

9.2 投緣 Hitting It Off

9.2a 演講比賽後 After a Speech Contest

A: 對不起，梁先生，我名字是亨利吳，我是演講比賽參賽者之一。

A: Excuse me, Mr. Liang. My name is Henry Wu. I am one of the speech contestants.

B: 喔，是的，亨利，你做得很好。

B: Oh, yes, Henry. You did well.

A: 謝謝，但是你的演講真的很吸引人，我無法想像我自己可以做到像你那麼棒的報告。

A: Thank you. But your speech was truly appealing. I can't imagine myself giving as great presentation as you.

B: 你這麼說真親切。

B: It's very nice of you to say that.

A: 我想知道你是否受過訓練。

A: I am wondering if you took any training.

B: 不算正式的，但我有參加英語演講的社團，那幫我很多。

B: Nothing very formal, but I do go to an English Speaking Club. It has helped me a lot.

A: 我不知道這裡有這個。

A: I've never heard about this being available here.

B: 喔，那不是大學為主的社團。我下週二晚上要去那裡，或許你可以一起去看看。

B: Oh. It's not a university-based club. I'm going there next Tuesday evening. Maybe you can come along and check it out.

A: 哇，那會很棒，我參加要付費嗎？

A: Wow. That would be great. Should I pay for attendance?

B: 是 7 元，但是沒有入會費。

B: It's $7. But there's no membership fee.

A: 好！	**A:** Good!
B: 下週二 5 點鐘在圖書館前面與我會面，我會載你去那邊。	**B:** Meet me in front of the library at 5 p.m. next Tuesday. I will drive you there.
A: 沒問題！謝謝，梁先生。	**A:** No problem! Thank you, Mr. Liang.
B: 請叫我傑克，到時候見。	**B:** Just call me Jack. See you then.

Word Bank 字庫

contestant [kən'tɛstənt] n. 參賽者
appealing [ə'pilɪŋ] adj. 吸引人的
presentation [ˌprɛzən'teʃən] n. 報告
attendance [ə'tɛndəns] n. 參加，出席

Useful Phrases 實用語句

1. 你這麼說真親切。
   It's very nice of you to say that.
2. 我想知道你是否受過訓練。
   I am wondering if you took any training.
3. 不算正式。
   Nothing very formal.
4. 或許你可以一起去看看。
   Maybe you can come along and check it out.

5. 我參加要付費嗎？

Should I pay for attendance?

9.2b 耶誕節 At Christmas Time

A: 耶誕快樂！

A: Merry Christmas!

B: 耶誕快樂！你是新來的鄰居嗎？

B: Merry Christmas! Are you new to the neighborhood?

A: 是的，我上週剛搬到這裡，我是黛比楊。

A: Yes, I just moved in here last week. I am Debbie Young.

B: 我是丹尼爾梅，幸會，我們在耶誕夜有一個派對，請帶你家人過來跟我們同樂。

B: I am Daniel May. Nice to meet you. We are having a party on Christmas Eve. Please bring your family over and have fun with us!

A: 那會很棒，你們住在哪裡呢？

A: That will be great. Where do you live?

B: 密雪兒街100號，我做了些裝飾，你跟其他鄰居來的時候，大家會很驚喜。

B: 100 Michelle Street. I have been doing some decorating. When you and the other neighbors come around, you will all be amazed.

A: 真的嗎？我跟我先生可以跟你一起裝飾嗎？我們很喜歡做這個。

A: Really? Can my husband and I join you with the decoration? We love doing this.

B: 這樣我們就是三人組了，我們可以這週末下午1點以後一起做。

B: That makes three of us! We can work together anytime after 1 p.m. this weekend.

A: 應該沒問題，你需要特別的材料或工具嗎？也許我們可以提供一些。

A: That should be no problem. Do you need any particular materials or tools? Maybe we can provide some.

B: 什麼都好，我們就即興(布置)吧。

B: Anything will be fine. Let's just improvise.

A: 聽起來已經蠻好玩了，我很期待這個週末。

A: This already sounds fun. I'm looking forward to the weekend!

B: 到時候見。

B: See you then.

decorate ['dɛkə,ret] v. 裝飾
particular [pə'tɪkjələ] adj. 特別的
provide [prə'vaɪd] v. 提供
improvise ['ɪmprə,vaɪz] v. 即興創作

實用語句 Useful Phrases

1. 我新到這個社區。
   I'm new to the neighborhood.
2. 你會很驚訝。
   You'll be amazed.
3. 我也是。
   That makes three of us!
4. 我們即興 (做某事) 吧。
   Let's improvise.

9.2c 在婚禮餐宴 At a Wedding Reception

A: 對不起，你知道我應該把禮物放在哪裡嗎？	**A:** Excuse me. Do you know where I should leave the gift?
B: 在那邊桌上，我帶你走過去。	**B:** Right over on that table. Let me walk you there.
A: 嗨，我是凱文李，里歐的同事。	**A:** Hi, I'm Kevin Lee, a colleague of Leo's.

B: 我是蒂娜布萊佛，新娘菲昂是我的表妹。

B: I'm Tina Bradford. The bride, Fion, is my cousin.

A: 我明白了，你知道我覺得這個餐會現場設計得很好。

A: I see. You know I find this reception party venue well designed.

B: 哇！謝謝你，我是設計師，這是我在行的。

B: Wow! Thank you. I'm the designer. This is what I am good at.

A: 你的品味真好，我經常看設計雜誌，但我很少見到像這樣高貴又有創意的設計，真的很精緻。

A: You do have great taste. I often look through designer's magazines, and I seldom see such an elegant and creative design. It's really delicate.

B: 我受寵若驚，所以你對活動設計有興趣？

B: I'm flattered. So you are interested in event designs?

A: 所有的設計，包含工業設計及建築，你呢？

A: All kinds of designs, including industrial designing and architecture. And you?

B: 當然，身為設計師，我們從各種元素裡找點子，譬如說，我的許多設計概念是從很棒的建築或甚至是從賽車來的。

B: Certainly, as designers, we draw ideas from all sorts of elements. For example, many of my design concepts derived from great architecture or even racing cars.

A: 這樣真的很酷，你有作品集嗎？我很想看看。

A: That's really cool. Do you have a collection album? I'd like to have a look.

B: 沒問題，我恰巧有一本在這間房子裡，在禮物區。我晚些在餐宴時過去那裡拿作品集給你。

B: No problem. I happen to have one here in the house, in the gift area. I'll go get the album for you some time during the reception.

A: 謝謝，我很期待。

A: Thanks. I look forward to it.

B: 沒問題，同時你可以讓自己自在地與別人聊聊。

B: Sure. Meanwhile, feel free to mingle.

A: 你真的很熱心款待，回頭見。

A: You are truly welcoming. I'll see you around.

Word Bank 字庫

elegant ['ɛləgənt] adj. 高貴的
creative [krɪ'etɪv] adj. 創意的
delicate ['dɛləkət] adj. 精緻的
industrial [ɪn'dʌstrɪəl] adj. 工業的
architecture ['ɑrkə,tɛktʃɚ] n. 建築
element ['ɛləmənt] n. 元素
derive [də'raɪv] v. 衍生
racing car n. 賽車
collection album n. 作品集

1. 你的品味真好。

   You have great taste.

2. 你有作品集嗎？

   Do you have a collection album?

3. 這是我在行的。

   This is what I am good at.

4. 我受寵若驚。

   I'm flattered.

5. 自在地與別人聊聊。

   Feel free to mingle.

6. 你真的很熱心款待。

   You are truly welcoming.

在社交場合，沒必要刻意迎合他人，誠實做自己就好，這可是很容易就看得出來的。談話音量也要注意，不要喧嘩。

9.2d 在政治聚會 At a Political Gathering

A: 嗨，我來參加今天的不公平審判抗議，我來早了嗎？

A: Hi, I'm coming to participate in today's protest against unfair trials. Did I show up too early?

B: 喔！不，你沒問題，謝謝你來參與這個活動，請在這裡登記。

B: Oh! No, you are fine. Thank you for being part of this campaign. Please register here.

A: 好。(寫下個人資訊) 我的名字是莎琳梅。

A: All right. (Writing down her personal information) My name is Charlene May.

B: 很高興認識你，莎琳，我是伊凡泰勒，這是你第一次志願參加這個活動嗎？

B: Nice to meet you, Charlene. My name is Evan Taylor. Is this your first time volunteering in this campaign?

A: 我上個月在網路上連署，我感到很憤怒，我發現有一些被告在判決時沒有被公平對待，這不是學校教我們的，你知道的—「無罪推定原則」。

A: I endorsed it online last month. I was really outraged to find out that some defendants have not been treated fairly during trials. This is not what schools teach us. You know-- “innocent until proven guilty”.

B: 沒錯，我們要正義伸張，所以以公平的過程尋找真理是很重要的，沒有人想被本來應該是公平正義的制度虐待。

B: That’s right. We do want justice to prevail, so seeking truth through a just process is essential. No one wants to be treated poorly by a system that’s supposed to be fair and just.

A: 你參加這樣的社會運動多久了？

A: How long have you been into such social movements?

B: 超過十年，要成為改革者並不容易，作為非營利機構，我們資源有限，但我們需要讓大眾注意嚴肅的社會議題。因此，有資源很重要。

B: Over 10 years. It's not easy to be a reformer. As a non-profit organization, we have limited resources, yet we need to get public attention for serious social issues. Therefore, being resourceful is important.

A: 這一定相當刺激。

A: That must be quite exciting.

B: 多數時候，是的。有時就只需要使勁地做行政工作，像黏信封、從一個地方搬重箱子到另一個地方。畢竟志工不是永遠有空。

B: Most of the time, it is. There are also times when you just need to do the arduous administrative work, such as sealing envelopes and moving heavy boxes from one place to another. After all, volunteers are not always available.

A: 你對改善社會一定很投入。

A: You must be highly devoted to bettering the society.

B: 我得到我雙親的遺傳，他們已從事社會運動數十年。

B: I picked this up from my parents. They have been involved in social reform for decades.

A: 你知道嗎？因為我現在大四，這年沒有很多課，或許我可以到你的辦公室多幫點忙，並且學習這個領域。

A: You know what, since I don't have many classes in my senior year now, maybe I can visit your office to help out more and learn about this field.

B: 那會很棒，有更多人來了。

B: That would be great. More people have arrived.

A: 過去接待他們吧，很高興跟你談話。

A: Go ahead to receive them. Nice talking to you.

B: 那回頭見了。

B: I'll see you around.

Word Bank 字庫

protest [prə'tɛst] n. 抗議
outrage ['aut͵redʒ] v. 激怒
defendant [dɪ'fɛndənt] n. 被告
prevail [prɪ'vel] v. 勝出，風行
resourceful [rɪ'sorsfəl] adj. 有資源的
devoted [dɪ'votɪd] adj. 投入的

1. 我陪你走到那裡。
   Let me walk you there.
2. 這是你第一次來這裡嗎？
   Is this your first time here?

3. 這樣令我很憤怒。
   This outrages me.
4. 過去招呼他們吧。
   Go ahead and receive [greet] them.

9.2e 在公園內 At a Park

A: 那是你的小（男）孩嗎？	**A:** Is that your boy?
B: 喔！是的，強納生是我的驕傲跟歡樂。	**B:** Oh! Yes. Jonathan is my pride and joy.
A: 你應當驕傲，他打棒球打得好極了，而且有討人喜歡的個性。	**A:** You should be proud. He plays baseball really well, and seems to have a pleasant personality.
B: 謝謝，這是真的，你有小孩嗎？	**B:** Thanks. That's really true. Do you have any kids yourself?
A: 沒有，但有兩個雙胞胎外甥女，她們8歲，我有時幫忙當褓姆帶她們。	**A:** No, but I have two twin nieces. The kids are 8. I help babysit them sometimes.
B: 她們也喜歡運動嗎？	**B:** Do they like sports as well?

A: 是的，她們喜歡游泳跟跳舞。

A: Yes. They are into swimming and dancing.

B: 所以你跟你的外甥女住得很近。

B: So you live close to your nieces?

A: 是的，這樣讓事情簡單些。

A: Yes, this makes things a lot easier.

B: 我想是的，我想過要跟我父母住近一點，但是強納生會想念他這裡的朋友。

B: I believe so. I have been considering moving closer to my parents, but Jonathan will miss his friends here.

A: 很困難的決定，不過你的兒子看來很獨立，也許你們按照現在這樣就可以了。

A: Tough decision. Nonetheless, your son looks independent. Maybe you two will be fine just the way it is.

B: 我希望如此，我的確常想太多，他經常叫我放輕鬆。

B: I hope so. I do tend to worry too much. He often tells me to relax.

A: 強納生真是個好孩子，順道一提，我是泰瑞莎陳。

A: Jonathan is definitely a good boy. By the way, I'm Teresa Chen.

B: 我是黛安娜沙勒斯，很高興認識你，也許我還會在這裡遇到你？

B: I'm Diana Salles. Nice to meet you. Maybe we will see you here again?

A: 當然囉，我在這附近工作，常到這公園，也許下一次你可以介紹強納生給我認識。

A: For sure. I work around here, and come to this park frequently. Maybe next time you can introduce Jonathan to me.

B: 一定！

B: Absolutely!

Word Bank 字庫

niece [nis] n. 甥 [姪] 女
tough [tʌf] adj. 困難的
independent [ˌɪndɪ'pɛndənt] adj. 獨立的

Useful Phrases 實用語句

1. 強納生是我的驕傲跟歡樂。
   Jonathan is my pride and joy.
2. 他有討人喜歡的個性。
   He has a pleasant personality.
3. 你有小孩嗎？
   Do you have any kids yourself?
4. 我有時幫忙當褓姆帶他們。
   I help babysit them sometimes.

5. 這樣讓事情簡單些。

This makes things a lot easier.

6. 我的確常想太多。

I do tend to worry too much.

7. 一定！

Absolutely!

願意主動做事的人 (包含主動開口) 看起來較容易親近，主動使許多機會得以發展。結交朋友當然須有所取捨，多數人希望獲得友誼及彼此的正向成長。

9.2f 在快速約會 At a Speed Date

A: 嗨！我是莫莉林。	**A:** A: Hi! My name is Molly Lin.
B: 我是羅伯特尼漢，很榮幸認識你，你看起來很漂亮。	**B:** I'm Robert Needham. Pleasure to meet you. You look really nice.
A: 謝謝！我該從問你從事什麼行業開始嗎？	**A:** Thank you! Should I start by asking what you do?
B: 好，我是旅館經理。	**B:** Sure. I am a hotel manager.

A: 那很酷，我的工作需要在國外開很多商務會議，我得住在不同的旅館。

A: That's cool. My job requires many business meetings abroad. I get to stay at different hotels.

B: 你喜歡這種忙碌的生活嗎？

B: Do you enjoy this kind of busy life?

A: 多數時候喜歡，但是我很難與我朋友和家人一起共度時光。

A: Yes, most of the time. But it has been difficult for me to spend time with friends or family.

B: 我們同病相憐，我經常加班很少有時間跟朋友相聚或真正結交朋友。

B: We are in the same boat. I often work overtime and seldom have time to hang out with friends or to actually meet friends.

A: 我很驚訝，我以為你每天可以與很多不同的人認識。

A: It's surprising to know that. I would think you got to meet many people every day.

B: 是的，但那些人來來去去。

B: True, but those people come and go.

A: 我明白了，跟我的情形很像，我希望可以有長遠的關係，有個令人信任的男友，有耐心，而且在我工作回來時陪在身邊。

A: I see. It's pretty much the same with my case. I wish to have a long-term relationship in which my boyfriend can be trusting, patient and be around when I'm back from work.

B: 很有意思，我也在找相同特性的女朋友。

B: Interesting. I'm looking for a girlfriend with the same traits.

A: 呃，也許我們還不知道我們是否適合彼此，但我肯定我們可以當朋友，因為我們很能認同彼此的工作情況。

A: Well, maybe we don't know yet if we are suitable for each other, but I certainly think we can be friends since we can relate to each other's work conditions well.

B: 我完全同意，我們保持聯絡吧！

B: I totally agree! Let's stay in touch!

A: 好。

A: Sure.

Word Bank 字庫

require [rɪ'kwaɪr] v. 需要
trusting ['trʌstɪŋ] adj. 信任的
trait [tret] n. 特質
suitable ['sutəbl̩] adj. 適合的
relate to v. 認同

1. 你看起來很漂亮。
   You look really nice.
2. 我該從問你從事什麼行業開始嗎？
   Should I start by asking what you do?

3. 你喜歡這種忙碌的生活嗎？

   Do you enjoy this kind of busy life?

4. 我們同病相憐。

   We are in the same boat.

5. 跟我的情形很像。

   It's pretty much the same with my case.

6. 我經常加班。

   I often work overtime.

7. 我很少有時間跟朋友相聚。

   I seldom have time to hang out with friends.

8. 我很少結交朋友。

   I seldom meet friends.

9. 我希望可以有長遠的關係。

   I wish to have a long-term relationship.

10. 我們很能認同彼此的工作情況。

    We can relate to each other's work conditions well.

11. 我相信是這樣。

    I believe so.

12. 我完全同意。

    I totally agree.

13. 我們保持聯絡吧！

    Let's stay in touch.

9.2g 在飛機上 On an Airplane

A: 嗨，我的座位在你旁邊。

A: Hi. I have seat next to you.

B: 好，我讓你過去。	**B:** OK. Let me get out of your way.
A: 謝謝，不用急。	**A:** Thanks. Don't hurry.
B: 沒什麼，我知道有人會很快過來。	**B:** No problem. I figured somebody would come soon.
A: 你覺得這班機會準時起飛嗎？	**A:** Do you think this flight will depart on time?
B: 誰知道呢？我想會吧，但是沒人料得準。	**B:** Who knows? I think it will, but you never know.
A: 對，我想我只是期待 (準時)。	**A:** True. I guess I'm just hoping.
B: 你要去辦重要的事？	**B:** Something important you're going to?
A: 對，我最好的朋友明天要結婚了，我可不想錯過。	**A:** Yes. My best friend is getting married tomorrow, and I don't want to miss it.
B: 我明白了，我知道你的感覺，我兩年前遇到一樣的情況。	**B:** I see. I know how you feel. I was in the same situation two years ago.

A: 你準時到嗎？	**A:** Did you make it on time?
B: 是的，雖然那時誤點讓我很擔心。	**B:** Yes, though there was a delay that worried me.
A: 好，我最好把手指交叉 (祈求好運)。	**A:** Well, I'd better keep my fingers crossed.
B: 我也會這麼做。	**B:** I will, too.
A: 謝謝。	**A:** Thanks.

depart [dɪ'pɑrt] v. 起飛
delay [dɪ'le] n. 誤點
cross [krɔs] v. 交叉

1. 我的座位在你旁邊。
   I have seat next to you.
2. 我讓你過去。
   Let me get out of your way.
3. 不用急。
   Don't hurry.
4. 你覺得這班機會準時起飛嗎？
   Do you think this flight will depart on time?

5. 誰知道呢？

Who knows?

6. 沒人料得準。

You never know.

7. 我只是期待。

I'm just hoping.

8. 我知道你的感覺。

I know how you feel.

9. 我最好把手指交叉 (祈求好運)。

I'd better keep my fingers crossed.

9.3 不投緣 Not Going Well

9.3a 在圖書館大廳 At the Lobby of a Library

A: 對不起，你在桌上留紙條要見我嗎？	**A:** Excuse me. Did you leave a note on the desk and ask to see me?
B: 是的。	**B:** Yes, I did.
A: 我可以為你做什麼呢？	**A:** What can I do for you?
B: 我過去三個月都坐在你對面桌子，我想知道我們是否可以做朋友。	**B:** I have sat across the desk from you over the last three months. I am wondering if we could be friends.

A: 我們又不認識，你不覺得這樣很尷尬嗎？	**A:** We don't know each other at all. Don't you think this is awkward?
B: 呃，這可能看起來有些唐突，但我很認真看待這件事。	**B:** Well, this may seem abrupt, but I am serious about it.
A: 我很抱歉，但我現在得走了。	**A:** I'm sorry, but I need to go now.
B: 你會至少考慮一下嗎？	**B:** Will you at least consider it?
A: 我得走了，再見。	**A:** I have to go. Bye.

Word Bank 字庫

awkward ['ɔkwɚd] adj. 尷尬的
abrupt [ə'brʌpt] adj. 唐突的

Useful Phrases 實用語句

1. 留紙條。
   Leave a note.
2. 我可以為你做什麼呢？
   What can I do for you?
3. 我們不認識。
   We don't know each other.
4. 這樣很尷尬。
   This is awkward.

5. 我現在得走了。
   I need to go now.
6. 我想知道我們是否可以做朋友。
   I am wondering if we could be friends.
7. 這可能看起來有些唐突。
   This may seem abrupt.
8. 我很認真看待這件事。
   I am serious about it.
9. 你會至少考慮一下嗎？
   Will you at least consider it?

以禮貌的藉口 (如 I have to go now.) 結束不投緣的對話是最好的，沒必要硬撐，對彼此都沒好處。

9.3b 尷尬時刻 An Awkward Moment

A: 嗨！記得我嗎？	**A:** Hi! Remember me?
B: 很抱歉，我不記得，我們認識嗎？	**B:** I'm sorry, but I don't. Did we meet before?
A: 我們大一美國歷史課是同學。	**A:** We were classmates in the freshman American History class.
B: 你是說傑克遜教授的課？	**B:** You mean Professor Jackson's class?

A: 是的，我們那時沒有機會說話，但我很開心遇到老同學。

A: That's right. We did not have a chance to talk back then, but I am so glad to bump into old classmates.

B: 對，我想是的，但我不是那堂課的學生，我是教授的助理。

B: Yeah, I would think so, except I wasn't a student there. I was the professor's assistant.

A: 喔！我很抱歉誤會了。

A: Oh! I'm so sorry for the mistake.

B: 沒關係，這樣的事總會發生。

B: It's okay. It happens.

A: 這樣很令人困窘，但可以給我你的電話嗎？

A: Now this is embarrassing, but may I have your number?

B: 嗯，我不確定，這樣吧，我可以交換電子郵件地址，我們目前可以那樣保持聯絡。

B: Well, I'm not sure. How about this? I can exchange email addresses. We can stay in contact that way for now.

A: 那樣也可以，謝謝。

A: That's fine, too. Thank you.

bump into 偶遇
assistant [ə'sɪstənt] n. 助理
embarrassing [ɪm'bærəsɪŋ] adj. 困窘的

1. 記得我嗎？
   Remember me?
2. 我們認識嗎？
   Did we meet before?
3. 我們見過面嗎？
   Have we met before?
4. 我很高興碰到你。
   I'm glad to bump into you.
5. 這樣的事總會發生。
   It happens.
6. 沒關係。
   It's OK.
7. 很抱歉誤會了。
   Sorry about the mistake.
8. 這樣很令人困窘，但是 (提出請求)
   This is embarrassing, but...
9. 可以給我你的電話嗎？
   May I have your number?
10. 這樣吧 (提出建議)？
    How about this?
11. 我們可以保持聯絡。
    Let's stay in contact.

9.3c 在飛機上 On an Airplane

Dialog 1 對話1

A: 對不起，我坐你旁邊。

A: Excuse me. I'm in the seat next to you.

B: 喔，好。

B: Oh. Fine.

(幾秒鐘後 a few seconds later)

A: 我希望這班飛機準時。

A: I hope this flight leaves on time.

B: 對。

B: Yeah.

A: 你經常搭這家航空公司嗎？

A: Do you fly with this airline often?

B: 不常。

B: No.

A: 好吧，那我就希望一切都好。

A: OK then, I guess I'll just hope for the best.

B: 嗯。

B: Uh.

1. 我坐你旁邊。

   I'm in the seat next to you.

2. 我希望這班飛機準時。

   I hope this flight leaves on time.

3. 你經常搭這家航空公司嗎？

   Do you fly with this airline often?

4. 我希望一切都好。

   I'll just hope for the best.

A: 嗨，我是傑克。	**A:** Hi, I'm Jack.
B: 哈囉。	**B:** Hello.
A: 你今天要飛到哪裡？	**A:** Where are you flying to today?
B: 我要去亞特蘭大。	**B:** I'm headed for Atlanta.
A: 你住在哪裡嗎？	**A:** Do you live there?
B: 不，我出差。	**B:** No. I'm on business.

A: 我明白了。

A: I see.

B: 抱歉，我要讀這些報告。

B: Sorry. I need to read these reports.

A: 喔，好的。

A: Oh. OK.

Notes 小叮嚀

搭飛機本身是件累人的事，人們通常不會想在飛機上與陌生人聊太多，有些人可能會多聊一些，但在機上與鄰座談話不要讓人覺得有壓迫感，可以觀察別人的肢體語言作判斷。許多人在機上想要利用時間做自己的事或安靜休息，不希望被困在想聊天的人旁邊。

9.3d 愛狗人遇厭狗人 Dog Lovers Meeting Non Dog Lovers

Dialog 對話

A: 請控制你的狗。

A: Please control your dog.

B: 抱歉，他[牠]跑開我一些些。

B: Sorry. He got away from me a little.

A: 呃，請離我遠點。

A: Well, please keep it away from me.

B: 好。

B: All right.

Useful Phrases 實用語句

1. 請控制你的狗。

   Please control your dog.

2. 請離我遠點。

   Please keep it away from me.

3. 抱歉，他 [牠] 跑開了。

   Sorry. He got away from me.

4. 他 [牠] 很友善。

   He is a friendly dog.

5. 請別害怕。

   Please don’t be afraid.

6. 他 [牠] 不會咬人。

   He doesn’t bite.

I'm really envious of them. I wish I had time to travel.

Unit 10 Common Topics for Chatting and Socializing

日常社交話題

以外語聊天是最讓人融入外國環境的學習方式，談些簡單的事是了解一個地方與人們最好的辦法，而最適合結交新朋友且在社交場合與他人輕鬆談論的就是日常話題，有一般的語言技能就能了解周遭的事情並進一步了解自己該做甚麼。

10.1 聊天氣 Chatting about the Weather

10.1a 好天氣 Good Weather

A: 今天天氣很好。	**A:** Good weather today.
B: 還不錯，但願每天都像這樣。	**B:** Not bad. I wish it were like this every day.
A: 那會很好，我喜歡這樣的天氣，在家裡或戶外做事都好。	**A:** That would be nice. I like this kind of weather for doing things inside or out.
B: 是，很好，你可以出去玩，或待在家，讓門開著，聽鳥唱歌。	**B:** Yeah, it's good. You can go out and play, or stay home, leave the door open and listen to the birds sing.
A: 是的，對精神很好。	**A:** Yes, it's good for the spirit.
B: 我想我要外出辦些雜事。	**B:** I think I'll go out and do some chores.
A: 我最好去建材行找些東西來修理我的房子。	**A:** I'd better run down to the building supply store and get some things to do repairs on my house.

B: 好，晚點見。

B: OK. Catch you later.

A: 晚點見。

A: Same to you.

chore [tʃor] n. 雜事
building supply store n. 建材行

1. 外面天氣很好。
   It's nice out.
2. 天氣如何？
   How's the weather?
3. 很好。
   Nice day.
4. 這樣對精神很好。
   It's good for the spirit.
5. 我要外出辦些雜事。
   I'll go out and do some chores.
6. 晚點見。
   Catch you later.

10.1b 天氣改變 Changing Weather

Dialog 對話

A: 嗨，莎莉，今天天氣很好。	**A:** Hi, Sally. Nice weather today.
B: 是的，我喜歡。	**B:** Yes, it is. I love it.
A: 你今天要出去嗎？	**A:** Are you going out?
B: 我今天沒計畫，但是天氣這麼好待在家裡很可惜。	**B:** I have no plans to, but it's so nice out, it seems a shame to stay in.
A: 對，也許我們可以找一些人去公園打網球。	**A:** Right. Maybe we should find a couple of more people and head down to the park to play tennis.
B: 呃，我聽到收音機說下午晚點會變天下雨。	**B:** Well, I did hear on the radio that it might cloud up and rain later today.
A: 不是開玩笑吧，那真讓我吃驚，想到現在天氣這麼好。	**A:** No kidding. That surprises me considering how nice it is right now.
B: 對，但你知道這裡的天氣說變就變。	**B:** True, but you know how the weather can change here pretty quickly.
A: 對，前一分鐘還天氣晴朗，下一分鐘就傾盆大雨。	**A:** You're right. One minute it's clear and the next it can be pouring.

B: 我們冒個險吧，就算是開始下雨也是晚點的時候，我們可以在公園旁邊不錯的小熟食店打發時間。

B: Let's risk it anyway. Even if it does start to rain it will be later, and we can hang out at that cool little deli near the park.

A: 我贊成，走吧！

A: I'm with you. Let's go!

Word Bank 字庫

pour [por] v. 傾洩
risk [rɪsk] v. 冒險
deli ['dɛlɪ] n. 熟食店
hang out 消磨

Useful Phrases 實用語句

1. 我沒有計畫。
I have no plans.

2. 我們出去。
Let's go out.

3. 可能會變天。
It might cloud up.

4. 可能下傾盆大雨。
It can be pouring.

5. 可能會變晴朗。
It might clear off.

6. 很可惜。
It's a shame.

7. 我們留在家裡。

   Let's stay in.

8. 我們去熟食店消磨時間。

   Let's hang out at the deli.

9. 我們冒個險吧。

   Let's risk it.

10. 我贊成。

    I'm with you.

10.1c 壞天氣 Bad Weather

A: 天啊！今天外面又冷、風又大！	**A:** Gosh! It's really cold and windy out today!
B: 我知道，天氣真的很糟。	**B:** I know. It's really nasty.
A: 天氣預報怎麼說？	**A:** What does the forecast say?
B: 接下來這兩天都像這樣。	**B:** It's supposed to be like this for the next two days.
A: 那我想是找本好書來讀的時候了。	**A:** Then I guess it's time to find a nice book to read.
B: 我懂你的意思。	**B:** I know what you mean.

nasty ['næstɪ] adj. 惡劣的
forecast ['for͵kæst] n. 預告

1. 天啊！
   Gosh!
2. 今天外面又冷風又大！
   It's really cold and windy out today!
3. 外面天氣真的很糟。
   It's nasty out.
4. 天氣預報怎麼說？
   What does the forecast say?
5. 我懂你的意思。
   I know what you mean.

10.1d 天氣警報 Weather Warning

A: 傑瑞，你有聽到氣象報告嗎？	**A:** Jerry. Did you hear the weather report?
B: 沒有，怎麼說呢？	**B:** No. What does it say?
A: 我們會受到暴風雪襲擊。	**A:** We're going to get hit by a snow-storm.

B: 什麼時候？

B: When?

A: 今晚。

A: Tonight.

B: 我們這裡這幾年沒下多少雪。

B: We haven't had much snow for the last few years here.

A: 我知道，但是天氣預報說一道阿拉斯加冷鋒今晚會經過這裡帶來很多降雪。

A: I know, but the weather service says an Alaskan cold front is going to pass through here tonight bringing a lot of snow with it.

B: 好，我想我最好到店裡買點食物及補給品。

B: OK. I guess I'd better go to the store and buy some food and supplies.

A: 我也要去，我想我們下週會處在不好的 (天氣) 狀況下。

A: I'm going too. I think we're in for bad conditions for the next week.

B: 我們最好走吧。

B: We'd better get going.

Word Bank 字庫

cold front n. 冷鋒
supplies [sə'plaɪz] n. 補給品

1. 氣象報告怎麼說呢？
   What does the weather report say?
2. 一道冷鋒今晚會經過。
   A cold front is going to pass through.
3. 我最好到店裡買點食物。
   I'd better go to the store and buy some food.
4. 我最好買點補給品。
   I'd better buy some supplies.
5. 我們處在不好的狀況下。
   We're in for bad conditions.
6. 我們最好走吧。
   We'd better get going.

10.1e 聊溫度變化 Chatting about Changing Temperatures

A: 哇！今天好冷。	**A:** Wow! It's cold today.
B: 是啊，昨晚氣溫驟降。	**B:** Yes. The temperature dropped fast last night.
A: 你穿得夠暖嗎？	**A:** Are you dressed warm enough?
B: 我想是的，你呢？	**B:** I think so. What about you?

A: 有吧，我沒問題，現在幾度？	**A:** Yeah, I'm OK. What degree is it right now?
B: 我聽收音機說現在零下 12 度。	**B:** I heard on the radio. It's -12.
A: 天啊！光聽到就讓我發抖了。	**A:** Man! That makes me shiver just hearing it.
B: 我也是，去年都沒這麼冷。	**B:** Me, too. It never got this cold last year.
A: 對，我希望不會一直這麼冷。	**A:** Right. I hope it doesn't stay this cold very long.
B: (氣象) 報導說至少一週。	**B:** Reports say a week, at least.
A: 啊。	**A:** Ugh.

Word Bank 字庫

temperature ['tɛmprətʃɚ] n. 溫度
degree [dɪ'gri] n. 度數
shiver ['ʃɪvɚ] v. 發抖

Useful Phrases 實用語句

1. 你穿得夠暖嗎？
   Are you dressed warm enough?

2. 現在幾度？

What degree is it right now?

3. 光聽到就讓我發抖了。

That makes me shiver just hearing it.

4. 我希望不會一直這麼冷。

I hope it doesn't stay this cold very long.

◆ **天氣 Weather**

Celcius	攝氏
Fahrenheit	華氏
cloudy	多雲的
minus	零下的
freezing	冰凍的
humid	潮溼的
humidity	溼度
breezy	有微風的
cold [warm] front	冷 [暖] 鋒
heat wave	熱浪
drizzling	下毛毛雨的
rainy	多雨的
pouring	傾盆大雨的
clear	晴朗的
overcast	陰霾的
windy	多風的
foggy	有霧的
smoggy	有煙霧的
hazy	有霾的
calm	平靜的
hurricane	颶風
tornado	龍捲風

lightening	閃電
thunder	打雷
snowflakes	雪花
snowy	多雪的
icy	結冰的
snowstorm, blizzard	暴風雪
sandstorm	沙暴
duststorm	塵暴
hail	冰雹
hailstorm	降雹
sleet (freezing rain)	凍雨 (雪加雨)
frosty	結霜的
nasty out	外面天氣壞透了
El Niño	聖嬰現象
La Niña	反聖嬰現象

聊天氣是安全的話題與人際關係的潤滑劑，無論熟悉與否，任何人都能回應。美國的天氣因地點而異，對不習慣冷天候的亞洲人而言，冬季即使在加州，許多地區室內也必須開暖氣，美國北部尤為酷寒，在室外要確保不致於受凍，毛衣、防寒大衣、手套、帽子、圍巾、雪鞋等皆是必要配備。公共場所開有暖氣，國人習慣穿著衛生衣或套頭毛衣到時會變得太熱，進出室內外溫度改變很大，按洋蔥式穿法一層層穿上或脫下才不致於感冒。壞天氣也表示會下雨或下雪，所以要帶把傘。下雪時當然就要確保足部保暖，必須選擇不受潮、保暖、防滑的鞋子，當然暖和的襪子及雪靴會很管用。

此外，下雪時的交通也會是個大問題，居民除了一大早必須鏟雪外，車子添加防凍劑、為輪胎上雪鍊、小心駕車及防止打滑等都要特別注意。因為冬天又冷又長，北美人們渴望春天快來，所以民俗上每年2月2日「Groundhog Day」(土撥鼠節)用來預測節令，如果土撥鼠出洞後看到自己的影子就表示春天至少還要等上 6 星期，反之，春天就不遠了。

10.2 聊交通
Chatting about Traffic

Dialog 對話

A: 今天的交通有夠糟。	**A:** The traffic is pretty bad today.
B: 還好我們共乘，否則我們會被塞在外車道。	**B:** Good thing we are car pooling, otherwise we'd be stuck in the slower lanes.
A: 對，或許我應該走里斯路出口。	**A:** Right. Maybe I should have taken the Reece Way exit.
B: 很難說，我曾在像今天這種路況時那麼做過，但沒省到時間。	**B:** Hard to say. I've done that in the past in conditions like this and saved no time.
A: 我想我們該更早出門。	**A:** I guess we should have left earlier.
B: 那是竅門，要避免尖峰時間。	**B:** That's the key. Avoiding the rush hours.
A: 對，但不可能永遠都能做到。	**A:** Yes, except you can't do it all the time.
B: 有時走港邊路會有幫助。	**B:** Taking Harbor Side Drive sometimes helps.

A: 也許，但那些大卡車怎麼辦？

A: Maybe, but what about all the big trucks?

B: 那條路有一大堆(卡車)，因為他們不被允許進入市區。

B: There are a lot along that way. That's because they aren't allowed to go through the city.

A: 有時我想乾脆忘掉所有這些，接受你何時到就到吧 (的想法)。

A: Sometimes I think it's better to just forget about it all and accept that you will get there when you get there.

B: 我贊成，就放輕鬆吧，放些音樂，要是天氣很熱、很冷、下雨天等等，待在車子裡要慶幸了。

B: I agree. Just relax, turn on some music, and be glad you're in a car if the weather is too hot, cold, rainy, etc.

A: 對！

A: Right on.

Word Bank 字庫

exit ['ɛksɪt] n. 出口
key [ki] n. 竅門
rush hour n. 尖峰時間

1. 很難說。
   Hard to say.

2. 我想我們該更早出門。

   I guess we should have left earlier.

3. 那是竅門。

   That’s the key.

4. 不可能永遠都能做到。

   You can’t do it all the time.

5. 你何時到就到吧。

   You will get there when you get there.

6. 忘掉所有這些。

   Just forget about it all.

7. 放輕鬆。

   Just relax.

8. 放些音樂。

   Turn on some music.

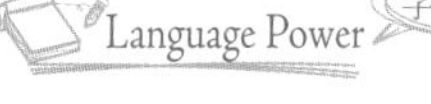

◆ **交通 Traffic**

northbound	北向
southbound	南向
highway	高速公路
exit 12	12 號出口
San Francisco 60 miles	距舊金山 60 英里
commute	通勤
stop sign	停車標誌
intersection	十字路口
crosswalk	行人穿越道
sidewalk	人行道
men working	人員工作中
construction ahead	前面施工
detour	繞道
do not pass	禁止超車

school zone	學校
lights on	開燈
tunnel	隧道
overpass	高架橋，天橋
underpass	橋下通道，地下道
ramp	斜坡 (高速公路引道)
no parking	禁止停車
4 way stop	四面來車停車
do not enter	禁止進入
no left turn	禁止左轉
no right turn	禁止右轉
slow	慢行
toll station	收費站
tollbooth	收費亭
exact change	不找零車道
change lane	找零車道
electronic pass lane (e-lane)	電子收費道
ticket only	回數票專用道
rest stop	休息站
rest area	休息區

10.3 聊工作 Chatting about Work

A: 最近工作如何？

A: How is your work going these days?

B: 不錯，但我有點累。

B: Not bad, but I'm kind of tired.

A: 睡眠不足嗎？

A: Not enough sleep?

B: 對，趕了幾個案子。

B: Yes, some projects had to be done.

A: 最近有人員流動嗎？

A: Has there been any turnover lately?

B: 有，有些人辭職了，你為何會問？

B: Yeah. Some people have quit. Why do you ask?

A: 好奇，我公司的人都待得好好的。

A: Curious. People have been staying at my company.

B: 那是個好工作環境，對嗎？

B: That's a pretty good place to work, right?

A: 他們的福利很好。

A: They have good benefits.

B: 那管理呢？

B: How's the management?

A: 很好，他們 (公司管理階層) 以訓練及晉升機會支持我們，你工作那裡好嗎？

A: Pretty good. They support us with training and advancement opportunities. Is it good at where you work?

B: 管理是很好，但是我碰過更好的。	**B:** Management is pretty good, but I've experienced better.

turnover ['tɝn͵ovɚ] n. 人員流動、汰換

benefit ['bɛnəfɪt] n. 福利

advancement [əd'vænsmənt] n. 晉升

1. 你的工作如何？
   How's work going?
2. 工作好嗎？
   Your job OK?
3. 我有點累。
   I'm kind of tired.
4. 事情很忙。
   Things are busy.
5. 我的工作沒問題。
   My job's fine.
6. 有些人辭職了。
   Some people have quit.
7. 他們的福利很好。
   They have good benefits.
8. 他們以訓練支持我們。
   They support us with training.
9. 我碰過更好的。
   I've experienced better.
10. 那是個獲得經驗的好地方。
    It's a good place to gain experience.

11. 那裡有一些好的機會。

    There are some good opportunities there.

12. 我喜歡我的工作。

    I like my job.

13. 打算辭職嗎？

    Planning to quit?

14. 人員流動率如何？

    How's the turnover there?

15. 最近有人員流動嗎？

    Has there been any turnover lately?

10.4 聊課業
Chatting about Studies

A: 凱若教授的課上得如何？	**A:** How is it going in Professor Kaizer's class?
B: 我想還可以，雖然有時我不懂。	**B:** OK, I guess. Sometimes I don't get it.
A: 對，我知道這種感覺，我對經濟學的上課內容很困惑。	**A:** Yeah. I know the feeling. I'm confused about what's being taught in my economics class.
B: 再兩週就期中考，我擔心是否能準備好。	**B:** Mid-Term tests are in two weeks. I wonder if I'll be ready.
A: 我們可以做到，但必須請求更多幫忙。	**A:** We'll make it. We have to ask for more help though.

B: 我想也是，你有常找助教嗎？	**B:** I suppose. Do you talk to the TAs much?
A: 還沒，但是唐姆笙教授的助教好像很聰明。	**A:** Not yet, but Professor Tomson's TA seems pretty smart.
B: 很好，對凱若教授的助教我一無所知。	**B:** That's good. I don't know anything about Professor Kaizer's TA.
A: 呃，我想我們兩個得跟他們熟一點。	**A:** Well, I guess we both need to get to know them better.
B: 那是一定要的。	**B:** That's for sure.

Word Bank 字庫

confused [kən'fjuzd] adj. 困惑的
economics [ˌikə'nɑmɪks] n. 經濟學
TA n. 助教 (= teaching assistant)
smart [smɑrt] adj. 聰明的

Useful Phrases 實用語句

1. 你的課業如何？
   How are your classes going?
2. 有時我不懂。
   Sometimes I don't get it.
3. 我知道這種感覺。
   I know the feeling.

4. 課程很難。

This class is tough.

5. 教授很好。

The professor is good.

6. 我聽不懂教授說的。

I don't understand the professor.

7. 我聽不懂那堂課。

I'm lost in that class.

8. 我那堂課上得不錯。

I'm doing well in that class.

9. 我喜歡助教。

I like the TA.

10. 有很多要讀的。

There's a lot to read.

11. 期中考快到了。

Mid-term is coming.

12. 我們明天有考試。

We have a test tomorrow.

13. 我們會辦到。

We'll make it.

14. 我們必須請求更多幫忙。

We have to ask for more help.

15. 我們得跟他們熟一點。

We need to get to know them better.

16. 那是一定要的。

That's for sure.

17. 作業何時到期？

When is the assignment due?

18. 作業星期一到期。

The assignment is due on Monday.

10.5 聊家庭
Chatting about Family

A: 你家人如何？	**A:** How is your family doing?
B: 呃，我們喜歡這裡，因為我們已經習慣這個地方了。	**B:** Well, we like it here now that we've gotten used to the place.
A: 那很好，我太太和小孩似乎也認為這裡不錯。	**A:** That's good. My wife and kids seem to think it's OK here, too.
B: 我們常常去城市的娛樂中心。	**B:** We've been going out to the city recreation center a lot.
A: 我聽說那裡不錯。	**A:** I hear that's not bad.
B: 那裡為小孩設計得很好，我太太跟我喜歡在那裡打網球。	**B:** It's set up well for children, and my wife and I like to play tennis there.
A: 你太太現在工作嗎？	**A:** Is your wife working now?
B: 她在一間學校找到一份兼職工作協助閱讀落後的小孩。	**B:** She got a part-time job in one of the schools assisting kids that are behind on reading.

A: 我太太也在找工作，但她還沒找到她喜歡的。	**A:** My wife is looking for a job, but hasn't found anything that she likes.
B: 找到適合的工作要花些時間。	**B:** It takes time to find something that fits.
A: 是的，你的小孩喜歡這裡的學校嗎？	**A:** Yes, it does. Do your kids like school here?
B: 似乎是，就我所知到目前為止沒有麻煩，你的小孩呢？	**B:** They seem to. So far no troubles that I know of. And yours?
A: 他們對新老師有點適應上的麻煩，我希望他們會很快完全融入。	**A:** They are having some trouble adjusting to their new teachers. I hope they'll settle in totally soon.

get used to 習慣
recreation center n. 娛樂中心
assist [ə'sɪst] v. 幫忙
adjust [ə'dʒʌst] v. 適應
settle in 融入

1. 我們已經習慣這個地方了。
   We've gotten used to the place.
2. 你太太目前在工作嗎？
   Is your wife working now?

3. 她找到一份兼職工作。

   She got a part-time job.

4. 你的小孩喜歡這裡的學校嗎？

   Do your kids like school here?

5. 他們對新老師有點適應上的麻煩。

   They are having some trouble adjusting to their new teachers.

6. 我希望他們會很快完全融入。

   I hope they'll settle in totally soon.

10.6 聊健康 Chatting about Health

Dialog 對話

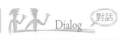

A: 你最近覺得如何？	**A:** How are you feeling these days?
B: 好多了。	**B:** Better.
A: 我聽說你有多運動了。	**A:** I hear you have been exercising more.
B: 對，我也有吃好一點。	**B:** Yes. I've been eating better too.
A: 那很好，我知道你生病兩個月。	**A:** That's good. I know you were sick for a couple of months.

B: 對，我沒照顧好自己，我工作過度而忽略健康。	**B:** Yes. I wasn't taking care of myself. I was working too much and neglecting my health.
A: 我也要改變生活方式，晚上太常出去了。	**A:** I've had to make some lifestyle changes also. Too much going out at night.
B: 對，很好玩，但是一陣子後就累了。	**B:** Yeah. It's fun, but you get tired after a while.
A: 確實是，我睡眠不足。	**A:** Exactly. I wasn't getting enough sleep.
B: 最好的醫療照顧幫不了我們，如果我們不照顧自己。	**B:** The best medical care in the world isn't going to help us if we don't take care of ourselves.
A: 對。	**A:** That's right.

neglect [nɪ'glɛkt] v. 忽略
lifestyle ['laɪfˌstaɪl] n. 生活方式

1. 你要照顧自己。
   Take care of yourself.
2. 飲食要健康。
   Eat healthy.
3. 做些運動。
   Get some exercise.

4. 我們去運動。

   Let's go work out.

5. 睡眠充足。

   Get enough sleep.

6. 以健康的生活方式過日子。

   Live a healthy lifestyle.

7. 你最近覺得如何？

   How are you feeling these days?

8. 你看起來很好。

   You're looking well.

9. 我覺得很好。

   I feel great.

美國沒有全國性的健康保險制度，醫療保險 (medical insurance) 所費不貲，多數人希望獲得一份有醫療保障的工作，可以省去購買醫療及意外保險的支出。醫療險需要繳交健康檢查報告，非吸煙者的保費比吸煙者低。因此，許多人熱中健身 (work out) 以保持健康的體格 (keep fit)。

10.7 聊嗜好
Chatting about Hobbies

A: 你空閒時喜歡做什麼，唐？	**A:** What do you like to do in your free time, Don?
B: 我喜歡園藝。	**B:** I like to garden.

A: 真的嗎？你種什麼？	**A:** Really? What do you grow?
B: 玫瑰。	**B:** Roses.
A: 不是在開玩笑吧？那好酷！	**A:** No kidding? That's cool!
B: 對，我覺得它們很漂亮。你喜歡做什麼？	**B:** Yes, I think they're beautiful. What do you like to do?
A: 我喜歡做鳥屋。	**A:** I enjoy building birdhouses.
B: 那很有趣，給什麼樣的鳥住呢？	**B:** That's interesting. What type of birds are they for?
A: 我給不同大小的鳥做不同類型的 (鳥屋)。	**A:** I make different types for all sizes of birds.
B: 你賣它們嗎？	**B:** Do you sell them?
A: 少數幾個，通常我直接送人。	**A:** A few. Usually I just give them away.
B: 我的玫瑰也是這樣。	**B:** I do the same with my roses.

Word Bank 

hobby ['habɪ] n. 嗜好
garden ['gardn̩] v. 做園藝
birdhouse ['bɝd,haus] n. 鳥屋

Useful Phrases 實用語句

1. 你有什麼嗜好？
   What's your hobby?
2. 你空閒時喜歡做什麼？
   What do you do in your free time?
3. 聽來很有趣。
   Sounds like fun.
4. 很有趣的嗜好！
   What an interesting hobby!
5. 會花很多時間嗎？
   Does it take a lot of time?
6. 是個很昂貴的嗜好嗎？
   Is it an expensive hobby?
7. 你是怎麼開始的？
   How did you get started in it?

Language Power 字句補給站

◆ **嗜好 Hobbies**

coin collection	收集硬幣
baseball cards	棒球卡
match boxes	火柴盒
board games	棋盤遊戲
figurines	小雕像
doll making	做娃娃

woodworking	做木工
doing crafts	做手工藝
building models	做模型
painting	繪畫
gardening	園藝
knitting	針織
cooking	烹飪
playing cards	打牌
reading	閱讀
writing	寫作
cinema	電影
photography	攝影
playing musical instruments	玩樂器
biking	騎腳踏車
ballroom dance	社交舞
doing yoga	做瑜珈
meditation	冥想

有機會與他人談談彼此的生活及興趣，可以增加對彼此的了解，注意聆聽並且適當回應是增進友誼的不二法門。

10.8 聊食譜與烹飪 Chatting about Recipes and Cooking

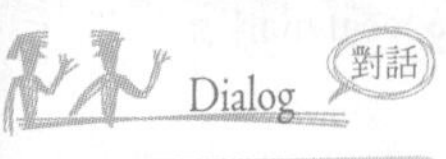

A: 我們來試試我發現的新食譜。	**A:** Let's try this new recipe I found.

B: 是什麼？	**B:** What is it?
A: 是一道雞肉料理。	**A:** It's a chicken dish.
B: 我喜歡雞肉，是墨西哥菜嗎？	**B:** I love chicken. Is it a Mexican dish?
A: 我不認為，我不知道它的起源。	**A:** I don't think so. I don't know its origins.
B: 沒關係，做這道菜我們需要什麼？	**B:** No matter. What do we need to make it?
A: 食譜說要帶骨的雞胸肉、麵粉、奶油、新鮮的羅勒及新鮮的大蒜。	**A:** The recipe calls for boned chicken breasts, flour, butter, fresh basil, and fresh garlic.
B: 大多數的東西我們都沒有。	**B:** We don't have most of those things.
A: 沒關係，我要走過去本地的市場。	**A:** That's OK. I'm going to walk down to the local market.
B: 我跟你去。	**B:** I'll go with you.

A: 我們先列清單才不會忘記東西。

A: Let's make a list first, so we don't forget something.

B: 好主意，我們也可以在市場挑些其他東西。

B: Good idea. We can pick up some other things at the market too.

A: 對，譬如說，我們沒有任何點心。

A: Right. For example, we don't have anything for dessert.

B: 嘿，說到這個，我想到兩星期前我找到一個特別的點心食譜。

B: Hey, speaking of that, it reminds me of a special dessert recipe I found a couple of weeks ago.

A: 你有食譜嗎？

A: Do you have it?

B: 在我房間。

B: It's in my room.

A: 帶著，我們也可以買那些材料。

A: Get it and we can buy those ingredients as well.

B: 好。

B: OK.

recipe ['rɛsəpɪ] n. 食譜
origin ['ɔrədʒɪn] n. 起源
flour [flaur] n. 麵粉
basil ['bæzḷ] n. 羅勒
garlic ['gɑrlɪk] n. 大蒜
remind [rɪ'maɪnd] v. 提醒，想起
ingredient [ɪn'gridɪənt] n. 原料，食材

1. 我發現一個好食譜。
   I found a good recipe.
2. 我在做點心。
   I'm making dessert.
3. 我們來試試這個新食譜。
   Let's try this new recipe.
4. 是雞肉料理。
   It's a chicken dish.
5. 我不知道它的起源。
   I don't know its origins.
6. 做這道菜我們需要什麼？
   What do we need to make it?
7. 我們先列清單。
   Let's make a list first.
8. 我們沒有任何點心。
   We don't have anything for dessert.
9. 我需要買食材。
   I need to buy ingredients.
10. 我沒有全部的食材。
    I don't have all the ingredients.

10.9 聊餐廳
Chatting about Restaurants

A: 有間新義大利餐廳下星期要開了，叫做「羅馬之桌」。	**A:** There's a new Italian restaurant opening up next week. It's called the Roman Table.
B: 我喜歡義大利食物，但我想去城鎮另一邊的法國餐廳。	**B:** I like Italian food, but I'd like to go to the French restaurant across town.
A: 我去過那裡，它裡面很棒，對吧？	**A:** I've been there. It's very nice inside, isn't it?
B: 對，很浪漫，(它的) 藝術作品讓你覺得自己像在畫廊。	**B:** Yes, it is. So romantic, and the art work makes you feel like you are in a gallery.
A: 記得兩個月前我們去過的墨西哥餐廳嗎？	**A:** Remember that Mexican place we went to a couple of months ago?
B: 記得。	**B:** Yeah.
A: 它關門了。	**A:** It closed.
B: 喔，真糟糕，我很喜歡他們的辣椒肉餡捲餅和袋餅。	**B:** Oh, too bad. I liked their enchiladas and fajitas a lot.

A: 我也是，但是「邊境之南」還開著。	**A:** Me too, but South of the Border is still open.
B: 「帕可之家」也是，這兩家都很棒。	**B:** Paco's Casa is too. They're both good.
A: 「西部馬車」午餐不錯，午間特餐很棒而且不貴。	**A:** Wagons West is not bad for lunch. They have great lunch specials, and they're inexpensive.
B: 說這些讓我覺得餓了起來。	**B:** All this is making me hungry.
A: 對，午餐時間到了沒？	**A:** Yes. Is it time for lunch yet?

Word Bank 字庫

enchilada [ˌɛntʃə'lɑdə] n. (墨西哥) 辣椒肉餡捲餅 (西班牙文)
fajita [fə'hitə] n. (墨西哥) 袋餅 (西班牙文)
lunch special n. 午間特餐
inexpensive [ˌɪnɪk'spɛnsɪv] adj. 不貴的

Useful Phrases 實用語句

1. 那是間好餐廳。
   It's a good restaurant.
2. 它裡面很棒，對吧？
   It's very nice inside, isn't it?
3. 它很浪漫。
   It is romantic.

4. 它關門了。

   It closed.

5. 這家餐廳午餐不錯。

   This restaurant is not bad for lunch.

6. 這家餐廳不貴。

   This restaurant is not expensive.

7. 這家餐廳很貴。

   This restaurant is pricey.

8. 我喜歡墨西哥食物。

   I like Mexican food.

9. 這讓我覺得餓了起來。

   This is making me hungry.

10.10 聊購物 Chatting about Shopping

A: 我覺得購物最好玩了。	**A:** I think shopping is the most fun thing to do.
B: 只要不太常購物就好了。	**B:** It is good as long as you don't do it too often.
A: 有道理。	**A:** That's a good point.
B: 我以前常去購物，但我發現如果太常去就沒有驚喜。	**B:** I used to go shopping a lot, but I found it offers no surprises if I went too often.

A: 我發現我會因為看到買不起的東西而感到沮喪。

A: I found I would get frustrated by all the things I saw that I couldn't afford.

B: 確實是。

B: So true.

A: 我現在一個月只去一次，你呢？

A: I only go about once a month now. How about you?

B: 差不多，雖然我現在差不多超過兩個月沒去了。

B: About the same, though I really haven't gone shopping for more than two months now.

A: 為什麼不去？

A: Why not?

B: 喔，我不知道，太忙了吧，或許。

B: Oh, I don't know. Too busy, maybe.

A: 你通常跟誰去？

A: Who do you usually go with?

B: 呃，其實就是這樣，我以前常跟其他朋友一起去，但他們多半搬家、結婚了或換了其他工作，所以很難湊在一起。

B: Well, that's the thing. I used to go with my other friends, but most have moved, married, found other jobs, so it's a lot harder to get together with anyone.

A: 打電話給我，我跟你一起去。	**A:** Call me. I'll go with you.
B: 真的嗎？你何時可以？	**B:** Really? When can you go?
A: 通常是週末。	**A:** Any weekend usually.
B: 好，橡園購物商場有拍賣，週六要去嗎？	**B:** Great. There's a big sale at the Oak Grove Mall. Want to go Saturday?
A: 沒問題。	**A:** No problem.

as long as 只要

frustrate ['frʌstret] v. 沮喪

afford [ə'ford] v. 買得起

mall [mɔl] n. 購物商場

Useful Phrases 實用語句

1. 我現在一個月去一次。
   I go once a month now.
2. 你通常跟誰去？
   Who do you usually go with?
3. 其實就是這樣。
   That's the thing.

4. 我以前常跟其他朋友一起去。

   I used to go with my other friends.

5. 購物商場有拍賣。

   There’s a big sale at the mall.

在美國的商場購物，如果售貨員不忙碌的話，會主動問好，問你是否需要幫忙或在找什麼「Hi, how are you? How can I help you? Are you looking for anything today?」，如果有需要幫忙就可以直接問。如果只是逛逛就說「Thank you. I’m just looking.」或簡單地說「Just looking」就好。許多歐美國家消費稅 (sales tax) 是外加的，購物殺價通常行不通並且可能招來異樣眼光，除非是在跳蚤市場 (flea market) 或車庫拍賣 (garage sale)。拍賣期間的折扣標示若為30% off，就是打七折，別搞混了。

◆ **購物 Shopping**

shopping mall	購物商場
outlet	名牌暢貨中心 (出售過季名牌)
shopping spree	購物欲望
supermarket	超級市場
membership	會員
discount	折扣
cashier	收銀員
checkout counter	結帳櫃檯
express lane	快速結帳通道
coupon	折價券
warranty	保固
local specialty	當地特產
clothing	衣服
accessories	飾品

style	樣式
color	顏色
material	質料
gift	禮物
wrap	包裝
buy one get one free	買一送一
on sale	拍賣
final sale	最後出清
exchange	換貨
refund	退錢
receipt	收據
credit card	信用卡
budget	預算

10.11 聊寵物 Chatting about Pets

A: 嗨，艾琳諾，我看到你有一隻寵物兔子。	**A:** Hi, Eleanor. I see you have a pet rabbit.
B: 對，我上星期才買的。	**B:** Yeah. I got it last week.
A: 真的？為什麼？	**A:** Really? Why?
B: 我喜歡兔子，牠們很可愛。	**B:** I like rabbits. They're cute.

A: 我想那是個好理由。	**A:** That's a good reason I guess.
B: 你有寵物嗎？	**B:** Do you have a pet?
A: 我有養一些魚。	**A:** I have some fish.
B: 什麼樣的？	**B:** What kind?
A: 金魚。	**A:** They are goldfish.
B: 我以前有養一些熱帶魚。	**B:** I used to have some tropical fish.
A: 牠們很棒，我想要養一些，但我聽說牠們很難照顧。	**A:** They're great. I'd like to have some, but I hear they are hard to take care of.
B: 不致於。牠們需要比金魚多些照顧，但很容易。	**B:** Not really. They need more care than goldfish, but they are pretty easy to care for.
A: 我應該多讀些關於牠們的東西。	**A:** I should read more about them.

B: 去「毛毛樂趣」寵物店，他們有關於各種寵物的書，那裡的人很有幫助而且知識豐富。

B: Go to Furry Fun pet shop. They have books about all kinds of pets, and the people there are very helpful and knowledgeable.

A: 好，我需要一些魚飼料，所以我會去那裡看看。

A: OK. I need fish food anyway, so I'll go there and check it out.

B: 保重 [再見]。

B: Take care.

A: 你也是，好好享受兔子 (的陪伴) 吧。

A: You too. Enjoy the bunny.

tropical fish n. 熱帶魚
furry ['fɝɪ] adj. 毛茸茸的
knowledgeable ['nɑlɪdʒəbl̩] adj. 有知識的
bunny ['bʌnɪ] n. 兔子 (口語，尤指小兔子)

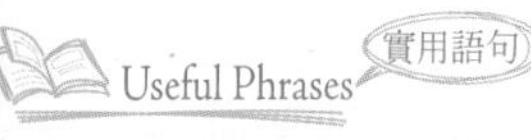

1. 牠們很可愛。
   They're cute.
2. 你有寵物嗎？
   Do you have a pet?

3. 我聽說牠們很難照顧。

   I hear they are hard to take care of.

4. 他們很容易照顧。

   They are pretty easy to care for.

5. 我會去那裡看看。

   I'll go there and check it out.

Do you have a pet?
I have some fish.

Language Power 字句補給站

寵 物 Pets

dog 狗

puppy 小狗

cat 貓

kitten 小貓

rabbit 兔子

guinea pig 天竺鼠

hamster 倉鼠

gerbil 沙鼠

bird 鳥

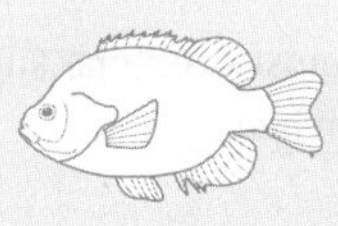

fish 魚

turtle 烏龜

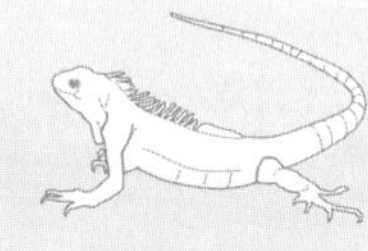

iguana 鬣蜥蜴

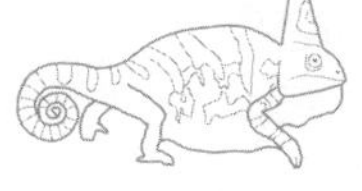

chameleon 變色龍

- toy 玩具
- cage 籠子
- birdhouse 鳥屋
- vet (veterinarian) 獸醫
- grooming 梳毛
- collar 頸圈
- (on a) leash (套上)鍊條，皮帶
- aquarium 水族箱
- doghouse 狗屋
- nutrition 營養

10.12 聊運動
Chatting about Sports

10.12a 聊棒球比賽 Baseball Game

A: 嘿！你昨晚有看棒球比賽嗎？	**A:** Hey! Did you see the basketball game last night?
B: 有，我興奮極了！連贏 12 場。	**B:** I did. I'm psyched! Twelve wins in a row.
A: 就是啊！我想他們今年可能贏到底。	**A:** Right on. I think they may win it all this year.
B: 如果成真，就太棒了，這個城市會爆掉！	**B:** That would be so cool if it happens. This city will erupt.
A: 對，這裡幾乎大家都支持這支球隊。	**A:** For sure. Almost everyone supports the team here.
B: 你想貝爾洛值得被選上最有價值球員嗎？	**B:** Do you think Belzer deserved to be chosen as MVP?
A: 我想是的，但是我也覺得塞蒙斯球賽打得很好。	**A:** I guess so, but I also thought Simmons played a great game.

B: 我也是。	**B:** Me too.
A: 我不敢相信有些裁判的判定。	**A:** I couldn't believe some of the calls by the refs though.
B: 我知道，很瘋狂，泰勒在那一次判定時被判犯規出場。	**B:** I know. It was nuts. Taylor fouled out on that one call.
A: 對，很瘋狂，他根本沒碰到那個人，我是說他根本沒近到可以碰到他。	**A:** Yeah, that was crazy. He didn't touch that guy at all. I mean he wasn't even close to touching him.
B: 那些裁判，有時我覺得他們是瞎子。	**B:** Those refs. Sometimes I think they're blind.
A: 確實是。	**A:** Definitely.

Word Bank 字庫

erupt [ɪ'rʌpt] v. 爆炸
MVP n. 最有價值球員 (= most valuable player)
refs [rɛfs] n. 裁判 (= referee)
call [kɔl] n. (棒球) 停止 (比賽)；(裁判) 判定
foul [faul] v. 犯規

Useful Phrases 實用語句

1. 我興奮極了！
   I'm psyched!
2. 連贏 12 場。
   Twelve wins in a row.
3. 這個城市會爆掉。
   This city will erupt.
4. 很瘋狂！
   It was nuts!
5. 他被判犯規出場。
   He fouled out.
6. 很棒的球賽！
   Great game!

10.12b 聊高爾夫球 Chatting about Golf

Dialog 對話

A: 你今天在球場上打得很棒。

A: You did well on the links today.

B: 謝謝，你也是。

B: Thanks. You too.

A: 你買了新球桿嗎？

A: Did you buy some new clubs?

B: 沒有，我在考慮，但是不確定新的球桿會對我的球賽有幫助。

B: No. I've been thinking about it, but I'm not sure new ones would help my game.

A: 或許你需要一些課程。

A: Maybe some lessons are what you need.

B: 我有想過，俱樂部有一些高手。

B: I thought about that. The club has some good pros.

A: 我知道，我幾個月前上過其中一個人的課。

A: I know. I took some lessons from one of them a few months ago.

B: 值得嗎？

B: Was it worth it?

A: 我想是的，我現在在這個球場可以穩健地打標準桿數或少於桿數。

A: I think so. I can steadily shoot par or under on this course now.

B: 真的，那上課之前呢？

B: Really? What about before the lessons?

A: 我很少打標準桿，我通常超出5桿以上。

A: I seldom shot par. I was usually five or more strokes over.

B: 哇，那很了不起。

B: Wow. That's really something.

A: 是啊，走吧，我們去俱樂部會所，我請你喝一杯。	**A:** Yes. Come on. Let's go to the clubhouse. I'll buy you a drink.
B: 謝謝，我到哪裡的時候會問一下課程。	**B:** Thanks. While I'm there I'll ask about lessons.

Word Bank 字庫

golf links n. 高爾夫球場
club [klʌb] n. 球桿
golf club n. 高爾夫球俱樂部
pro [pro] n. 高手，職業選手
shoot [ʃut] v. 揮桿
par [pɑr] n. 標準桿
golf course n. 高爾夫球場
stroke [strok] n. 桿數
clubhouse ['klʌbˌhaus] n. 俱樂部會所

1. 值得嗎？
   Was it worth it?
2. 我請你喝一杯。
   I'll buy you a drink.
3. 那很了不起。
   That's really something.

◆ **運動 Sports**

news	新聞
sports	運動

win	贏
lose	輸
loss	損失
golf	高爾夫
caddy	桿弟
golf pro	高爾夫職業選手
baseball	棒球
league	聯盟
basketball	籃球
basketball court	籃球場
basket	籃框
net	籃球網
slamdunk	灌籃
three point shot	三分球
score	分數
final	總決賽
game	局，場
tennis	網球
football	美式足球
soccer	足球
badminton	羽毛球
volleyball	排球
icehocky	冰上曲棍球
serve	發球
coach	教練
goal	球門
goal posts	球門門柱
time out	時間到
team	球隊
fans	球迷

10.12c 聊規律運動以保持身材 Chatting about Regular Exercise to Keep Fit

A: 你喜歡什麼樣的運動？	**A:** So what kind of exercise do you like to do?
B: 我每星期打兩次網球，你呢？	**B:** I play tennis a couple of times a week. And you?
A: 我喜歡游泳。	**A:** I like to go swimming.
B: 你多久去一次？	**B:** How often do you go?
A: 一星期 3 次。	**A:** Three times a week.
B: 你體格一定很棒。	**B:** You must be in great shape.
A: 我想我還可以，但是你看起來也很強健。	**A:** I'm OK I guess, but you look really fit as well.
B: 網球似乎讓我保持苗條，但反正我體格偏瘦就是了。	**B:** Tennis seems to keep me trim, but I'm sort of slightly built anyway.

A: 所以你沒有變胖過，對嗎？	**A:** So you never look fat, right?
B: 沒錯，我總是看起來體格不錯，但事實上我身材經常變形。	**B:** Exactly. I always look like I'm in shape, but actually I am often out of shape.
A: 為什麼？	**A:** Why's that?
B: 我網球約會缺席很多次。	**B:** I miss a lot of my tennis dates.
A: 太忙了嗎？	**A:** Too busy?
B: 對，我的工作使我沒有足夠的運動。	**B:** Yes. My work keeps me away from exercising enough.
A: 我了解你的意思。	**A:** I know what you mean.

Word Bank 字庫

fit [fɪt] adj. 強健的
slightly built 體格偏瘦
in shape 體型健美
out of shape 身材變形
tennis date n. 網球約會

1. 你喜歡什麼樣的運動？
   What kind of exercise do you like?
2. 你體格一定很棒。
   You must be in great shape.
3. 你多久去一次？
   How often do you go?
4. 你看起來很強健。
   You look really fit.
5. 我體格偏瘦。
   I'm slightly built.
6. 我身材經常變形。
   I am often out of shape.
7. 我的工作使我沒有足夠的運動。
   My work keeps me away from exercising enough.

10.13 聊車子 Chatting about Cars

A: 嗨，傑瑞，我看到你買另一輛車。	**A:** Hi, Jerry. I see you bought another car.
B: 我以 (舊) 車換 (新) 車。	**B:** I traded in the other one.
A: 這部車看來很好。	**A:** This one looks nice.

B: 它很有力而且很舒適。	**B:** It's pretty powerful and comfortable.
A: (車子的) 耗油呢？	**A:** How's it on gas?
B: 不賴，一加侖跑 27 英里路。	**B:** Not bad. I get 27 to the gallon.
A: 我很嫉妒，我的只跑 23 英里。	**A:** I'm envious. Mine gets 23.
B: 但是你的車全付清了。	**B:** Yours is paid for though.
A: 對，沒有分期付款很好。	**A:** That's true. It is nice to have no monthly payment.
B: 我現在每個月要付 280元。	**B:** I'm paying $280 a month.
A: 我可以看看裡面嗎？	**A:** Can I have a look inside?
B: 當然，請便。	**B:** Oh, sure. Go ahead.
A: 嘿，這些座位真的很舒服。	**A:** Hey. These seats are really comfortable.

B: 對，音響也很好，開 CD 吧。	**B:** Yeah. The sound system is good too. Turn on the CD player.
A: 聽來很好，很清楚。	**A:** Sounds great. Very clear.
B: 我喜歡上下班通勤時聽。	**B:** I love it on my commute to work back and forth.
A: 讓我也想以車換車了。	**A:** Makes me want to trade my car in.
B: 對，嗯，記得那些分期付款嗎？	**B:** Yeah. Well, remember those monthly payments?
A: 對。	**A:** Right.

trade in 以 (舊) 車換 (新) 車
monthly payment n. 月付款
commute [kə'mjut] n. 通勤

1. 我以 (舊) 車換 (新) 車。
   I traded in the other one.
2. (車子的) 耗油呢？
   How's it on gas?

3. 我一加侖跑 27 英里路。

I get 27 to the gallon.

4. 我很嫉妒。

I'm envious.

5. 你的車全付清了。

Your car is paid for.

6. 沒有分期付款很好。

It is nice to have no monthly payment.

7. 我可以看看裡面嗎？

Can I have a look inside?

Language Power 字句補給站

汽車 Cars

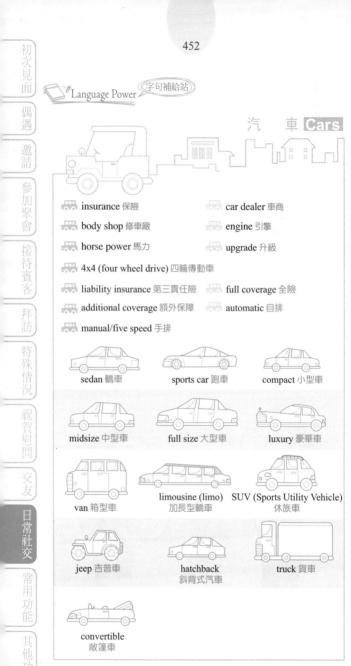

- insurance 保險
- car dealer 車商
- body shop 修車廠
- engine 引擎
- horse power 馬力
- upgrade 升級
- 4x4 (four wheel drive) 四輪傳動車
- liability insurance 第三責任險
- full coverage 全險
- additional coverage 額外保障
- automatic 自排
- manual/five speed 手排

sedan 轎車

sports car 跑車

compact 小型車

midsize 中型車

full size 大型車

luxury 豪華車

van 箱型車

limousine (limo) 加長型轎車

SUV (Sports Utility Vehicle) 休旅車

jeep 吉普車

hatchback 斜背式汽車

truck 貨車

convertible 敞篷車

10.14 聊旅遊、度假
Chatting about Travel Experience and Vacationing

A: 嘿！你回來了！	**A:** Hey! You're back!
B: 昨晚回來的。	**B:** Got back last night.
A: 那裡如何？	**A:** How was it?
B: 真的很不錯。	**B:** Really nice.
A: 你在那裡做什麼？	**A:** What did you do there?
B: 駕風帆 (船)、做日光浴、上夜店、游泳、吃東西。	**B:** Sailing, tanning, clubbing, swimming, eating.
A: 真好。	**A:** Sweet.
B: 對，美好的兩星期。	**B:** Yeah, it was a wonderful two weeks.

初次見面
偶遇
邀請
參加聚會
接待賓客
拜訪
特殊情況
祝賀慰問
交友
日常社交
常用功能
其他功能

A: 看起來你晒得很黑。	**A:** Looks like you got a pretty deep tan.
B: 對，我常躺在太陽下。	**B:** Yes. I laid around in the sun a lot.
A: 那裡物價如何？	**A:** How are prices there?
B: 不全然那麼糟，我很高興。	**B:** Not all that bad really. I was pleased.
A: 那很吸引人，我一直想要去度那樣的假，但很怕物價。	**A:** That's encouraging. I've been thinking about going on that kind of vacation, but fear the price.
B: 你應該去，那裡比這裡至少便宜一半。	**B:** You should go. Prices there are at least 50% less than here.
A: 就這樣，我要去了。	**A:** That's it. I'm going.

Word Bank 字庫

sailing ['selɪŋ] n. 駕風帆 (船)
tanning ['tænɪŋ] n. 日光浴
clubbing ['klʌbɪŋ] n. 上夜店

1. 我有個很棒的假期。

   I had a great vacation.

2. 你的假期如何？

   How was your vacation?

3. 那裡的物價如何？

   How are prices there?

4. 花費不會太糟。

   The cost was not bad.

5. 那很吸引人。

   That's encouraging.

6. 食物很棒。

   The food was really good.

7. 我想再去。

   I'd like to go there again.

8. 天氣很好。

   The weather was beautiful.

9. 我的飯店很好。

   My hotel was nice.

10. 很令人放鬆。

    It was very relaxing.

11. 我買了很多紀念品。

    I bought a lot of souvenirs.

◆ **度假 Vacationing**

vacation ideas	度假點子
vacation packages	套裝行程
itinerary	行程
visa	簽證

ski resort	滑雪度假村
castle	城堡
villa	別墅
beach house	海邊房舍
safari	非洲獵奇
ranch vacation	農莊之旅
cruise	郵輪
camping	露營
trekking	健行
horseback riding	騎馬
kayaking	划獨木舟
rafting	划木筏
white-water rafting	泛舟
hot-air balloon	熱氣球
architecture	建築
museum	博物館
scenery	風景
historical site	歷史地點
ruins	遺跡
natural wonder	自然奇景
landmark	地標
a must-see	必看 (之地、物)
affordable	負擔的起的
reservation	預定
vacation hangover	假期結束症候群

10.15 聊娛樂 Chatting about Entertainment

10.15a 聊歌唱比賽 Chatting about a Singing Contest

A: 你昨晚有看「下個明星」嗎？	**A:** Did you see *Next Star* last night?
B: 有，我看了，我認為珊蒂巴奈斯很棒。	**B:** Yes, I did. I thought Sandy Barnes was great.
A: 真的嗎？她 20 分只得了 11 分。	**A:** Really? She only got eleven out of twenty points.
B: 我知道，但是我覺得評審們錯了，她很棒。	**B:** I know, but I think the judges are wrong. She was great.
A: 事實上，我也喜歡她。我想她挑了大家都喜歡的歌。	**A:** I like her too actually. I think she picks songs that everyone likes.
B: 對，對我而言，那使她具有娛樂性，她也是個好舞者。	**B:** Yeah. That makes her entertaining to me. She's a good dancer too.
A: 那是真的，她是唯一能歌善舞的參賽者。	**A:** That's true. She is the only contestant that can sing well and dance at the same time.

B: 你想她真的有機會被選為優勝者嗎？

B: Do you think she really has a chance to be chosen the winner?

A: 很難說，但是她很有原創性而且有幽默感。

A: Hard to say, but, she's pretty original and has a sense of humor.

B: 好見解，即使她在某個時間點被淘汰，她或許還是可以變成流行歌手。

B: Good point. Even if she does get eliminated at some point, she may still go on to become a pop star.

A: 對啊！很多人喜歡她。

A: Right on! Lot's of people like her.

Word Bank 字庫

original [ə'rɪdʒənḷ] adj. 原創性的
humor ['hjumɚ] n. 幽默
eliminate [ɪ'lɪmə,net] v. 淘汰
pop star n. 流行歌手

Useful Phrases 實用語句

1. 她很有原創性。
   She's pretty original.
2. 她有幽默感。
   She has a sense of humor.
3. 她或許還會繼續。
   She may still go on.
4. 那使她具有娛樂性。
   That makes her entertaining

5. 你想她真的有機會贏嗎？

Do you think she really has a chance to win?

6. 對啊！

Right on!

傳播媒體與網路的發達對大眾的影響無遠弗屆，受歡迎的娛樂是人們時常談論的話題，與生活息息相關的新聞報紙或雜誌上的文章也是朋友間經常交換的訊息。

10.15b 聊表演團體 Chatting about an Acting Group

A: 嗨，克萊兒，你這個週末要做什麼？	**A:** Hi, Claire. What are you going to do this weekend?
B: 我不知道，有什麼建議嗎？	**B:** I don't know. Any suggestions?
A: 城市演員團這個週末要登臺。	**A:** Yes. The City Actors Group is on stage this weekend.
B: 我聽說他們很好。	**B:** I've heard they are good.
A: 我想是的，我看過一些他們的表演。	**A:** I think so. I've seen several of their performances.

B: 兩個月前在為孩童的義演我看過一些演員。	**B:** I saw some of the actors at a benefit for kids a couple of months ago.
A: 那很酷，怎麼樣呢？	**A:** That's cool. How was it?
B: 很好，他們為那裡的小孩演了一齣短喜劇。	**B:** Good. They did a short comedy for the children there.
A: 真棒！你有想過要當演員嗎？	**A:** Neat! Have you ever thought about being an actor?
B: 沒有，我真沒想過。你呢？	**B:** No, not really. How about you?
A: 我幻想過。	**A:** I've fantasized about it.
B: 我知道你的意思，我也一樣。	**B:** I know what you mean. I do the same thing.

Word Bank 字庫

benefit ['bɛnəfɪt] n. 義演
comedy ['kɑmədɪ] n. 喜劇
fantasize ['fæntəˌsaɪz] v. 幻想

1. 你這個週末要做什麼？
   What are you going to do this weekend?
2. 有何建議？
   Any suggestions?
3. 那很酷。
   That's cool.
4. 真棒！
   Neat!
5. 你有想過要當演員嗎？
   Have you ever thought about being an actor?
6. 沒有，絕不會。
   No, not really.
7. 我幻想過。
   I've fantasized about it.
8. 我知道你的意思。
   I know what you mean.

10.15c 聊新電影及演員 Chatting about New Movies and Movie Stars

A: 嗨，喬伊，我昨天晚上開車經過時看到你在電影院。	**A:** Hi, Joy. I saw you at the movie theater last night as I drove by.
B: 真的嗎？我跟一個朋友在一起。	**B:** Really? I was there with a friend.

A: 你看什麼？

A: What did you see?

B: 唐登特拉的新電影。

B: The new Don Dontela movie.

A: 他是個好演員，又帥。

A: He's a good actor, and handsome.

B: 是的，我的朋友跟我都很喜歡他。

B: Yes, he is. My friend and I both love him.

A: 去年我看了一部他與雪莉蕭的電影。

A: I saw him in a movie last year with Shelly Shaw.

B: 喔，我知道！我看過，一部動作片，我不記得片名。

B: Oh, I know! I saw it. An action film. I can't remember the name of it.

A: 「三殺」，那電影有時很性感。

A: *Triple Shot*. It was pretty sexy at times.

B: 是的，特別是那些床戲，我想你很喜歡。

B: Yes, it was. Especially those love making scenes. I'll bet you liked those.

A: 對，我猜你也是，因為你先提了。

A: I did. I guess you did too since you mentioned them first.

B: 被你說中了。

B: You got me.

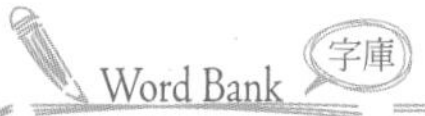

action film n. 動作片
scene [sin] n. 場景

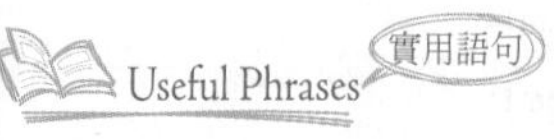

1. 你最喜歡的演員是誰？
   Who's your favorite actor [actress]?
2. 我最愛的是……。
   My favorite is....
3. 最近有看些好電影嗎？
   Seen any good movies lately?
4. 我上週看了一部好片。
   I saw a good movie last week.
5. 我黏在椅子上了。
   I was glued to my seat.
6. 很無聊。
   It bored me.
7. 很拖戲。
   It was a drag.
8. 我看到一半就走了。
   I walked out half way through.

Language Power 字句補給站

◆ **電影 Movies**

1. 類型 Gener

western	西部片
detective	偵探片
drama	戲劇片
horror	恐怖片

science fiction (sci-fi)	科幻片
comedy	喜劇
tragedy	悲劇
documentary	紀錄片
romance	愛情片
mystery	推理片
thriller	驚悚片
epic	史詩片
musical	歌舞片，音樂片
adventure	冒險片
fantasy	夢幻劇
war	戰爭片
classic	經典片
animation	動畫
foreign film	外語片

2. 製作 Production

box office	票房
director	導演
actor / actress	演員 / 女演員
leading role	主角
supporting role	配角
cast	卡司
star	明星
stunt person, double	替身
understudy	候補演員
extra	臨時演員
dub	配音
voice dubber (actor)	配音員
setting	背景
role	角色
theme	主題

script	劇本
playwright	編劇，劇作家
movie review	電影評論
critic	評論人
music	音樂
soundtrack	電影配樂
subtitle	(翻譯的) 字幕
costume	服裝
make up	化妝
photography	攝影
special effect	特殊效果
A-list	一線的
celebrity	名流
masterpiece	傑作
blockbuster	賣座片
movie buff	影迷
sequel	續集
car chase	車輛追逐
action-packed	充滿動作的
preview (trailer)	預告片

3. 評價 Review

award-winning	獲獎的
outstanding, marvelous, fantastic, wonderful	精彩的，出色的
thought provoking	引人深思的
lousy	差勁的
boring, dull	無聊的
rediculous, absurd	荒謬的
dumb, silly	愚蠢的
drag	歹戲拖棚
junk	大爛片

因為大眾傳播的影響，許多人對不同國家人民及其生活的認知，來自片段擷取的新聞或是電視電影裡為搏取收視率而充滿戲劇效果的情節，難免有誇張或扭曲的成分，與真正的生活當然不同。

10.15d 聊電視與廣告 Chatting about TV Programs and Commercials

A: 我喜歡這個電視節目。	**A:** I like this TV show.
B: 還不錯，我也看了幾次。	**B:** It's not bad. I've watched it a few times too.
A: 演技好，故事也妙。	**A:** The acting is good, and the stories are clever.
B: 對。	**B:** True.
A: 但是廣告讓我抓狂。	**A:** The commercials are driving me crazy though.
B: 我知道，廣告太多了。	**B:** I know. There's too many.

A: 我錄下節目之後再看。	**A:** I record the shows and watch them later.
B: 我應該要那樣做，可以跳過廣告。	**B:** I should do that. Then you can just skip the ads.
A: 正是。	**A:** Exactly.
B: 我想已有一些服務可以讓你更容易那麼做。	**B:** I guess some services exist that let you do that easily.
A: 對，但是我可不想付那個錢。	**A:** Sure, but I don't want to pay for any of that.
B: 我也不要。	**B:** Me neither.

Word Bank 字庫

commercial [kə'mɝʃəl] n. (電視、廣播) 廣告
ad [æd] n. (報章、雜誌) 廣告 (= advertisement)

Useful Phrases 實用語句

1. 你看過那個節目嗎？
   Have you seen this program?
2. 廣告太多。
   There are too many commercials.

3. 我覺得廣告也不錯。

   I think the ads are entertaining too.

4. 過來陪我一起看。

   Come on over and watch it with me.

5. 廣告很好笑。

   This ad is funny.

6. 我看不懂這個廣告。

   I don't get this ad.

7. 他 [她] 的演技很棒。

   His [Her] acting is great.

◆ **電視 TV**

TV guide	電視節目表
channel	頻道
cable TV	有線電視
remote (control)	遙控器
sitcom	情境喜劇
cartoon	卡通
soap opera	肥皂劇
docudrama	以事實事件編成的戲劇
melodrama	通俗劇
children's program	兒童節目
educational and cultural program	文教節目
game [quiz] show	益智節目
travel program	旅遊節目
nature show	自然節目
talk show	脫口秀
variety show	綜藝節目
singing contest	歌唱比賽

cooking show	料理節目
sports program	運動節目
shopping program	購物節目
shopping channel	購物頻道
MTV	音樂電視
TV movies	電視電影
mini series	迷你影集
news	新聞
business news	財經新聞
news commentaries	新聞評論
live	現場
couch potato	電視迷

10.15e 聊歌手、樂團及演唱會 Chatting about Singers, Bands, and Concerts

A: 伊莉莎，你看！我拿到吉艾斯卡林斯的新CD。	**A:** Elisa, look! I got the new Giles Collins CD.
B: 嘿，那很酷！	**B:** Hey, that's cool.
A: 我來放。	**A:** I'll put it on.
B: 我聽說他下個月會來這裡開演唱會。	**B:** I hear he's going to have a concert here next month.

A: 我們該買票。	**A:** We should get tickets.
B: 我會上網查，可能會很貴。	**B:** I'll check it out online. It could be expensive.
A: 對，但願音樂別這麼貴，我想要更多。	**A:** True. I wish music wasn't so expensive. I want to have more.
B: 那是每個人都在抱怨的。	**B:** That's what everyone complains about.
A: 你又說對了。	**A:** True again.
B: 「硬斃」樂團今晚將在「蹦跳廳」演奏。	**B:** The Rough B Band is playing tonight at Skips Lounge.
A: 最低消費是多少？	**A:** What's the cover?
B: 免費，今晚是女士之夜。	**B:** Free. It's Ladies Night.
A: 喔，對，我忘了，今天是星期三。	**A:** Oh, yeah. I forgot. This is Wednesday.
B: 我們要去嗎？	**B:** Think we should go?

A: 當然，我們該穿什麼？	**A:** Sure. What'll we wear?
B: 我們現在開始想吧。	**B:** Let's start figuring that out now.
A: 好！	**A:** Yes!

concert ['kɑnsɝt] n. 演唱會
cover ['kʌvɚ] n. 最低消費 (表演費、娛樂費)
Ladies Night n. 女士之夜

1. 我買了新 CD。
   I bought a new CD.
2. 我們來放吧。
   Let's play it.
3. 我來放。
   I'll put it on.
4. 好音樂！
   Great music!
5. 他要開演唱會。
   He's going to be in concert.
6. 我們要買票。
   We should buy tickets.
7. 票價多少？
   How much are tickets?

8. 他們今晚演出。

   They're playing tonight.

9. 有最低消費嗎？

   Is there a cover charge?

10. 他們幾點開始？

    What time do they start?

11. 我們早點去。

    Let's go early.

◆ **音樂與歌曲 Music and Songs**

rock (and roll)	搖滾
pop	流行
reggae	雷鬼
salsa	騷莎
classical	古典
jazz	爵士
opera	歌劇
gospel	福音
country	鄉村
folk	民謠
heavy metal	重金屬
hip hop	嘻哈
electronic music	電音
blues	藍調
fusion	融合
new age	新世紀
world music	世界音樂
duo	二重唱
trio	三重唱
quartet	四重唱

band	樂團
oldies but goodies	好聽的老歌
composer	作曲家
song wrtier	歌曲作曲家
lyrics	歌詞
lyricist	作詞者
copy right	著作權
pirated	盜版
Internet radio station	網路音樂電臺
radio station	電臺
radio program	廣播節目
download	下載
legal	合法的
illegal	非法的
royalty	版稅
hit	賣座

10.16 聊書籍與雜誌文章
Chatting about Books and Magazine Articles

A: 辛蒂，你讀了「成長」雜誌裡這篇關於經濟的文章嗎？

A: Cindy, did you read this article about the economy in *Going Up* magazine?

B: 沒有，我根本還沒看到新的一期。

B: No. I haven't seen the new edition at all.

A: 真的很有啟發性，我認為一大堆問題出自華爾街。

A: It's pretty revealing. I think a lot of trouble is coming for Wall Street.

B: 真的嗎？我得讀一讀。

B: Really? I'll have to read it.

A: 別錯過了。

A: Don't miss it.

B: 我不會，嘿，你有讀我告訴你的「休息5分鐘」裡的那篇文章嗎？

B: I won't. Hey! Did you read that article I told you about in *Take Five*.

A: 有，那篇也很好，跟我剛提到的文章有關。

A: Yes. That was good too. It relates with the article I just mentioned.

B: 你知道，寫這篇文章的人下週將要在一個研討會上講這個主題。

B: You know, the man that wrote that article is going to be at a conference to speak on the topic next week.

A: 研討會在哪裡？

A: A conference where?

B: 在城內。

B: Here in this city.

A: 不是玩笑吧，誰可以參加？

A: No kidding. Who can go?

B: 先到先贏，在本市的會議中心。

B: It's first come first serve at the city's convention center.

A: 誰主辦的？	**A:** Who's putting it on?
B: 本地的日報贊助。	**B:** It's being sponsored by the local daily newspaper.
A: 我們應該去。	**A:** We should go to it.
B: 或許，如果時間允許的話。	**B:** Maybe. If time allows.
A: 當然，當然。	**A:** Sure, sure.

article ['ɑrtɪkḷ] n. 文章
edition [ɪ'dɪʃən] n. 期，版
revealing [rɪ'vilɪŋ] adj. 啟發性的
Wall Street n. 華爾街
conference ['kɑnfərəns] n. 研討會
convention center n. 會議中心
put on 上演，演出
sponsor ['spɑnsɚ] v., n. 贊助 (者)
daily newspaper n. 日報

1. 這是本好雜誌。
   This is a good magazine.

2. 你該讀一讀這篇文章。

   You should read this article.

3. 我有訂閱。

   I subscribed to it.

4. 我每個月都讀。

   I read it every month.

5. 用我的書。

   Take my copy.

6. 我可以借你的雜誌嗎？

   Can I borrow your magazine?

7. 先到先贏。

   First come, first serve(d) .

8. 誰主辦的？

   Who's putting it on?

9. 如果時間允許的話。

   If time allows.

10.17 聊他人
Chatting about Other People

A: 我看到蓋瑞走向圖書館，我叫他，但他沒停下來。

A: I saw Gary going towards the library. I called to him, but he didn't stop.

B: 他大概要去莎琳的家。

B: He's was probably going to Charlene's house.

A: 為什麼？

A: Why?

B: 他們最近在約會。	**B:** They've been dating.
A: 真的啊，我不知道。	**A:** Really. I didn't know that.
B: 對，他們約會大概快要一個月了。	**B:** Yeah. They have been seeing each other for close to a month.
A: 我有點驚訝。	**A:** I'm kind of surprised.
B: 我倒不會。莎琳很好看而且相處起來又有趣。	**B:** I'm not. Charlene is good looking and fun to be with.
A: 那是真的，我猜我真的也沒什麼好驚訝的。	**A:** That's true. I guess I have nothing to be surprised about really.
B: 蓋瑞也是一個好人，他為一個兒童協會工作。	**B:** Gary is a good guy too. He works for a children's association.
A: 做什麼？	**A:** Doing what?
B: 他負責公眾體認活動以增加 (大眾) 對虐童的體認。	**B:** He manages a public awareness program to increase awareness of child abuse.
A: 不是開玩笑吧？那很了不起。	**A:** No kidding? That's something.

B: 是的，總之，我認為他們很適合。	**B:** Yes. Anyway, I think they are a good match.
A: 聽起來是的。	**A:** Sounds like it.

date [det] v. 約會
good looking 好看的
child abuse n. 虐童
awareness [ə'wɛrnɪs] n. 體認，察覺
match [mætʃ] n. 匹配

1. 他們最近在約會。
   They've been dating.
2. 不是開玩笑吧？
   No kidding?
3. 我不知道。
   I didn't know that.
4. 我有點驚訝。
   I'm kind of surprised.
5. 我感到驚訝。
   I'm surprised.
6. 與她相處很有趣。
   She is fun to be with.
7. 他們很適合。
   They're a good match.

10.18 聊網路
Chatting about the Internet

Dialog 對話

A: 我傳一個好用的網站連結給你。

A: I sent you a link to a good website.

B: 謝謝，我會看看。

B: Thanks. I'll look at it.

A: 是，我想你會喜歡。

A: Yeah. I think you'll find it to your liking.

B: 我喜歡看新網站，但很討厭有時候收到一些從註冊網站而來的垃圾郵件。

B: I like checking out new sites. I just hate getting the junk mail that sometimes comes with registering on some sites.

A: 我知道，那真的很煩，我的電子郵件現在過濾的不錯，所以現在不像以前一樣是個問題。

A: I know. It's a drag. My email system filters well now, so it's not the problem it used to be.

B: 你還有在寫部落格嗎？

B: Are you still running your blog?

A: 有啊，我最近有點散漫，但我一週至少更新1次。

A: Yeah. I've been kind of lax about it lately. But, I update it once a week at least.

B: 那很好，我放棄我的了，我最近沒時間。	**B:** That's good. I gave up on mine. I don't have time for it these days.
A: 我了解。	**A:** That's understandable.
B: 對啊，什麼事都沒空。	**B:** Yes. No time for anything.
A: 至少一週要收一下電子郵件。	**A:** Make sure you at least check you email once a week.
B: 我還是每天都收，如果不這麼做會完全脫離現實。	**B:** I still do that everyday. If I don't I'll get totally out of touch.
A: 對。	**A:** Exactly.

Word Bank 字庫

junk mail n. 垃圾郵件
filter ['fɪltɚ] v. 過濾
blog [blɑg] n. 部落格，網誌
lax [læks] adj. 散漫的
update [ʌp'det] v. 更新
out of touch 脫離現實

Useful Phrases 實用語句

1. 看這個連結。
   Check out this link.

2. 我在上網。

   I'm surfing the net.

3. 我傳一個連結給你。

   I'm sending you a link.

4. 我收到太多垃圾郵件。

   I've got too much junkmail.

5. 我必須在這個網站註冊。

   I have to register at this site.

6. 我得更新。

   I need to update.

7. 網站被駭客入侵了。

   The website is hacked.

10.19 聊新聞 Chatting about News

A: 哈囉，吉米。	**A:** Hello, Jimmy.
B: 嗨，卡爾，怎麼樣啊？	**B:** Hi, Carl. How's it going?
A: 還好吧，我想，我有點擔心我昨晚在電視上所聽到的。	**A:** OK, I guess. I'm kind of worried about what I heard on the TV news last night.
B: 為什麼？你聽到什麼？我昨晚沒看新聞。	**B:** Why is that? What did you hear? I didn't watch news last night.

A: 電視說本地的房市很糟，沒人要買。	**A:** It said that the local housing market is bad. Nobody is buying.
B: 我想那對你很不好因為你是木工，對嗎？	**B:** I guess that's bad for you because you are a carpenter, right?
A: 對，因為如果沒人買房子，那我幾乎就沒工作了。	**A:** Yes. If no one buys houses, then I have little work to do.
B: 那也會影響到我的工作，因為我的雇主賣（貨）給這裡的五金店。	**B:** It can impact my work too because my employer sells to hardware stores in the region.
A: 對啊，對我們這裡許多人都很不好。	**A:** Yeah. It's not good for a lot of us here.
B: 確實是的。	**B:** That's for sure.

Word Bank 字庫

housing market n. 房市
carpenter ['kɑrpəntɚ] n. 木工
impact [ɪm'pækt] v. 影響
hardware store n. 五金店

Useful Phrases 實用語句

1. 我有點擔心。
I'm kind of worried.

2. 那會影響到我的工作。

   It can impact my work.

3. 確實是的。

   That's for sure.

◆ **新聞與報紙 News and Newspapers**

headlines	頭條
breaking news	號外，快報
political news	政治新聞
international [world] news	國際新聞
Asia News	亞洲新聞
local news	本地消息
news commentaries	新聞評論
entertainment news	娛樂新聞
fashion news	流行新知
crime news	社會新聞
sports news	運動新聞
business news	商業新聞
(chief) editor	(總) 編輯
editorial	社論
gossip column	八卦專欄
paparazzi	狗仔隊
job ads	徵才廣告
classified ads	分類廣告
comics	卡通漫畫
weateher report	天氣預報
trend	趨勢
strike	罷工
crisis	危機
conflict	衝突

riot	暴動
war	戰爭
warm	溫馨的
depressing	令人沮喪的
news stories	新聞故事
news update	新聞更新
current news	時事
making news	製造新聞
publicity	知名度
anchor	主播
news reporter	主播，新聞記者
journalist	文字記者
live	現場

10.20 聊國際新聞 [全球議題]
Chatting about International News [Global Issues]

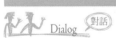

A: 你在做什麼？	**A:** What are you doing?
B: 看國際新聞。	**B:** Catching up on International news.
A: 是嗎？有什麼新消息？	**A:** Yeah? What's new?
B: 我最近讀到非洲動向。	**B:** I've been reading up on what's going on in Africa right now.

A: 我聽說安全協議有些問題。

A: I heard there are some problems with security agreements.

B: 對，墨西哥的貿易也有些問題。

B: Yes. There are also some problems in Mexico with trade.

A: 要了解那一堆事很難。

A: It's hard to understand all that stuff.

B: 對，我了解，我日復一日在讀，但還是不能完全理解問題的根源。

B: Yeah. I know. I keep reading about it day after day, but still don't fully understand the causes of the problems.

A: 我想「美國國家公共電臺」及「美國公共電視網」是最好的，讓我們獲得最深刻的了解。

A: I think *National Public Radio* and the *Public Broadcasting System* are the best for getting insights.

B: 真的不錯，一些網站也很好，但決定相信哪些網站很花時間。

B: They're really not bad. A lot of sites on the net are good too, but it takes time to decide which ones to trust.

A: 最好可以打聽或看其他的部落格，並看看你喜歡的作家是否有在你查看的新網站上。

A: It's good to ask around, check other blogs, and see if writers you like are found on new sites you look at.

B: 好建議。	**B:** Good advice.

security agreement n. 安全協議
cause [kɔz] n. 原因
National Public Radio n. 美國國家公共電臺 (NPR)
Public Broadcasting System n. 美國公共電視網 (PBS)

1. 我喜歡讀新聞。
   I like to read the news.
2. 我喜歡本地的報紙。
   I like the local newspaper.
3. 我每天看新聞。
   I watch the news every day.
4. 這是我最喜歡的新聞臺。
   This is my favorite news station.
5. 我覺得新聞的報導很不好。
   I think the news coverage is poor.
6. 我不太關心新聞。
   I don't care much about news.
7. 我偏好國際新聞。
   I prefer international news.

Unit 11 Common Functional Expressions

常用功能性用語

語言為表達工具，人們因應不同場合與情境來表達自我，彼此溝通。本章列出人們溝通時經常碰到的情境及各種功能性用語。

11.1 表達了解
Expressing Comprehension

A: 你去工作室前記得來辦公室與我會面。

A: Remember to meet me at the office before you go to the studio.

B: 為何我不能在工作室跟你碰面？

B: Why can't I just meet you at the studio?

A: 因為傑瑞要帶一些我們需要的東西過來我們辦公室。

A: Because Jerry is going to drop off some things we need at the office.

B: 你不能把那些東西拿到工作室嗎？

B: Can't you bring those things to the studio?

A: 我會在他到那裡之前就離開了。

A: I'll be gone before he gets there.

B: 但你說在我們去工作室之前記得到辦公室跟你碰面。

B: But you said to remember to meet you at the office before we go to the studio.

A: 不是，我要你到辦公室這裡來跟我碰面。

A: No. I want you to come to the office and meet me here before you go.

B: 我明白了，你要我在辦公室跟你碰面，一起等傑瑞，然後將他帶來的東西拿到工作室。

B: I see. You want me to meet you at the office. Then wait for Jerry, and then bring the things he drops off to the studio.

A: 你答對了。

A: You got it.

B: 好，沒問題。

B: OK. No problem.

studio ['stjudɪ,o] n. 工作室
drop off 放下

Useful Phrases 實用語句

1. 他的意思是什麼呢？
   What is he getting at?
2. 你知道我在說什麼嗎？
   Do you know what I am saying?
3. 你知道我的意思嗎？
   Do you know what I mean?
4. 你答對了。
   You got it.

回答別人「我懂了」是「I see」，而不是「I know」。(「I see」表示經過別人解釋弄明白了，是比較謙虛的說法；「I know」意味著本身就知道不需別人告知，可能讓人覺得自大)。

11.2 表達不了解 Expressing Non-Comprehension

A: 對不起，我不確定怎麼處理這個表格。	**A:** Excuse me. I'm not sure what to do with this form.
B: 你要先填好再帶到人事室。	**B:** You need to fill it out first. Then, take it to the personnel office.
A: 我要先預約嗎？	**A:** Will I need to make an appointment?
B: 你只要在5點以前到那裡。	**B:** You only need to get there by 5 p.m.
A: 我要在人事室等很久嗎？	**A:** Will I have to wait long at the personnel office?
B: 你只要先把表格拿到那裡就可以。	**B:** You only need to take the form there.

A: 真的嗎？我只要把它放在那裡就可以嗎？

A: Really? I just need to drop it off there?

B: 是的，那樣就可以了。

B: Yes. That's right.

A: 多謝你的幫忙。

A: Thanks for your help.

B: 沒什麼。

B: No problem.

form [fɔrm] n. 表格
fill out 填寫

1. 我不確定怎麼處理這個表格。
   I'm not sure what to do with this form.
2. 我不懂。
   I don't understand.
3. 我不懂。
   I don't get it.
4. 我感到困惑。
   I am confused.
5. 你可以示範 [指] 給我看嗎？
   Can you show me?
6. 我要等很久嗎？
   Will I have to wait long?

7. 真的嗎？

   Really?

8. 對。

   That's right.

「Excuse me.」(不好意思，對不起；用於必須打斷別人、引人注意、請問事情時)，「I'm sorry.」(對不起；用於道歉)。聽不懂時，不要裝懂也不要著急，冷靜地請對方重述或示範給你看就好，這是學習的機會，多數人了解這種情形，並且樂意幫助他人使溝通更順暢。

11.3 請求說明
Asking for Clarification

A: 嗨，鮑伯，明天七點半碰面。	**A:** Hi, Bob. We'll meet at 7:30 tomorrow.
B: 你說早上還是晚上的七點半呢？	**B:** Do you mean 7:30 a.m. or p.m.?
A: 我指的是晚上。	**A:** I mean p.m.
B: 那我們在你家還是其他地方碰面？	**B:** So we'll meet at your place or elsewhere?
A: 抱歉，我該說清楚，我們在網球場的停車場集合。	**A:** Sorry. I should make things clear. We'll meet at the tennis court parking lot.

A: 不好意思，菜單上的有些東西我不大懂。	A: Excuse me. I don't understand something on the menu.
B: 是什麼問題呢？	B: What is your question?
A: 標準早餐包括咖啡及馬芬鬆糕嗎？	A: Does the standard breakfast include coffee and a muffin?
B: 是的，如果在 10 點前點餐的話，否則就沒有了。	B: Yes, if you order before 10:00 a.m., otherwise they are not.
A: 只包含一杯咖啡嗎？	A: Is only one cup of coffee included?
B: 不是，續杯都是免費的。	B: No. Refills are always free.

Word Bank 字庫

muffin ['mʌfɪn] n. 馬芬鬆糕
refill ['riˌfɪl] n. 續杯

1. 這個我不是很確定，請再解釋一次。
   I'm not sure about this. Please explain it again.
2. 很抱歉，我只是想確定我了解 (然後提出問題)。
   I'm sorry. I just want to make sure I understand.

3. 抱歉打擾你，你剛才是說……？

Sorry to bother you, but did you say...?

4. 請再說一遍。

Say once more please.

5. 你是指 [你的意思是] ……？

Do you mean...?

6. 你剛才的意思是……？

Did you mean...?

「I have a question.」或「I have a problem.」兩者別混淆了。「question」指的是要問的問題，「problem」則是指造成的問題或麻煩。

馬芬鬆糕 (muffin) 與杯型蛋糕 (cupcake) 皆為杯狀，但馬芬鬆糕不甜且尺寸較大，常見核桃、巧克力、藍莓口味，口感厚實，作為早餐或午茶點心溫熱食用；杯型蛋糕造形低矮，上綴糖衣奶油，口感輕甜，作為 (特殊場合) 甜點。

11.4 確認 Confirmation

A: 請問，這是今晚會面的房間嗎？	**A:** Excuse me. Is this the room we should meet in tonight?
B: 不是，直走，在住宿登記處對面。	**B:** No, it's not. That room is down the hall and across from the check-in desk.
A: 有兩扇紅色大門的那間嗎？	**A:** The one with two large red doors?

B: 對，就是那間。	**B:** Yes. That's the one.

hall [hɔl] n. 走廊
across [ə'krɔs] prep. 對面
check-in desk n. 住宿登記處

A: 我可以幫你嗎？	**A:** May I help you?
B: 可以，我要買兩張下週的棒球票。	**B:** Yes. I'd like to buy two tickets for next week's baseball game.
A: 哪天晚上呢？	**A:** Which night?
B: 星期四晚上。	**B:** Thursday night.
A: 你希望坐在棒球場的哪一區呢？	**A:** Which area of the stadium do you want to be in?
B: 本壘附近。	**B:** Near home plate.

A: 好的，這是兩張下週四晚上靠近本壘的票。還需要什麼嗎？

A: OK. That's two tickets near home plate for next Thursday night's game. Anything else?

B: 不用，就這樣，謝謝！

B: No. That's all. Thanks.

stadium ['stedɪəm] n. 體育館
home plate n. 本壘

1. 這樣對嗎？
Is this right?
2. 我們走對方向嗎？
Are we going in the right direction?
3. 你確定沒問題？
Are you sure it's no problem?

◆ 確定與否的說法 **Expressing Certainty**

1. 確定的說法 Sure

①我確定。
I'm certain.

②我 (很/相當) 肯定。
I'm (very/pretty/really/fairly) sure.

③我絕對肯定。
I'm absolutely sure.

④肯定！
Positive!

⑤我確定。

I'm positive.

⑥我絕對確定 (以生命保證)。

I'm dead sure.

2. 不確定的說法 Not Sure

①我不確定。

I'm not really sure.

②我不是那麼確定。

I'm not so sure.

③事實上我不太確定。

I'm not sure actually.

11.5 請求重述
Requesting Repetition

A: 對不起，你可以告訴我荷曼博物館的地址嗎？	**A:** Excuse me, could you please tell me the address of the Holman Museum?
B: 當然可以，北 7 街 1254 號。	**B:** Of course. It's 1254 North 7th Avenue.
A: 您是說北7街1254號嗎？	**A:** Did you say 1254 North 7th Avenue?
B: 對。	**B:** Yes, that's right.
A: 非常謝謝你。	**A:** Thank you so much.

Dialog 2 對話2

A: 嗨！我可以怎麼幫你呢？	**A:** Hi. How can I help you?
B: 明天的旅遊還有名額嗎？	**B:** Are there still seats available for tomorrow's tour?
A: 有。	**A:** Yes, there are.
B: 行程是從早上 7 點開始嗎？	**B:** Does the tour start at 7:00 in the morning?
A: 對的。	**A:** That's right.
B: 我可以直接在這裡買票嗎？	**B:** Can I buy tickets right here?
A: 可以的，沒問題。	**A:** Sure, no problem.

1. 請您再重複一次好嗎？
   Could you repeat that please? (could 較客氣)
2. 請你再重複一次好嗎？
   Can you repeat that please? (can 較直接)
3. 請你再重複一次好嗎？
   Pardon? (即 May I beg your pardon? 音調提高請求重述)

4. 你剛說……？

   Did you say...?

5. 請你再重複一次。

   Say that again, please.

6. 可以請你說慢點嗎？

   Could you say that more slowly, please?

聽不懂或不知道怎麼做時，避免說「What?」(此字雖可表示疑問，但也經常表示驚訝、難以置信，有時具有挑釁意味)，而是說「Excuse me?」(加上列用句)，或說「Pardon?」即可。放輕鬆，請對方再說一遍，即使是同種族說相同語言的人也會有這種情形，重複說明是很稀鬆平常的事，也是學習必然且重要的過程。

11.6 請求幫忙
Asking for Favors

A: 嘿，山姆，你可以幫我個小忙嗎？	**A:** Hey, Sam. Can you do a small favor for me?
B: 或許吧。是什麼忙呢？	**B:** Maybe. What is it?
A: 我需要搬動這些行李箱。	**A:** I need help moving these suitcases.
B: 好，你要放到哪裡？	**B:** Oh, OK. Where do you want to put them?

A: 放到那邊吧。	**A:** Let's put them over there.

Dialog 2 對話2

A: 傑瑞，我需要幫忙。	**A:** Jerry, I need a favor.
B: 需要幫什麼忙呢，布魯斯？	**B:** What do you need, Bruce?
A: 我的車在（修車）廠裡，所以我需要搭便車。	**A:** Well, my car is in the shop, so I need a ride.
B: 我可以幫你，而且不管如何，我還欠你個人情。	**B:** I can do that for you. Besides, I owe you a favor anyway.
A: 為什麼？	**A:** For what?
B: 你不記得了嗎？兩星期前你載過我。	**B:** Don't you remember? You gave me a ride a couple of weeks ago.

Word Bank 字庫

shop [ʃɑp] n 修車廠 (= auto shop)

Useful Phrases 實用語句

1. 你可以幫我一下嗎？
   Can you help me out a minute?

2. 你可以幫我嗎？

Would you lend me a hand?

3. 對不起，我需要人幫忙。

Excuse me. I need a little favor done.

4. 需要幫忙嗎？

Need a hand?

11.7 請求許可
Asking for Permission

A: 我可以現在離開嗎？	A: Would it be all right if I left now?
B: 可以，你另外有約嗎？	B: Yes. Do you have another appointment?
A: 是的，在此鎮的另一邊，我可以使用電話嗎？	A: Yes, I do. It's across town. Can I use the phone?
B: 當然可以，在這裡。	B: Sure, of course. It's in here.
A: 抱歉這麼叨擾。	A: Sorry to be such a bother.
B: 沒關係的。	B: Forget about it.

「Would it be all right if I left now ？」是客氣的用法，用過去式「would 」及「left 」，是種假設的口氣。若被拒絕，彼此不會尷尬。

「appointment」指的是職業或商業上的約定，如「an appointment with Mr. Carson」(與卡森先生約定碰面) 或「a doctor's appointment.」(看醫生)；男女朋友間的約會用「date」。

Dialog 2 對話2

A: 我可以把這些東西留在這裡嗎？	**A:** Is it acceptable for me to leave these things here?
B: 我想可以吧，讓我先把其他東西挪開。	**B:** I think so. Let me move these other things first.
A: 你確定沒問題嗎？	**A:** Are you sure it's no problem?
B: 我肯定。	**B:** I'm certain.
A: 我也想在行李保管處放一份。	**A:** I would also like to put one in luggage storage.
B: 我現在就替你拿一份放進去。	**B:** I'll take it now and put it in for you.
A: 太好了，謝謝。	**A:** Terrific. Thanks.

acceptable [ək'sɛptəbḷ] adj. 可接受的

storage ['storɪdʒ] n. 保存；放置

請求許可 Asking for Permission

1. 這個可以嗎？

   Is this OK?

2. 我們可以現在進去嗎？

   May we go in now?

3. 我可以使用電話嗎？

   May [Can] I use the phone?

4. 我可以在這裡停車嗎？

   May [Can] I park here?

5. 我可以在這裡抽菸嗎？

   May [Can] I smoke here?

6. 你介意我抽菸嗎？

   Do you mind if I smoke?

7. 這裡可以抽菸 [露營，釣魚，游泳，跳水] 嗎？

   Is smoking [camping, fishing, swimming, diving] allowed here?

8. 我可以把這個留在這裡嗎？

   May I leave this here?

9. 我可以問一個問題嗎？

   May I ask a question?

10. 我可以摸你的狗嗎？

    May I pet your dog?

11. 我可以跟你的小孩玩嗎？

    May I play with your kids?

12. 我可以帶走這份簡介嗎？
    May I keep this brochure?
13. 我可以跟你照相嗎？
    May I take a photo with you?
14. 我可以替你拍照嗎？
    May I take a picture of you?
15. 可以給我你的簽名嗎？
    May I have your autograph?

許可 **Giving Permission**

1. 可以，沒問題。
   Yes, no problem.
2. 可以，請便。
   Yes, be my guest.
3. 可以，當然。
   Yes, by all means.
4. 可以，沒問題。
   Yes, that's fine.
5. 可以。(你被允許)
   Yes, you may.
6. 當然。
   Sure.
7. 請便。
   Go ahead.
8. 自己來。
   Help yourself.
9. 自由使用，不必客氣。
   Feel free to use it.

否定 (但客氣) 的說法 **Denying Permission Politely**

1. 我不確定。
   I'm not sure.

2. 我不認為你可以 (這麼做)。

I don't think you can.

3. 恐怕不能。

I'm afraid not.

4. 你大概不能。

You probably can't.

不允許 Denying Permission

1. 但願你不要 (抽菸)。

I'd rather you didn't (smoke).

2. 事實上我介意。

I do mind actually.

3. 不行。

No, you can't.

4. 不行。

No, you may not.

5. 不行。

No, it's not allowed.

用「may」請求較正式、有禮貌，用「can」較直接、不正式，國人習慣看到別人的寵物或小孩很可愛就伸手去摸或逗小孩，未先徵得主人或父母同意，是很不受歡迎的舉動。因為小孩抵抗力弱，有些父母不希望不熟識的人隨意觸碰小孩。

11.8 表達道謝及回應 Thanking and Responding

A: 那景點很棒，真高興你邀我來。

A: It was a great viewing spot. I'm so glad you invited me.

B: 我很高興你樂在其中。	**B:** I'm happy you enjoyed it.
A: 下次我們一定要在那裡待到日落。	**A:** Next time we must be there at sunset.
B: 那一定會很好玩。我們下週去吧。	**B:** That would be fun. Let's do it next week.
A: 好，那就這麼說定了，我會打電話給你。	**A:** OK. It's set. I'll call you.
B: 我迫不及待了呢。	**B:** I can't wait.

viewing spot n. 景點

Useful Phrases 實用語句

1. 說定了。
   It's set.
2. 我迫不及待。
   I can't wait.
3. 我很高興你樂在其中。
   I'm happy you enjoyed it.

「It's a deal!」是「It's set.」的另一種說法。更簡單些，直接問「Deal?」即可，回答也是「Deal!」另外常用的「Promise? Promise!」是保證的意思。

A: 你問了鮑伯週末會不會來與我們聚會嗎？	**A:** Did you ask Bob about coming with us this weekend?
B: 問了。	**B:** Yes, I did.
A: 他怎麼說呢？	**A:** What did he say?
B: 他說他一定會來。	**B:** He said he'd come for sure.
A: 好極了！謝謝你打電話給他。	**A:** Great! Thanks a lot for calling him.

1. 你聯絡鮑伯了嗎？
   Did you contact Bob?
2. 你打電話給鮑伯了嗎？
   Did you call Bob?
3. 謝謝你做了那件事。
   Thanks for doing that.

Dialog 3 對話3

A: 這裡就是你問起的餐廳。	**A:** Here is that restaurant you asked about.
B: 哇！我們來得真快。	**B:** Wow, we got here quick.
A: 我知道你真的很想嚐一嚐這裡有名的肋排。	**A:** Well, I know you really want to try the famous ribs here.
B: 當然了，再一次謝謝你是這麼一個好主人。	**B:** I sure do. Thanks again for being such a good host.
A: 這是我的榮幸。	**A:** My pleasure.

◆ **道謝與回應 Expressing Appreciation and Responding**

1. 道謝及不客氣有好幾種說法很常見

①非常謝謝你。

Thank you very much.

②多謝。

Thanks a lot.

③十二萬分感謝。

Thanks a million.

④我很感激。

I really appreciate it.

⑤謝謝，我非常感激這件事。

Thanks, I appreciate this a lot.

⑥我很感激。

I'm grateful.

⑦謝謝你的幫忙。

Thanks for all your help.

⑧謝謝你為我做的每件事。

Thanks for everything.

2. 有時再加上一兩句話，顯現對方的重要

①沒有你，我不可能辦到。

I couldn't have made it without you.

②謝你再多都不夠。

I can't thank you enough.

③沒有你，我不知道我會怎麼做。

I don't know what I would have done without you.

3. 回應 Responding

①不客氣。

You're welcome.

②當然的事 (我很開心幫到忙)。

Sure. (I'm glad I could help.)

③沒什麼。

No problem.

④那沒什麼。

It was nothing.

⑤無論何時都樂意幫忙。

Any time.

⑥樂意之至。

My pleasure.

4. 再加一兩句互挺對方的話

①這是朋友之道！

That's what friends are for!

②你也會這樣對我的。

You would have done the same for me.

11.9 表達稱讚 Complementing

A: 嘿，莎拉，你看起來很棒。	**A:** Hey, Sarah. You look great!
B: 謝謝。	**B:** Thanks.
A: 那件洋裝在你身上看起來很漂亮。	**A:** That dress looks lovely on you.
B: 你看起來 (也) 很好。	**B:** You look pretty good yourself.
A: 謝謝你的讚美。	**A:** Thank you for the compliment.
B: 我也要恭喜你的晉升。	**B:** I want to congratulate you on your promotion.
A: 喔！謝謝！我不知道我是否已為那個位子做好準備。	**A:** Oh! Thanks. I don't know if I'm ready for that position.
B: 我想你是的，你會做得很好，我確定。	**B:** I think you are. You'll do very well, I'm sure.

A: 謝謝你的支持，我有些緊張。

A: Thanks for the support. I'm sort of nervous about it.

B: 任何人都會的，但是你會做得很好，毫無疑問。

B: Anybody would be. You'll do fine though. No doubt about it.

Dialog 2 對話2

A: 嗨，凱莉，你看來令人驚豔。

A: Hi, Kelie. You look fabulous.

B: 謝謝，你看起來(也)很好。

B: Thank you. You look pretty good yourself.

A: 你這麼覺得嗎？

A: You think so?

B: 是的，我想你穿那顏色很好看。

B: Yes. I think that color looks very good on you.

A: 多謝，很高興聽到這句話。

A: Thanks so much. It's nice to hear that.

B: 我也要恭喜你昨天的簡報。

B: I also want to congratulate you on your presentation yesterday.

A: 喔，那沒什麼。

A: Oh, it was nothing.

初次見面
偶遇
邀請
參加聚會
接待賓客
拜訪
特殊情況
祝賀慰問
交友
日常社交
常用功能
其他功能

B: 不，真的！你做得很好，報告很棒。

B: No, really! You did well. It was very good.

A: 我花了很多時間準備。

A: I spent a lot of time preparing for it.

B: 看得出來。

B: It showed.

A: 我很受寵若驚。

A: I feel so flattered.

Word Bank 字庫

fabulous ['fæbjələs] adj. 令人驚豔的

Useful Phrases 實用語句

1. 你看起來令人驚豔。
   You look fabulous.
2. 你穿那顏色很好看。
   That color looks very good on you.
3. 我要恭喜你昨天的報告。
   I want to congratulate you on your report yesterday.
4. 你做得很好。
   You did well.
5. 做的不錯喔！
   Way to go!
6. 做得好！
   Well done!

7. 做得好！

Good job!

8. 很高興聽到這句話。

It's nice to hear that.

9. 你看起來也很好。

You look pretty good yourself.

10. 我花了很多時間準備。

I spent a lot of time preparing for it.

11. 看得出來。

It showed.

12. 我很受寵若驚。

I feel so flattered.

A: 嘿，傑瑞，你好嗎？	**A:** Hey, Jerry. How are you doing?
B: 好，謝謝，你呢？	**B:** Fine, thanks, and you?
A: 我也很好，我要告訴你我很喜歡你上週開的派對。	**A:** I'm OK too. I wanted to tell you how much I enjoyed your party last week.
B: 喔，太好了，很高興聽到你這麼說。	**B:** Oh, great. Glad to hear it.
A: 對，很好玩，你是個很好的主人。	**A:** Yeah. It was a lot of fun. You're a great host.

B: 謝謝你的讚美。	**B:** Thanks for the compliment.
A: 你應得的，我們都有段好時光。	**A:** You deserve one. We all had a great time.
B: 再次謝謝你。	**B:** Thanks again.

1. 我很喜歡你上週開的派對。
   I enjoyed your party last week.
2. 你是個很好的主人。
   You're a great host.
3. 很好玩。
   It was a lot of fun.
4. 我們都有段好時光。
   We all had a great time.
5. 很高興聽到你這麼說。
   Glad to hear it.
6. 謝謝你的讚美。
   Thanks for the compliment.
7. 你應得的。
   You deserve one.

A: 安，你是個好廚師。	**A:** Ann, you're a great cook.

B: 謝謝你，非常感謝你這樣說。

B: Thank you. That's kind of you to say.

A: 你在哪裡學會烹飪？

A: Where did you learn how to cook?

B: 我大多自己學的，但我也從我媽那裡學到一些技巧。

B: Mostly I'm self-taught, but I picked up some skills from my mother too.

A: 這道菜肴很棒，而且這雞肉美味到讓人口水直流。

A: This dish is wonderful, and the chicken is mouth watering delicious.

B: 你真是過獎了。

B: You praise me too much.

A: 我不認為，你媽一定很為你感到驕傲。

A: I don't think so. Your mother should be proud of you.

B: 她的確好像喜歡在她朋友面前誇耀我的廚藝。

B: She does seem to enjoy bragging to her friends about my cooking.

A: 嗯，她應該的，憑你這麼棒的食物可以開間餐廳了。

A: Well, she ought to. You could have a restaurant with food this good.

B: 謝謝，但不必了，我想我會為我的家人和朋友煮下去。

B: Thanks, but no thanks. I think I'll stick to cooking for my family and friends.

Word Bank 字庫

mouth watering 口水直流
brag [bræg] v. 說大話，自誇
stick to 堅持

1. 你是個好廚師。
   You're a great cook.
2. 你在哪裡學會烹飪？
   Where did you learn how to cook?
3. 你媽一定很為你感到驕傲。
   Your mother should be proud of you.
4. 非常感謝你這樣說。
   That's kind of you to say.
5. 我大多自己學的。
   Mostly I'm self-taught.
6. 我學到一些技巧。
   I picked up some skills.
7. 你真是過獎了。
   You praise me too much.

讚美別人的加強語氣不要用有負面意涵的「too」而是「very, really, pretty, so」等字。所以「You are too nice.」「You are too kind.」另有所指，意為你是濫好人，你「太」好心了或其他影射；「You are very nice! You are really kind!」(你真好！你真好心！) 才是真正的稱讚。

11.10 同意與附和
Agreeing and Responding to Agree

11.10a 演講 Speech

A: 我認為演講者很有趣。	**A:** I think the speaker was very interesting.
B: 我同意，有些想法很值得思考。	**B:** I agree. Some ideas are really thought provoking.
A: 對，我甚至沒像他一樣想到政府措施的後果。	**A:** Right. I haven't ever considered the consequences of government action the way he has.
B: 我也沒有，我想他真的讓我大開眼界。	**B:** Me either. I think he really opened my eyes.
A: 我懂你意思，下一回我聽到政府官員說話我會多想想。	**A:** I know what you mean. I'll think twice the next time I hear government officials speak.
B: 我也是。	**B:** I will, too.

Word Bank 字庫

provoke [prə'vok] v. 挑起，激起

consequence ['kɑnsə͵kwɛns] n. 後果

government action n. 政府措施

Useful Phrases 實用語句

1. 他真的讓我大開眼界。

   He really opened my eyes.

2. 我會多想想。

   I'll think twice.

3. 我懂你的意思。

   I know what you mean.

4. 我也沒有。

   Me either [neither].

5. 我也是。

   Me too.

◆ 同意 Agreeing

1. 肯定句的同意

A：我喜歡這個演講。

A: I like the speech.

B：我也是。

B: So do I./I like it too./ Me too.

2. 否定句的同意

A：我不喜歡這個演講。

A: I don't like the speech.

B：我也不喜歡。

B: Neither do I./ I don't like it either./ Me neither.

3. 否定的同意用 either 或 neither?

因為「Neither = not + either」，所以如果「not」出現在句子中就用「either (I don't like it either.) 」，沒有「not」，就用「neither.」，簡便口語正確用法為「Me neither.」，但「Me either.」也有人使用。

11.10b 電影評論 Movie Review

Dialog 對話

A: 我們今晚去看這部電影吧。	A: Let's go to this movie tonight.
B: 好，我聽說這部電影很棒。	B: All right. I've heard it's good.
A: 我讀到報紙的一篇關於它的影評說很值得看。	A: I read a review in the paper about it. It said it's worth seeing.
B: 我也讀了一篇。	B: I read one too.
A: 哪一篇？	A: Which one?
B: 柯林戈塔的評論。	B: Colin Goldtop's review.
A: 正是我讀的那篇！	A: That's the one I read!
B: 真的嗎？我想他的評論很精確。	B: Really? I think his reviews are pretty accurate.
A: 我也這麼想。	A: I think so too.

B: 好，那我們都覺得看這部電影好，對嗎？

B: Great. Then we both feel good about seeing this movie, right?

A: 沒錯！

A: No doubt!

review [rɪ'vju] n. 評論
accurate ['ækjərɪt] adj. 精確的

11.10c 選購衣物 Shopping for Clothes

A: 你覺得哪個顏色的上衣好看，藍色還是綠色？

A: Which color of these two tops do you think is better, the blue or the green?

B: 我覺得綠色的比較漂亮。

B: I think the green one is prettier.

A: 真的嗎？我也喜歡那件。

A: Really? I like it too.

B: 我認為綠色那件跟你穿的其他衣服比較搭。

B: I think the green one will go better with the other clothes you wear.

A: 聽起來有道理。

A: Sounds right to me.

B: 我認為這頂帽子也很可愛。

B: I think this hat is cute too.

A: 你說的對，它是很可愛。你想我該買它嗎？

A: You're right. It is. Do you think I should get it?

B: 是的，它讓你看起來可愛又聰明。

B: Yes, I do. It makes you look cute and smart.

A: 我喜歡你的品味。

A: I like your taste.

B: 謝謝。

B: Thanks.

1. 聽起來有道理。
   Sounds right to me.
2. 你說的對。
   You're right.
3. 我喜歡你的品味。
   I like your taste.

11.10d 討論重要事情 Discussing Something Important

A: 你認為他說的對嗎？

A: Do you think what he said is right?

B: 我不確定。	**B:** I'm not sure.
A: 我想至少我們可以想一想。	**A:** I think it's at least worth considering.
B: 我同意。	**B:** I agree with that.
A: 你認為我們今天該再和他談談嗎？	**A:** Do you think we ought to talk to him again today?
B: 是啊。	**B:** Yes, I do.

1. 你同意嗎？
   Do you agree?
2. 這個我不確定。
   I'm not sure about this.
3. 我們想一想吧。
   Let's think about it.
4. 值得考慮。
   It's worth considering.
5. 我們晚點再問。
   Let's ask again later.

11.10e 選擇餐廳 Choosing a Restaurant

Dialog 對話

A: 你想吃些什麼？	**A:** What do you want to eat?
B: 你有何建議嗎？	**B:** Do you have any suggestions?
A: 我知道有家不錯的墨西哥餐廳。	**A:** I know of a good Mexican restaurant.
B: 我不會反對這個提議。	**B:** I won't argue about that choice.
A: 他們也有不錯的墨西哥啤酒。你覺得呢？	**A:** They have good Mexican beer, too. What do you say?
B: 走吧！	**B:** Let's hit the road!

1. 我同意。
   I agree with that.
2. 我不會反對。
   I wouldn't argue about it.
3. 聽起來不錯。
   Sounds good to me.

4. 我想你是對的。

I believe you are right.

5. 毫無疑問。

No doubt.

6. 好主意。

Good idea.

7. 好，我會做這事。

OK, I'll do it.

8. 沒問題。

No problem.

9. 走吧！

Let's hit the road!

Unit 12 Other Functional Expressions

其他功能性用語

在日常生活裡，表達相反的意見很平常，但如果要向別人表達不滿，希望別人改進，就要小心使用語言並保持情緒平靜，以免傷了和氣。通常對方未必知道他們對你造成麻煩，因此口氣要婉轉，別人才能接受，當然平日碰面時的問候還是有其必要。

12.1 表達不同意 Expressing Disagreeing

12.1a 演講 Speech

A: 我認為演講者很好。	**A:** I think the speaker was really good.
B: 真的嗎？我認為他不怎麼有趣。	**B:** Really? I don't think he was very interesting.
A: 真的嗎？為什麼？	**A:** Really? Why not?
B: 我認為他講了一大堆沒人在乎的事情。	**B:** I think he talked about a lot of things no one cares about.
A: 那不是真的。	**A:** That's not true.
B: 是真的，誰想到政府時會想到那個？	**B:** It is true. Who thinks about that stuff when they think about governments?
A: 那才是重點！我們應該想到。	**A:** That's the point! We should think about it.

B: 我不同意。

B: I don't agree.

A: 你不同意那個？為什麼？

A: You don't agree with that? Why?

B: 我不懂有何道理要去想多數人不注意的事。

B: I don't see any reason to think about things that most of the population is totally unaware of.

A: 我想你沒抓到重點。

A: I think you're missing the point.

B: 什麼重點？

B: What point?

A: 教育大眾為何事情會按照現在的模式發生，才是唯一真正讓事情得以改變的方式。

A: That by educating people about why things occur the way they do is the only way things can ever really change.

B: 我不相信那樣會成功。

B: I don't believe it works.

A: 我想關於這個，我們必須同意彼此意見不一了。

A: I guess we will just have to agree to disagree about this.

B: 看起來似乎是。

B: So it seems.

educate ['ɛdʒəˌket] v. 教育
occur [ə'kɝ] v. 發生
agree to disagree 同意彼此意見不一

1. 那才是重點！
   That's the point!
2. 我不同意。
   I don't agree.
3. 但我不認為是這樣。
   But I don't think so.
4. 我不懂有何道理。
   I don't see any reason.
5. 你沒抓到重點。
   I think you're missing the point.
6. 我不相信會成功。
   I don't believe it works.
7. 我們意見不一。
   We just have to agree to disagree.

12.1b 電影評論 Movie Review

Dialog 對話

A: 我們去看那部電影。	**A:** Let's go to this movie tonight.
B: 我聽說那部不好。	**B:** I heard that it's bad.
A: 真的嗎？我讀了一篇關於它的評論說它很好。	**A:** Really? I read a review about it that said it's good.
B: 誰寫的評論？	**B:** Who wrote the review?
A: 柯林戈塔。	**A:** Colin Goldtop.
B: 喔，他喔！他的評論很差。	**B:** Oh, him! His reviews are poor.
A: 我認為他很精確。	**A:** I think he is quite accurate.
B: 我不認為，我從不同意他的電影評價。	**B:** I don't. I never agree with his assessment of a movie.
A: 我很驚訝，我認為他的評論相當好。	**A:** I'm so surprised. I think his reviews are pretty good.

B: 你應該看傑克亞庫曼的評論，他好多了。

B: You should read Jack Acuman's reviews. He is much better.

A: 呃，關於這部電影我認為你錯了，但是我會讀亞庫曼的評論。

A: Well, I think you're wrong about this movie, but I will read Acuman's review.

B: 很公平。

B: Fair enough.

1. 我從不同意他的評價。
   I never agree with his assessment.
2. 關於這個我認為你錯了。
   I think you're wrong about this.
3. 很公平。
   Fair enough.

12.1c 選購衣物 Shopping for Clothes

A: 你覺得哪個顏色的上衣比較好，藍色或綠色？

A: Which color of these two tops is better, blue or green?

B: 我喜歡藍色的。

B: I like the blue one.

A: 是喔，我以為你會挑綠色的。

A: Really. I thought you'd choose the green one.

B: 綠色在你身上沒那麼好看。

B: Green doesn't look that good on you.

A: 我認為好看。

A: I think it does.

B: 我認為你的膚色跟綠色不搭。

B: I think your skin color is wrong for green.

A: 沒有人注意那個。

A: Nobody notices that.

B: 你在開玩笑嗎？每個人都注意到了。

B: Are you kidding? Everybody notices that.

A: 才沒有。

A: They don't.

B: 他們會的。

B: They do.

A: 我想你太挑了。

A: I think you are being too picky.

B: 我不認為我很挑。真的！

B: I don't think I am. Really!

A: 呃，我不確定，我會考慮一下。	**A:** Well. I'm not sure. I'll think about it for a while.
B: 相信我，我是對的。	**B:** Trust me. I'm right.
A: 嗯，或許吧。	**A:** Hmmm. Maybe.

Word Bank 字庫

top [tɑp] n. 上衣
picky ['pɪkɪ] adj. 挑剔的

1. 綠色在你身上沒那麼好看。
   Green doesn't look that good on you.
2. 我認為你的膚色跟綠色不搭。
   I think your skin color is wrong for green.
3. 沒有人注意那個。
   Nobody notices that.
4. 你太挑了。
   You are being too picky.
5. 我會考慮一下。
   I'll think about it for a while.

「Everybody notices that.」(大家都注意到那個) 或「The color is wrong for you.」(這顏色不適合你) 不同意的口氣很強，要小心使用，通常僅限於家人、熟人或被允許用這種口氣說話的權威及專家們使用。「Some people might notice that.」(有些人可能會注意到，might 表示較低的可能性)，「The color doesn't seem right for you.」(這顏色似乎不適合你，加上「seem」（似乎）口氣較為緩和)，一般交情的人較容易接受。

12.1d 交通 Traffic

A: 8 點左右出發似乎是最好的主意。	**A:** It seems that going around 8 a.m. is the best idea.
B: 真的嗎？你確定嗎？我不認為。	**B:** Really? Are you sure? I'm not.
A: 為什麼？	**A:** How come?
B: 我認為交通會很糟。	**B:** I think the traffic will be bad.
A: 喔，對。那我們什麼時候去？	**A:** Oh. Good point. When should we go then?

初次見面 偶遇 邀請 參加聚會 接待賓客 拜訪 特殊情況 祝賀慰問 交友 日常社交 常用功能 其他功能

B: 很早去或10點左右。	**B:** Either very early or around 10.
A: 我不認為 10 點好。	**A:** I don't think 10 is good.
B: 會有什麼問題？	**B:** What would be the problem?
A: 我們很可能會遲到。	**A:** We'd most likely arrive late.
B: 對，你說的對，我們最好早點出門。	**B:** Yes, you're right. We'd better leave very early.

1. 會有什麼問題？

   What would be the problem?

2. 我們很可能會遲到。

   We'd most likely arrive late.

3. 我們最好早點出門。

   We'd better leave very early.

12.2 表達拒絕 Refusing

A: 我很抱歉，那天真的沒辦法參加。	**A:** I'm sorry, but I really can't participate that day.

B: 但是我們真的需要你，你一定要來。

B: But we really need you. You must come.

A: 不，我真的很抱歉，我沒辦法，我有別的重要約會必須要去。

A: No, I'm really sorry, but I can't. I have another important engagement I must go to.

B: 至少你可以來參加活動的後段部分嗎？

B: Can you at least make it to the later part of the event?

A: 不行，我真的很抱歉，真的沒辦法。

A: No. I'm terribly sorry. I really cannot.

Word Bank 字庫

participate [pɑr'tɪsə,pet] v. 參加
engagement [ɪn'gedʒmənt] n. 約定 (正式的說法)

Useful Phrases 實用語句

1. 我真的很抱歉。
   I'm really sorry.
2. 我非常抱歉。
   I'm terribly sorry.
3. 我那天真的沒辦法參加。
   I really can't participate that day.
4. 我有別的重要約會必須要去。
   I have another important engagement I must go to.

拒絕時，只說「No」是不夠的，必須說明理由，才不會顯得冷淡或無禮。

12.3 表達遺憾 Regretting

Dialog 1 對話1

A: 我很後悔我接了這份新工作。	**A:** I'm sorry I took this new job.
B: 為什麼？	**B:** Why?
A: 我的舊老闆好多了。	**A:** My old boss was a lot better.
B: 哪些方面？	**B:** In what ways?
A: 她比較有組織也較有耐性。	**A:** She was more organized and more patient.
B: 你可以回去嗎？	**B:** Can you go back there?
A: 不幸地，太遲了。	**A:** Sadly, it's too late.

organized ['ɔrgən,aɪzd] adj. 有組織的

Useful Phrases 實用語句

1. 我很後悔我接了這份新工作。
   I'm sorry I took this new job.
2. 我的舊老闆好多了。
   My old boss was a lot better.
3. 不幸地，太遲了。
   Sadly, it's too late.
4. 哪些方面？
   In what ways?
5. 你可以回去嗎？
   Can you go back there?

A: 嗨，鮑伯，我可以跟你談一分鐘嗎？	**A:** Hi, Bob. Can I talk to you a minute?
B: 好。	**B:** OK.
A: 我要因我昨晚說的話向你道歉，那很無禮。	**A:** I want to apologize for what I said last night. It was rude.
B: 好，沒關係，我也說了侮辱人的話。	**B:** OK. It's all right. I said some insulting things too.

A: 我想我們都有一點激動了。

A: I guess we both got a little carried away.

B: 我想是吧，我也很抱歉。

B: I think so. I'm sorry too.

A: 好，我們忘掉它吧。

A: OK. Let's forget about it.

B: 好，我們和解吧。

B: Right. Let's bury the hatchet.

Word Bank 字庫

insulting [ɪn'sʌltɪŋ] adj. 侮辱的
hatchet ['hætʃɪt] n. 短柄斧頭

Useful Phrases 實用語句

1. 我們都有一點激動。
   We both got a little carried away.
2. 我錯了。
   My mistake.
3. 是我不好 (不正式)。
   My bad.
4. 我們忘掉它吧。
   Let's forget about it.
5. 我們和解吧。
   Let's bury the hatchet.

Dialog 3 對話3

A: 真希望我沒挑上這件裙子。	**A:** I wish I hadn't picked this skirt.
B: 為何？	**B:** Why?
A: 跟我的上衣不搭。	**A:** It doesn't go well with my blouse.
B: 我覺得不錯。	**B:** I think it's not bad.
A: 謝謝，但我真的後悔這個選擇。	**A:** Thanks, but I really regret this choice.

1. 真希望我沒有挑上這件裙子。

   I wish I hadn't picked this skirt.

2. 跟我的上衣不搭。

   It doesn't go well with my blouse.

3. 我真的後悔這個選擇。

   I really regret this choice.

A: 你喜歡這電影嗎？	**A:** Did you like the movie?

B: 不喜歡。	**B:** No.
A: 抱歉我拉你來。	**A:** Sorry I dragged you to it.
B: 沒關係，我因愛而來。	**B:** That's OK. I did it for love.
A: 真的嗎？	**A:** Really?
B: 真的。	**B:** Yes.
A: 下一次我會陪你看任何你想看的電影。	**A:** Next time I'll go to whatever movie you want to see.
B: 你可能會後悔。	**B:** You might be sorry.
A: 如你說的，為了愛。	**A:** Like you said, for love.

Useful Phrases 實用語句

1. 抱歉我拉你來。
   Sorry I dragged you to it.
2. 我因愛而來。
   I did it for love.

3. 你可能會後悔。

You might be sorry.

12.4 表達情緒 Expressing Emotions

12.4a 表達驚訝 Expressing Surprises

A: 哇！這是何時發生的？	**A:** Wow! When did this happen?
B: 昨晚深夜，有人侵入。	**B:** Late last night. Somebody broke in.
A: 警察來過了嗎？	**A:** Have the police been here?
B: 他們現在在這裡。	**B:** They're here now.
A: 每樣東西都一團亂，我們怎麼工作啊？	**A:** Everything is a mess. How can we do our jobs?
B: 沒辦法，我們可以回家。	**B:** We can't. We can go home.
A: 你在開我玩笑！	**A:** You're kidding me!

B: 不，珍說我們最好休一天假。	**B:** No. Jane said we might as well take the day off.
A: 我想那樣有道理。	**A:** I guess that makes sense.
B: 讓我告訴你一件事。	**B:** Let me tell you something.
A: 什麼呢？	**A:** What's that?
B: 他們懷疑是安德魯做的。	**B:** They suspect Andrew did it.
A: 什麼！我無法置信！	**A:** What! I can't believe it!

Word Bank 字庫

break in 侵入
take off 休假
suspect [sə'spɛkt] v. 懷疑

Useful Phrases 實用語句

1. 老天！
   Gee!
2. 天啊！
   My goodness!

3. 我的天！

My God!

4. 哇！

Wow!

5. 你在開玩笑！

You're kidding me!

6. 什麼！

What!

7. 我無法置信！

I can't believe it!

8. 這是個玩笑嗎？

Is this a joke?

9. 我無法相信我的眼睛 [耳朵]！

I can't believe my eyes [ears]!

10. 這令人無法置信！

This is unbelievable [incredible]!

11. 你在開我玩笑！

You're pulling my leg!

12. 你一定在開玩笑！

You must be joking!

13. 我很震驚！

I'm shocked!

14. 我一定在作夢！

I must be dreaming!

15. 到底發生什麼事？

What on earth happened?

16. 那 (事件) 到底何時發生的？

When on earth did that happen?

12.4b 表達憂慮 Expressing Worries

A: 我不確定這個計畫。	**A:** I'm not sure about this plan.
B: 你擔心什麼？	**B:** What are your concerns?
A: 看起來我們似乎沒有足夠的時間把全部東西整理好。	**A:** It seems that we don't have enough time to pull all this together.
B: 我知道你的意思，我也很擔心。	**B:** I know what you mean. It worries me a lot too.
A: 我也不確定預算會支付這個計畫。	**A:** I'm not sure the budget will cover this project either.
B: 我在上次會議中表示過疑問。	**B:** I expressed doubts about that at the last meeting.
A: 我記得，你說資金何時會進來並不清楚。	**A:** I remember that. You said it isn't clear that the funding will come in on time.
B: 對，那就是問題，這個計畫的財源仍然沒有完全確定。	**B:** Yes, that's the problem. The finance of this project is still not completely settled.

Word Bank 字庫

fund [fʌnd] v. 提供資金
finance [faɪ'næns] n. 財源

Useful Phrases 實用語句

1. 你擔心什麼？
What are your concerns?
2. 我很擔心。
It worries me a lot.
3. 你為何不開心嗎？
What's bothering you?
4. 你為何鬱卒？(不正式)
What's eating you?
5. 你為何鬱卒？(不正式)
What's bugging you?
6. 開心點。
Lighten up.
7. 保持冷靜。
Stay [Keep, Be] cool.
8. 冷靜下來。
Calm down.
9. 放輕鬆。
Take it easy.
10. 放輕鬆。
Chill out.
11. 放輕鬆。
Relax.

12.4c 表達悲傷 Expressing Sadness

Dialog 對話

A: 我看到莎琳離開很傷心。

A: I'm sad to see Charlene go.

B: 我也是，她迷人又有趣。

B: Me too. She is so charming and fun to be around.

A: 我同意，我真的會想念她。

A: I agree. I'll really miss her.

B: 我很遺憾沒去她的生日派對。

B: I'm sorry I didn't make it to her birthday party.

A: 我也錯過了，但我寄了禮物。

A: I missed it also. I did send a gift.

B: 我沒有，我一直把買東西給她的事拖到來不及了。

B: I didn't. I kept putting off getting her something until it was too late.

A: 你可以在生日之後給她。

A: You could have given it to her after her birthday.

B: 我知道，但我一直閒晃沒做個決定買什麼給她，現在我覺得很蠢。

B: I know, but I kept fooling around not making a decision about what to get for her. Now I really feel foolish.

A: 你看起來像快要哭了。

A: You look like you're going to cry.

B: 她是個好朋友及同事，我覺得很傷心。

B: She's a good friend and a great coworker. I feel sad.

Word Bank 字庫

charming ['tʃɑrmɪŋ] adj. 迷人的

put off 拖延

fool around 胡搞，瞎混

Useful Phrases 實用語句

1. 言語不足以說明我的悲傷。

   Words are not enough to express my sadness.

2. 我看到 [聽到，知道] ……很悲傷。

   I am sad to see [hear, know]...

3. 這真是令人傷心。

   This is really heartbreaking.

4. 我很想哭。

   I feel like crying.

5. 我的淚水湧了上來。

   I'm tearing up.

6. 你的眼淚湧了上來。

   Your eyes are welling up.

7. 你要哭了嗎？

   Are you welling up?

8. 你在哭嗎？

   Are you weeping?

9. 她因為失去小狗而悲傷。

   She was saddened by the loss of her dog.

10. 她讓朋友們流淚。

    She made her friends in tears.

11. 她哭得很傷心。

    She was crying her heart out.

12.4d 表達失望 Expressing Disappointment

Dialog 對話

A: 我昨晚沒去看我女兒的表演。	**A:** I didn't make it to my daughter's performance last night.
B: 那真可惜。	**B:** That's too bad.
A: 對，但願我可以早點離開那個不得不去的會議。	**A:** Yeah. I wish I could have got out of having to go to that meeting.
B: 她會有別的表演嗎？	**B:** Will she do another performance?
A: 不會，但願他們會有另一場，但我知道他們沒有。	**A:** No. I wish they would do another, but I know they won't.
B: 你怎麼知道？	**B:** How do you know?

A: 它是學校的年度活動。	A: It's an annual event the school does.
B: 你錯過實在很可惜。	B: It's really a shame you missed it.
A: 對，我女兒也很失望。	A: Yeah. My daughter is disappointed too.
B: 她會原諒你的。	B: She'll forgive you.

annual event n. 年度活動
shame [ʃem] n. 憾事

Useful Phrases 實用語句

1. 我昨晚沒去成 [沒做到]。
   I didn't make it.
2. 但願他們會有另一場。
   I wish they would do another.
3. 她很失望。
   She is disappointed.
4. 它是學校的年度活動。
   It's an annual event.
5. 實在很可惜。
   It's really a shame.
6. 真可惜！
   What a shame!

7. 她會原諒你。
   She'll forgive you.

12.4e 表達煩惱 [憤怒] Expressing Annoyance [Anger]

Dialog 對話

A: 這真的讓我很火大。	**A:** This is really annoying me.
B: 什麼事？	**B:** What is?
A: 這個電腦程式。	**A:** This computer program.
B: 為什麼？	**B:** Why?
A: 它每隔10分鐘就一直重複下載。	**A:** It keeps reloading itself about every ten minutes.
B: 那很奇怪。	**B:** That sounds odd.
A: 我很生氣，我想把這部電腦從窗戶丟出去。	**A:** It's making me angry. I want to throw this computer out a window.
B: 別這麼做，打電話給技術部門。	**B:** Don't do that. Call tech. services.

A: 他們也讓我火大，他們到這裡要花一輩子的時間。

A: They drive me crazy too. It takes them forever to get here.

B: 讓珍妮打電話給他們，她知道怎麼讓他們快一點。

B: Have Jenny call them. She knows how to make them hurry up.

A: 那又讓我更火大，她可以那樣做只因為那些傢伙認為她漂亮。

A: That just angers me too. She can do that just because those guys think she's pretty.

B: 對，但至少那讓他們來這裡。

B: True, but at least it gets them here.

A: 好，要不那樣我就要爆炸了！

A: OK. It's either that or I explode!

annoy [ə'nɔɪ] v. 惹惱

reload [ri'lod] v. 重新裝填

1. 真煩！

   It's annoying!

2. 我被電腦氣死了。

   I'm very upset by the computer.

3. 它把我氣瘋了。

   It drives me crazy.

4. 它讓我抓狂！

   It drives me nuts!

5. 噪音真是不勝其煩。

   The noise is getting in my hair.

6. 我被惹毛了。

   It's getting on my nerves.

7. 我在扯頭髮了。

   I'm tearing my hair.

8. 這真荒謬！

   This is ridiculous!

9. 這真荒謬！

   It is absurd!

10. 這完全令人無法接受！

    This is totally unacceptable!

每種語言都有髒話 (dirty words) ，中文有許多三字經，英語裡則有許多的四字經，既使是憤怒的時候也不應出口成髒 (foul-mouthed) ，那只會使情況更糟。

12.4f 談惹人厭的事 Talking about Pet Peeves

Dialog 對話

A: 我真受不了卡拉在工作時講手機。	**A:** It really bothers me when Carla talks on her cell phone during work hours.
B: 我懂你的意思，她說話的方式讓人討厭。	**B:** I know what you mean. She has such an annoying way of talking.
A: 還有她說的內容。	**A:** And what she talks about.

B: 對，她總是不斷地說她家人多蠢。

B: Right. She is always going on about how her family is so stupid.

A: 而且說太大聲了，讓我快抓狂。

A: And she is so loud about it. It drives me nuts.

B: 我也是，讓我快瘋了，她每天都這樣。

B: Me too. It's making me crazy. She does it every day.

A: 如你所言，她在工作時間都這樣。

A: Like you said, she does it during work time.

B: 對，她至少該等到午餐時間，大家才不會被迫聽到。

B: Yeah. She ought to at least wait till lunch so we all don't have to listen to her.

A: 我想那很難去要求。

A: I guess that's too much to ask.

B: 似乎是如此。

B: Apparently so.

Language Power 字句補給站

◆ 談惹人厭的事常用句型

Expressions for Talking about Pet Peeves

①人們說話大聲讓我討厭 (bother 也可以用 upset 或 annoy代替)。

It bothers me when people talk loudly.

②我討厭 [受不了] 無禮的人。

I hate [can't stand] it when people are rude.

12.5 表達期許與抱怨
Expressing Wishes and Complaints

A: 嗨，抱歉打擾你，但我希望你能把電視關小聲點。	A: Hi, sorry to bother you, but I wish you would turn the TV down.
B: 喔，抱歉，我不知道那麼大聲。	B: Oh, sorry, I didn't know it was loud.
A: 我必須準備明天的報告。	A: I have to prepare for a report tomorrow.
B: 好，我會保持小聲。	B: OK, I'll keep the volume down.
A: 謝謝你，我感謝你這麼做。	A: Thanks. I appreciate it.

turn down 關小聲
volume ['vɑljəm] n. 音量

1. 抱歉打擾你。
   Sorry to bother you.
2. 我希望你能把電視關小聲點。
   I wish you would turn the TV down.

3. 我必須準備明天的報告。

I have to prepare for a report tomorrow.

4. 我感謝你這麼做。

I appreciate it.

5. 我不知道那麼大聲。

I didn't know it was loud.

6. 我會保持小聲。

I'll keep the volume down.

A: 嗨，杜立德先生，你好嗎？	**A:** Hi, Mr. Doolittle, how are you?
B: 我很好，你呢，莎莉？	**B:** I'm fine, and you, Sally?
A: 我也很好，但是我需要跟你談談你的狗。	**A:** I'm fine too, but I need to talk to you about your dog.
B: 是什麼事呢？	**B:** Yes, what is it?
A: 牠很可愛，可是我希望牠不會來花園吃我的花。	**A:** It is a cute dog, but I wish it wouldn't come eat my flowers in the garden.
B: 喔，我真的很抱歉，這隻狗在長牙齒並且在這年紀很好奇。	**B:** Oh, I'm really sorry. The dog is teething now and is quite curious at this age.

A: 我也怕牠會生病。	**A:** I'm afraid it might get sick too.
B: 你可以帶我看牠吃了什麼嗎，莎莉？	**B:** Can you show me what it ate, Sally?
A: 當然可以，杜立德先生，跟我來。	**A:** Of course, Mr. Doolittle, just follow me.

teethe [tið] v. 長牙齒

1. 我可以跟你談一下嗎？
   Can I talk to you a minute?
2. 我需要問你一件事。
   I need to ask you about something.
3. 你有一點時間嗎？
   Got a minute?
4. 關於這個我很抱歉。
   I'm sorry about this.
5. 關於這個我真的很抱歉。
   Really sorry about this.
6. 我會馬上處理。
   I'll take care of this right away.
7. 恐怕有個問題。
   I'm afraid there is a problem.
8. 我要跟你談一個問題。
   There's a problem I need to talk to you about.

向他人提出抱怨及期待改進並不是件簡單的事，心裡即使不舒服，在言語上要格外小心，可能別人根本不知道他們對你造成什麼困擾，尤其鄰居之間常常會碰面，關係弄僵會使雙方都很不自在。因此提出問題時要加幾個字婉轉地說「Sorry to bother you, but...」或「I am afraid there is a problem.」，而非毫不考慮地說「Excuse me. The music is too loud!」「You have a bad dog！」，咄咄逼人的口氣馬上使關係降到冰點。使用「wish」接過去式，用「但願」的口吻「I wish you would turn the TV down.」「I wish your dog wouldn't eat my flowers.」給人感受完全不同，禮貌堅定地要求自己的權益 (通常美國人會反應而非委屈自己)，也別忽略維持平時的問候。

12.6 表達道歉及回應
Apologizing and Responding

A: 抱歉，我遲到了，我被困在車陣裡了。	**A:** Sorry, I'm late. I got stuck in traffic.
B: 沒關係。	**B:** That's all right.
A: 我以後不會再犯了，真抱歉。	**A:** I won't let it happen again. I'm really sorry.
B: 算了，沒什麼大不了的。	**B:** Forget it. It's no big deal.

道歉 Apologizing

1. 抱歉。

   Sorry.
2. 我很抱歉。

   I'm very sorry.
3. 我非常抱歉。

   I'm terribly sorry.
4. 我非常抱歉。

   I'm awfully sorry.
5. 那件事很抱歉。

   Sorry about that.
6. 請原諒我。

   Please forgive me.
7. 因為這個我很不好意思。

   I'm so embarrassed by this.
8. 我很抱歉造成你的困擾。

   I'm very sorry for causing you trouble.
9. 我以後不會再犯了。

   I won't let it happen again.
10. 下不為例。

    It will never happen again.

解釋原因 Explaining Reasons

1. 我被…困住了。

   I got stuck in...
2. 我的手機沒電了。

   My cell phone was out of battery.

3 突然有事。

Things came up.

詢問原因 [表達關心] Asking for Reasons [Showing Concerns]

1. 怎麼了？

   What was wrong?

2. 發生什麼事？

   What happened?

3. 你為何耽擱？

   What was holding you up?

回應 Responding

1. 沒關係。

   That's all right.

2. 算了。

   Forget it.

3. 沒關係，算了。

   Never mind.

4. 沒關係。

   It doesn't matter.

5. 沒什麼大不了的。

   It's no big deal.

A: 喔，你來了。你發生了什麼事嗎？	**A:** Oh, there you are. What happened to you?
B: 我必須為昨天沒來而道歉。	**B:** I must apologize for not being here yesterday.
A: 你昨天怎麼了？你去哪裡了？	**A:** What happened to you yesterday? Where were you?

B: 昨天我必須去醫院。	**B:** I had to go to the hospital.
A: 為什麼？	**A:** Why?
B: 我生病了所以去了醫院，我告訴導遊了。	**B:** I got sick and went to a hospital. I told our tour guide.
A: 我想他忙到忘了告訴我們。	**A:** I guess he was too busy to tell us.

Useful Phrases 實用語句

1. 真遺憾聽到這件事。
   I'm sorry to hear that.
2. 我希望你接受我的道歉。
   I hope you accept my apology.
3. 抱歉，我今晚沒辦法來。
   Sorry, but I can't make it tonight.
4. 請為此原諒我。
   Please forgive me for this.

Notes 小叮嚀

道謝和道歉一樣是基本禮儀，大小事情都適用。「Where were you?」(你去那裡了) 要看交情及情況問，並非每個人都樂意回答這個問題。

12.7 表達建議 Giving Suggestions

Dialog 1 對話1

A: 嘿，瑪莉，我想學個新技藝，你有什麼建議？	**A:** Hey, Mary, I'm thinking about learning a new skill. Do you have any suggestions?
B: 做陶器如何？	**B:** How about pottery?
A: 哇，聽起來很酷！	**A:** Wow. That sounds cool!
B: 我一年前學過，很好玩。	**B:** I took it up a year ago. It's fun.
A: 你在哪裡學？	**A:** Where did you learn?
B: 本地的社區大學有很棒的課，老師也很有趣。	**B:** The local community college has great classes. The teacher is funny too.
A: 貴不貴？	**A:** Is it expensive?
B: 不算貴，我付了250元，包含所有材料。	**B:** Not really. I paid $250 for everything including all the materials.

A: 不會弄得很髒嗎？	**A:** Don't you get dirty?
B: 你會有一件圍裙，但是最好穿件可以弄髒的衣服。	**B:** You have an apron, but it is best to wear clothing that's OK to get messy.
A: 我需要買什麼？	**A:** What do I need to buy?
B: 學校幾乎提供所有東西，你只要出現就行。	**B:** The school provides almost everything. You only need to show up.
A: 我今天就打電話給他們。	**A:** I'm going to call them today.

Word Bank 字庫

pottery ['pɑtərɪ] n. 陶器製造
community college n. 社區大學
apron ['eprən] n. 圍裙
messy ['mɛsɪ] adj. 髒亂的

Useful Phrases 實用語句

1. 你有什麼建議？
   Do you have any suggestions?
2. 很好玩。
   It's fun.
3. 我需要買什麼？
   What do I need to buy?

4. 你只要出現就行。

You only need to show up.

Tips 小祕訣

維持友誼的辦法是不要隨便就給人建議 (有時朋友只是想要有人傾聽)，除非別人向你尋求意見。

Dialog 2 對話2

A: 嗨，亞倫，你有去過俄羅斯嗎？	**A:** Hi, Allan, Have you been to Russia?
B: 有。	**B:** Yes.
A: 你可以推薦那裡的一些地方給我嗎？	**A:** Can you recommend any places there to me?
B: 當然，我知道很多好地方，你對哪類地方有興趣？	**B:** Sure. I know of a lot of great spots. What kind of places are you interested in?
A: 我喜歡建築。	**A:** I like architecture.
B: 好，那，我想你會喜歡莫斯科跟聖彼得堡。兩者都有很美妙的建築。	**B:** Well, then, I think you can enjoy Moscow and St. Petersburg. Both have wonderful architecture.
A: 很難找嗎？	**A:** Is it hard to find?

B: 不會，現在有很多旅行團可以選擇，或者你可以用地圖找建築物。	**B:** No. There are many tours available these days, or you can just find buildings by using a map.
A: 聽起來很方便。	**A:** Sounds convenient.
B: 很不錯。	**B:** It's not bad.

Russia ['rʌʃə] n. 俄羅斯
recommend [ˌrɛkə'mɛnd] v. 推薦

1. 你可以給我一些建議嗎？
   Can you give some advice?
2. 你推薦什麼？
   What do you recommend?
3. 我需要一些主意。
   I need some ideas.
4. 我該去哪裡？
   Where should I go?
5. 我該做些什麼？
   What should I do?
6. 我該找誰談？
   Who should I talk to?
7. 你覺得我的計畫 [點子] 如何？
   What do you think of my plan [idea]?

8. 何時是去那裡的好時機？

When is a good time to go there?

Tips 小祕訣

當你請別人推薦時，要仔細聽答案，眼睛直視對方，注意自己的肢體語言，不要分心看不相干的東西，如果別人知道你是認真地在請教，會樂於給更多、更內行的資訊。

12.8 表達鼓勵 Encouraging

A: 嗨，芭芭拉，今天好好表現。	**A:** Hi, Barbara. Do well today.
B: 謝謝，我有些緊張。	**B:** Thanks. I'm kind of nervous.
A: 那很正常。	**A:** That's natural.
B: 我知道，但那是不好的感覺。	**B:** I know, but it's a bad feeling.
A: 你會沒事，你準備得很好。	**A:** You'll be fine. You're well prepared.
B: 我知道，但我從來沒有在這麼多人面前這麼做。	**B:** I know, but I've never done this in front of so many people.

A: 你可以做到的，我知道你可以。 → **A:** You can do it. I know you can.

B: 好，謝謝你的鼓勵。 → **B:** OK. Thanks for encouraging me.

1. 今天好好表現。
   Do well today.
2. 你準備得很好。
   You're well prepared.
3. 昂首向前。
   Keep your chin up.
4. 你可以做到！
   You can do it!
5. 我知道你可以。
   I know you can.
6. 你具有所需要的一切能力。
   You've got everything it takes.
7. 要有自信。
   Be sure of yourself.
8. 盡你最大的努力！
   Do your best!
9. 盡力去做。
   Give it your best shot.
10. 要有信心！
   Have faith!
11. 我相信你。
   I believe in you.

12. 我相信你。

I have faith in you.

Dialog 2 對話2

A: 我真的為明天的大考緊張。	**A:** I'm really nervous about tomorrow's big test.
B: 為什麼？	**B:** Why?
A: 我有在衝刺，但我不覺得已準備好。	**A:** I've been cramming for it, but I don't feel ready.
B: 嘿，記住，這科你很拿手。	**B:** Hey, remember, you're good at this subject.
A: 謝謝，但這個考試是最重要的。	**A:** Thanks, but this test is the most important one.
B: 所有考試你都考得很好，你會再次考得很好。	**B:** You've done well on all the tests. You'll do well again.
A: 我想是吧，我真的想拿到證書。	**A:** I suppose. It's just that I really want to get the credential.
B: 你會的。	**B:** You will.

A: 謝謝你的鼓勵。

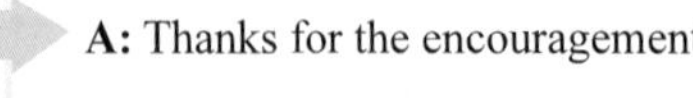

A: Thanks for the encouragement.

B: 沒什麼，你會通過的，沒問題。

B: It's nothing. You'll pass, no problem.

nervous ['nɝvəs] adj. 緊張的
cram [kræm] v. 強塞硬擠、衝刺
credential [krɪ'dɛnʃəl] n. 證書

1. 這科你很拿手。
   You're good at this subject.
2. 你會再次考得很好。
   You'll do well again.
3. 沒什麼。
   It's nothing.
4. 你會通過的。
   You'll pass.
5. 沒問題。
   No problem.
6. 要樂觀。
   Be positive.
7. 正面思考。
   Think positive.
8. 加油！
   More power to you!

Dialog 3 對話3

A: 做得好，莎莉！

A: Way to go, Sally!

B: 我做得好嗎？

B: Did I do well?

A: 是！你做得很好。

A: Yes! You did.

B: 我想我只是幸運。

B: I think I just got lucky.

A: 才不是，你可以做到，你剛剛證明了。

A: No way. You can do it. You just proved it.

B: 我不確定我可以再做一次。

B: I'm not sure I can do it again.

A: 你可以，我知道你可以，我們都知道。

A: You can. I know you can. We all know it.

B: 謝謝。

B: Thanks.

「希望」與「愛」可說是人類共同的信仰，家人、朋友、同事之間有機會給人讚美及鼓勵就不要吝嗇，鼓勵他人可以讓人保有更堅定的意志去克服困難。

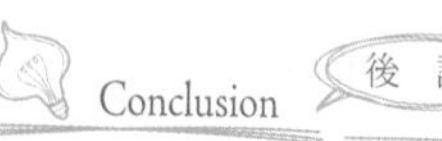

參與社交活動除對他人開放心胸，向他人學習之外，如有機會擔任世界志工 (world volunteer) 盡己之力，以英語或其他語言作為溝通工具，實現國際社會互助互愛理念，使世界更美好，個人也必然獲得豐碩的國際觀與歷練！

Appendices

附錄

1. 不規則變化動詞 Irregular Verbs
2. 溫度換算 Temperature Conversion
3. 美國假日 Holidays in the USA
4. 電影分級 Movie Ratings in the United States
5. 美國中央情報局世界百科：世界與美國人口資料 CIA-The World Factbook: Population Data (the World and the United States)

1. 不規則變化動詞 Irregular Verbs

現在	過去	過去分詞
be 是	was	been
begin 開始	began	begun
blow 打擊	blew	blown
break 打破	broke	broken
bring 帶來	brought	brought
build 建造	built	built
buy 買	bought	bought
catch 抓住，趕 (巴士)	caught	caught
choose 選	chose	chosen
come 來	came	come
do 做	did	done
drink 喝	drank	drunk
drive 開車	drove	driven
eat 吃	ate	eaten
fall 掉下	fell	fallen
feel 感覺	felt	felt
find 找	found	found
fly 飛	flew	flown
forget 忘記	forgot	forgotten
get 得到	got	gotten
give 給	gave	given
go 去	went	gone
have 有	had	had
hear 聽到	heard	heard
hold 握	held	held
keep 保持	kept	kept
know 知道	knew	known
leave 離開	left	left
lose 遺失	lost	lost

make 做	made	made
meet 遇到	met	met
pay 付款	paid	paid
ride 騎(馬)，搭(車)	rode	ridden
run 跑	ran	run
say 說	said	said
see 看	saw	seen
sell 賣	sold	sold
send 寄	sent	sent
sing 唱	sang	sung
sit 坐	sat	sat
sleep 睡	slept	slept
speak 說	spoke	spoken
spend 花(錢、時間)	spent	spent
stand 站立	stood	stood
swim 游泳	swam	swum
take 拿	took	taken
teach 教	taught	taught
tear 撕	tore	torn
tell 告訴	told	told
think 想	thought	thought
throw 丟	threw	thrown
undertand 了解	understood	understood
wear 穿	wore	worn
write 寫	wrote	written

2. 溫度換算 Temperature Conversion

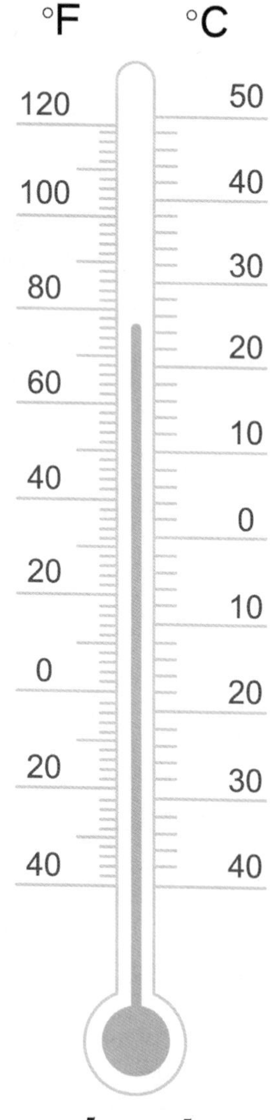

℃=(℉-32)5/9　℉=5/9℃+32

3. 美國假日 Holidays in the USA

比起歐洲人，美國人的休假時間算是少的，從聖誕節到新年期間是美國的年假，家人們聚在一起享受佳肴、交換禮物或出遊。一年中的休假假日並不多，如果有週休二日加上少數放假或補假的星期一才有 long weekend，許多節日並不休假。

☑ **Official Holidays 國定假日 (為休假日，若碰到週末，則週一補假)**

1. New Years Day - Jan. 1　新年 (一月一日)
2. Martin Luther King Day (MLK Day) - 3rd Mon. of Jan.　馬丁路德金恩誕辰 (一月的第三個星期一)
3. Presidents Day - 3rd Mon. of Feb.　總統紀念日 (二月的第三個星期一)
   包括 Lincoln's Birthday - Feb. 12th　林肯誕辰 (二月十二日)
   Washington's Birthday - Feb. 22nd　華盛頓誕辰 (二月二十二日)
4. Memorial Day - last Mon. of May　陣亡將士紀念日 (五月的最後一個星期一)
5. Independence Day - July 4th　獨立紀念日 (國慶日) (七月四日)
6. Labor Day - 1st Mon. of Sept.　勞動節 (九月的第一個星期一)
7. Columbus Day -12th of Oct.　哥倫布紀念日 (十月十二日)
8. Veterans Day - 11th of Nov.　退休軍人節 (十一月十一日)
9. Thanksgiving Day - 4th Thurs. of Nov.　感恩節 (十一月的第四個星期四)
10. Christmas - Dec. 25th　聖誕節 (十二月二十五日)

☑ **Not Official Holidays 非國定假日 (不休假)**

1. Groundhog Day - Feb. 2nd　土撥鼠日 (二月二日)
2. Valentines Day - Feb. 14th　情人節 (二月十四日)
3. Saint Patrick's Day - March 17th　聖派屈克節 (三月十七日)
4. April Fools Day - Apr. 1st　愚人節 (四月一日)
5. Easter - A Sunday in Mar. or Apr.　復活節 (春分滿月後的第一個星期天)
6. Mother's Day - 2nd Sunday of May　母親節 (五月的第二個星期天)
7. Father's Day - 3rd Sunday in June　父親節 (六月的第三個星期天)
8. Halloween - Oct. 31st　萬聖節 (十月三十一日)

4. 電影分級 Movie Ratings in the United States

美國電影協會 (Motion Picture Association of American, MPAA) 分級制度將電影依其內容及適合觀眾觀賞年齡分成 5 類，臺灣採用類似制度：

G-General Audiences (所有人皆可觀賞)

PG-Parental Guidance Suggested (兒童須由父母陪同)

PG-13-Parents Strongly Cautioned (13歲以下須由父母陪同)

R-Restricted (17歲以下須由父母或成年人陪同)

NC-17- No Children under 17 admitted (17歲以下不得觀賞，以前標示為X級)

電影預告上之NR (not rated) 代表尚未送檢分級 (This film is not yet rated)。

5. 美國中央情報局世界百科：世界與美國人口資料 CIA-The World Factbook: Population Data (the World and the United States)

A. 世界人口 the World Population

1. 總人口 (Total Population) ：67億9千多萬 (2009年7月)

2. 世界人口宗教信仰 (Religions) 比例：

基督徒Christians 33.32%

- 天主教徒 Roman Catholics 16.99%
- 新教徒Protestants 5.78%
- 東正教徒Orthodox 3.53%
- 英國國教徒Anglicans 1.25%

回教徒Muslims 21.01%

印度教徒Hindus 13.26%

佛教徒Buddhists 5.84%

錫克教徒Sikhs 0.35%

猶太教徒Jews 0.23%

大同教Baha'is 0.12%

其他宗教other religions 11.78%

無信仰者non-religious 11.77%

無神論者atheists 2.32%

(2007 年)

3. 世界人口語言 (Languages) 比例：

中文Mandarin Chinese 13.22%

西班牙語Spanish 4.88%

英語English 4.68%

阿拉伯語Arabic 3.12%

(北) 印度語Hindi 2.74%

葡萄牙語Portuguese 2.69%

孟加拉語Bengali 2.59%

俄語Russian 2.2%

日語Japanese 1.85%,

標準德語Standard German 1.44%

法語French 1.2%

(2005 年)

註：1. 將人口數乘上百分比可得人口數。例如：基督徒約22億人，回教徒約14億人，印度教約9億人，佛教徒約4億人。

2. 語言為母語人口 (Native Speaker) 之比例。

B. 美國人口 USA Population

4. 總人數 (Total Population)：3億7百多萬 (2009年7月)

種族 (Ethnic Groups) 比例：

白人white 79.96%
非洲裔black 12.85%
亞裔Asian 4.43%
原住民Amerindian and Alaska native 0.97%
夏威夷及其他太平洋島民native Hawaiian and other Pacific islander 0.18%
兩種族以上two or more races 1.61%
(2007年7月)

註：1. 拉丁裔Hispanic占美國人口15.1% (CIA將此資料分開計算於百分比外另外列表)。
　　2. 白人比例內含中東裔。

宗教信仰 (Religions) 比例：

基督徒Christian 78.5%
　新教徒Protestant 51.3%
　天主教Roman Catholic 23.9%
　摩門教Mormon 1.7%
　其他基督教派other Christian 1.6%
猶太教Jewish 1.7%
佛教徒Buddhist 0.7%
回教徒Muslim 0.6%
其他及未明other or unspecified 2.5%
不屬於任何宗教派別unaffiliated 12.1%
無宗教信仰none 4%
(2007年7月)

註：新教徒教派繁多含浸信會Baptist、衛理會Methodist、路得會Lutheran、長老會Presbyterian、聖公會Episcopalian、靈恩派Pentecostal、基督教會Church of Christ、聯合基督教會Congregational United Church of Christ、耶和華見證人 Jehovah's Witnesses、神召會Assemblies of God等。

語言 (Languages) ：

英語English 82.1%
西班牙語Spanish 10.7%
其他印歐語other Indo-European 3.8%
亞洲及太平洋島語Asian and Pacific island 2.7%　(2000年)
其他 other 0.7%

註： CIA-The World Factbook，網址：https://www.cia.gov/library/publications/the-world-factbook/
由美國中情局 (Central Intelligence Agency) 發行及更新 (現僅供網路版服務)，提供世界及 265 個國家與政治實體之檔案查詢，包含簡介、地理、人口、政府、經濟等各方面之統計資料。

附錄

國家圖書館出版品預行編目資料

開口就會社交英語／黃靜悅, Danny Otus Neal 著.
——初版. ——臺北市：五南, 2011.07
面；　公分

ISBN 978-957-11-6301-7（平裝附光碟片）

1. 英語　2. 會話

805.188　　100010093

1AC5

開口就會社交英語

作　　者　黃靜悅、Danny Otus Neal
發 行 人　楊榮川
總 編 輯　龐君豪
企劃主編　鄧景元、李郁芬
責任編輯　溫小瑩
內頁插畫　吳佳臻
地圖繪製　吳佳臻
封面設計　吳佳臻

出 版 者　五南圖書出版股份有限公司
地　　址：台北市大安區 106 和平東路二段 339 號 4 樓
電　　話：(02)2705-5066　傳真：(02)2706-6100
網　　址：http://www.wunan.com.tw
電子郵件：wunan@wunan.com.tw
劃撥帳號：01068953
戶　　名：五南圖書出版股份有限公司

法律顧問　元貞聯合法律事務所 張澤平律師

出版日期　2011 年 7 月　初版一刷

定　　價　390 元整

Time Zones of the United States

WA

OR

ID

MT

ND

SD

WY

NE

PACIFIC
（太平洋時區）

MOUNTAIN
（洛磯山時區）

CENTR
（中央時

NV

UT

CO

KS

CA

AZ

NM

OK

TX

HI

Honolulu

HAWII-ALEUTIAN
（夏威夷-阿留申時區）

AK

ALASKA
（阿拉斯加時區）

Juneau

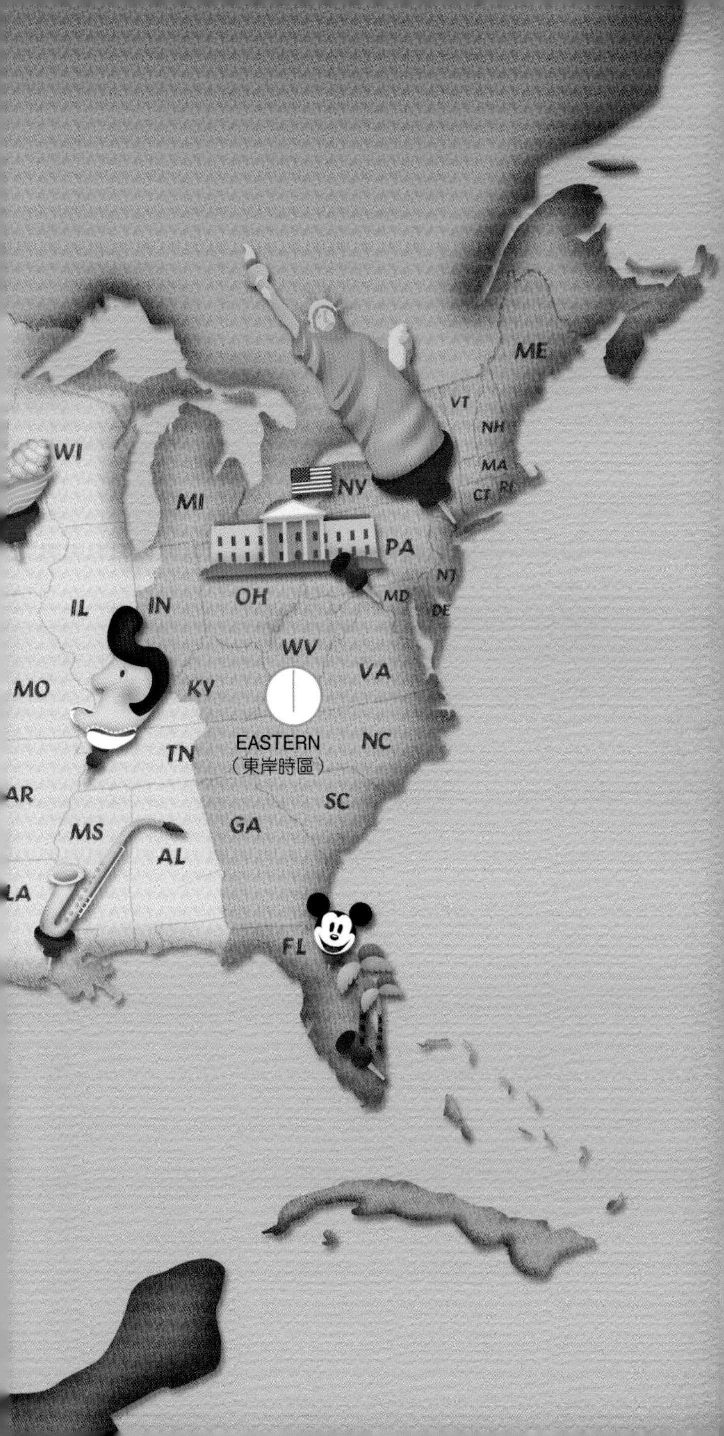
ME
VT
NH
MA
RI
CT
NY
WI
MI
PA
NJ
MD
DE
OH
IL
IN
WV
VA
MO
KY
EASTERN
（東岸時區）
NC
TN
AR
SC
GA
MS
AL
LA
FL